FORGOTTEN RAGE

FORGOTTEN RAGE

NEVER FORGIVE. NEVER FORGET.

MELODIE HERNANDEZ

Forgotten Rage

Copyright © 2018 by Melodie Hernandez

ISBN (978-1-7320990-0-5)

Printed in the USA

For my husband and children who have taught me that life
is too short and there's no time like the present to reach
your dreams. For my parents, both of whom always believed
in me as an author and who were my first fans.
For my sister, my first best friend and biggest supporter.
Thank all of you for supporting me and my writing,
it's because of your faith that I kept writing all these years
and will continue to keep writing because it's
who I am and what I love.

JANUARY 18TH, 1995

"Objection!" Nicholas Mason shot out of his chair in the courtroom.

The judge heaved a sigh. "You are not the trying attorney in this case, Mr. Mason, and while I understand that you *are* an attorney, in this instance you are to remain silent. Please allow Mr. Marx to state any and all objections on behalf of the prosecution."

Nicholas slowly sat, shooting the prosecuting attorney a scathing look. He bent over the banister so that Marx would hear him. "Why didn't you object?" he spat.

Adam Marx turned only halfway toward his friend. "Because I don't object to the defense attorney's cross examination," he harshly whispered back. "The only thing I object to is *you* trying to do my job for me. Now sit down and try to control yourself." He turned forward, facing the witness stand and effectively dismissed his friend.

Nicholas clenched his jaw but took his seat. He and his partners had wanted to work this case all the way up through

1

trial, but due to the conflict of interest, the court had demanded he find another attorney to chair the case from outside his firm. His friend, Adam Marx, had taken over and from the beginning assured Nick that he would see justice done.

Nick sighed and put his head in his hands. The case was slipping away. It had been six months since Adam had taken the case and they were losing points left and right. It began in week five of the trial when crucial evidence was thrown out due to contamination, and since then, they'd had one witness change her story, another disappear, and—currently—their only star witness was being ripped apart by the defense team's cross-examination.

The judge seemed as blind as lady justice herself and the jury had looked bored throughout the entire trial. Nick badly wanted to shake them all and make them see what a son of a bitch Anthony Yates really was. Nick's fingers ached from clutching the armrests in a white-knuckled grip, *why couldn't anyone else see it?* he wondered desperately.

"Hey, Nick, let's go." Adam lightly shook Nick's shoulder.

"What happened?" Nick asked, snapping out of his thoughts. People were filing out the door at the rear of the courtroom.

"The judge called a recess; the jury is deliberating. We'll be called once they reach a verdict."

Nick waited for Adam to gather his notes and place them into his briefcase before following him out of the courtroom.

The press crowded the hall. They flashed pictures and yelled questions as they followed Nick and Adam like a hungry pack of wolves, salivating for even the tiniest soundbite.

"Mr. Mason, given the validity of the defense, how can you believe the jury will find Mr. Yates guilty of murder?" shouted Emily Watkins, top news anchor from Channel four. She led the group of reporters, her designer heels annoyingly clicked against the marble floor as she kept pace with them.

Nick squeezed his eyes shut and kept walking, while the morbid slideshow of the murder scene flashed through his mind. Leah, his wife, lay dead in a pool of her own blood. Found on their houseboat with her throat cut from ear to ear.

Bile rose in his throat and he shook his head to distinguish the violent images, but the acidic taste remained, almost choking him.

"Mr. Mason has no comment," he heard Adam reply as they pushed their way through the throng of reporters.

Nick stopped walking and looked around. The reporters fell silent and watched him. Their ravenous looks should have given him pause but he was too aggravated to care. He took a deep breath and began. "Mr. Yates is a power-hungry politician and I have no doubt that he has risen to his post as city council president through deception and scandal. Given his background as a police detective, he of all people would know how to cover his tracks after committing a murder. He's guilty. I'd bet my career on it! And I hope the members of the jury remember that the victim here is *not* Mr. Yates but Leah Mason... my... my wife." He got stuck on her name but continued. "She lost her life seven months ago at the hands of this monster and I pray to God that he gets punished!" Nick stopped to catch his breath; whenever he spoke of Leah he couldn't help the rage that built inside.

She was so young, had so much to offer this world. Why couldn't it have been me, instead? Over the last few months, he had pleaded with the universe for answers, but none ever came so he had dug his heels in and gone after the person responsible for tearing his life apart.

Cameras flashed, and reporters threw more questions out; hungry as ever after being fed the morsels they craved. Adam, however was not prepared to satisfy their appetite. He steered Nick into the nearest office and slammed the door.

"What the hell are you doing?" he demanded, keeping his voice low.

Nick looked at him. "What?" he asked dully, feeling no remorse over his display in the hallway.

"What? What do you mean '*what?*'" Adam snapped, the vein in his forehead angrily pulsing. "What if the jury finds him innocent? He could sue us for slander. Or worse. I don't think the DA's office would appreciate you betting *their* careers on this case, I know *I* wouldn't." Adam's eyes widened—in what Nick assumed was surprise and regret at his own words—and he backed away from Nick with his hands in the air. Nick looked at him, slack-jawed. He waited a beat before addressing the betrayal he felt.

"You don't think Yates is guilty, do you?" he asked. "Well shit, Adam, if I would've known, I sure as hell wouldn't have asked you to take on this case!" Nick shook his head. "I can't believe this. Yates kills my wife and I have to justify my emotions to my best friend of all people. If I were trying the case—"

Adam exhaled and placed a hand on Nick's shoulder, speaking softly to him. "Nick, she was your wife, which is why I'm handling the case. Normally, it would be a conflict of interest for the friend of a victim's husband to take such a case, so I was careful not to mention that we knew each other when I was named first chair. I want whoever killed Leah punished just as much as you do, but how can we be sure it was Yates? You've heard the defense's case every day for six months now, and you have to admit, our case isn't exactly solid." Nick began to shake again, but Adam kept talking. "I know we've had some bad luck with evidence and testimonies, so I want you to be prepared if the jury comes back with a not guilty verdict, okay?"

Nick sighed and shook his head. The pity in his friend's voice was too much to bear. "Adam, you know how much Leah meant to me. How can you tell me to let go?" He looked up at his friend.

"I'm not telling you to let go. If Yates is guilty, he'll go to prison, but if he isn't, the police will continue the investigation. The best thing for you is to not waste time appealing the case and to help them as much as possible. Now I'm going to get something to eat. Would you like to join me?"

Nick stared at his friend and forced a smile. "No, I don't think I could hold anything down. You go ahead. Meet me back here when you're done."

"You sure?" Adam's hand hovered over the doorknob.

"Yeah, go ahead. I'll be fine." All Nick wanted was to be left alone. He had too many emotions to deal with and he didn't need an audience.

"Okay but I don't want you talking to the press, and I don't want you going after Yates, either. Just promise me you'll stay here—"

"Just leave me the fuck alone!" Nick snapped. "I said I'd be fine." Looking up at his friend's face, he knew he'd offended Adam, but he couldn't muster up the effort to apologize.

"Whatever," Adam said stiffly. He left the room, closing the door a little too hard behind him.

Nick sat and looked around the office. How the hell had all this happened? When the case began, it was open and shut. But now there was a chance Yates would walk. Nick briefly considered killing Yates himself, but he could never kill another human being, even one who had murdered his wife. Nick wiped at the tears that flowed down his face.

Leah, I'm so sorry, he thought, *I should have been there for you.*

There was a knock at the door and Fredrick James popped his head in. "Nick, the jury's back with a verdict. Adam's been paged."

Nick stood up and headed for the door. "Thanks, Fred." Nick walked down the hall to the courtroom. He paused before opening the door and composed himself; a quick deliberation by the jury usually meant a guilty verdict but he didn't want to get his hopes up. He took a deep breath, walked into the courtroom and took his seat. He clasped his shaking hands on his lap, trying to breathe deep and stay calm.

The courtroom buzzed with anticipation. Nick scanned the room and waited. Soon after, Anthony Yates walked in behind his defense attorney. Yates was the picture of health at forty-seven; six feet two, with a medium build. He wore an impeccably tailored suit, as always, lending him an air of importance. Nick glanced down at his own rumpled suit with distaste. He had lost so much weight dealing with this case and mourning his wife, he had stopped bothering with his appearance months before.

He looked at Yates, whose face was set in a grim expression, but Nick could tell in the way he carried himself that Yates basked in the glow of the press; he was a politician, after all. His lawyer was enjoying the publicity as well, but publicity was nothing new to Paul Cummings.

Cummings and Nick had worked at the same firm until the year before, when Cummings left to work for the DA. They had worked side by side on many cases as prosecutors and eventually became good friends. But Paul had taken on a big case and lost, which garnered negative publicity for the firm. It was because of that publicity that the firm lost a significant amount of business and, in the end, the partners had cut their losses and let him go. Paul moved on to work for the DA where he built his reputation as a defense attorney. He then developed a massive ego and cut ties with everyone from his past, including Nick. Since that time, Nick and Paul had enjoyed a healthy rivalry in the courtroom.

But Paul had taken things too far with this case. Instead of treating it sensitively for Nick's sake, he had been the most vicious Nick had ever seen him. He guessed working with hoodlums and criminals would do that to a person. One whiff of Nick's emotional state and Paul had attacked and insisted he represent Yates. Every time Paul was in the same room as Nick, he smiled smugly, which infuriated Nick and wore down his patience.

But Nick wasn't looking at Paul. His interest was in Yates. Yates, who sat at his counsel table, pompous and calm; Yates who had killed Leah with his bare hands; Yates who might get off and walk away a free man. Nick's hands trembled harder and he felt nauseous.

Adam asked, "Are you going to be okay?"

Nick looked up at Adam. "Adam—" he started pleadingly but was cut off by the bailiff's booming voice.

"All rise, the Honorable Judge Melbourne presiding!"

Everyone stood as a short, stumpy old man shuffled out of his chambers up to the bench. Judge Melbourne was an impatient man but was usually fair with his cases. Melbourne took his seat and ordered the jury brought back into the courtroom.

The jury filed in and took their seats, all the while trying to avoid eye contact with Yates. Nick took that as a good sign but held his breath anyway.

Judge Melbourne put on his glasses and faced the jury box. "Members of the jury, have you reached a verdict?"

Complete silence took over and the foreman—a pudgy, thirty-something man with a bad comb-over and sweat stains at his armpits—stood and replied, "We have, Your Honor."

"What say you?" snapped Melbourne.

The foreman cleared his throat. "In the matter of the State verses Anthony Alan Yates on the count of murder one—"

Nick closed his eyes.

"We, the jury, find the defendant not guilty."

Murmurs rose from the crowd and Melbourne banged his gavel and called for order. Nick exhaled slowly as he watched the expression on Yates's face turn from despair to surprise and finally to one of victory. Nick watched him shake hands with Cummings and watched Cummings turn to Nick with his arrogant smile.

"You bastard!" Nick yelled, starting across the room. Several reporters swung their cameras in his direction. "This isn't finished, Yates! I know you killed her! I know you killed my wife!"

It was Adam's hand that pulled him back. "Don't do this. Let it go, man!" he hissed in Nick's ear.

But Nick shoved him off and sat down. Again, he gripped the arms of his chair until his knuckles were white. The room spun, and he felt sick.

A timeline of images played in his mind: meeting Leah at law school, asking her on a date, asking her to marry him, their wedding day, their beautiful honeymoon in Hawaii, the look on her face when they closed on their first house, the two of them celebrating with a bottle of wine at their favorite restaurant when he made partner at the firm, Leah sleeping soundly in their bed, her long hair fanned out on the pillow and her head resting on her arm. She had looked so peaceful... so beautiful... so... alive. He would never know that kind of happiness again.

Without warning, images from the murder scene flashed through his mind—all that blood, and the way her life had drained away, the way her eyes were no longer bright but dull and fixed. Even in death, Nick believed her eyes had stared at him asking him the question he'd asked himself ever since: "*Why weren't you there?*"

Nothing mattered. Not the case. Not his job. Nothing.

Completely numb, Nick got up and, without looking at anyone, shoved through the reporters and left the building.

Nicholas Mason was no more.

CHAPTER ONE

The rage inside has found its way free
The evil has long been restrained inside of me
The way to quench the thirst to kill
Is to succumb to this wicked thrill

MAY 12ᵀᴴ, 2002 2:05 AM

Garbage was meant to be discarded and left alone. Yet the woman in the alley dug through it as if she'd discovered lost treasure. *Disgusting,* thought the spectator who watched the woman's face light up when she pulled a half-eaten sandwich from the dumpster near the building. The woman tore off the moldy pieces of bread and greedily ate the remainder of the sandwich, licking each of her filthy fingers when she was done. She then took her cart and pushed it to the next dumpster. Carefully, she climbed in, using the three-wheeled shopping cart as a step stool, and rummaged around. The spectator moved then, entering the alley while listening for any signs that they were not alone. Satisfied there would be no interruptions, the killer pulled out a knife and crept toward the dumpster.

• • •

Mildred Jamison thought she'd hit the jackpot. Inside the dumpster, she found boxes of discarded Thai food. It had been years since she'd eaten Thai. She salivated at the memory of savoring it before she'd become homeless.

Mildred once rented a small, run-down house in south Seattle. It wasn't hers alone—she split the rent with another woman, Anne. Mildred and Anne had fixed that house up so that it looked almost new. They were great friends and often confided in each other over rocky road ice cream and a pack of Newports.

One day, Anne came home from work late with track marks on her arm. Mildred tried talking to her, but Anne wouldn't listen, saying the heroin wasn't an addiction; that it was just for fun. But as time passed, Anne lost her job and began stealing to pay for her "fun". Mildred tried to get her help but didn't have enough money to send her friend to rehab. When the rent was due, Mildred couldn't afford it on her own. Anne had sold everything of worth in the house.

Mildred didn't have a husband or any family to go to for help. Anne was her only friend. So she stayed as long as she could until the power was shut off and she was escorted off the premises. Soon after that, she lost her job and was forced to live on the streets. She'd seen Anne twice downtown; the first time, Anne was offering her body to a passerby. The second time had been more recent. Anne was walking down the street with two other women; she was clean, well-dressed and looked very healthy. She looked as though she'd gotten the help Mildred had always wished for her and had turned her life around. So Mildred approached Anne to talk, hoping Anne would be able to help her now that she'd helped herself. But Anne barely recognized Mildred, and when there *was* a flicker of recognition, Anne had scoffed at her; told her she had no time for pathetic homeless people and walked off. Mildred's face reddened, and her stomach sank. She felt hurt and abandoned as Anne walked away.

Since then, Mildred had fended for herself. She went hungry most of the time. Stomach pains kept her up at night in whatever shelter she landed in—if she found room. Food was hard to obtain, and the other homeless people were very territorial.

But that night, she had struck gold. She dug her hand in the Styrofoam container and scooped up a handful of day-old noodles and was about to thrust them into her mouth when someone grabbed her head from behind. Mildred, stunned, dropped the container of Thai food. A searing pain creased her neck and her breath left her body in one loud, final gasp. The last thing she saw before she died was the bottom of the rusted dumpster.

MAY 16TH, 2002 3:36 AM

Headlights cut through the darkness, illuminating the small figure drenched in blood and the sound of tires screeching pierced the silence
Luz jerked awake gasping for air, her eyes wildly searching

the room for something to anchor her back to reality. She tried to steady her breathing by slowly counting to ten and taking deeper breaths.

Her phone rang, startling her. She quickly tried to block the effects of the nightmare and answered the phone.

"Santos."

"Luz, this is Mike. Sorry to wake you, but we need you downtown. We got a body."

Luz sat up straighter in bed. "I'll be right there, give me the address." She reached into her nightstand for her pen and paper.

"Just come to the corner of James and Second."

"Come on, Mike, just give me an address, I'll find it," she said, irritated that her boss wasn't more forthcoming with the information. *God, I need some coffee,* she thought.

"That *is* the address, Santos," Mike said, sounding a little annoyed himself. "The vic's a dead homeless person."

Luz pulled the phone from her ear and stared at it for a beat before speaking to her boss again. "Oh... okay. Well then, that's not my problem, Mike. Homeless people die all the time—disease, old age and exposure to the elements."

"This one was murdered, so get up and get your ass downtown. I'll expect a full report when I get in." He hung up.

Luz laid back, looked up at the ceiling. She shook off the panic from her nightmare and sighed. "Well, chica," she said to herself, "another day another peso." And with that, she jumped out of bed and headed toward the bathroom.

She had a modest-sized living space with two bedrooms and one bathroom, a large kitchen with a connecting dining room and a living room. Her favorite aspect of the house was the fact that it was a boat.

No other houseboat on Lake Union had cost as little as hers. But nobody else on the lake had a father like hers. Her father once worked for a man who owned property all over the Puget Sound. When Luz had moved out on her own, her father convinced his old employer to let her move in at a huge discount. Once she graduated the academy and made detective, she not only could afford the place, she could afford to furnish it right. It was adios to Swedish furniture and hello to something plush, things more her style.

She hopped out of the shower and over to the mirror to dry her hair. She surveyed herself closely; promising to get her roots done as soon as she could. She preferred honey brown to her natural black; it made her look much more glamorous. She chuckled to herself; not that she needed to be glamorous—she was the only female detective in her precinct and she had already turned down offers from half the men in her department. She didn't need to attract more attention. She smiled, gave herself an appraising look and returned to her bedroom to dress.

Once dressed she grabbed herself a Pepsi from the fridge and put on her coat. She didn't normally drink soda but there was no time to brew coffee. On the way to the front door, she spotted her Chihuahua sleeping under the window. She went to the closet, pulled out a puppy piddle pad and laid it on the kitchen floor.

"Hey, Cheech," she called, and the small dog popped up

and came over wagging his tail. "Sorry, boy, no time for a walk. I gotta go." She looked up at the clock and scowled; seven-fifteen.

"¡Dios mío!" she exclaimed, "traffic's gonna be shit!" She ran out the door.

MAY 16TH, 2002 8:01 A.M.

Officer Leroy Sacks had been with the Seattle Police Department for eleven months and had yet to see a body so sickening as the one he was looking at. They'd carefully removed the woman's corpse from the dumpster—to not disturb evidence—and laid it on the ground. Leroy considered himself lucky that the crime scene guys got stuck with moving her. They had a very difficult job doing it.

Rigor mortis had come and gone, leaving the body as dead weight. What complicated things was the dumpster. It was so deep that after the body was photographed, one of the guys had to climb in and haul the corpse part of the way out before anyone could give him a hand. Once the body was freed, it was laid out on a plastic sheet for examination.

At this point, Leroy assumed he was no longer needed at the scene, so he'd gone to his patrol car, intending to go home. Unfortunately, his boss spotted him and ordered him to stick around until the crime scene crew finished up. Leroy had gotten out of his car and taped off the area so that passersby wouldn't get the urge to rubberneck.

He couldn't guess why anyone would want a glimpse of

what he had seen. The woman they found had been dead a while and her pasty skin and glossy eyes were enough to give him nightmares. If that wasn't bad enough, she was found with her throat cut from left to right, and thousands of maggots eating away at the tissue in the gash. The smell alone was enough to make him lose his breakfast and when he saw the body extracted from the dumpster, he found that he hadn't gotten rid of all his eggs and bacon. Just thinking about it made his stomach churn.

"You're looking green today," a voice came from behind him.

Leroy relaxed when he saw it was his mentor. "You would be green, too, if you saw what they pulled out of that alley this morning," he replied, shaking his head.

Eddie Lopez smiled. "Yeah, I just took a look, poor woman. Probably never saw it coming," he said calmly.

Leroy looked at his friend, surprised. "That's it? You didn't even gag?"

Eddie shook his head. "No, it's not like it's the first time I've seen a murder vic like this, I've seen worse... way worse," he said.

Edward Lopez transferred from East LA four years before and Leroy had no doubt his partner had seen more than his share of violent crime.

"But I guess you wouldn't have seen much like this back in Rhode Island, would you?" Eddie asked him.

"No. The closest thing I've seen to this was an old man hit by a bus—there was blood everywhere—but at least he lived."

Eddie patted him on the shoulder and smiled. "Leroy, my

man, unfortunately you've been sheltered. But you'll get used to it. For now, let me handle this scene and you can handle the paperwork. I'll meet you back at the office. Deal?"

Leroy groaned; he hated paperwork, but the alternative was to spend more time with the body, so he readily agreed. "Sure," he said. As he got into his car and closed the door, a silver Mitsubishi Eclipse, tires screeching, came peeling around the corner and pulled up to the curb.

"Here comes Speedy Gonzales," Eddie called, the corner of his mouth lifting in a grin.

Leroy snorted. "That's Detective Santos, right? Lutz is her first name?"

"Her name is Luz, pronounced like the word 'lose'," Eddie explained, keeping one eye on Luz as she got out of her car."

"Got it. If you're gonna go over and say hi, wipe the drool off your mouth first," Leroy said giving his partner a smug grin.

Eddie shot him a stern look and asked, "Don't you have paperwork to do?"

Leroy laughed and started his car. He watched Detective Santos head straight for the alley. Then he glanced at his partner, who stared as she walked by him in a rush, not even acknowledging his presence. Eddie had harbored a flame for Santos since the beginning. He'd asked her out several times and she'd always turned him down. It seemed she had a policy about dating other cops—not to. But that hadn't stopped Eddie. Every time he saw her he put on that, "You're Latina, I'm Latino" routine. Leroy thought it was time for Eddie to come up with new material, but his partner was determined. He watched Eddie follow Santos to the crime scene like a dog in heat. *When will he learn?* thought Leroy. He chuckled and drove away.

• • •

"What have we got, Ben?" Luz asked the medical examiner as she approached the body. She was aware that Officer Lopez was tailing her.

"White female, approximately thirty-nine, been rotting here for about four days now," Ben said as he bent down to examine the body.

Luz crouched as well. The smell almost knocked her over. Atop the scent of death lay an aroma of rotting food and garbage. Luz did not regret skipping breakfast that morning. "Cause of death?" she asked, swallowing a gag.

Ben pulled back the sheet. Luz stood and backed away. She put her hand over her mouth then turned and spit. *It's not the first dead body you've seen, Santos,* she thought. *Get a grip.*

"Knife wound. Looks like someone came up from behind and sliced her," Ben said, tracing the wound from ear to ear with his latex-covered hand. "Why? I don't know. She didn't have any money or valuables on her. But these homeless people can get violent when their space is compromised."

Luz looked down at the body and shook her head. She took a pair of gloves from Ben and pulled them on. "This doesn't look like it came from just any knife. Look at the way the skin was cut, not a rip—a clean slice. It must have been a very sharp knife."

"Could've been glass or a razor blade," she heard someone behind her say. Edward Lopez leaned against the alley wall.

"Officer Lopez, don't you have something better to do?" she asked and turned back around. "And I don't mean checking out my ass while I'm investigating this murder scene," she added.

Luz heard the others snicker, and Eddie snorted and walked over to the body.

"Don't flatter yourself, Santos, not everybody wants to jump into bed with you," he said with a smug smile.

Luz blushed slightly. She knew she'd embarrassed him in front of the other cops, but she had more important matters to attend to. She couldn't worry about wounded pride. Instead of egging him on, she turned his attention to the victim.

"Did you find any identification on the body?" she asked. She saw his disappointed look and knew he'd wanted a chance to confront her in front of the group. She congratulated herself for not letting her temper get the best of her. *This is why I don't date cops*, she thought. *This is why I don't date at all.*

"Mildred May Jamison," he read off of a driver's license, "last known address is located down south toward the town of Whitecenter. Officer Sacks and I will check it out."

Luz looked up at him and scowled.

"What? We were the first officers on the scene. I'm just following up," he said, shrugging.

Luz thought this over. Her workload had been piling up and she could use all the help she could get. "Okay, thanks," she replied reluctantly. She hated depending on Eddie for anything. The only thing she could count on was his desire to get into her pants, and as she looked up at him she could see that very thought written all over his face.

"Well, aren't you going to leave?" she snapped

He smiled down at her. "Yeah, I'm going. Did you want to get some dinner later to discuss the details of the case?" he said in a way that Luz thought was an attempt to sound professional, but he failed miserably.

Luz narrowed her eyes and stood up so that her face was level to his. "You never give up, do you?" she asked, pointing a finger at him.

He smiled mischievously. "Not until you say yes and since that won't be for a very long time, if ever, get used to having me around. I'll stop by your office later if I come up with anything. Adios!"

Luz couldn't help but smile as he walked away. As persistent as he was, Eddie was a good guy and a good cop. She just wished he wouldn't look at her like a piece of meat whenever they were in the same room. She turned back to the body and found Ben smiling at her.

"What?" she asked raising her eyebrows.

"Why don't you just give him a chance?" Ben asked. "He's been after you for two years now. It's not like you're dating anybody."

"I don't date cops," she snapped. "And if I did, I wouldn't date that one. He's got trouble written all over him."

"How would you know?" Ben asked.

"I wouldn't, but I have a feeling. He's a typical jock cop and I don't have room in my schedule to fit his ego." She looked at Ben squarely. "Can we get back to work now?"

Ben threw his hands up and bent back over the body. He pointed at the throat where the skin had been sliced. "See here how the skin was cut? The wound is deep, the blade on the knife was wide as well as long. I'll know more when I get the autopsy report back."

"You don't sound so sure," Luz said, watching his expression.

"Well, something tells me this wasn't an ordinary steak knife. But I'll have to do some research and get back to you. You can see where the skin goes from ripped to sliced. That means the blade is serrated in some aspect near the hilt. I've seen only one other cut like this and it's got me thinking," he said, his brow furrowed.

Luz looked at the body. The woman's face was pale and bloated. She wore a torn, matted wool coat and a wool hat that had seen better days. She was a small woman; maybe about five-foot two, a hundred pounds, and Luz wondered why anyone would want to kill someone so helpless.

"Why do you think someone would have wanted her dead?" she asked Ben.

He shrugged again. "That's your job. However, homeless people are very territorial. They get greedy over food. I would, too, if I hadn't eaten in days. But," he paused and looked down at the body. "I don't think this was your run-of-the-mill bum scuffle. There are no signs of a struggle, no bruises or scratches. If you ask me, she never saw it coming."

Luz made some notes on her pad and approached the dumpster where the crime guys were working. "Anything?" she asked them.

The young blond guy working on the ground looked up at her. "Nothing so far," he said. "I'm not sure anything will turn up. This alley has nothing but garbage in it. Even if we covered every beer bottle and gum wrapper, I wouldn't expect to come up with anything."

Luz sighed and walked back to Ben. "All right. Call me when you get something, even if it's just a hunch, okay?"

Ben began packing up his things and ordered the body loaded into the coroner's van. Ben glanced at her. "If I get a hunch, you'll be the first to know," he said with a warm smile.

Luz left it at that. She knew him well and trusted he would come to her if he thought of something that pertained to her case. She decided she would ask him after she had more information from the autopsy. "Okay then," she said heading back to her car. "You know how to reach me."

"Hey!" called Ben. She stopped and turned around. "Be nice to Lopez, he really likes you."

Luz gave him a sour look and grinned. "I'm done being nice. I was nice to you and look what happened."

Ben smiled at her with a gleam in his eye. "Yeah, but we had our good times," he said with a wink.

Luz shook her head and laughed "Yeah, Torres, we had a blast," she said sarcastically and got in her Eclipse. She rolled down the window as she drove by him.

"Ben," she said, her tone serious. "I'm glad we're still friends."

"Me too, Luz. I only ever wanted you to be happy," he said. He bent down and kissed her cheek. "We'll talk later. I have to finish up here, but it was good seeing you again. Don't be a stranger. You got my number, too."

He turned and walked back to the crime scene and talked to the other officers. Luz watched him go, rolled up her window and took off.

She drove down to First Avenue, took a right and headed north. The sky above was unusually cloudless for a Seattle day, and the sun was climbing to the east. Days like that one made living in the Pacific Northwest worth it. She turned onto Westlake Avenue and noticed all the well-dressed people on their way to work. Many of them looked as though they were taking their time, soaking up as much sunlight as they could before beginning their dreary day behind a desk, in front of a computer. Luz didn't blame them; days when the rain stayed away were few and far between, and she planned on spending her free time outdoors. She drove into the parking garage of the West Precinct building and pulled into her parking spot. Before going into the building, she took one last look at the sun-drenched streets, hoping she would be able to have that sort of free time.

CHAPTER TWO

Once forgotten, I was alone
My need for love remained unknown
But rejection cut, and the wound did grow
Into malicious intentions I can't shove below

MAY 16TH, 2002 1:50 P.M.

"More tea?" the woman asked.

A few of the women nodded but most kept their eyes on their cards. There were six women in all but only four were serious canasta players. They all lived in the same neighborhood, in cookie-cutter houses located in the suburbs of Seattle. It was a nice, neat area, and the women got together once a week to play a mean game of cards. The women were homemakers—and with their husbands at work, children at school and the housework done—they had plenty of time to socialize. That week it was Antoinette's turn to host.

She went to the kitchen and prepared more tea. She filled the kettle with water while she heard the TV from the other room. She enjoyed playing hostess; she had a big house and expensive taste in furnishings and took pleasure in showing them off. She didn't consider herself a snob—she was just lucky. A few years back she had had a brush with death. After that she found a renewed interest in life and turned it all around. It hadn't been easy for her. *But I'm here now and that's what matters!* she thought with a smile.

During her transformation, Antoinette had met a man and fallen in love. They'd married five months later and were still in love with one another. It was by chance that her husband worked at Microsoft as head of software development. But the money he brought in made for a comfortable life for both of them and she was more than happy with the way things turned out.

The whistling kettle brought her back from her reverie and she poured the water into the china cups, each with a tea bag, and placed the kettle back on the stove. As she scooped in the sugar, she heard gasps from the other room.

She quickly placed the cups on a tray, straining to make out the voices in the other room. She heard Emily Watkins, the news anchor from Channel Four doing the noon news. She placed a plate of shortbread cookies on the tray and headed for the dining room.

Antoinette passed through the doorway and found all five women absorbed in the television.

"What is it?" Antoinette asked, looking from worried face to worried face.

"Shh!" someone snapped.

A little annoyed, Antoinette took her seat and asked again.

This time her friend, Eve, turned to her.

"Some poor woman was found murdered in downtown Seattle this morning. Apparently, it wasn't just a bum killing another filthy bum," she said. "God forbid," she added, laying her left hand on her chest calling attention to the giant rock of a diamond set into her wedding ring. "Wouldn't that just solve everything? Then we wouldn't have to worry about those dirty people begging us for money every time we shop downtown."

Antoinette knew her friend would ramble away from the point, so she turned her attention to the television. Emily Watkins of Channel Four, with her too-perfect hair and five-hundred-dollar business suit, stood on a downtown corner going on about the problem of homelessness in Seattle.

"If those people would bathe once in a while, they could get a good job and find themselves a home," Eve said huffily, while pulling out a compact from her Coach purse and checking her reflection for the twentieth time since she arrived. The plastic surgeon had done a great job on her nose, but did she really have to check on it every five minutes?

"Shh!" It was Antoinette's turn to snap. She was annoyed that her friend was so close-minded. Bathe? Where were the homeless supposed to bathe? Shaking her head, Antoinette sipped her tea and turned up the volume. Emily's voice filled the room:

"...found this morning only feet from where I stand, this woman," the screen cut to a picture of a middle-aged woman smiling out at them. "Mildred Jamison was found in a dumpster with her throat slashed. If any of our viewers are able to help the Seattle Police Department with information regarding this poor victim, please call the number shown below."

Antoinette didn't hear the rest of the report. Her mind seemed to stop, and a loud ringing filled her ears. Her friends turned to her with concerned looks, but Antoinette couldn't speak. She tried to stand, and the room tilted, then everything went dark.

MAY 16ᵀᴴ, 2002 7:30 P.M.

Luz turned off the ignition and rested her head back on the seat. It had been another long day. In addition to the murder of the Jamison woman, she had a vehicular homicide case, a Jane Doe case with no leads, a gang banger suspected of shooting up a parking garage—causing thousands of dollars' worth of damage as well as taking out the lot attendant—and she had to deal with the owner of a gay bar on Capitol Hill who was worried about hate crimes occurring in the area. He was concerned because the body of a popular local drag queen had been discovered in the parking lot of his bar the previous week. All in all, it had been an extremely busy, albeit slow-moving, day and she was exhausted. She lazily got out of her car and trudged down the dock, at the end of which she unlocked the door to her house. She'd almost walked inside when she remembered she'd left her dinner in the car. Grudgingly, she shuffled back to the car, turned off the alarm and pulled out the plastic bag that held her dinner. She heard her phone ring and found it on the front seat.

"Santos," she barked into the phone.

"Whoa, is this a bad time?" a tentative man's voice asked.

Luz locked the car and enabled the alarm before responding. "No, Eddie, what's up?"

He hesitated. "Well," he began, "Sacks and I checked out that address in south Seattle today and the place is pretty much condemned. I mean, there are boards on the windows and weeds growing out of every crack. I was positive no one lived there, but Leroy wanted to be sure, so we knocked on the door and nobody answered. We found mail in the box—mostly junk."

Luz was back at the boat; her stomach growling as she set her food on the kitchen counter. "Did you find out who owned the property?" she asked, pulling out two Styrofoam containers from the plastic bag.

"Way ahead of you on that one," he chirped. "I called a friend of mine at the King County Assessors' office and had him track down the owner. It belongs to a Mr. Don Mullen. So I called my other friend at the Department of Licensing and got a current address for Mr. Mullen. He lives down in Tacoma now, small house off the waterfront. I couldn't track down a phone number for him though. I was thinking maybe you'd wanna drive down and ask him a few questions tomorrow morning."

"You were correct thinking that. Hold on, let me get a pen." She grabbed a pen from her desk and snagged a Post-it note. "Okay, shoot." Eddie recited the address and Luz thanked him for his help.

"So what time should I pick you up tomorrow?" he asked.

Luz closed her eyes and took a breath. "Eddie, I'm grateful for all the time and effort you've put into this for me. But—"

"But you'd rather handle this on your own, right? Jeez, Santos, can't you lighten up? I wasn't asking you on a date, I just want to help."

He was angry, and Luz could hear the disappointment in his voice. She had known there would be consequences to letting him help her out. She thought back to what Ben told her that morning and all the fight went out of her.

"Seven," she stated into the phone.

She took his silence for shock. She gave him time to compose himself.

"Um, sure, seven it is," he replied. "Did you want to get breakfast, too? I know a little place right on the water that—"

"Eddie, don't push it. See you in the morning." She hung up before he could reply. She found herself smiling.

She opened the containers and inhaled the aroma of her native food. She had left work knowing she would be too tired to cook, so she stopped off at the taco truck and ordered dinner to go. She usually liked to eat heathy but that night, she was too tired to care.

She sat down with her food and her Corona with a slice of lime, which she squeezed onto the steak tacos. She dropped the lime into the Corona, then turned on the TV while pouring dog food into Cheech's bowl. Cheech scurried over and noisily devoured his dinner. As Luz dug into her rice, she channel-surfed until she landed on the Speed Channel.

Her older brother had gotten her interested in cars at an early age. After dropping out of school in tenth grade, Hector decided to be a mechanic, and presently owned his own speed shop. She remembered when he'd first come home after three years at Job Corps. She had barely recognized him. When he left, he was young, scrawny, bored and untidy but when he returned, he'd grown into his body. He had defined muscles in his arms; he was clean and determined to make the most of his education. He enrolled in a vocational college and got his degree in auto mechanics soon after. In the past ten years he'd gone from mechanic to owner. Luz was proud of his success and appreciated all the things he'd taught her along the way. He was the one who suggested she buy her Mitsubishi Eclipse, and when she made the purchase he went to work on the car. After he customized her car, he gave her a few pointers on driving and maintenance. She frequently drove around Seattle at high-speed, passing up state patrol vehicles without hesitation.

She finished dinner and went to the couch to lie down. Cheech trotted over to Luz and quietly whined.

"Hey there, boy," she said sleepily. He jumped on her face and licked her wildly—his tail wagging.

Luz giggled. She couldn't resist her pup. "All right. Let's go." She got up from the couch and grabbed the leash, fastened it to Cheech and headed out. The night air was warm, but a cool breeze blew up off the bay. She walked the dog down the dock and up toward the parking lot, where they reached the trail and Cheech took his time finding a place to do his duty.

31

Once he was done, Luz cleaned up after him by dumping the plastic bag in the designated receptacle.

They continued on the path for a while and when it became harder to see the trail they headed back. Watching the sun sink toward the horizon, Luz was filled with dread. She wondered if the killer would strike again. Seattle wasn't one of the best cities in the world for safety, but it wasn't the worst. Luz lived on Lake Union and had yet to see more than a burglary since she'd chosen to live there. But Luz had been fortunate to live in such a well-kept area. Mildred Jamison hadn't. A shudder rippled through Luz and she picked up her pace. Cheech seemed to sense his owner's discomfort and let out a soft whine. When they got back to the boat Luz turned on the news. Channel four was doing a run-down of the murder. The nightly news anchors threw around theories on why the poor woman was killed, but they had no answers.

Luz was confused as well, but her curiosity was genuine. After a thorough background check on the dead woman, Luz found that the victim had no living relatives. Mildred's parents had died when she was twenty-eight—Luz's own age— and she had no friends to speak of. Mildred had been in debt for years, but from the looks of it, she was slowly pulling herself out of the hole. Even at thirty-four she'd attended South Seattle Community College to take culinary art courses. Luz suspected that Mildred planned to turn her life around. But what landed her on the streets? Luz wondered. And why had someone taken her life?

Luz turned off the television, locked the doors and went to

bed. She lay in bed for a while pondering Mildred's fate until she drifted off to sleep.

It was half-past midnight when her phone rang. The sound jerked her into consciousness so that she had to collect her scattered thoughts before she could pick up the phone.

"Santos," she answered.

"Wake up sleeping beauty, we have another one." Her boss's voice sounded as tired as she felt.

"Are we going to make this a habit?" she mumbled.

"No, because we found the killer this time," he stated matter-of-factly.

Luz sat straight up in bed. "What?"

"Yeah, the guy was stupid enough to get caught at the scene."

"Are you sure?"

"Sure as I'm going to get. Now you be sure to get your ass down to First and Columbia ASAP. I don't want anyone talking to the press."

"I got it. I'll be there in twenty." She hung up and swung her legs over the side of the bed and headed for the bathroom. She spotted her academy sweatshirt and pulled it on over the t-shirt she wore to sleep in. She didn't want to bother with a bra but knew she might not make it home until late, so she put one on. She pulled on some fresh socks and found her running shoes. When she reached the bathroom, she pulled a comb through her hair with one hand and brushed her teeth with the other. She pulled her hair up with elastic, wincing when she noticed her dark roots. "I'll get you my pretties," she cackled to the mirror. She had bigger things to worry about then getting her hair colored. She looked herself over in the full-length mirror on the door before grabbing her keys and rushing out. She wouldn't have to worry about traffic so early in the morning.

She should have been happy, but she wasn't.

The killer hadn't wasted any time finding another victim.

MAY 17TH, 2002 1:00 A.M.

Luz pulled up to the scene twelve minutes later. There were people everywhere and she required a policeman to help make room for her to get out of the car.

"What's going on?" she asked. "Who are all these people?"

The officer tapped his watch. "It's still party time for these people. Most of them were just heading home. Ladies' night at the club up the street, this is a typical Thursday night." He waved his arm toward the crowd and Luz noticed a man leaning on her car.

"Hey, watch the paint job, idiot! I didn't wax my car so drunks like you could scratch it up! Get lost!" she yelled

"Bite me, bitch!" the man yelled back but trotted off.

She was about to chase the man down and tell him where he could bite her, but her eyes snagged on Ben, who waved her over. She shot an icy glare at the drunk idiot before she approached the scene. Ben just grinned.

"If you drove a piece of junk like I do, you wouldn't have to worry about the paint getting scratched."

Luz pictured his beat-up Toyota and smirked. "If I drove

a bucket like yours I'd have to worry whether my car would start up every morning."

"Hey, it may look like crap but it's dependable," he said, weeding his way through the officers. They reached the body and Luz slipped on some gloves and pulled back the sheet. She was surprised to see the face of someone she knew.

"Dammit, Matty. Wrong place at the wrong time once again, I see," she said, sadly shaking her head.

"You know this guy?" asked Ben, glancing up at her.

"Yeah, a couple months ago I was working this drug case and had a problem finding information on a certain dealer. When I was investigating the area, Matty gave me some useful information. Well, *gave* would be the wrong word, more like he *sold* me information. That information checked out and helped solve the case, so I was grateful. He's been a contact for me ever since. I hadn't seen him in a while. I assumed he was strung out or something. He was always wandering the streets with a smile on his face, like he had an inside joke." She looked at the cut and noticed sadly that the gash resembled a sort of second smile but this time the joke was on Matty. She stared a minute longer at his lifeless eyes and pulled the sheet back up.

"Whoever is doing this must prey on the weak because this man is skin and bones," she said, looking up at Ben.

"You'll have a chance to ask the perp that yourself. He was taken downtown about an hour ago. He wasn't a big guy, either, so of course he would have picked someone easy to overcome. But he's not talking."

"The weapon was found on him?" she asked.

"Yeah, it was literally found *on* him, right on top of him."

"What? It wasn't concealed? He wasn't running?"

"I don't know. When I showed up, he was already in the cruiser. The odd thing was that he was sleeping. The man was just picked up and arrested for murder and he's catching some Z's. Pretty strange, right?"

Luz nodded. She'd have to wait until she made it back to the station before figuring things out. First, she had to process the scene and piece together her own version of events.

CHAPTER THREE

The relief floods their stark-white faces.
While I hide in more obvious places.
They've caught their death-man and I'm elated.
To watch from afar the game I've created.

MAY 17ᵀᴴ, 2002 3:15 A.M.

The cell was warm, and the blanket was cozy if not a little scratchy. It had been a long time since he had slept in a real bed; too long. He closed his eyes, pretending to sleep but he heard the officers talking in the hallway. They were discussing the two murders he was accused of. He turned over and huddled closer to the wall, intending to nap, but his eyes were closed no more than five minutes when his cell door slid open. He resisted the urge to turn around but opened his eyes and listened. He heard the guard tell whoever entered that he would be right outside the cell if they needed him. He was surprised when the reply that came was a woman's voice. At this, the prisoner turned to see her wondering why she would want to speak to him. As she walked toward him, the light caught on the badge hanging around her neck; she was a cop. *Not again,* he thought. She stopped at the foot of the bed and stared at him for a moment, as if trying to decide something.

"I'm Detective Santos. I work in homicide." She paused, her eyes roving over him, assessing. "So, you're the sick bastard who likes to cut up homeless people, huh?" she asked in a tone of utter disgust. The prisoner lay unmoving, staring back. She was about five-foot six, with a slim build, though one could hardly tell with the oversized sweatshirt she wore, and long light brown hair with dark roots peeking through. Her face was oval-shaped, and her lips were pouty and full. She wore no makeup and her russet skin was smooth and clean. The most striking feature was her eyes. They were big, round, the color of emeralds and devoid of emotion.

"You won't talk, eh? You know, when you keep silent, the assumption around here is that you're guilty. You were found at the scene of the crime with the murder weapon on you, and none of our witnesses saw anyone else in the area, so that leaves you." She stared at him intensely, but he gave no reply. She shook her head and her ponytail bounced around her neck. She then called for the guard to let her out. Before she left, she gave the prisoner one last look.

"It's sad that you don't want to cooperate with me, I might be the only one who really wants to help you." She spun on her heels and walked away.

The prisoner sat up and rubbed at his beard, wondering why the woman wanted to help him. He laughed at himself for questioning her motives; he could use all the help he could get. He was being accused of murder! He needed someone on his side; he hadn't needed anyone for anything in a long time. But an image of her face came to mind and he thought about the way she had talked to him—strong willed and determined to get answers. He lay back down and rolled himself up in the blanket, he wouldn't worry about her; he would just enjoy the free room and board.

Luz rode the elevator up to the fifth floor and headed straight for her boss's office. Three steps from his door his secretary ran interference, blocking her way, Luz nearly ran into her.

"He's busy, Santa, doesn't want to be disturbed," she stated while examining her manicured nails. Rosa always knew how to push Luz's buttons; they hadn't gotten along from the day Rosa sashayed in with her designer clothes and applied for the secretary position. Luz wondered why a woman who obviously had enough money to spend on couture needed a job at a police precinct and she got the distinct impression Rosa herself believed she was slumming it there.

"Rosa, you know damn well my name is Santos, not Santa. The joke is getting old, and I don't care how busy the captain is, I need to speak with him right now. So either you take your skinny ass back to your desk or I'll have your job." Luz had never threatened Rosa before, but what she had to tell her boss couldn't wait. Rosa delayed a second longer then resentfully backed away. Luz could feel the secretary's eyes boring holes into the back of her head.

Luz opened the door as she knocked. Captain Andrews sat at his desk, speaking to someone who faced away from her.

"Captain, I realize you're busy, but I have some pressing news I think you need to hear regarding the murders downtown."

He nodded and waved her over to the unoccupied chair by his desk. "Luz, I'd like you to meet Mayor Yates. Mayor, this is Luz Santos, one of our top detectives in homicide. She solved the Grant case two years ago."

As she rounded the desk, she got a clear view of the man in the chair. He was tall, gray-haired, and judging from the wrinkles on his face, she estimated him to be in his late fifties.

"Yes, of course, Jonathan Grant; murdered his wife and her mother, made it look like a murder/suicide. He got life in prison; good job on that one, detective." Yates rose and stepped forward to take her hand. His grasp was strong and she winced when he pumped her hand hard and fast before finally letting go. Her boss waited until they had taken their seats before speaking again.

"Now, what is this pressing news, detective?" the captain asked.

She cleared her throat. "The suspect accused of killing both the Jamison woman and Matthew Hanson was found in the same alley as his second victim with the murder weapon on him." She paused, looking from one man to the other. "The problem with this is that he was found sleeping with the knife resting in his hand. The other discrepancy is that there's one set of prints on the knife and they aren't his. The knife looked clean otherwise."

Andrews looked at her squarely. "But I hear the man isn't talking. We don't know who he is, if he has a criminal history or if he's mentally ill. If he won't cooperate, it's likely he's hiding something."

"We're running his prints right now and I should have that information in a couple of hours. As for his cooperation, I'd say that has nothing to do with hiding something. He's old and looks like he's been on the street for a long time. I think he's taking advantage of the free food and shelter. I don't think he cares that he's in a jail cell."

The Mayor shifted in his chair and looked at the captain. "Mike, let's just hope this is our guy. We don't need a serial killer loose in this city. This man was found at the scene with the victim's blood on his hands as well as the weapon. What more do we need?" he asked, turning to Luz. *Maybe a motive?* she thought. She could see her boss rolling his eyes behind the mayor's back, probably in anticipation of the remarks she wanted to make—so she smiled politely.

"Good," Yates said happily. "Then this whole situation should be contained and solved by the end of the day."

Andrews stood and extended his hand. "I can't promise that, Tony, but we'll do the best we can. Thanks for coming by. I'll keep you updated."

They shook hands and the mayor saw himself out. Luz's boss loudly exhaled and plopped down in his chair. "That man gives me a headache," he said, massaging his temples. "He thinks because he was a cop back who-knows-when and who-knows-where that he knows the ins and outs of my precinct. He's used to open and shut cases, a murder, man found with the weapon, guilty verdict and put him away. This isn't an episode of C.S. fucking – I. That's not how this shit works."

41

Luz agreed and pushed on. "One more thing, boss, this knife that was used; it's not your basic kitchen knife. This knife looks like an antique. It's oddly shaped and it's got engraved designs on it. Davis down in evidence says it must have cost nearly two-thousand dollars; his grandfather used to collect."

"And?"

"So, what the hell is a bum doing with an expensive knife like that? Davis said that this particular knife is rare. He said it would have to be from a serious enthusiast's collection."

Her boss put his head in his hands moaned. He opened his desk drawer and pulled out a rumpled pack of Marlboros. In most buildings, the recent smoking ban was in effect. However it was far from enforced in their department mostly due to the fact that the boss smoked when he was stressed.

Luz raised her eyebrows. "I thought you quit, Mike?"

He laughed and shook out a cigarette. He lit it, took a long drag and blew out a big cloud of rolling smoke. "Well, I quit quitting." He said.

MAY 17TH, 2002 7:38 A.M.

"Help me!" the boy shouted. Blood dripped all over his tiny frame, and her stomach hurt thinking about whatever horror had caused him to look that way. She took a step towards him, but he quickly backed away, his eyes feral and afraid.

"Let me help you," she told him, gently trying to creep closer to him. He eyed the darkness behind her but when she was a step away from reaching him his eyes widened and focused on her.

"What is it?" she asked, confused. "What's wrong?"

"Run."

She felt someone shake her shoulder and she grabbed their arm and pulled, ready to execute a self-defense maneuver she'd learned at the academy.

"Oww! What the hell Santos!"

Her eyes snapped open "Eddie?"

"Yeah it's me. Dammit. Let me go."

She immediately released his arm as she recognized where she was. The office was mostly empty, but a few people were looking in her direction.

"You fell asleep at your desk, Santos," Eddie said rubbing his arm. "I went to pick you up at your place and your car was gone. So I came here. You could have called."

She checked her watch and cringed, she'd been sleeping for a half hour. "I'm sorry Eddie; I got zero rest last night. They found another body this morning and I've been up all night."

Eddie stared at Luz, his mouth slightly open. "So, are… are we going to talk about what just happened? What were you dreaming about that had you react to me like that?"

She felt the tears on her face and quickly wiped them away. It was one thing to have nightmares at home, where she could calm herself down but at work she was a different person and didn't want people seeing her vulnerable. She took a deep breath to calm her nerves.

"It was nothing, really. Just a bad dream. I'm sorry if I hurt you, I was acting instinctively." She stood up and stretched out the kinks that had settled in during the nap at her desk.

She couldn't believe she'd fallen asleep. It was time for some caffeine. She turned back to Eddie, who was watching her stretch. Suddenly she felt like she was on display. Clearing her throat, she got his attention and his eyes shot back to her face as a blush crept up his neck. At least he had the decency to look embarrassed. "Okay, Lopez. I might take you up on the breakfast offer; I could use coffee and a good meal."

Eddie's face shifted from anger to excitement. "Really? Cuz the place I was thinking of makes great coffee and their omelets are excellent!"

Luz grabbed her coat off the back of her chair and let him go on about the restaurant; she was too tired to ask him to shut up. She had to wake up somehow and Tacoma was a long drive. "Eddie?" she asked, cutting him off. "I have to check in with Andrews before I leave, would you mind running down and getting me a coffee from the Starbucks on the corner?"

He stopped talking and eyed her suspiciously. "I thought we were getting coffee at breakfast. Is this your way of ditching me?"

She laughed. "No, and to prove it to you…" she threw him her car keys, "you can hold on to these. Meet me at my car in ten minutes."

He caught the keys and smiled. "Ten minutes, you better be there, Chiquita, or I'm going for a joy ride in your flashy car."

"Do it and die," she yelled over her shoulder. "I'll be down in a sec. Just hurry. I need that caffeine." She watched him jog toward the elevators and felt a bit guilty. The only reason he put up with her shit was because he had a crush on her. It was wrong of her to use that to her advantage; she would have to be more careful not to lead him on.

She stopped by the captain's office, but he wasn't there. She decided to leave him a message, but Rosa was in one of her moods and after their little scene earlier, Luz doubted she would be much help. She returned to her office, grabbed her stuff and headed downstairs.

• • •

"I wasn't sure what you liked in your coffee. I got you a caramel Macchiato," Eddie said when Luz met him by her car.

"What did you get?" she asked, eyeing the cup he kept close to his chest.

"Just black with cream," he replied.

She reached for his cup and smiled. "You assumed wrong, Lopez. I like my coffee dark and mild. Let's go"

They hopped in the car. Eddie looked sullen and Luz felt guilty. "Okay, let me have a taste," she said.

"Hey if you don't like sweet, that's okay, I don't want to force you." He winked at her.

"Just give me the damn coffee!" she snapped and took the cup from him. She took a sip and, with great effort, swallowed the rich liquid. It was so sweet it hurt her teeth. She must have made a face because Eddie started laughing.

"Hey, you have to give me credit. I tried it," she said, smiling broadly. She inserted the key in the ignition and rolled out of the parking lot into the street. In a matter of minutes, they were cruising down Interstate 5 toward Tacoma. Luz rolled down her window to feel the wind on her face. Eddie was the first to break the silence.

"You handle this car so easily. How long have you had it?"

"About three years now, but I take care of her, even spoil her a little."

"A little?" he asked then listed off the car's features as he saw them; there was a tachometer, with a shifting light and Indiglow gauges installed, not to mention a top-notch stereo system, complete with a CD changer. The windows were tinted dark and he heard the turbo every time she shifted. He also told her that he'd taken time earlier to admire the custom paint and the flashy rims, as well as the custom spoiler on the back of the car. "You call this a little?"

She laughed and noticed his face lighting up.

"Okay, I admit I splurged, but blame my big brother. If it wasn't for him, I wouldn't have given this car a second glance."

They casually chatted about family and hobbies for the rest of the drive. Eddie occasionally stopped speaking to grip the door handles and hold his breath as Luz pushed her speed and wove through traffic. He was relieved when they reached their exit and Luz dropped the speed of the Eclipse back down to the legal level. They drove down on the waterfront where they faced heavier traffic. The sun shone, and the area was bustling; couples rollerbladed down the promenade and kids played in the grass. A few boats sat on the water and business was booming for the restaurants along the docks.

Eddie signaled for her to turn into the next parking lot and she found a space right in front of the eatery.

Boat ropes lined the walls of the restaurant, the windows were shaped as portholes, and the employees wore blue and white striped shirts and navy blue bottoms.

The hostess showed them to a booth near the back of the restaurant next to a large rusted anchor, where they sat and ordered more coffee.

"This place is…" Luz paused. "…different."

"Yeah, it's a little much, but the food makes up for the décor," he said rubbing his stomach. "My ex used to come here all the time and, boy, did she have a set of pipes. They have karaoke every Thursday and Saturday night."

"Your ex came here? You mean, she didn't stay home cooking and cleaning for you like a good Mexican woman?" Luz folded her arms and leaned back.

"Ha, ha, very funny. Actually, she wasn't Hispanic."

"Really? How surprising. I assumed you only dated Latinos. I guess we're both learning new things today, aren't we?" She smiled at him and he realized what she meant.

"Listen—" he started

"Don't worry about it, Eddie. I was just making a point. Clean slate from here. You won't assume things about me and vice versa. Deal?"

He took a moment to think and held out his hand. "Deal."

CHAPTER FOUR

Sleep comes quick and pulls me under
My heartbeat booms like rolling thunder
The evil inside burns so bright
It waits for release with the fall of night.

MAY 17TH, 2002 10:14 A.M.

Luz and Eddie finished breakfast and headed back. After a few blocks they took a right and followed the hill all the way to the top and turned down a narrow street. Most of the houses were small but there were a few newer homes that were larger, which made them look out of place in the neighborhood. Luz pulled into the driveway at the end of the cul-de-sac and sat in the car.

"This is the place?" she asked Eddie.

"Yeah, this is it. Kinda ugly, isn't it?" he said scrunching up his nose.

Salmon-colored stucco encased the house, and its shutters were the color of plums. The roof had gray Spanish-style tiles, and different-colored flowers grew all along the fence.

Everything clashed, and Luz pitied the neighbors who had to look at the monstrosity every day. It was as if whoever had chosen the layout had been colorblind.

They got out of the car and strolled up the walk to the wine-colored door. Eddie knocked, and they waited. A dog barked on the other side of the door—a big dog from the sound of it.

"Hello?" came a woman's muffled voice.

"Hello, ma'am. My name is Officer Lopez. I'm with the Seattle Police Department, with me is Detective Santos. Can we have a word?"

"The police? Why on earth would you want to speak with me?"

Luz was quick to make sure she hadn't startled the woman. "Please, ma'am, we're not here to harass you, we just have a few questions." Maybe the sound of another woman's voice comforted her because she unlocked the door and peered out. She looked to be in her mid-seventies; her hair was snow white and her skin was loose on her bones, like she was wasting away, but the strength of her gaze told another story.

"Well, aren't you a pretty little thing," she cooed at Luz. "Just want to ask me some questions, huh? Okay, come on in. She pushed open the screen door and let them inside. They were about to follow her into the living room, but a huge black mass stood in their way, growling protectively. The woman took no notice and kept walking.

Eddie cleared his throat. "Um, ma'am, could you call off your dog?"

Luz was surprised at the fear in his voice and made a mental note to tease him about it later.

The old woman stopped, turned slowly and whistled. The huge beast stood his ground.

"Hamlet, you come here right now!" she hollered, and the dog stopped snarling and sat next to her. "Well, all right then, you make yourself at home and please, by all means, call me Nelly." She took a seat in an old oak rocking chair and patted the dog's head.

Luz sat on the cream-colored sofa closest to the old woman while Eddie opted for a blue Lazy Boy across the room. He sat down, eyeing the dog, Luz enjoyed his uneasiness.

Nelly pursed her lips. "Now then, what is it I can help you with, Ms. Santa?"

Luz ignored the mispronunciation of her name and began. "We were hoping to speak with Mr. Mullen about a property he owns up north in Whitecenter."

"Well, you can't speak with him, I'm sorry." Nelly folded her hands in her lap.

"He's not in trouble. We just need some information," Luz clarified.

Nelly closed her eyes and began to rock. The silence in the room stretched for two minutes. Finally, she opened her eyes and fixed her stare on Luz, the sadness in Nelly's gaze was immense.

"Young lady are you married?"

Luz, bewildered, answered the question. "No, ma'am, I'm not."

"Well, do you know what it is to be in love?"

Luz felt Eddie's eyes on her. It was her turn to be uneasy.

She didn't answer. "Nelly, a woman lived in the house your husband rented out two years ago. I need to know if she had any roommates, or a boyfriend who stayed with her."

Nelly slowly shook her head. "Well, do you? Don't be rude. It's a simple question. Yes or no?"

Luz lowered her eyes and stared at her hands, then lifted her chin and said, "No." Hearing herself say the word made it sound so final. Her eyes shifted to Eddie. Instead of his usual smirk, she found pity in his gaze. Luz didn't want to be the object of anyone's pity. Trying to steady her voice, she turned back to Nelly. "What relevance does this have to the purpose of our visit? And why can't we speak with Mr. Mullen? We're working on an important case."

The room went silent again—this time the tension ran high.

"He's dead," Nelly whispered. Hamlet whined, sorrowfully nudging her thigh with his huge snout.

Luz's heart sank. She felt guilty for having pushed the old woman to speak to them. "I'm so… I'm so sorry. I never meant to…" she trailed off, feeling intrusive.

"Don't be sorry. He was a great man. He gave me the best years of my life, fifty-three to be exact. The last year was the most difficult to get through; he had cancer. Watching the man I love waste away, watching the cancer eat away at him day after day, month after month, was the hardest thing I've ever had to do. But I stayed with him, I stayed by his side." She cried and choked on her words. Hamlet licked her hand, clearly in an attempt to comfort his mistress. She watched Hamlet for a while; lost in her memories, then she wiped her eyes and smiled.

"Look at me," she exclaimed. "Crying like a loony old woman. I'm sure you didn't drive all the way here to watch me cry my eyes out." She stood and headed for the hall. "Come now, follow me, I think I may have some answers for you."

They obeyed and trailed her down the hall to the last room on the right. Luz looked around the room and wondered when someone had last been in there. Sheets covered the furniture and what wasn't covered in cloth was coated in a thick layer of dust.

"Mr. Finnity, our attorney, took care of the legal matters, the properties, the cars and the house, but I still have most of Don's records in here. What was the address?"

Eddie recited it and they waited while Nelly sorted through a musty file cabinet. "Oh, yes, here it is," she said, pulling out a file and opening it. "I remember now. He rented it to two women. I went with him when they signed the lease. They were delightful young ladies. Said they planned to spiff up the place. They had such an energy about them. I had no doubt that, given enough time, they would have made that house look like new. God knows Don and I didn't have the strength for it."

"Mildred Jamison is the one we're here about," Eddie said.

Nelly smiled. "Yes, yes, Milly. She was the older of the two. She was working on becoming a chef; told me she was a waitress at some upscale place on Lake Union. She wanted to take some courses to impress her boss, hoping he would give her a job in the kitchen. She was so ambitious. What happened to her? The last time I heard from her she was asking to pay her rent late, said something about family problems. I remember thinking that was strange because she never mentioned having family in the area. But months went by and we never saw the funds. Don was worried about losing money. He had just found out about his cancer and knew the medical bills would be sky high. Eventually, we had to ask them to move out, but we weren't happy about it. Those two were so nice."

Luz's assumptions about Mildred had been correct; she had been trying to turn her life around.

"When did this happen?" asked Eddie.

"About two years ago, I believe."

"What was the name of the roommate?"

Nelly handed him the file and he read it over. "Antoinette Lesheaux. No forwarding address. I'll call in the name and run a check." He walked toward the door, keeping a wide berth from Hamlet, who dutifully stood next to his mistress.

"Nelly, was there anything left in the house when your husband cleaned it out?"

Nelly shook her head. "Don never made it up there. He was too sick to leave the house and eventually had to stay in the hospital. Our attorney assured us the property would be taken care of. Have you been there? It's a cute little house."

"I haven't seen it, but Officer Lopez went down and said the house was boarded up and deserted. The grounds weren't kept up at all," Luz replied.

The old woman pursed her lips again. "I'll have to speak with Mr. Finnity about that," she said absently.

Luz followed the woman back into the living room and grabbed her coat. "Thank you, Nelly, you've been a great help. I am terribly sorry about your husband."

Nelly followed her to the door where Hamlet stood, looking out at Eddie. "Don't worry about it, dear. Don was a great man with a big heart. It was just his time to go. But I will tell you this, when you find a love as special as the one I shared with Don, you must be ready to give yourself entirely to that person. The love you'll share will bond you physically, emotionally and spiritually for the rest of your lives. So when you find it, hold on to it with both hands, and never let go." Tears pooled in her eyes and instinctively Luz leaned over and hugged her.

"Here I go again," mumbled Nelly. "I'm sorry. I just get caught up sometimes."

"It's okay. I haven't been lucky enough to find a love like that, but if I do I will remember your words."

Nelly smiled at her and touched her cheek. "Not *if* dear, *when*," she said softly. "*When* you find love. And you'll find it."

Luz didn't share the woman's optimism. She smiled and said goodbye. Nelly invited her back to visit. Eddie walked up to shake Nelly's hand but was stopped short when Hamlet let out a low growl. Eddie waved goodbye as he backed up to the car.

When they were back on the road, Luz laughed. "Are you dry yet?" she asked.

"Dry?"

"When you saw that Rottweiler, you looked like you pissed

your pants," she joked.

"It's not funny," he said flatly.

"It was to me. You squirmed in your seat when that dog breathed too hard. What's that about?"

He pulled down the collar of his shirt to reveal a scar, about six inches long. It started at his neck under his ear and wound down in a crescent, ending above his collarbone.

"See this? When I worked narcotics in LA, I was conducting a bust at this crack house. I chased a dope head through the house to the backyard and had him cornered against the fence. I was about to handcuff him, but when I got close, he whistled really loud. I wrestled him to the ground and had him cuffed, and he was whistling the whole time. Then, as I dragged him to his feet, I was tackled by this Rottweiler, must've been a hundred twenty-five-pound dog. Hit me like a bus. Anyway, it went straight for my throat. I tried to fight it, but it clamped on and had *me* pinned to the ground. The shithead I arrested stood there, laughing. I could taste my own blood and he was laughing..." he cringed as he trailed off.

"So I was basically stuck on the ground with this dog's teeth sunk into my neck, waiting for back-up. After my partner cleared every room in the house he came out back and saw me on the ground. He ordered the guy to call his dog off, but the guy just kept on laughing. I don't know what happened after that because I passed out. I had lost a lot of blood. My partner tried distracting the dog. But the dog stayed put, so in the end, he had to shoot him. I was rushed to the ER and they pumped some blood into me and stitched me up. Since then I don't piss off any dog, even Chihuahuas."

Luz swallowed. She felt guilty having teased him about the dog but recovered quickly. "That's too bad; I think Cheech would like you." Luz smiled, trying to diffuse the tension created by Eddie's story. She was relieved when he smiled back.

"Cheech?" he asked.

"He's my Chihuahua. It takes a while for him to get used to you, but after that he's pretty amiable. Now, if you were to bring him peanut butter cookies, he'd be putty in your hands."

Eddie arched a brow. "Cookies, huh? So are you planning to introduce me to Cheech?"

Luz detected eagerness in his voice and realized she'd steered the conversation in the wrong direction. After spending the day with Eddie, her feelings had shifted, but not in a way he'd like. If anything, he felt more like a brother, but she didn't dare tell him that. Men hated hearing that. *And women hate saying it*, she thought glumly. She would just have to keep him at arm's length and not take any more day trips with him. By now he would want to continue helping her with the case, but that didn't mean they had to work side by side. He also had his own job and his own life, but that hadn't stopped him from getting himself involved. Luz glanced sideways at Eddie. "Yeah, you'll meet Cheech one of these days," she said noncommittally. Then she boosted the car to ninety-five miles per hour and she was sure that Eddie was too busy holding on for dear life to worry about whether she was lying.

MAY 17ᵀᴴ, 2002 1:30 PM

The prisoner slept soundly until angry voices woke him. He opened his eyes and watched a large man argue with the guard. His voice was demanding; he sounded like a man who was used to getting what he wanted. After the verbal battle, the guard reluctantly led the man to the cell door and unlocked it. The larger man stormed into the cell and headed straight for the prisoner.

"Wake up, asshole. Judgment time," he yelled in the suspect's ear.

The man on the bed cringed but remained still. The large man squatted down so they were level. "Oh, you want formalities? Okay. Well, hello. I'm Detective Harris," he said mockingly and held out his hand.

The inmate shifted into a sitting position and reached for the detective's hand, but Harris snatched it back with a coarse laugh.

"You'd have to be crazy to think I was going to touch your grimy hand! Look at you—your beard is horrendous and probably housing five species of insects. Your clothes are covered in filth, and I could smell you from the Space Needle! But you know what?" he spat, his face inches from the prisoner's own. "What really makes me sick is the fact that you butchered two helpless people and you're just lying there, enjoying this place like it's the goddamn Hilton," he roared.

Harris paced the cell from end to end, glaring maliciously at the man on the bed. The man calmly stared at him. This did not please the detective.

"Okay, you sick bastard. You're quiet now, but when you're on trial for the murder of these people, I'm sure you'll have plenty to say. Just tell me one thing," he said and bent low so the inmate could smell the coffee on his breath. "Was it worth it?"

Harris waited for a reply and when one didn't come, the detective swung his fist hard. His punch landed right between the suspect's shoulder blades.

"Huh? Was it worth it?" he yelled, his face reddening. Harris hauled the prisoner off the bed by his collar and threw him to the floor. The man didn't fight; just got to his knees and stared at the cop. He remained silent but the hate in his eyes was likely evident.

Harris stepped forward. "What? You got something to say? Are you proud of yourself? You must feel pretty big killing two defenseless homeless people." He waited, took a breath and continued. "Or maybe you're feeling a little defenseless yourself right now." He chuckled.

The suspect looked up at Harris just as the cop brought up his knee and slammed it into the prisoner's ribs.

"What the hell is going on here?" Detective Santos yelled from outside the cell with fury in her voice "Harris, what the fuck do you think you're doing?"

Harris turned to her and wiped the sweat from his brow. He spit at the floor missing the injured man by an inch. "I'm doing your job, since you can't do it yourself." He stated.

The suspect watched as Detective Santos jerked open the jail door and marched up to Harris, who was a half a foot taller than her, but she managed to get in his face. "My job is to serve and protect innocent people. This man is innocent until proven guilty, you got that?"

"Whatever, Santos," Harris said and shrugged.

Detective Santos shot him an icy stare. "Harris, assholes like you should not be wearing a badge. One day *you'll* end up rotting in a cell somewhere, pulling shit like this. But you'll have a lot more to worry about than a beating. I'm reporting you to Andrews. I hope you like patrol duty," she finished and stepped out of the way. "Now, if you will excuse me, I need to speak to *my* suspect." When Harris didn't move, she pushed past him, shoulder first, and managed to shove him out of her way as Officer Lopez followed her into the cell.

Harris sucked in his gut and walked away. "Fucking beaners," he mumbled.

Detective Santos grabbed Officer Lopez's arm as he shot toward Harris. "It's not worth it, Lopez. Harris is just a hothead. He uses his muscle to get results."

Lopez was breathing heavily. "Yeah, well, I can use muscle too! Who the hell does that puto think he is, anyway?"

"Hey," Santos snapped, tugging his arm. The suspect watched their interactions and wondered if they were partners. They treated one another like old friends. "Let it go, Lopez! I'm serious. The guy has cobwebs in his brain." She held her finger to the officer's temple. "But use yours. He's not worth it," she repeated more sternly, releasing her grip on his arm.

"Yeah, I know. How did that prick ever make it to detective?" Officer Lopez asked.

"Heard of Dick Harris?" she asked.

"You've got to be shittin' me! So, daddy's the district attorney, huh?"

It seemed that the detectives had forgotten about the prisoner. He watched them talk, amused, but not showing it.

"Which comes in handy for a guy like Rick Harris every time he does something, like beat up a suspect," she said, pointing to the inmate on the floor of the cell. "Guess who's there to bail him out?"

She kneeled next to the prisoner. "Are you going to be okay?" she asked, looking him over for injuries.

The prisoner coughed and stood, holding his ribs tightly. "Title 21, section 210402 of the Violent Crime and Law Enforcement Act of 1994 has data on the use of excessive force by police officers. Police misconduct will often constitute a violation of common criminal statutes. In addition, the US Congress and many state legislatures have passed criminal statutes that prohibit a police officer from willfully interfering with another person's civil rights. Yet criminal prosecutions of police officers for misconduct in the line of duty are exceedingly rare."

Luz's jaw dropped, and she stared at him in amazement, then looked at Eddie who displayed the same shocked expression. The man in front of her wore rags, smelled like garbage, was covered in grime and was homeless. This man—who hadn't spoken a word to anyone—was articulately speaking about police brutality. Not only did he seem to know the law, he spoke clearly and enunciated every word. Too stunned to speak, they listened.

"Because Officer Asshole's father is the District Attorney, he will most likely never be prosecuted. Because of their close working relationship, prosecutors tend to be reluctant to bring charges against police officers, on whom they so heavily depend as a group. Perhaps as a result, local prosecutors' offices traditionally dedicate limited resources to police prosecutions. Probably more so when daddy sweeps it under the rug." He stopped and sat down on the bed, wincing in pain.

Luz picked her jaw off the floor and walked over to him. "That's incredible."

The man looked at her, a bit of anger in his stare. "What's incredible? That I'm educated? I can understand why you would think that someone who looks like me would be brainless. It's that kind of limited thinking that has our society in ruins."

Luz frowned then looked back at Eddie. "I guess there are a lot of assumptions floating around today, huh?"

Eddie shrugged and checked his watch. "Listen, you obviously have your hands full here. I've gotta go. I'm on in fifteen and I need to suit up. If you need any more help, give me a call."

She smiled. "Sure, and thanks for everything today.".

"No problem. See ya." He stepped out of the cell and walked down the hallway, Luz waited until his footsteps faded before she focused her attention on the injured man.

"First of all, I came down here because you called and left a message asking to speak with me. Second, if you want to sue Rick Harris, be my guest. I could care less. And lastly, I want to apologize if you thought I was judging you based on your looks. Any common man wouldn't be able to recite the law

61

verbatim, but you aren't the common man, are you? You're a lawyer, right?"

He stared, holding his ribs tightly.

Her gaze softened, and she grew serious. "I will make sure Harris is punished for what he did to you. That man has been accused numerous times of police brutality but because of who his father is, he's still got a badge. Nobody's happy about it but that's the way it is. That's all beside the point. You called and wanted to talk. I'm here, so talk."

He was about to say something but was cut off by the sound of Luz's cell phone.

"Hold that thought," she said, pointing a finger at him. Then she flipped open her phone. "Santos"

"What's up, Senorita?" said a male voice.

"Hey, Sonny. Did you get a track on those prints?"

"Yes siree. They belong to a Mr. Nicholas Mason. Thirty-five years old, been missing for some time now. Seven years or so. Used to be some big-shot lawyer downtown. Hope he still has connections, 'cuz if he killed those people, he'll need a good lawyer."

Luz shut her eyes and thought for a minute. "Thirty-five you say?"

"Yup, why?"

"No reason, it's just," she paused and looked at the man sitting beside her on the bed. "It just didn't seem that way at first. Thanks, Einstein. I'll call if I need anything else."

"No problem, sweetie, glad I could help. Be careful around this guy though. He's been laying low for a long time. Sounds like trouble to me."

"I will. Thanks." She flipped the phone shut and shoved it in her pocket. She smiled and turned her attention back to the inmate. "You were saying?" she asked.

"I wanted to know why you think I'm innocent. Due to the incriminating evidence thus far, I could be considered guilty."

"I've been doing my homework. But I just spoke with someone who may have changed my mind."

He looked doubtful. "You still believe me to be innocent, don't you?"

"I don't know, Nick, are you?"

His expression turned to one of surprise. "How did you know my name?"

"I got a friend upstairs who did some checking. Your name is Nicholas Mason; you were a successful attorney seven years ago. Now how did you get from there to here?"

Luz watched as he battled with his emotions; he seemed hurt and damaged. All the strength he'd shown earlier ebbed. She waited for his reply, but none came.

"All right, you aren't ready to talk yet. If you'd like to wait until your attorney is present, I get it. But I need some answers. What were you doing in that alley last night?"

He hesitated before answering and for one moment she thought he'd wait until he had legal counsel present to answer any questions from her. When he finally spoke, she felt relief wash over her. She didn't know why, but it pleased her that he trusted her enough to keep talking. "Sleeping. I had scored enough money to buy myself a couple of cheap beers and I drank alone in that alley and eventually fell asleep."

"Scored? Like drugs? Theft?" she asked.

"No," he stated, his cheeks reddening. "As in sitting on the street begging for money."

"Okay." She'd have to take his word on that. "Did you hear anything or anyone else in the alley?"

"No. I pick that spot because a lot of the homeless people congregate farther east. I'm usually left alone."

"Do you know anyone by the name of Mildred Jamison or Matthew Hanson?"

He looked at her blankly. "No."

"Does the name Gil Billion ring a bell?"

"No, should it?" he asked.

"You tell me."

The silence stretched for a couple of minutes and Luz began pacing the cell.

"So you woke up when the police were cuffing you?"

"Yes. I was sleeping, rudely awakened, and read my rights. I had no idea what was happening until I was brought down to the station and questioned."

Luz searched for any signs of acting, but could find no twitching, fidgeting, or eye movements that would have given him away. His voice was stern and strong like a lawyer trying a case in court. But she wasn't the judge who could set him free.

"Mr. Mason, tonight I have a charity function to attend at the mayor's estate. He has already begun congratulating my boss for catching the killer in this case, which would be you. I will speak with my boss on the matter of your innocence. I believe that you are innocent, so either you're telling the truth or very good at lying and being a lawyer. That's an asset to the trade, am I right?"

"I'm no longer practicing law. I've left that life behind," he stated in a bitter tone.

"You left it purposefully?" she asked, surprised. Instantly she felt his walls go up again. She stopped pacing and stood in front of him.

"Whatever the reason, it must have been traumatic, and you don't have to tell me if it doesn't pertain to this case. One more question; do you have a bank account?"

She watched him hesitate for a fraction of a second before he nodded.

"Yes. I have a savings account that's been collecting interest for a while now. I had a friend who worked at a credit union lock up my account for ten years so the money wouldn't be touched. I gave him special instructions so none of that money would be accessible to me for at least the first five years. When I got used to being homeless, I taught myself to never want for anything more than existence. It was hard at first. I had a good job and a wi—" his hands began to tremble, and he stopped. "Anyway, there's a substantial amount of money in the account but I haven't spoken to Fredrick in years." Mason scoffed. "He wouldn't recognize me anyway."

Luz took a moment to process this information. The pieces weren't fitting, but Nicholas Mason was a puzzle worth solving. *Not on your schedule,* she thought and checked her watch.

"Okay. I have to run. I'll check in with you again tomorrow.

In the meantime, get some rest. If you need a doctor to examine you or to check for broken ribs, tell the guard and he will arrange it. If you need to speak with me, call my cell. I will leave the number with dispatch on the way out." She bent down and stared into his eyes, noticing at once how sharp and clear they were; the blue hue was so light they bordered on gray.

"Was there anything else?" he asked.

Luz blushed, realizing she'd been staring. She got up quickly and walked away.

"No, that's all." She called the guard over to lock the cell. She held onto the bars for a moment and stared at the broken man on the bed.

"Mr. Mason, I'll do my best to get you out of here, but if for one moment I think I made the wrong decision in helping you, you will be very sorry."

Mason raised his head and stared at her warily and Luz realized she had come across a lot harsher than intended, but she'd made her point. She released the bars and walked away.

• • •

Nick kept his eyes fixed on the spot where she had stood. He'd made a fool of himself when he jabbered on about police brutality. He wanted to sound smart and to make the cops feel stupid, but it backfired when he was left alone with Detective Santos. After answering her questions, he was the one left feeling dim-witted. He had a very successful life, very capable of flying, but he had chosen to walk, and risk being trampled by society's expectations.

It was a risk he'd been willing to take. He wondered if his reasons for staying homeless were the same now as they were seven years ago. His wife's horrific murder still haunted him, and he hadn't forgiven himself for not being there for her when she needed him. But now that he had slept in a real bed and eaten real food and had an intelligent conversation with someone, he knew the time had come to stand up and take back a place in society.

An image of Detective Santos flashed through his mind and a genuine smile lit his face for the first time since his imprisonment. He'd gotten a better look at her that time; her clothes were of expensive taste and he picked up the faintest scent of Michael Kors perfume when she sat near him. He inhaled slowly trying to pick up any trace of the alluring fragrance.

When she'd stepped up to Harris's face, she had a take-no-crap attitude and had proven she was stronger than she looked. During the whole ordeal her voice had gone from cold to warm and back again, and he knew that she could either be a powerful ally or one's worst enemy. He was glad she'd chosen to go to bat for his team. If she'd been on the other side, he would have been doomed. It was one reason he felt safe talking to her without his lawyer present.

He slid himself onto the bed and winced when a sharp pain tore at his ribs. He lifted his shirt and assessed the damage. The ribs on the right side were red and beginning to swell. He remembered Luz's suggestion of a doctor and decided against it. The pain would remind him to seek vengeance. Yes, Harris would learn his lesson and Nick would be his teacher. Nick rubbed his ribs a bit longer while he thought of the torment he would inflict on the son of a bitch. He fell asleep with a wicked smile on his face.

CHAPTER FIVE

My body shakes with anticipation
I calm my nerves with some complication
The smell of blood I mournfully long
Tonight the evil is very strong

MAY 17ᵀᴴ, 2002 4:30 P.M.

Luz was typing at a pretty good pace when her computer froze. She stared blankly at the screen then got up and banged on the monitor. "Dammit!" she shouted. She tried several keystrokes to restart her computer, but they were useless. She took a deep breath and tried them again. When they didn't work, she cursed furiously at the screen.

"Whoa, I haven't heard words that dirty since the Navy."

She looked up, startled, and found Sonny grinning at her from the doorway of her office. "Sorry," she said quickly and banged on the monitor again.

"Whoa, whoa, whoa. Hold on there, honey. That's no way to treat technology," he said, stepping protectively in front of her monitor.

She ignored the "honey" since it was just the way he spoke. Sonny worked in the forensic department on the third floor; he had been hired by the Seattle Police Department right after announcing his retirement from the US Navy. He enjoyed his work and the people he worked with and had always been like a grandfather to Luz. He was constantly doing her favors; rushing fingerprint jobs or other reports that usually took forever to get back. Sometimes she would take him to dinner, or get him tickets to a Mariner's game, but no matter how many times she did something nice for him he would top her with three more favors. Sometimes she felt as though she would never catch up. She smiled thinking of his frizzy gray hair. He bore a strong resemblance to Albert Einstein. So strong, in fact, that the other cops had started calling him that and it stuck.

"Technology, my ass. I just spent the last three hours typing up reports on five different cases and suddenly the computer decided to make my job twice as hard."

Sonny put his hands on her shoulders and forced her to sit down. "I got this, just hold on." He turned his back to her and typed furiously. The computer emitted a series of beeps and when he stepped away, all her data was restored safe and sound on the desktop. She sighed as the tension melted from her muscles. "What would I ever do without you, Einstein? Thank you. I owe you lunch."

He waved her off and took a seat on the corner of her desk. "Glad I could save you, but that's not the reason I came up here. I lifted the fingerprints off the knife and one pair came from your boy, Mason, and the other I can't seem to locate. I'm running an extensive search on them now and should have results in a couple of days. But the unidentified prints were stronger and easier to lift. Mason's prints were barely on the knife at all. I'm writing up a report, but you may want to mention it to Andrews tonight."

"Oh shit!" Luz jumped out of the chair and grabbed her purse and coat. "I'm sorry, Sonny, I just remembered I have that charity dinner at the mayor's. I have to go, but thanks for all your help. Let me know what comes up." She ran from her office to the elevators, tapping her foot as she waited for one of the cars to stop on her floor. The doors finally opened, and she almost collided with another woman.

"Excuse me," the woman stammered, stepping back. She was at least a half foot taller than Luz, and she wore navy slacks and a cream-colored cardigan. The woman looked lost as her manicured hands fussed with the pearls around her neck.

"I'm so sorry. I'm kind of in a hurry," Luz said, backing into the elevator.

"That's okay, I was wondering who I should speak to if I have information on a case."

Luz stopped the closing doors and pointed to the right. "There's a secretary over there who will take your information and help you find someone to speak with."

"Thank you... Ms.?"

"Santos. Detective Santos, and your name?" Luz asked as the elevator doors began to close again.

"Antoinette Peterson."

"Okay, Mrs. Peterson, have a nice day." She let the doors close and felt the elevator coast to the ground floor. Luz nearly stepped out of the elevator when the name clicked. Cursing herself, she got back in and returned to the fifth floor. She found Mrs. Peterson in the front office, sitting in one of the chairs staring at the wall.

"Mrs. Peterson, would you please come with me?" she called. The woman was obviously confused at the sight of her. "I know I told you I was in a hurry, but my schedule just opened up. I believe I may be the person you want to speak with anyway."

She led the woman to her office and shut the door, took her seat behind her desk and motioned for Mrs. Peterson to sit, too.

"Now, you're here about the Jamison murder, am I correct?"

The woman looked at her with amazement, her blue eye going wide. "How did you know that?" she asked.

Luz ignored her question. "Your maiden name was Lesheaux and you used to rent a house with Mildred in Whitecenter."

Antoinette brought her hand to her mouth and stared. "I... I don't know how you know, but you're correct."

Luz crossed her arms across her chest. "We looked into Mildred's past, seeking a reason someone would want to take her life. We didn't come up with much, but we did get your name. We couldn't trace it and now I know why. Did you marry?"

"Yes, a year ago next Friday," she whispered. Luz detected a slight tremble within that whisper.

"Congratulations," Luz said. "When did you first hear about the murder?"

Antoinette lowered her head—her long blond hair became a curtain, closing off Luz's view of her face—then mumbled something.

"I'm sorry? I didn't catch that," Luz said, leaning forward a little. "Yesterday."

"And you didn't come forward until now? Mrs. Peterson, I don't know if you know this, but that makes you a suspect. First Mildred is murdered and then another victim is found last night, and you don't show up until now." She bent down to see the woman's reaction but could only make out the top of her head.

"Why did you wait so long?" Luz asked. The woman's body shook and was soon racked with sobs. Antoinette lifted her tear-streaked face to look at Luz. Luz offered her a tissue. She took it and wiped at her nose while Luz gave her time to collect herself.

"In a way I *did* kill her. We lived together for quite a while and we enjoyed each other's company. She was the only person who could make me laugh back then." She smiled weakly and wiped her nose again. "I lived in Spokane in ninety-three. I grew up there and I had a boyfriend who was moving to Seattle. I followed him here but shortly after the move, he up and left me. Of course he left with my money and my car. Typical of the man. I didn't have a job, either, so I couldn't keep the apartment. I looked for a month for a place to stay, and on the day of my eviction, I met Milly.

"She worked at a ritzy Thai restaurant downtown and I applied there as a waitress. When I was walking out, Milly called me over and wished me good luck on the job. She was so sweet…" she dabbed her eyes with another tissue and continued. "Anyway, I got the job, thanks to her, and she told me she was looking for a roommate. I moved in the next week and we became best friends. I mean we told each other *everything*. Back then she called me Anne, which was a lot less Renaissance than Antoinette. We had a lot in common. I could trust her, and she could trust me…" she trailed off.

"What happened?" Luz asked.

"One day my ex-boyfriend showed up again and I was stupid enough to take him back. He began partying and asking for money. Knowing his past, I should have said no. But one night he gave me a taste of heroin. Then, I began asking Milly for money. Pretty soon she cut me off. She saw what the drugs were doing to me and tried to stop me. Being the addict I was, I mistook her concern for betrayal and blew up. From there, I sold everything I owned and most of her belongings to pay for my habit. It cost me my home, my friend and almost my life. Even though we went our separate ways, we both ended up on the street. But I did see her shortly after, when one time I was, um… earning money for drugs—"

Luz cut in, "Earning money?"

She sighed impatiently. "I don't like to talk about it, and it only happened that one time. I'm not proud of it at all."

Understanding dawned on Luz and she nodded slowly. She'd seen what drugs could reduce people to. When she worked the street, she had busted her fair share of prostitutes. "Go on," she urged.

"Well, I was about to get into this van with this scumbag and I looked across the street and there she was, staring at me like I was trash. I didn't see her for a long time after that. After I overdosed on the heroin and was rushed to the hospital, I decided my life needed changing. So here I am, born again and living it up while my friend is lying on a cold slab at the morgue." She sobbed again, and Luz handed her the box of tissues.

"I'm not sure I understand—if you went your separate ways, when was it that you saw her again?"

Antoinette cried harder. Luz watched as her eyes swelled again and felt sorry for the woman. After a few minutes, Ms. Peterson forced herself to be calm and wiped her eyes.

"A couple of months ago I was shopping downtown with some of my friends. Mind you, my friends are very close-minded and know nothing of my past... nothing. We were shopping, and Milly approached me on the street and told me how good I was looking and if there was any way I could help her out. I just stared at her for a minute, and my friends glanced at me, then at Milly, their faces full of disgust, trying to figure out the connection between me and this homeless woman. I started to feel as if the perfect new world I'd created for myself was falling apart... so, I acted like I was revolted by Milly. I tried to mirror my friends' expressions. I... I yelled at Milly to get away from us and walked off.

"I thought about what I'd done for the rest of that day and the weeks that followed. I couldn't eat or sleep without thinking about her. One day I woke up early and drove to Seattle hoping to find her. I must have looked in every alley, under every bridge, and in every shelter. I finally went home exhausted from my efforts and I cried. It took me weeks to get over how I'd treated her. I figured Milly was really smart and resourceful and would have found a way to pull herself up. But when I saw her face on the news, when I heard what happened, I couldn't believe it, and to think that if I hadn't been such a pretentious bitch and had done the same that she'd done for me—she would be alive."

Luz watched Antoinette work her way through the box of tissues on the desk. She wanted to tell the woman that she had done everything possible to find her friend, but that's what the woman had come to her for; redemption. Luz wasn't going to give her that. The woman in front of her was selfish, ungrateful and didn't deserve forgiveness.

"So you never held a grudge against Mildred?" Luz asked, arms folded and eyebrows raised.

"No. Why would I? I wouldn't be the person I am today without her."

"She didn't have money stashed away that you knew about?"

"Well, she had saved up some money for her culinary classes but that's all I knew. Why is this starting to feel like an interrogation?" she asked, gripping the used tissues tightly in her hands.

"Well, Mrs. Peterson, what you've told me about yourself has led me to believe that you're a manipulative liar." Luz registered the shock on the woman's face. "And I am going to need you to come downstairs with me for fingerprinting."

Antoinette's shock gave way to anger and she slammed her hand on the desk in a surprising show of confidence. "Now see here, detective, I came here to offer information and now I'm being treated as a suspect? This is bullshit!"

Luz got up and walked around the desk, her eyes never leaving Antoinette's. "First of all, you took quite a long time to come forward. As I said before—there was another murder last night, so you could be a suspect."

Antoinette stood and looked at her defiantly. "I watched the news this morning and you've already caught the killer, so don't try and intimidate me."

Luz clicked her tongue. "Tsk, tsk, tsk, Mrs. Peterson. You shouldn't believe everything you see on TV. The man caught at the scene is clean. Turns out he's just another homeless person for you and your friends to turn your noses up at."

Antoinette hung her head.

"Please follow me, Mrs. Peterson. It's a relatively short procedure," Luz said, formally opening the door.

Antoinette collected her coat and purse and followed Luz out. The elevator ride down was a quiet one; in fact, they didn't speak until it was over.

"I suggest you stay in town. I'll need to ask you some more questions," Luz said.

The woman simply nodded and left, still shaken. Luz was walking back to her office when her cell rang.

"Santos," she answered.

"Where are you, Luz? I've been here for almost an hour waiting for you. The mayor asked if my date's even coming!"

"I'm so sorry, sir. Something came up."

"It better damn well be important, because I'm sitting here

dressed like a penguin only because you said you'd be my date for the night. Otherwise, I would have asked Rosa to accompany me, but I chose you because I wanted to have intelligent conversation. I hate these stupid functions. I sat here all night and listened to the mayor ramble on and on about all his accomplishments and contributions to society. It's all a crock of the steaming pile, ya know?"

"Mike, a woman came to see me today about the Jamison murder. She says they used to be friends but that she didn't help Mildred to get off the streets when she had the chance."

"Yeah, so what? She feels guilty. Anything else?"

"She was a pretty big woman, I mean, physically strong-looking. She could have easily handled a person Mildred's size."

Luz heard the music in the background fade and assumed her boss had found a quieter place to talk. "Okay. What's her connection with the other victim?"

"When she told me about her past, she mentioned a boyfriend who had stolen a lot from her; he ruined her life. That could have been Matthew Hanson, right?"

Mike sighed. "Luz, that's a little far-fetched—" he began.

"I know, but I fingerprinted her just in case. Those could have been her prints on the knife as well as Nicholas Mason's. I had to be sure."

"When will we know?"

"I was going to stay all night and work with Sonny until we got a match."

"So I guess I'm going stag for the rest of the night?" Luz could picture the look on her boss's face and tried not to snicker but failed.

"I heard that. You think this is funny, do you, Santos?"

"No, sir," she said, suppressing another laugh.

"Yeah, well laugh all you want, cuz you're coming with me next Tuesday."

"What's next Tuesday?" she asked, the smirk disappearing from her face.

"Next Tuesday, Mayor Yates plans to outdo himself and throw a bigger, more extravagant party than the one that I'm sitting alone at right now."

Luz groaned. "I don't think I can make it, Mike. I've got to wash my hair."

"Har, har, Santos, it wasn't a request; it was an order. You *will* be coming with me."

"Well since you put it that way, I'll see you at seven."

"Good, I have to go now. The mayor is about to blow some more hot air."

Luz laughed. "All right. Will you be in tomorrow?"

"Probably. It's a Saturday and I don't have a life."

"Great, then we can not have a life together. I need to talk to you about Nicholas Mason in the morning."

Her boss moaned. "Morning? I was hoping to sleep in. This thing doesn't end until eleven tonight."

"If I bring in some Krispy Kremes will you be in by ten?"

"Oh yeah, throw in some premium coffee and I'll make it by nine." He perked up.

"Will do. See you at nine." She hung up and went to find Sonny and some coffee for herself.

It was going to be a long night.

CHAPTER SIX

The moon is shining, it's far from dawn
Time to choose another pawn
Then my rage will subside
Only to surge, only to rise.

MAY 18TH, 2002 12:00 A.M.

I awoke in a cold sweat and sat up in bed, images from the dreams stuck to my consciousness. My body shook badly as I got up and went to the bathroom. I let the water run until it was frigid and splashed it on my face. Shortly after the shaking stopped, the itching began. It started along the back of my neck and spread down to the tips of my fingers. I opened the medicine cabinet for some calamine lotion and slowly rubbed onto my skin. I knew the itching was mental—but the ritual helped me calm down in the past, so I continued to rub it in.

Memories of the dream drifted into my mind and I lifted the lid to the toilet and retched. When my stomach settled down I put the lotion away and got dressed. I quietly tiptoed downstairs to the kitchen and opened the back door. There was only one way to make the itching stop. I stepped outside and disappeared into the night.

• • •

Luz drove home in a daze. She had been up for twenty-four hours and was in desperate need of sleep. She had worked with Sonny all night—breaking only once to go home and let Cheech out—and it still hadn't made a difference. They would still have to wait until morning for the results. It could have been on a subconscious level, but she ended up cruising the streets downtown. She stopped at a corner store and bought a Snickers bar. She hadn't eaten since breakfast. On her way back to the car she decided to take a walk through Pioneer Square. She grabbed her windbreaker from the backseat, pulled it on and strolled down toward the park.

She passed a lot of homeless people, some sleeping in the doorways of buildings and some on the sidewalk; vulnerable and exposed. She thought about how easy it must have been for the killer to choose his prey. The number of homeless people in Seattle had multiplied significantly in the last five years. Unfortunately, the number of shelters and missions had stayed the same. She wished there was some way to keep them all inside until they could find the sicko who was now stalking them. But there were too many homeless, and not enough resources to do the job.

She thought back to when her own family faced poverty and was grateful that someone had taken them in. Her father,

Luis Santos, had come to the United States stuffed into a tiny truck with fifteen other Mexicans. He was born and raised in Jalisco, Mexico. He had come to the States after Luz's youngest brother, Raul was born. After Luz's mother had given birth she became ill and Luis had come to the United States to find work to afford the medication she needed to get well. He sent money almost every month but when Raul was eleven months old, she passed away. After that, Luz's aunt and uncle took her and her two brothers in, but after her mother's funeral her dad insisted he could raise the children on his own. After four separate attempts and many pesos, Luis got himself and his three children passage to the US.

Luis worked hard in the orchards of California, making ends meet for his family. But when it came time for Hector to attend school, there wasn't enough money to send him. One day Luis got word of the apple orchards of Washington and how much money was to be made there. So he packed up his children and headed to up to Yakima, Washington. It was rough at first, trying to provide for his family. There was a point when an unexpected drought left no work for the immigrants. Luis was forced to take his family from the house they had grown up in. Luckily the Mexican community was strong and took pride in helping others of their culture. They lived there until Luz was twenty, and by then her father was too old for physical labor. So they moved to Seattle with another family and Luis got a job as a gardener/handyman for a wealthy family. Moving to a big city had been intimidating for Luz. She was used to a small community, but she adapted and soon found life in the city exciting. After trying to attend a community college for six months, she had taken interest in law enforcement.

Her older brother, Hector, had chosen Job Corp, and her younger brother, Raul was still in school at the time and she knew her father didn't have enough money to send her to a decent college. So she called around and interviewed at the Seattle Police Department. After she completed all the testing, she was sent to the academy. She excelled at every level and started her career as a police officer at twenty-one. People who mattered took notice of her hard work and devotion, and she made detective five years later. She had a better track record than the other detectives in her department for solving cases, which earned her many awards along the way. It was difficult working in a male-dominated field, but instead of alienating herself, she tried her hardest to tolerate the men she worked with. She had already received two job offers with the FBI, but she declined because she felt she needed more experience. She was very proud of her accomplishments and grateful for the opportunities in her life.

She stopped walking and surveyed her surroundings. She was close to Chinatown near an overpass, underneath she saw people sleeping in cardboard boxes or wrapped in plastic for warmth. Instead of walking toward the makeshift shelters, she turned and headed for her car. She decided to visit the murder scenes to figure out a pattern. She was a few blocks from where they had found Matty's body and decided to take another look. The police tape was still intact, but the area was deserted. She walked around the alley, breathing through her mouth; the stench of rotting garbage was overpowering.

She exited the alley onto a quiet street. She looked up and down the road and after turning right, walked for a while, crossed the street and headed back. As she passed a doorway, someone grabbed her ankle.

"What the?" she shouted and kicked away the hand.

"Could you spare some change, miss?" came a scratchy voice.

Luz's heart pounded wildly and instinctively she pulled her gun. The old man's eyes grew wide when he saw that. He held his hands in front of his face and reeled backward.

"Sorry, I'm sorry. Please don't shoot me. I'm only hungry." he said, peeking through his fingers and eyeing the weapon.

She relaxed and put the gun away. The man was leaning against the wall and one of his legs ended at the knee; the stump was wrapped in an old t-shirt. "You shouldn't grab people when they walk by. You're likely to get yourself in trouble. I could have shot you just now."

The man hawked up some spit and launched it in her direction. "Shot, huh? Well I woulda shaken your hand but as you can see," he rubbed a hand over the nub, "I can't stand up too fast. What's a pretty thing like you doing with a gun anyway?" he narrowed his eyes and looked her over.

She pulled out her badge and showed it to him. "I'm a detective; guns are part of the job. Listen, you shouldn't be alone on the street like this," she said.

"You're right, detective. I'll just hop in my Mercedes and drive home to my mansion and sleep in my fifty-thousand thread count sheets," the bum replied.

Luz sighed. "Why don't you take yourself over to the bridge? I can help you. There are more people over there."

"That's the reason I'm not over there. Those people are thieves. I'd never get any sleep because I'd be too busy watching my back. Why do you care anyway?" he asked, scratching at a scab on his face.

Luz glanced up and down the dark street. "There have been two murders in this area in the last two days. If I were you, I'd migrate to well-populated spaces."

"Well, you ain't me and if you ain't gonna give me any money, leave me alone," he said before hawking up more spit.

Luz gave up. "Okay. Do what you want. I did warn you. Just don't let your guard down."

He launched another glob of mucus at Luz, and it landed a little too close for comfort. A cool breeze blew through the buildings and she pulled her coat closer and walked away. She could still hear the man laughing when she crossed the street. She felt guilty for not forcing him to go. She was about to turn the corner when the laughter died, and a gurgling noise replaced it. Luz stopped and listened. Footsteps pounded on the pavement from the direction of the man, but it was dark, and she couldn't make out any features. She knew it couldn't have been the bum unless he had a prosthetic leg she hadn't noticed.

She ran back up the street and pulled up short. The bum was staring up at the sky with his mouth open. Blood covered his shirt in random splatters and his head dropped back to reveal a nasty gash stretching from one ear to the other. Luz stood for a second before the shock wore off, and she ran in the last direction she heard the footsteps. She drew her gun and took the safety off. Peering into the darkness she could make out somebody running about thirty yards away.

"Stop! Police!" she shouted. The figure stopped and turned. Then it disappeared around a corner. She picked up her pace, heart pounding against her rib cage. When she reached the corner, she stopped and held her breath. She held up the gun and cleared the corner. Maybe it was because she was so tired, but her reflexes fell short. Something sharp pierced her abdomen and she doubled over in pain. Quickly, she looked up to find the person responsible for the attack, but a strong fist punched her face. She fell over, groping at the wound in her side. The attacker kicked her in the head and took off. She tried to focus on the retreating figure but failed to observe any defining features. Her vision was blurred. She gave up and lay still in the middle of the street, unable to move.

She heard a car door slam and screeching tires. Smelling the burnt rubber, she looked up and saw headlights coming at her; fast—too fast. She cried out and tried to get up, but the pain in her side was immense. The car sped toward her and she managed to roll out of the way; hot pain coursing through her with the effort. The car barely missed her and continued up the street. She squeezed off two shots, one shattering the back window and the other taking off a hubcap. The car fishtailed, and she thought she'd hit her mark, but the driver regained control and the car disappeared from sight. Luz watched the hubcap roll lazily to the curb where it stopped and landed with a sharp *clang* that echoed in her head.

Weak and lightheaded, Luz dropped her gun and clutched at her side. She brought her hand up to inspect it and saw that it was covered in blood. She let out an agonized, alien cry that she didn't recognize as her own voice. She blinked rapidly and knew she would lose consciousness soon. Slowly, she reached into her pocket and pulled out her phone. She opened it with one hand and punched a couple of buttons. She couldn't remember if it rang but she heard the voice on the other end say hello.

"Ben..."

"Hello? Who is this?" he said.

"...help... hurt..."

"Luz? Luz is that you?" he shouted frantically. "Where are you? Luz! Say something, dammit!"

"...towndown...." She was having trouble speaking.

"Town down? Downtown? Where are you, are you okay?"

With her vision cloudy she barely saw the green and yellow neon sign across the street.

"Subway near homeless bridge.... Please, hurry... I can't..." she trailed off as her pain intensified.

"Luz, I'm getting help. Hold on, okay? Help is on the way!"

He continued to speak, but she didn't catch anymore of his words. Before long, she was out cold.

MAY 18TH, 2002 10:30 A.M.

Luz opened her eyes and shut them quickly when the light from the florescent bulbs burned her vision. She whimpered and turned her head, immediately regretting the movement when bolts of pain shot through her skull causing flashing lights behind her eyelids.

"Don't try to move, the doctor wants you to rest," a voice said. Familiar. It took Luz a moment to guess who the speaker was.

"Ben?" she whispered and could hear his footfalls as he walked to her side.

"It's me, Litebrite, I'm here," he said, and the fear in his voice unsettled her. "I thought we lost you there for a moment."

She smiled. "Luz" in Spanish means "light" and when they were dating, Ben had chosen the nickname Litebrite. She hadn't heard it in a long time. A small smile creased her lips.

"What happened?" she murmured.

He took a deep breath and exhaled slowly. "Luz, just rest now. We'll talk when you're feeling up to it, okay?"

"Please, Ben? I need to know. There was a guy, a bum. He was killed. I should've... I ran after the killer and—"

"You don't have to tell me what happened next. I'm guessing he stabbed you and knocked you down and you called me. God, Luz, it scared the shit out of me, hearing you near death and not knowing where you were and if I could get help in time. You sounded so... so... weak."

Luz grimaced. Ben wasn't used to seeing her as weak. While they dated she had been careful not to show weakness. When they broke up she made him believe that she'd be okay because she was a fighter, but he didn't know she'd spent many nights crying thinking about him and deeply missing him.

"What happened after I called you?" she asked, slowly

opening her eyes. He stood by her bed looking down at her with concern. He wore an old Guns N Roses t-shirt and his hair was rumpled as if he'd just woken up.

"I called 911 and told them about the call. Luckily, gun shots were reported in the vicinity of the attack. I told the dispatcher you said something about a Subway being close by and since Seattle doesn't have a subway system I assumed you meant the sandwich shop and they narrowed it down to two in the area. They found the homeless man two blocks away... he was dead. They called me, but I sent a replacement so I could be here when you woke up."

Luz attempted to smile, even though it hurt. "Thank you."

Ben looked away, his face reddening. "Anyway, they found your gun next to you and figured you must have fired the shots. Across the street they found a hubcap with a slug lodged in it that matched the ones in your nine-millimeter. They assumed that the killer was driving a Honda since the hubcap bore the emblem." He paused and stared down at her. "They said they found you on the street in a puddle of blood. Your face was swollen, and you had a pretty good-sized bump on your head. Jesus, Luz, what were you thinking chasing a killer by yourself? You should have called for backup."

"My car was blocks away and I hadn't remembered my cell phone until I thought to call you. If you want to call it a thought. I was really woozy. I'm surprised I could think at all."

"The doctor says you have a concussion in addition to the wound in your side and that shiner on your face."

She lifted her arm and noticed the IV drip, then she

touched underneath her right eye and flinched. Ben laughed. "That was smart," he said. "You didn't believe me? Seriously, you look like Sylvester Stallone in *Rocky*."

Luz closed her eyes against the pain. *Good job, Luz, you landed yourself in the hospital,* she thought.

Ben's voice softened, and he reached for her hand. "Hang in there, Santos. The doctor said the knife barely missed a major organ but cut a few arteries on the way in. After the operation they stitched you up and pumped you full of painkillers. You've been asleep for hours, but you'll be fine. I'm gonna go get some coffee. I'll be back."

He released her hand and walked toward the door. He paused in the doorway and turned around. "Oh, yeah, you might want to thank Eddie for saving your life. His blood type matched yours and they ran out here at the hospital. Busy night, I guess. You owe him big time." Ben smiled playfully and walked out.

Luz groaned but this time it wasn't from the pain.

CHAPTER SEVEN

The stakes are higher, the rules keep bending
My sinful pleasures never ending
All eyes on me but they can't see
The monster I have come to be

MAY 18ᵀᴴ, 2002 2:30 P.M.

When Luz opened her eyes, the room was empty. Or so she thought.

"Hello," came a soft voice from her right. She jumped.

She turned her head and saw a well-dressed man sitting in a chair across the room. He looked relaxed, wearing Dockers, a chestnut polo shirt and matching brown Oxfords. His hair was freshly cut, and his face looked clean-shaven and flawless. His bone structure was angular with prominent cheekbones; as if he were a little underweight. Nevertheless, Luz thought him absolutely striking. There was something familiar about him.

"Can I help you?" she asked, her voice croaking through her parched throat.

He stood and crossed the room stopping a few feet from

her bed. "Even if I came here for help, I doubt you could do much in your condition," he said, the corners of his mouth turning up slightly.

Luz realized that her room was dark and—from the sounds of it—the hallway deserted. She clenched the blanket that covered her and kept her eyes on the nurse call button at the side of her bed. When the stranger let out a short laugh she flinched and cursed at him.

"Very constructive vocabulary you have. I guess I should have introduced myself before invading your personal space. I assumed you would have recognized me, but I forgot you suffered a concussion."

Luz stared at him, trying to figure out who he was. His voice seemed just as familiar as his eyes, but for the life of her she couldn't remember. She hoped she wasn't suffering temporary amnesia. "I'm sorry, I don't mean to be rude, but I really can't seem to place where I know you from," she said.

He held out his hand. "Nicholas Mason, cellblock A."

Luz tried her hardest to hide her shock. She must not have done a very good job because he laughed again.

"It's okay. I know, I went from one extreme to the next. It's amazing how soap and a razor can change a man. I was surprised I still knew how to use a razor after being on the streets for so long." He eased his way back into the chair across the room.

A uniformed police officer stuck his head in the doorway. "Everything okay in here, detective? Is this man bothering you? I told him to make his visit short."

Relieved there was a guard posted outside her room, she

smiled. "It's okay officer, thank you for checking on me."

Luz was still recovering, and it was hard for her brain to process that the old homeless man with the beard and grime had transformed into the handsome specimen sitting before her. Giving her time to cope, Nick began again.

"They let me out after you were attacked. Your friend, Sonny, pulled some strings. It seems that my prints were non-existent on the knife, but I've been told to stick around. So I cleaned up a little and headed over to thank you properly. Your boss tells me that you were more responsible for my release than anyone, so... here I am. Thank you."

"You're welcome. I'm glad I could be of assistance," she said slowly.

"I'm sorry my innocence was proven this way. You almost lost your life."

Luz thought back to the attack and shuddered. She had been close to death and it wasn't something she wanted to remember.

Nick took the shudder for a shiver. "Would you like another blanket? I can call the nurse?"

"No, I'm fine, thanks," she said but pulled her covers up anyway. She let him stare at her for a while before she broke the silence. "Mr. Mason, how did you get the money to... clean yourself up?"

He surveyed his clothing and grinned. "I do clean up nice, eh?" he joked. "I had a little stash put away. It's not much but it bought me a hotel room for the week."

"So this isn't the same money you had your friend protect

for you?"

His face grew grim and Luz wondered why his mood had suddenly changed.

"No, it wasn't the same money. That money is going to stay where it is for now."

"Have you spoken to anyone since your release?"

He slowly shook his head. "Wow, you don't waste any time getting back to being a detective. To answer your question, no, I haven't, except for your officers, of course."

"Did you call anyone from jail?"

"Just you, why? I thought you believed me to be innocent?"

"Well, brushes with death cause one to reconsider things."

He seemed to think this over for a while before retrieving his coat from the back of the chair. "Well, detective, I'm staying at the Ramada Inn on Fifth, room twenty-eight if you feel the need to investigate me. I came here to thank you for your help and to offer my legal expertise. But I have a feeling you won't be needing it. Take care."

"Mr. Mason," she said, and he paused at the door. "I'm glad you're free and I will call you if I need legal advice." She managed a small smile.

He smiled back and walked out of the room. Luz wondered if she would see him around. She'd already closed her eyes when she heard the door open again. Thinking it was Mason coming back to see her, she opened her eyes and smiled broadly. After seeing who it was, her smile waned, but just a little.

"That's no way to greet the man that saved your life."

"Eddie, I'm so glad you're here," she said feebly.

"Well, it didn't seem that way a second ago. Who were you expecting?"

She thought about Mason and remembered the way he looked at her.

"No one in particular," she lied but Eddie didn't seem to notice.

"So anyway, everyone is talking about you back at work. That move you pulled downtown was impressive. Of course, Andrews doesn't see it that way. He said, and I quote; 'Santos is a fine detective, but what she did was reckless and landed her in the hospital. I don't want any of you pulling that kind of stunt. We're a team here. Call for backup.' He came down on us hard, but I think it's because he almost lost his top investigator," he said, chuckling.

"You flatter me, Lopez," she said flatly. "Mike hasn't been to see me yet. I'm sure he's prepared to rip me a new one when I get back to work."

"When do you think you're coming back? You were stabbed, and you think they're going to release you, what? Today?"

"It's not their choice. I'm giving it until Monday morning. If the doctor doesn't let me go by then, I'll leave on my own."

Eddie whistled. "You sure are hard-headed, Santos. It's no wonder you do what you do."

"I'm going to take that as a compliment because I'm too weak to reach over and slap you."

He laughed and after a few moments, she laughed, too. When they settled down Luz grew serious.

"Thank you, Eddie."

"For the compliment?" he asked, beginning to laugh again.

"For my life," she said, tearing up.

"Aw, shucks ma'am, it was nothing. I was just doin' my job," he teased, but grew more serious as he noticed the tears on her cheeks.

"Luz, really, it was nothing. You would have done the same for me. Please don't cry." He reached for a tissue and dabbed her face.

"I'm sorry Eddie. I don't usually cry like this."

He stared into her eyes. "I know, but you don't have to play tough cop in front of me. You *are* human, you know. Crying is what we do."

She stared back into his eyes, which were shiny too. She felt awkward sharing such an intimate moment with Eddie of all people. But she was glad he was there with her. They shared a comfortable silence for a while, then Eddie bent down and kissed her cheek.

"Have you called your family?" he asked.

Luz brought her hand up and hit her forehead. "Damn! With all the drugs they've been giving me for the pain, I must have forgotten."

He eyed her warily. "Forgot to call your family? You're kidding, right?"

"No," she said sadly. "You don't understand. I grew up with my father and brothers. I was the only girl and they all wanted me to be a nurse or a flight attendant, anything but a cop. My dad's not happy with my decision to serve and protect; says it's a man job. If I tell him I got hurt, he'll only say, 'I told you so, mija'.'"

"Yeah but I'm sure he'll be happy that he got the chance to tell you at all. You almost died, Luz! Call your familía!" he scolded and handed her the phone.

She hesitated but took the receiver when he glared at her. "Okay, okay, let me call my brother first."

Eddie shrugged. "Whatever. Just remember to call your father when you're done." He looked at the clock on the wall. "I have to go, but I'm not leaving until I hear you talking to someone." He stood, arms crossed, and looked expectantly at her.

She sighed and dialed Hector's home number. A girl answered. "Hola, Karlita, is your papi home?" Luz asked.

"Oh hi, Tía, Daddy's outside working on the car. I'll get him for you." Luz listened as Karlita put the phone down and ran away calling her daddy's name. Karlita was Hector's oldest and Luz loved how eager she always was to help. Luz smiled at Eddie and he mouthed "call your dad" and left the room. Luz waited three more minutes before her brother got on the line.

"Hey, sis, haven't heard from you in a while, what's up?" he asked.

"Nothing much. Just, uh, sitting here in the hospital passing time."

"What? Hospital? Luz, what happened?" he asked. His protective instinct had kicked in and Luz could hear it in the rush of his words, the panic behind them.

She recounted the event that landed her there and he listened, interrupting her with questions and concerns. Then he filled her in on the happenings in his life. Martha, his wife, was pregnant with their third child.

"That's wonderful, Hector! If it's a girl, you name her after me, right?"

"We find out the sex next week, but I'll keep your name in mind. Martha's grandmother passed away a few months ago and she's leaning on the name Guadalupe."

"Ouch."

"Yeah, it's old-fashioned, but you know how stubborn Martha can be. Anyway, I need to finish up on the car. Can I come visit you?"

"Um, I think they're going to let me out soon. I'm still in the middle of this case but I'll make time to come out and see you soon. Do me a favor though, call Dad and tell him I'm all right."

She could picture Hector frowning on his end. "Luz, *you* need to call Dad. He'll want to hear it from you. I'm too old to be doing this for you anymore."

"Okay, okay. You are such a big pain sometimes," she said, already anxious of her father's reaction to her recklessness, bracing herself for yet another lecture regarding her career choice.

"Well, it runs in the family. By the way, have you heard from Raul lately?"

Luz's younger brother had moved out on his own four years earlier and once in a while he would fall off the map. Two years before he had a bout with drugs but had checked himself into rehab and changed his ways.

"He's clean, Hector. Don't worry. The last time I saw him he was talking about enrolling in the army."

"The army? That sounds a little drastic for Raul, qué no?"

"Well, the boy has dreams. It seems like he's craving order in his life. What better way to get it than joining the armed forces?"

"Yeah, you're right, but you'd think he'd call and let us know before he went and did something like that."

"He would. I don't think that's where he's at. I'll ask Dad when I talk to him."

"Good, let me know. So. I'll talk to you later, okay? Take care."

"You too. Tell Martha I'll be in touch. Love you."

"Love you too! Bye."

"Oh wait!" she shouted, suddenly remembering Cheech.

"Yeah?"

"Could you please pick up Cheech? He's probably starving, and his bladder will bust if he's not let out. Just take him to the house and I'll pick him up when I'm out."

"Sure. The kids will love having a dog to chase around."

"Thank you so much, Hector."

"No problem. Gotta go. Bye."

Luz was stuck listening to dead air. She knew she should call her father, but pride kept her from dialing his number. She placed the phone on the table beside her bed and closed her eyes. She felt guilty, but she felt tired too, and eventually her fatigue won out. She dropped off into a dreamless sleep.

MAY 18TH, 2002 8:30 P.M.

Luz jerked awake and, automatically reached for her phone. Its ringing had woken her. "Santos," she answered, groggy, still assessing her surroundings.

"Mija!"

Luz heard the anger in the deep voice at the other end of the line.

"Uh, hi, Dad. I—."

"Luz I can't believe you," her father interrupted. "You get stabbed, almost killed and you don't call? What's wrong with you? Had I not talked to Martha I would have never known you were hurt."

"Calm down, Dad. I'm okay now," she said, hoping it would alleviate his stress. The last thing she needed was for him to have a heart attack.

"That would have been nice to know sooner. Why on earth didn't you call me?" he said a little more calmly.

"Dad, I've barely been conscious for more than twenty minutes at a time. I was going to call earlier but the pain killers put me to sleep," she said, hoping he would understand.

He didn't. "That's no excuse. You should have called. I know you think you're a hotshot cop, but you are my daughter first. It was bad enough you shut us all out after that shooting years ago. We were sick with worry and you wouldn't talk to anyone. I was so happy when you started reaching out again. You weren't the same, but who is after something like that? I'm not going to let you go through it again. We are familía, and that means we're here for the good, the bad and the ugly. Comprendes? Now, I hope you'll think about quitting to find a job that doesn't involve risking your life."

Luz heaved a sigh. "Dad, I'm sorry I didn't call you sooner.

I won't insult you by lying to you, but I knew you would act like this. I like my job and when I recover I'm going back. I'll just have to be more careful. I promise to stay more connected, you know how much my family means to me."

There was silence on the other line before he spoke again, softly this time. "Yeah, I think I have *some* idea how much. Mija, I worry about you. I don't want to be one of those fathers who outlive their children; you are my only daughter. I want you to live long enough to get married and have kids." He paused, as if waiting for Luz to say something. She sighed. The silence didn't last long. "I understand that you have chosen your path in life but you are my daughter and I need to know that you are okay. It's hard for a father to let go and let his children live their own lives." There was another silence. Luz could practically hear the question her father was preparing to ask.

"Speaking of children . . . are you seeing anyone?" There it was. Luz groaned.

"Please don't start with that. When the right man comes, he'll come. I don't want to rush it."

"What about Ben? He was nice."

Luz remembered how Ben had held her hand and shown her tenderness earlier. Under the circumstances, that behavior was expected, but she wouldn't fall for him again.

"Ben and I are just friends now, Pop."

"Well, promise me you'll keep an open mind when it comes to men—you are so independent sometimes, and it can scare them off."

Luz knew about that first hand, but she didn't dare admit it to her father. "I promise, but for now don't plan on grandchildren from me any time soon."

He chuckled. "I wasn't being selfish when I said I wanted you to have kids. I just can't wait until you worry about them as much as I worry about you."

She smiled. "Thanks a lot. Now I can't wait," she said dryly. "Oh yeah, that reminds me; you haven't heard from Raul lately, have you?"

Her father stopped laughing. "Actually, I have. He called a couple of days ago asking for money. He got himself kicked out of his apartment; I think he's back on drugs."

Luz's chest tightened. "Drugs? Come on, Dad, he's been clean for a long time now. Plus, his probation officer gives random UA's. He wouldn't risk going back to jail."

Her father grunted. "Well, whatever. I didn't give him the money."

"What? Where is he?"

"I don't know," he replied curtly. "He could be on the street for all I know."

Luz's stomach twisted into a knot. "Dad, don't you watch TV?" she asked.

"I work all day and come home and sleep. I barely have time to do anything, why?"

"The case I've been working on involves the murder of homeless people downtown. If Raul is on the street, we need to find him ASAP!"

"What are you talking about, Luz?" Now there was a slight

tremble to her father's voice.

"Dad, he could be in danger."

"I… I didn't know. What should I do?" he asked.

"Don't worry about it. I'll put out an APB and have him brought in."

"Are you sure? There's nothing I can do?" he asked, his voice higher, more frantic.

"Call his friends. Maybe they can tell you something. I wouldn't worry though; he's probably staying at someone's house. You know Raul, he's surrounded by friends."

This seemed to make sense to her father because his tone evened out.

"You're right. I'll do that."

"Good. Call me if you find anything out. Love you, Pop."

"Love you too, mija. And for once, being a cop helps. Bye"

Luz said bye and hung up the phone smiling. Maybe he was finally starting to support her career. The smile dissolved when she thought of Raul. She made some calls to the station and was promised full cooperation by her peers as well as getting razzed for playing Superwoman out in the field and ending up in a hospital bed. Dinner came but she didn't have much of an appetite, so she drank the juice and left the food untouched.

She felt helpless lying in a hospital while the person who tried to kill her was free to plan their next kill. She prayed to God that next kill wouldn't be Raul.

CHAPTER EIGHT

The sun is fading as darkness comes fast
I'm free to hunt and kill at last
My mission is slowly becoming clearer
As my endgame is drawing nearer

MAY 19TH, 2002 11:15 P.M.

Raul Santos wandered the streets of Seattle. He'd just left a friend's house but had no place to go. He thought about calling his sister—she lived about twenty minutes from where he stood—but decided against it. He had been drinking and the last thing he needed was a lecture. Luz was the only one in the family who usually left him alone, but it wouldn't be his sister lecturing him, no, it would be her cop alter ego chewing him out. He didn't need that.

He hadn't had the best of luck lately. He'd lost his job at the video store because he was accused of stealing from the register. He hadn't taken the money, but he knew who had. Tim was the other guy who worked on his shift. Tim had asked him to party a couple of times, but Raul declined—he'd been clean a while and wanted to keep it that way. Tim was offended and became bitter toward Raul, but still asked him for money one day. Not wanting to support Tim's drug habit, Raul said no but offered to get him help. That didn't go over well at all. Tim made a scene and stormed off. When Raul was called into his supervisor's office and accused of stealing, he knew Tim had set him up.

Raul tried to explain the situation, but his boss had made up her mind. She simply told him she'd been screwed over too many times and that she took a giant risk hiring people his age. She threatened to call the police if he didn't leave the premises.

Soon after, Raul's roommate kicked him out because Raul had been short on rent. Raul gave him all the money he had; he even skipped meals for a week so he would have enough. But his roommate had planned to kick him out anyway so that his girlfriend could move in. Raul wasn't at all surprised.

Since then, he'd hopped from place to place staying with friends here and there. During all his moving around, he managed to go speak with a recruiter at the Army Center. Sergeant Nickerson had been enthusiastic and assured Raul that he had a future with the US. Army.

Raul proved the sergeant right when he scored ninety-two on his ASVAB test. For three whole weeks, Raul wanted to share the good news with his family, but he knew that telling them would mean revealing he'd lost his job and home. They would think him irresponsible and reckless. He called his dad on Tuesday asking for help, but his father only argued with him and hung up.

Feeling dejected, Raul kicked an empty Coke can across the pavement and yawned. What he needed was a place to crash. It would be two more months before he would report to Sergeant Nickerson and be shipped off to boot camp. He couldn't drift around; he had to get his head together, had to figure things out.

He checked his digital watch—eleven thirty. It was getting late and he'd landed himself an interview at Westlake Mall for the morning. He had washed up at his friend's place and secretly used Jack's deodorant and toothbrush. He didn't want to smell like a bum at Sam Goody in the morning. But when it came time to leave, Jack hadn't asked him to stay another night. Raul didn't blame him. He had already allowed him three nights of free room and board.

Feeling like a burden, he'd left and made his way across town. Looking up he saw the Space Needle in the distance, its lights winking at him. He walked up Denny Way and found a deserted building on the end of the street. He climbed up to the first level of the rickety fire escape and looked down. The streets were empty of pedestrians and he knew he'd be left alone. It was a warm night, so he took off his coat and used it as a pillow when he lay down.

He looked at the sky, wondering what the army would be like. He knew his father would be proud. Pride was a byproduct of the armed forces, as was responsibility and honor. He rolled over and tried to find a comfortable position but on his side the aroma of the dumpsters below proved to be too strong. He rolled on his back, knowing he'd smell like a bum in the morning whether he liked it or not.

MAY 20TH, 2002 2:20 A.M.

Nick grabbed the remote and turned the television off. His eyes were heavy and felt grainy when he blinked. He wasn't used to watching TV.

He shuffled his way to the bathroom. He didn't know how he was still awake; he must have been running on reserve energy. He looked in the mirror above the bathroom sink. It had been so long since he'd seen himself bathed and primped. He looked like his old self, except for the crow's feet around his eyes and the hollowness of his cheeks. He'd ordered Chinese food, a favorite of his, and ate it in his room but his stomach ached—he was not used to so much food. During dinner he had watched the news, and he was relieved to see that his release hadn't been announced.

He had caught the clip about Luz Santos's attack two nights ago. The newswomen had interviewed Captain Mike Andrews, who hadn't hesitated to defend his detective's actions—he even went so far as to congratulate her for her bravery. Nick thought what she'd done was foolish, even if it had earned him his freedom. It wasn't that he was ungrateful, but when he'd heard of the attack, he was worried for her safety and recovery.   On his way to the hospital he tried to convince himself that he was going to see her only to thank her for what she'd done for him, but the truth was that he wanted to be sure she was okay. She'd been kind to him—the first person to be kind to him in a long while. The first person to treat him like a human. He wanted to thank her for that. Maybe he also wanted to be treated like a human again.

He thought the visit was going quite well until she shifted into work mode and began grilling him. He was pretty sure that any bond developed between them had expired, but when he bade her farewell, he thought he saw a small spark of kindness or softness in her eyes.

He walked from the bathroom to the main room and took in his surroundings—a typical hotel room: a queen-sized bed with a nightstand; a dresser and a desk with decorative lamps; a television and heater—all bolted down tight. Even though it was just a hotel, it certainly felt more like home than the streets had. He walked to the window, drew the curtains aside and looked out into the night. He stayed there for a while thinking about the others who still lived outside, sleeping on the hard concrete. He had made some acquaintances along the way and hoped they would be safe.

He listened to the cars go by and thought about taking a walk, though he knew he should go to bed. He wouldn't sleep, not with so much to do and so little time in which to do it.

He went to the closet and grabbed his coat and hat, then he went back to the bathroom to take one last look at himself before he left. He did not like who he saw. Worst of all, he did not like what he was about to do. But he had to carry out his plan. He shut off the bathroom light and the light from the adjoining room threw shadows over his reflection, casting a sinister look upon him.

MAY 20ᵀᴴ, 2002 8:17 A.M.

The one-legged bum sat on the street looking up at her.

"Aren't you a cop?"

"Yes" she replied.

"Why didn't you help me? I'm dead, and it's your fault. You should've helped me."

"I... I tried, you said—"

"You should've helped me!" he screamed and then morphed into a little boy, the little boy.

"Help me!" he pleaded.

Luz was horrified and confused at the transformation. All she could do was stand, stare, and try to speak. It wasn't easy. But she did it. "I did help you, don't you remember?" she asked him softly.

"You killed my daddy, you didn't help. You killed him!" The boy came towards her, his little fists flying as if he would attack her.

Her eyes sprung open and she couldn't catch her breath. A shrill alarm went off beside her bed and a nurse came rushing into the room.

"Everything okay miss?" she asked as she took Luz's vitals. "Your blood pressure is elevated, and it looks like you're having trouble breathing".

Luz shook her head. "I'm fine. I'm okay now. Just woke up and forgot where I was for a moment. It must've been a panic attack. I'll be fine in a few minutes."

Not looking convinced, the nurse finished her examination and changed the bandage on Luz's wound. The quick stabbing pain helped Luz focus and soon she felt her breaths even out to a normal level. Once the nurse left she gathered her thoughts and started thinking about her nightmare. That was the third time this week. She'd have to talk to someone soon if this continued.

Her phone rang, and she reached over and answered it.

"Have you found your brother yet?" Mike asked immediately.

"No, my father called and told me that he spoke to one of his friends and that he stayed with them two nights ago but hasn't seen him since. I tried his other friends all day yesterday but to no avail. Why, you hear something?"

He paused before speaking. "I'm afraid so. It's not good news, Luz."

Her body went cold. "What? What happened, Mike?" she asked. Her panic returned; thicker. It blanketed her goosebumped flesh and filled the room. Voice strained by tears that had yet to fall, she whimpered into the phone. "No-no! He's not. No. He can't be! What the fuck happened, Mike?"

"Luz calm down—"

"Where is he?" she screamed.

"We're not even sure it's him. The body found this morning was a young hispanic male, matching the description you put out Saturday night. That doesn't mean a thing. There are thousands of young hispanic males in this city."

Luz fought hard to keep her composure, but it took every ounce of her strength. "Mike, please tell me it's not him." Her hands shook so bad she could barely hold on to the phone.

"I wish I could, but I haven't been down to see the body yet. I'm on my way now."

"Come and get me," she demanded.

There was a strained silence before Mike replied. "What? No, I can't do that. You shouldn't be out of bed. The doctor said—"

"I'll find my own way if I have to," she said, angrily throwing off her blanket.

"You don't even know where the murder scene is," he stated flatly.

"Dammit, Mike, if you don't come and get me, you'll have my resignation on your desk first thing tomorrow morning. Now, I don't want to hear your voice, I want to see your face. I'm in room B-two thirty-seven, on the second floor. No arguments. I'll see you soon."

She hung up before he could argue. She found herself still violently shaking. Luz pushed the nurse button repeatedly until the she arrived.

"Miss, you only have to push the button once and—"

"Get me a doctor, now," Luz ordered.

"If you need something I can"

"I'm not going to ask you again. If I don't see a doctor in five minutes, I'll pull this IV out and leave."

The nurse gave her a sour look and disappeared into the hall. Luz got up and retrieved her clothes from the closet, each step causing her to flinch from the pain in her side. By the time she had her jeans fastened the doctor walked in.

"What do you think you're doing?" he asked, his voice tinged with anger.

"What does it look like? I'm leaving," she replied.

"We need to keep you here for at least twenty-four more hours. Ms. Santos. You've suffered a concussion and a serious wound to your abdomen. It would be best if you stayed to recover a little longer."

She stopped tying her shoe and shot him an icy glare. She walked over to him with some difficulty, but her face remained impassive.

"I don't have a choice, doctor. I have to leave *now* on police business. My boss is on the way and he will authorize my release, so the best thing for you to do is cooperate or we'll have your ass for interfering with a police investigation."

He looked at her boldly. "Ms. Santos, I realize you are working a big case, but when you're here, you are under my care and I don't think you're well enough to leave. Those stitches need time to set in order to help you heal properly." Arms crossed, he held her gaze until she looked away.

Luz sat on the bed and folded her arms. "Fine. We'll wait for my captain to get here, and you can have words with him. I doubt you'll convince him to keep me here."

They waited twenty minutes before her boss arrived. Mike spoke with the doctor out in the hall and Luz could hear his tone go from business to casual to business again. When he was through, he came back into the room, looking grim.

"You sure know how to talk your way into trouble." He gave her a grin.

"Cut the small talk, Mike. Can we go now?"

He nodded toward the door. "The good doctor is getting the release forms ready but he's less than happy about it."

"I could give a rat's ass. Has anyone found ID on the body yet?"

"No. I called from the parking garage. Luz, this might not

be Raul."

"Don't say another word. I'm trying not to think about it." But her eyes welled up and she broke down. Her boss stood awkwardly for a moment, then tentatively put his arms around her. Her body tensed immediately, and he let her go. She wiped her face with her sleeve and looked at him.

"Sorry," she said, shaking her head, embarrassed for having cried in front of her superior.

"You can cry all over me if you want, I'll just send you my dry-cleaning bill."

She managed a small laugh and the tension eased out of her. Doctor Cleveland viewed the scene from the doorway and stepped inside holding a clipboard.

"Here are the release papers along with a form stating that if your injuries worsen we won't be held responsible."

Luz took the forms, scanned the fine print and signed on the dotted line. The doctor unhooked her IV and gave her a bottle of prescription Tylenol with codeine.

It took them forever to get down to the car because Luz repeatedly stopped to rest. After being laid up for a few days her muscles were weak, and she couldn't keep up with Mike's long strides.

Mike radioed for an update once they got in the car, but there was nothing new. They were still waiting for the ME to arrive. In this case that would be Ben, and if he got there before she did, he'd be able to identify the body. He and Raul had gotten along great when he'd been involved with Luz. She secretly hoped she wouldn't have to view the body at all.

You're a cop, that's what you do, she told herself, but if it was Raul—she couldn't do it.

They drove onto Denny Way and pulled up next to a local news van. As soon as Luz stepped out of the car she was bombarded by the press. Mike covered her and walked her back behind the police tape, where the media wasn't allowed.

"Goddamn vultures," he mumbled but she saw him straighten his tie.

The last thing Luz needed was the media watching her every move and reaction. If indeed the body belonged to Raul, she didn't want her tears splashed all over the eleven o'clock news. Even worse, she didn't want her father and brother to find out about it from the TV.

She slowly walked toward the crime scene, half because she couldn't limp any quicker due to her wound and half because she was in no hurry to see the body on the white sheet under the fire escape. She stopped to take a deep breath and felt a hand on her shoulder. She spun around and came face to face with Ben.

"Ben," she said and embraced him.

"I just heard what happened. I'm so sorry, Luz."

She paled and looked up at him wide eyed. "So, Raul *is* dead?" she asked, backing away from him. Her hand flew up to her trembling lips. *This can't be happening, not Raul, please God!*

"I thought it was confirmed?" he asked, confused. "Hold on." He called one of the officers over and asked a few questions. Luz was too numb to listen. Too many emotions stirred inside her, and she felt faint.

Ben turned back to her. "Luz, I'm going over to ID the body. Stay here. I'll be right back." He walked away, and Luz was left to think the worst.

"You look white as a ghost," someone said, and she looked up to find Eddie, watching her with worry. "Are you okay?"

But she couldn't talk. She could only cry. He steered her away from the prying eyes of the press and sat her in his cruiser. He didn't speak to her but stayed close in case she needed him. A couple of minutes later Ben came back looking tense, Luz took one look at his face and sobbed uncontrollably. He bent over and took her hand.

"Litebrite, it's not Raul. It's someone named Morales."

She stopped crying and stared up at him. "How would you know his name if there was no identification?

"Unless Raul tattooed someone else's name on his chest—" he began

She shook her head. "No… no, Raul has one tattoo from his gang banger days, but that's on his hand." She shook off her grief and got up and hugged Ben tightly.

"Now do you want the bad news?" he asked, his voice muffled though her hair. She pulled away, puzzled.

"Bad news?"

"Our killer strikes again. Same knife used on this guy. At least it looks that way."

"Shit." She pushed her hand through her hair in frustration.

Ben gripped her shoulders, looking her square in the eyes. "But don't worry about that now. Find your brother and let him stay with you for a while. I don't care what you have to do but get him off the street."

"That was my next step," she said pulling herself together. She heard someone clear their throat and forgot that Eddie was leaning on the car the whole time.

"I get off in ten minutes if you need help. You don't look too good," he said staring her up and down. She could imagine what she looked like in her jeans and disheveled sweatshirt, but fashion was the last thing on her mind. She had to find Raul.

"Thanks, Eddie, but I need to start looking now. Ten minutes could make a difference," she said solemnly, not allowing herself to recall how close she'd come to thinking she'd lost her brother for good.

He hopped in the driver's seat. "Okay get in. I'll tell Leroy to finish my shift, he won't mind."

"Are you sure?"

"Is the Pope catholic?" he teased and buckled in.

Luz rolled her eyes and got in the passenger seat. Ben crouched down to the window. "Call me later, so I know you're all right," he said, kissing her lightly on the cheek.

She beamed at him and winked. "You'll hear from me either way."

"Ha, ha. Just try and stay out of trouble. I don't know how you weaseled your way out of the hospital but now that you're out, try and stay safe."

Eddie squared his shoulders. "She'll be safe with me," he said, eyeing Ben. Luz suppressed a laugh, but Ben reacted differently; he shook Eddie's hand, looking dead serious.

"I know. Now get going." He slapped the side of the car and

walked away.

• • •

They started looking in the surrounding area and slowly worked their way out.

Luz checked in with her father and brother but neither had heard from Raul.

Eddie cleared his throat. "So are you and Ben back together?" he asked.

"No, and this is not the time to talk about this," she snapped.

Eddie apologized and lapsed into silence.

They were driving past Pike Place Market when Eddie's cell phone rang. Eddie picked it up.

"Lopez, what've you got?........ uh-huh… great. Where?" he looked over at Luz and gave her a thumbs-up. She sat up and anxiously listened, hoping to hear where her brother was found. Eddie hung up the radio and looked at her, eyes bright.

"They picked him up in the mall. They're holding him now."

"Westlake Mall? We'll be there in a second." They drove to Pine Street and pulled over in front of the mall. Inside, they walked towards the Sam Goody store where Luz spotted Raul sulking along the wall. She ran over and embraced him, despite her pain, and held on tight.

"I love you," she said, practically choking him to death.

He tried to squirm away, but she wouldn't let go.

"Oxygen, Luz. I need to breathe," he said calmly and

untangled himself from her.

"What's going on? I just finished up a job interview at Sam Goody, which went very well, by the way, and this officer comes up and asks me my name. As soon as I told him, he made me wait here. Now my would-be boss is looking out at me like I'm some kind of hoodlum and I probably won't get the job. I deserve an explanation," he huffed, crossing his arms over his chest.

Luz smiled and recounted all the events of the last week, including the body they found that morning. Raul appeared dumbfounded by the news; four murders, an attack on his sister and a frantic search to find him. He admitted he was pretty spooked that both he and his sister could have been in grave danger.

"Wow, I'm so sorry, sis. I should have called you last night. I didn't mean to put you through all that."

"It's fine now. You're alive and you'll come home with me tonight," she said and linked her arm in his. Eddie led them back to the patrol car and they drove straight to the marina. They rode in silence. When they pulled into the parking lot, Luz saw her car.

"How did you get my car here?" she asked, looking at Eddie quizzically.

He shrugged. "I kinda stole your keys while you were in surgery and had Leroy give me a lift home. It was worth it, too, that car was fun to drive." He winked.

She snickered. "Thanks. I was worried it was still parked downtown, stripped down to the bare metal frame. I owe you," she said and got out of the car. Her brother walked over to survey the Eclipse and she shuffled around to the driver's side of the cruiser.

"Eddie, you've been so helpful, thank you so much. I really do owe you. Maybe I'll buy you lunch sometime."

"Maybe you'll let me cook for you sometime."

"Wow he cooks?" she joked.

"I'm serious. Come over for dinner tomorrow night and I'll whip up my famous enchiladas," he said, beaming at her.

"I'm sorry, I can't. Big date with the boss tomorrow. Mayor's having a shindig." Eddie looked so crestfallen. "But Wednesday is good."

"Can't. I work the four to midnight shift. How about Thursday?"

"We'll see. I believe I can squeeze you in. Call me later in the week."

"Will do, now go and rest. You're not Wonder Woman."

She spread her arms and managed to spin around once before her side ached. "Ow," she cried.

"You don't listen too well, do you, Santos? I said you're *not* Wonder Woman. But you would look cute in her uniform."

Luz threw back her head and laughed. "In your dreams, Lopez, in your dreams."

CHAPTER NINE

The demons lurk within my mind
A thread of sanity I strive to find
The power that comes with ending a life
Grows with every slice of the knife

MAY 20TH, 2002 11:47 P.M.

I watched as the old man on the corner did a sloppy rendition of Frank Sinatra's "New York New York". It infuriated me that someone who lived on the streets and ate from the garbage had the gall to sing a song by one of the classiest musical artists of all time. Sinatra's sophistication could not be imitated by a sixty-year old has-been who danced in rags for booze money.

I continued to view the bum's performance with forced indifference, which quickly bloomed into disgust. I grew very disturbed by the macabre performance and thought it would be better if the bum was *in* New York instead of infesting the streets of Seattle.

When the night grew long, the old man packed up his

cardboard stage and collected his daily earnings from a ragged hat and started down Pine Street toward the water. I followed silently, trying to blend in with the pedestrians. The bum stopped at a park bench and sat down, humming to himself while trying to get comfortable. A car drove by and the driver flicked a cigarette out of the window. The homeless man jumped up and hurried into the street to pick it up, taking a long satisfying drag and returned to his seat on the bench. I gagged at that wretch, not wanting to imagine what kind of bacteria was left on the cigarette. I curiously watched the man as he finished it off and snubbed it out with his worn-out boot.

The man got up and began walking again and I continued to stalk the oblivious trash. We walked down under the Alaska Way Viaduct and crossed the street to the Ferry Docks. The old man passed the shops and restaurants closing up for the night and turned down a dock near the Ivar's Seafood counters.

I hesitated, looking for anyone who might be watching and proceeded to follow the bum down the dark pier. For a moment I couldn't see where the bum had gone but then I heard coughing a few feet ahead of me.

I crept along and unsheathed my knife. The old man sat on the end of the dock leaning against a post, whistling the tune to Sinatra's "Strangers in the Night". I thought how apt that was as I stepped behind the bum. The old man must have heard something because he started to turn, but he never got a chance to see the face of his murderer because I'd grabbed his head with one arm and sliced his throat with the other. I dutifully stepped back to avoid the splatter of blood. The bum went down quickly with a dull thud as his body bounced off the wood of the dock.

I smiled and wiped the blood from the knife. One less parasite for the good people of Seattle to worry about, and one less "human" to loathe. The night was still young and my craving to take worthless lives wasn't yet sated. I slinked off into the darkness of the night humming Sinatra's "My Way".

I was free to kill again and eager to do so.

MAY 21ST, 2002 7:59 A.M.

Luz woke with a start, aware of another presence in her home. She peered through the darkness and made out a lump across the room on her couch and remembered that Raul had spent the night. She listened to him breathe for a while before she got up.

She showered, awkwardly trying to clean her wound as best as she could. Afterward she went to the kitchen and brewed coffee. She pulled out a slice of bread intent on making toast but the mold on the corner had her throwing the entire loaf in the garbage. Her food had gone bad during her stay in the hospital.

"Morning, sis," Raul said, stumbling into the kitchen stretching his arms.

"I'm sorry Raul. Did I wake you?"

"Nah, don't worry about it. I would've woken up around this time anyway. What's for breakfast?"

"I wish I could tell you. Everything went bad while I at the hospital. How about going out for breakfast?"

His face lit up. "Sure, let me wash up," he said and headed toward the bathroom.

Luz picked out some black Capri pants and a red tank top from her closet. She grabbed a pair of matching sandals and slid them on then quickly brushed her hair, remembering that she had to get her hair done before going to the banquet with Mike. She phoned her hairdresser and made an appointment for that afternoon. By the time she made it back to the kitchen, Raul was dressed and ready to go.

They left the boat and cruised north for a while and got onto Highway 99, heading towards Hector's house. They stopped and ate at Denny's, discussing Raul's plans for the army.

"That's great, I'm glad you've decided what to do with your future," Luz said between bites of waffles. She made sure to wash down Advil with some orange juice. Even though Advil wouldn't cover all her pain, she couldn't take her prescription narcotics and drive all day.

"Yeah, I still feel behind. I mean, Hector had a steady job by my age and you were already on the force at twenty-two and *I'll* be twenty-two in about a month. I wish I had figured this all out a little sooner," he said, taking a swig of orange juice.

"The past is the past. All you can do now is think about the future. Dad will be so proud of you when you tell him." She beamed.

Raul stopped eating. "You mean, you didn't tell him when you spoke to him yesterday?"

"No. I thought I'd leave you the honor," she said. "After breakfast we're going to see Hector and Martha. Dad said he'd meet us there."

Raul frowned and stared at his eggs for a while.

"What's wrong?" she asked.

"Nothing. It's just… he was really mad at me the other day. He accused me of taking drugs again, and, well, I don't know." he looked down at the table.

Luz sternly eyed her brother. "Raul, remember when I began working as a cop? Dad went through the roof, but that didn't stop me. I knew what I wanted and nothing he said or did could have stopped me from reaching my dreams. Yeah, he's our dad but that doesn't mean he always knows best. Just tell him and if he doesn't like it, tough, it's your life." She reached up and patted his shoulder.

He went quiet for a while, then slapped the table. "You're right, Luz. I'll just tell him, and he'll deal with it."

"That's what I want to hear; optimism. Now finish your breakfast. I'm on a tight schedule."

• • •

Their father was waiting for them at Hector's house. Raul shared his news with the family and to his surprise, his father was very pleased. They asked Luz about the case and she told them about the murders, leaving out the confidential aspects of the ongoing investigation. Raul brought up her attack and the subject seemed to make everyone tense so Luz decided to switch the group's focus.

"So, Martha, I hear you're going to name the baby after me," she said, winking at her sister-in-law.

Martha looked at Hector disapprovingly and he shrugged. "What?" he asked backing away from Martha, a grin on his face. "It was just a suggestion." He turned to his sister. "See what kind of trouble you get me into?"

Luz laughed. "I'm only kidding, Martha, it was my idea. I wanted—" she was cut off by her cell phone. "Excuse me," she said, leaving the room. Once she was sure she was out of earshot she answered.

"Luz, it's Mike. Guess what?"

"You called to tell me that the mayor cancelled for tonight?"

"Yeah, don't you wish? No. I called because our killer has grown pretty bold; we found two bodies this morning. We need to wrap this thing up. Our forensic guys are going nuts without any evidence to go on. The medical examiner says the wounds match those of the other victims but the only thing they have in common is that they're homeless. He's escalating, Santos."

"Have you spoken with the mayor? Does he want to hold a press conference? Six bodies in less than a week… we're talking a serial killer here, Mike."

"I know. I'm up to my ears in calls from news stations because we have a leak somewhere, and if I find out who it is, they'll never work in this city again."

"Okay, I'm going to wrap it up here. I'll see you soon."

"If you need the time off I can get someone to cover. I know you had quite a scare yesterday with your brother and you just got out of the hospital."

Luz reached down and touched the tender spot in her side. Replacing the bandages earlier had been painful but the Advil she took had kept the pain to a minimum. "I'll be fine. Raul is safe and will be staying with my brother for a while. I'll be in. Besides, who would cover for me? Harris?"

"That asshole. After that stunt he pulled the other day, he'll be lucky if I let him work meter reader duty. You're right. I don't have anyone to cover for you. I was just being polite." He chuckled.

"Thanks, I appreciate it," she said.

"Hey, it's all part of being the sensitive man I am."

Luz snorted. "Yeah, you're sensitive all right, and I'm just being polite."

He immediately backpedaled. "Okay, you know shit when you smell it. Just get down here, okay?"

"Okay, bye." She hung up and rejoined everyone in the living room. Hector had Raul in a headlock and the kids were screaming with excitement.

"Get him, Dad," Erik, Hector's youngest, shouted, pumping his fists in the air.

"Yeah, Dad, give him a wedgie," screamed Karlita, hopping up and down on the couch. Cheech ran in circles around the kids, excited by the display, his little tail wagging rapidly.

Luz giggled, grabbing her jacket and purse. "You better watch out, Hector. When Raul gets back from the army, he'll have *you* in a headlock."

Hector took his fist and rubbed it on Raul's head making him wince. "Yeah right, I'd like to see him try."

"I have to go. Duty calls," she said and hugged everybody goodbye.

"But you just got here," her father argued. "¡Dios mio! I can't believe they want you back. You're recovering from being stabbed for God's sake!"

Luz hugged him and gave him a kiss on the cheek. "It was my call. I need to find the bad guy and put him away for good. Thanks again for watching Cheech. Don't give him too many treats; he'll be farting for days." She rolled her eyes, knowing they would spoil her dog—they always did. "I'll call you later, okay?"

Her dad grunted, and she took that for a goodbye and moved on to Raul. She gave him a big hug and kiss as well. "You better stay out of trouble, hombre."

"I will. Now go to work. Oh yeah, and say hi to Eddie for me," Raul said, batting his lashes.

Instantly her father perked up. "Eddie? Who's this Eddie?"

Luz sighed and elbowed Raul in the ribs. "No one you have to worry about, Pop."

"Is he Mexican? When do I get to meet him?"

"Look, Dad, I wish I could stay and chat, but I'm needed downtown. We'll talk later." She opened the door and was outside before he could say any more. She hadn't thought about Eddie all day. She ran to her car and drove off, thinking of how complicated her life was becoming.

• • •

Luz met Ben at the morgue. He'd just unloaded the second body and had a ton of paperwork to go through. He compared the autopsy photos at his desk as Luz entered.

"I don't know, Luz, this killer is good. Not one piece of evidence. He surprises his victims so there are no defense wounds to be found. No bloody footprints or witnesses, and he's getting confident."

"But that's how we usually catch them. They get arrogant, think they're invincible, then they screw up and we got' em." She snapped her fingers.

"Yeah. I have a feeling this one isn't going to mess up. Already six victims and not so much as a fingerprint. Actually, we think it may be eight victims. I checked the database for similar crimes and it looks like there were two other unsolved homeless murders in the last six months. The wounds are consistent with what we're looking at here. I told you these wounds reminded me of something, I just had to do my homework."

"What are you talking about? We got prints. Sonny's working on them as we speak."

"If he hasn't traced them by now, I doubt he will."

"This killer's already escalated considerably. He's bound to make a mistake sooner or later. I'd rather it to be sooner. Don't be such a pessimist."

"I work with dead people for a living. I can't help it," he said.

She noticed Ben's pale skin, and that the lids of his eyes

excessively drooped. "This is taking a toll on you, isn't it?" she asked.

He fingered the stubble of his beard and managed a smile. "Yeah. Between the bodies turning up and the ex-girlfriends needing rescued, I haven't been getting a lot of sleep."

"Of course you'd blame me," she joked, shoving her shoulder into his. "That's okay, I'm used to it. So, can I see the bodies?"

He led her downstairs. The room was sterile and very cold. Two of the walls were lined with drawers and the room was empty except for three examining tables set in the middle of the room. The scent of death hung in the air despite all efforts to conceal it. Ben took out a card and counted his way to the fifth row, second drawer up. He pulled it open.

"Curtis Miller, sixty-two. Cause of death; open gash to the throat made by a sharp instrument. Again, I'm seeing the ripped skin and then the clean slice in each gash." He unzipped the body bag and the smell of decaying flesh hit Luz instantly. She stepped back, covering her nose and mouth. Ben gave her some mentholated gel to rub under her nostrils. She hastily unscrewed the jar and applied the gel before the smell caused her to lose her Grand Slam breakfast.

She bent low to inspect the wound. The skin was beginning to wrinkle and fold over on itself. It looked exactly like the others.

"Both of the victims were male?" she asked, zipping the bag and pushing the drawer closed.

"Yes. All the victims are the same build and race. The Jamison woman doesn't fit the pattern."

"So there's a possibility she wasn't killed by the same person?"

"The same type of knife has been used for every killing. Whether it's the same person using that knife is *your* job to figure out."

"It just doesn't make sense. Wait. All the victims *weren't* the same race. They found that Latino kid yesterday."

"But he was light enough to pass as Caucasian. Living in Seattle, we Latinos don't get very dark," Ben said, holding out his arm for inspection. "Vitamin D deficiency."

Luz held her arm out for comparison. "Yeah? Then what's my excuse?"

"Tanning bed and good genes?" he guessed, looking at her pointedly.

"Damn right," she said and pulled her arm away. "So where do we stand on all of this?"

He flipped up a couple of sheets on the clipboard he held. "Basically, we have a serial killer who likes to use expensive knives to cut people. He must be intelligent because we've got nil for evidence. I'd keep checking on that knife. Call the manufacturer and figure out how many were produced. Sometimes they keep lists of collectors. It's somewhere to start, anyway. The rest is up to you. Now, I have a ton of paperwork to fill out on these two new guys so if you'll excuse me." He pushed the table back into the wall and closed the latch securing it.

"Sure. No problem. Thanks for letting me see the bodies," Luz said.

She caught his eye again. "I may need your help later. Can

I call you?" Her mind was already working on possible scenarios and she wanted to bounce some ideas off him. It's what they did when they dated, and she missed the exercise. It helped her think.

"I'll be here. Maybe you can stop by later and bring me some food. I'll be too busy to get something myself."

Luz tried to find any hidden meaning in his words and failed—much to her relief. "I have that charity thing at Yates's tonight but if you want I can stop by Chan's and grab some chicken chow mien. But I don't understand how you have an appetite, smelling these stiffs all day."

"Oh, don't worry about it. I can call and have something delivered, though it's hard to get places to deliver to a morgue. Creeps people out, you know?" he looked up and smiled.

"Can't imagine why," she teased. "Okay, well I have a lot of work ahead of me, see you around." She walked toward the door and was about to leave when he called to her.

"Don't work too hard, Litebrite!"

"You know I will," she yelled back and left. She welcomed the fresh air when she stepped outside. It was reaching midday and the sun streamed down through the skyscrapers. She got in her car and pulled open the sunroof, wishing she could spend the day outside; forget the horrible murders of the past week. But those images would stay with her for a while—fueling her need to find the lunatic before more helpless people lost their lives.

CHAPTER TEN

I once lived in an infestation
From the hell around me there was no vacation
All I ever feel are wants and needs
And the madness inside breeds and breeds

MAY 21ST, 2:15 P.M.

Elaine Murphy kneeled in the grass by her husband's grave and placed red carnations at the base of his tombstone. She usually only visited on Sunday afternoons, but she felt she owed him an apology that couldn't wait five more days.

She prayed as she always did and placed a kiss on the cool marble before getting to her feet. The whole process took about thirty minutes. The praying went rather fast. It was the getting up that took the most time. Elaine was pushing ninety and if she tried to move faster than her years, she was likely to throw out a hip.

She folded her arms and forlornly read her husband's name carved in the stone. It was getting harder to make out the words. It had been eleven years, and the headstone showed

132

some wear. It read:

EUGENE ALEXANDER MURPHY, A LIFE THAT
TOUCHED SO MANY. WONDERFUL HUSBAND
AND FATHER. LOVED BY ALL. 1911 – 1986.

To Elaine, Eugene was still alive; in spirit and in her heart. Even when she wasn't visiting his grave, she felt his presence. She still lived in the house they bought after they were married. It was a wonderful two-story farm-house set on ten acres of land in Carnation, a dairy town that had grown into an immense rural community. Where there were once pastures and a small local grocer, there were now houses and small shopping centers. It wasn't the same place she and her husband had chosen to live sixty years ago but she liked it all the same.

The cemetery was north of the center of town, only blocks from where she lived. On sunny days—like that one—she enjoyed walking outside. She'd chosen to visit the cemetery because her guilt was too heavy to bear.

Eugene was a man whom everyone had loved; his generous ways had earned him many friends throughout his life. When he had returned from the war at age thirty-two, he was worn and suffered from mild shell shock, or what the navy doctors called "gross stress reaction". Either way, Elaine knew he'd returned a changed man, but she still loved him, and he loved her. By that time, they'd had a son and were ready to add to the family. Their home was bright and cheerful, always full of friends and family—the kind of home anyone would want to raise a family in.

But their home wasn't always happy. Eugene would sometimes wallow in his war memories and grieve for those who hadn't made it home. He would sit for hours in his study going through his memorabilia. There were medals, scraps of uniforms, rusted dog tags, old weapons and many letters and photos. There was one particular knife he spent a lot of time holding; it belonged to his best friend, Frank Addams. Frank had been an avid knife collector and had taken his favorite knife with him into war. He and Frank had been friends for years—they were like brothers—and Frank was their son's godfather.

When they went off to war, only Eugene came home. As he lay dying on the battlefield, Frank asked Eugene to take the knife and give it to his godson, like his father had given it to him. Eugene reluctantly took the knife, not wanting to accept the loss of his best friend, but in the end, he didn't have a choice. Frank hadn't gotten to the medical base fast enough and passed away.

It took Eugene years to get over his friend's death. In a way, he blamed himself for not protecting Frank better. Elaine told him many times that his friend had died protecting his country and because of that, many people lived free, but that didn't comfort Eugene when he was awash in memories. He would never let her into that part of his life, much to her disappointment, but she'd made peace with that early on.

Their son, Robert, had held onto the knife until his death in the Vietnam War years later. It was then passed on to Robert's son, Adam, who gave it back to his grandfather for his fiftieth birthday. Over the years, Eugene became obsessed with collecting knives of all shapes and sizes. At the time of his death, he owned over three hundred knives. Each knife was different, and many were rare. Some originated overseas and some in the US, but somehow Eugene found the means to locate and purchase each one. Soon, their savings dwindled but every time Elaine tried to talk with Eugene about it, he would shut her out and disappear into his study with a bottle of brandy.

The post-traumatic stress he suffered from the war led Eugene to take over Frank's hobby of knife collecting, but it had also led him to drink excessively. Eugene became an alcoholic and their once-untroubled home became a place of harsh words and hurt feelings. Elaine never gave up on Eugene; he had his good days, and she remained married to him because he was the only man she ever loved, the only one she ever *would* love.

When he died, he left her the house and whatever remained in it. His life insurance hadn't been much, but it paid the bills for years after his death. When that money ran out, Elaine had nowhere to turn. Her grandson sent money from San Francisco (where he'd moved his family eight years before), but it wasn't enough to pay for her frequent hospital visits and her medication. A spring chicken she was not.

One day someone from the church visited and noticed her husband's collection of knives. He went on and on about how much each knife was worth and asked if she would like to sell some of them. She declined and asked the man to leave.

That was seven months ago. Since then she had sold half of her land and her old jewelry—but refused to sell the knives.

She no longer had a choice. She had suffered a stroke and needed a full-time nurse to take care of her at home. Her doctor suggested she move to a nursing home, but Elaine told him that if she were to die, it would be in her home. So she called up Cliff, a gentleman from church, and he helped her put together a website for her collection. She let him take care of the computer aspect of it; she wanted nothing to do with the technology of the last twenty years. She preferred her typewriter and rotary telephone to the computers everyone seemed to always be looking at.

Within weeks she pulled in over ten thousand dollars' worth of sales from the knives. Cliff then asked her if she would like to sell the rest of the items. She hesitated, worried that if she sold them all she would sell everything that meant something to Eugene. So she kept one small knife for herself in honor of her husband. According to Cliff and the papers for the knife, it appeared to be worth a lot of money, but Elaine needed to keep it; for herself and for Eugene.

The month before, Cliff informed her that a wealthy bidder was looking for a knife like the one she had saved. At first, she waved Cliff off, but he said the bidder would pay anything. With the bidder's insistent emails and phone calls, Elaine ordered Cliff to shut down the website. With all the other knives gone she wanted nothing more than to live her life in peace.

Peace was the last thing she got. She suffered another stroke and was in the hospital for four and a half weeks. From the cost of the hospital stay, medication, the ambulance and the additional cost of maintenance on her house, Elaine could not pay her bills.

She called Cliff and sadly declared that she would sell the knife, but Cliff said the bidder was long gone.

Elaine panicked, prepared to sell her home.

Six nights before, there was a knock on her door. Slowly, she'd hobbled to the door, with the aid of her new walker. She found a man standing on her doorstep, dressed in all black, his fingers folded over a manila envelope.

"I'm here for the knife," he said in a soft voice, almost feminine.

Elaine was confused for a moment, then remembered that Cliff had called her earlier. He'd found person who wanted the knife.

She invited the man in, but he declined, claiming he was in a hurry. So she went to the back room and retrieved the knife in its wooden box. She returned to the front door and gave the box to the man. He then handed her an envelope. The bottom half of the envelope dropped and swung like a pendulum. Elaine knew there was a lot of money inside because of its weight.

She looked up to thank the man, but he was halfway down the walk heading back to his car. She watched him drive away before she went back inside and closed the door.

She shakily opened the envelope. And counted out six thousand dollars. It seemed like too much for just the one knife, and at first, she didn't spend the money. She lived off donations from the church congregation and the money Adam sent her. But when her nurse announced that she could no longer work for so little pay, Elaine knew she would have to dip into the manila envelope and remove the last reminder she had of Eugene's knife.

All those events had led her to the cemetery on a Tuesday afternoon. She had come to apologize and explain to her husband why she'd done what she did. She wiped the tears from her wrinkled cheek and took one last look at the grave before walking away. She looked up toward the heavens pleadingly, hoping with all her heart that Eugene would forgive her.

MAY 21ST, 2002 6:30 P.M.

Mike Andrews whistled then stared open-mouthed at Luz as she walked toward the car. She flashed a cheesy, million-dollar smile his way and turned full circle, ignoring the pain in her side. It was a dull pain—thanks to the Advil she'd been popping like Skittles. Another day in the hospital would have helped, but she didn't have time to lay up and mend. The case took priority. It always did. Mike opened her door for her.

"Here you go, madam, and may I say, you look ravishing."

Luz laughed, though she was flattered by his compliment. "Why, thank you, good sir. I'm sure there's a human resources violation in there somewhere but I'm feeling too good to care," she replied and slid into the backseat of the town car. *You better look good, you just spent two hours getting ready*, she thought and pulled at the straps of her dress. She owned seven gowns and they ranged from cocktail to super elegant. But they were reserved for occasions like this: political functions, charity events, whatever the event of the month was. That night she wore a Sue Wong full-length rosebud embroidered gown with a matching embroidered shawl. The ensemble, plus shoes and jewelry, had come to over seven hundred dollars, but it was worth every penny for the reaction it elicited from those who had seen her in it at previous functions.

It not only complemented her figure, it lent an elegance she would not have in a department store dress. It also did wonders for her ego—men couldn't help but stare when she strolled by. She was sure that night would be no exception. She was glad she had managed to get her hair colored and styled, as well as a manicure. For the first time in days she felt at ease, like she would enjoy herself, even though she was escorting her boss around town. At least he was good company.

"How are you feeling?" Mike asked, shutting the door and motioning the driver to take off.

"Great. I thought the dress would catch on the bandages," she said pointing to her injury. "But I've been dressed for twenty minutes without incident. Cross your fingers and hope it stays that way."

He looked her up and down once more and shook his head sadly. "If only I wasn't your boss and *was* twenty years younger," he said.

She laughed so loud the driver glared at her in the rearview mirror. "Now *that* was definitely sexual harassment," she said. "Save it, Mike, you're not my type." She patted him on the shoulder.

"Don't get a big head, Santos, I said 'if'. Besides, word around the office is you're dating Officer Lopez down at the station."

Luz moaned and rolled her eyes. "Great, that's just great. The guy helps me out on one case and suddenly we're bed buddies."

"No, we were all thinking: the guy *saves your life* and suddenly you're bed buddies. Did you forget that you've got his blood in your veins?"

She shuddered at Mike's use of words, but he was correct. "No, but that's how it feels with Eddie. Like we're related. He's like a big brother, you know?" She looked at Mike, hoping to find understanding in his eyes.

Mike held his hands up. "Hey, you don't have to explain anything to me. I know you're smart enough to not date a cop. That's why I knew I was off limits," he said with a like chuckle.

They talked about the case as they rode across town. Antoinette Peterson was cleared as a suspect but filed a formal complaint against Luz's actions towards her during her visit. Mike dismissed the complaint immediately. Working homicide, one had to check every angle, even if that meant pissing people off.

Sonny had yet to find a match for the prints found on the knife. What they did know was that the knife the killer used must have been a duplicate of the one found on Nicholas Mason. Luz had done some work that afternoon and found that only twenty versions of that particular knife had been made, back in 1929, by an American bladesmith in Georgia. She had to leave a message with the guy's secretary requesting a list of buyers for each knife. The woman told her they no longer made knives—only sold them for a partnering company, and she wasn't sure they held records dating so far back but she promised to deliver the message.

"Now all we can do is wait," Luz told Mike.

"There's nothing else?" he asked.

"Well there's so much trash at the lab from each murder scene. That's taking the longest; from cigarette butts to chewed gum, they have their hands full."

Mike sighed. "So the waiting game continues," he said and looked out the window as they pulled up to the mayor's palace.

The grounds had been recently manicured and the fountain in the center of the driveway beamed with lights slowly fading from one color to another as water ran over a sculptured stone rosebush with budding roses. Luz found the sculpture beautiful and got out of the car for a closer look. The water ran over stone petals that seemed to change shape every time the colors changed. She wondered if the fountain belonged to the mayor before his election or if the good residents of Seattle had paid for it. She guessed the latter was likely, since Anthony Yates wasn't as well off back in his days as the senior policy advisor to the former mayor.

Mike took her arm and led her to the entrance of the house. Classical music drifted through the doors as they walked from the foyer to the ballroom beyond. The room had a high ceiling with several crystal chandeliers lined down the center. Small lamps on the surrounding walls cast softer light, which gave the room a more intimate feel. Linen the color of pearls covered the tables which were and set with china dishes and crystal glassware. They formed six rows with ten tables to each that all arced around the podium and the stage on the far wall. Each chair was made of polished redwood and upholstered with the finest fabric.

Luz and Mike wandered around the room and Luz found that the music was performed live by a string quartet on a platform lavishly decorated with white lilies and a cream-colored silk backdrop. She thought the whole affair was a bit much for a charity auction but recalling the mayor's love of attention and praise (never mind his need to flaunt his wealth), she knew that despite all the decorations, the evening was toned down a bit.

They hobnobbed with the deputy mayor and his wife, who had just returned from a cruise in the Caribbean, the governor's wife and her son, a junior at Harvard Law, and several city council members—all promoting their committees. With everyone it was the same conversation; they all wanted to know about the serial killer stalking Seattle and how long it would to take to catch him. Mike politely tried to change the subject many times but failed. Luz could see how relieved he was when it was announced that dinner would be served, and the auction would begin.

Mike and Luz were saved from discussing the case during dinner; they sat with a group of art collectors who had flown in for the auction. Luz was grateful.

The items up for auction ranged from sailboats and paintings to oddly shaped statues and famous items of clothing.

But what caught Luz's attention was the last item on the block. It was brought out in a glass case and the bids were up past two-thousand dollars before she realized what it was. It was a duplicate of the knife they had in evidence. Her breath caught in her throat and she looked at her boss for confirmation, but Mike was engaged in conversation with the woman to his left. She took the heel of her shoe and brought it down gently on the toe of his size twelve wingtip Barringtons. He whipped around and looked at her, baffled.

"Excuse me for a moment," he said to the woman and turned back to Luz. "Is there a reason you're playing footsies?" he asked.

"Look up there." She nodded toward the stage and watched his expression morph from irritation into utter shock.

"What the fu—" he began.

"I know. It looks just like the one we have. There were only twenty of that version made. Where did that one come from?" she was cut off when the audience began clapping. The last bid was in and the knife had sold for four thousand dollars. The announcer's voice boomed throughout the room.

"Congratulations to Mr. Petry of Petry's Rare Knives and Swords based in Philadelphia, Pennsylvania. Not only is this rare knife in mint condition, it comes from the mayor's personal collection."

The crowd applauded as Anthony Yates rose from his front-row seat and enthusiastically waved. He then walked to the stage to shake Mr. Petry's hand and posed for photographs taken by the select members of the press who were invited to attend.

The dinner plates were cleared from the tables and the music played once more. A few people strolled out to the dance floor. Mike grabbed Luz's arm and dragged her to join him. She tried to protest but he was insistent, so she gave up and let him lead.

"You know what we have to do now, don't you?" he asked, softly dipping his head towards hers so that he could whisper and not be heard.

"Waltz?" she replied.

"Luz, this is serious. If Yates has more of those knives lying around, he's a potential suspect and I don't want to have to bring that to his attention," he said looking around, likely for any members of the press who might be listening. "Dammit. How do we find out?"

She lifted her head and stared at him. "Where did you get your badge, a Cracker Jack box? We just go up and ask him. As long as he doesn't know about the knife we have, he'll have no reason to suspect anything."

Mike looked doubtful, but he continued to sweep her around the floor until the classical piece concluded, then he steered her toward a group of politicians who had congregated near the French doors that led to the terrace. Mike used his conversation expertise to propel them through the crowd toward the mayor. Yates spotted them and approached with his hand outstretched and ready to shake.

"Ah, there you are, Michael. I was hoping to see you tonight. How's the case coming along?" he asked and the people around them fell silent.

Mike cleared his throat and leaned in toward the mayor. "I'd love to discuss it with you, but it *is* official police business," he said with a wink.

Yates smiled and winked back. "Yes, of course," he said a little too loudly. "I completely understand." He turned to Luz and smiled graciously. "Mike, I don't believe I've met your date."

The volume of chatter returned to a normal level and Luz blushed.

The last time she had seen the mayor she'd worn her hair tied back and was dressed in jeans and a sweatshirt. *It's no wonder he doesn't recognize you,* she thought and held out her hand.

"Luz Santos," she said. He kissed the top of her hand and bowed slightly. "Detective Santos," she corrected.

His eyes grew wide with recognition and he dropped her hand. It was at that moment she understood what she must have looked like when Nicholas Mason revealed his identity.

"I'm terribly sorry, Ms. Santos. I meet new people all the time in my line of work, so it becomes easy to lose track. But I won't forget your face again. You look exquisite this evening," he said giving her an appraising look.

Luz accepted his lie and let him kiss her hand once again, raising her eyebrows at Mike in the process. Mike rolled his eyes as if the whole experience was amusing rather than uncomfortable.

"Anthony, darling, I can't leave you alone for one moment without you kissing the hand of an attractive young woman."

The tone was meant to be playful, but Luz detected ice in those words.

Luz turned and the first thing that came to her mind was that Princess Diana was, indeed, still among the living. The woman bore such a strong resemblance to the late princess that Luz had some difficulty convincing herself that there was *not* a ghost standing before her. The woman wore a long-sleeved gown of gold silk that trailed behind her when she walked up to take her husband's arm. Luz wondered how the woman managed to look tasteful when the front of her dress dropped low and revealed enough cleavage to attract attention. Diamonds dripped from her ears and neck and she held herself gracefully, seeming to float rather than walk across the floor. She was stunning with her high cheekbones and slanting eyes. Her blond mane fell around her shoulders in luscious golden locks. Her husband didn't seem too pleased to see her; he stood, looking like a child caught with his hand in the cookie jar.

"Mr. Andrews, your wife is trés chic. Where on earth did you find her?" she asked smiling tightly at Luz. The smile didn't quite reach her eyes—eyes that sized Luz up with unwavering scrutiny.

"Luz Santos, I would like you to meet Annabel Yates, the mayor's wife and his better half, I might add," Mike said laughing uncomfortably. The mayor joined in, sounding equally uncomfortable. "Mrs. Yates, may I present Luz Santos, not my wife, but my top homicide detective on the force."

The compliment had Luz flush as she held out her hand

which Annabel looked at as if it were diseased and turned to her husband. "Darling, Richard and Jennifer Harris are here. I think it would be polite to say hello. He *is* the district attorney after all," she said, looking at Mike and Luz.

Yates coldly stared at his wife. "Annabel, don't be rude to our guests. I was in the middle of an important conversation with Captain Andrews and Detective Santos. The district attorney can wait," he said, effectively dismissing her.

A look of shock crossed her face but only for a second, as she quickly replaced it with indifference and spoke to him in a chilled voice. "I apologize. By all means, don't let me keep you." And with that, she shot a nasty look at Luz and stalked off.

Any similarity Annabel had held to Princess Diana was washed away in Luz's mind, and she wondered if Prince Charles would disagree. In any case the mayor's wife had proven to be nothing short of a patronizing snob and Luz didn't doubt their marriage was a complicated one. She smiled politely at the mayor and he shook his head.

"I'm terribly sorry for the interruption. Now, what were we talking about?" he asked.

Luz summoned her most charming tone. "I was wondering about that last item in the auction. They said it was from your own collection," she said.

The mayor brightened a bit at the inquiry. "Oh yes, I have quite the collection. It began with my great grandfather; he had quite a passion for collecting medieval weaponry. As the hobby passed down through the generations, my family accumulated many artifacts and rare items from past wars and famous bladesmiths. My father was more interested in pistols of the past, but my fascination lies in knives. My collection is quite extensive, therefore allowing me to auction off a couple pieces a year. I was quite surprised at how much that knife sold for tonight. It's a rare piece but not impossible to find for less," he said, rubbing at his mustache. "At least the profit will go to charity," he absently added.

"Would you mind showing us your collection?" Luz asked. "My grandfather collects as well."

"Really?" Yates said. "What is his main focus?"

Luz thought quickly. "Weapons of the Mayan and Aztec tribes. He is, after all, Latino."

The mayor appeared intrigued by that. A slight smile could be detected beneath his mustache. He raised his eyebrows and cocked his head to the side. "Those are very rare indeed, most of the items found at those sites are protected and kept in museums. How on earth has he managed to get his hands on them?"

Luz took a long sip of her drink while she thought of her reply. "There's a lot of land yet to be excavated by archeologists in Mexico and the surrounding countries. Collectors like my grandfather spend a lot of time and money locating these sites. You'd be surprised what they've found."

"Hmm... you'll have to tell me more about this. I have only one knife in my entire collection from the Aztecs; it's very crude—but priceless—and it would be nice to add similar makes. Maybe your grandfather would be willing to part with some of his findings?" he asked.

Luz tried her best to sound clever. "There's a right price for everyone, Mr. Yates."

"Of course. Please remind me to get his number from you," he said, and Luz could practically see the gears turn in his mind. "But first, allow me to give you a tour." He held out his arm and Luz smoothly slid hers into it.

As they walked out onto the terrace, Luz marveled at the view of the lake. The terrace stretched a good forty yards over the water. The boathouse near the edge of the lake housed two large sailboats. There were also two boats docked; one small yacht and a sleek speedboat. Mike was silent as he stared out at the water.

"You have beautiful boats, Mr. Mayor," Luz commented, letting a little awe slip through to boost his ego. It was a balancing act trying to stroke his ego and not give herself away, but she was up to the task. They badly needed a lead on the case and if it meant pretending to like the pompous ass attached to the arm she was holding—so be it.

"Ah, yes. Knives aren't the only thing I like to collect," he replied.

Mike shot Luz a look behind his back and mimed a kiss while pointing to Yates's butt. Luz shrugged; kiss-ass or not, she was getting results. They stepped off the terrace onto a path that ran behind the house to the bottom half of the building. Yates pulled down the cover of a security console and blocked it from their view while he dialed the pass code and pulled out a key. He unlocked the door and they walked through, finding themselves in a small foyer with another door at the end. Again, the mayor dialed in his password disabling the alarm.

They walked through the doorway and Luz was amazed. Along the walls were hundreds of glass cases with knives set in velvet stands. Luz walked the perimeter and noticed that the smaller knives were kept along the wall. The larger, more expensive knives were set in separate cases and placed in glass islands around the room. The knives had brief descriptions engraved on small bronze plates attached to the top of each case.

Yates moved through the room, speaking with pride. "As you see, I'm a very serious collector. I'm a member of the National Knife Collector's Association and the Art Knife Collector's Associates, as well as many others. One day my collection will be passed to my son. Assuming, of course, that he'll follow in my footsteps. He graduates next year from Harvard Law. He's one year ahead of the governor's son," Yates boasted.

Always trying to one-up the next guy, Luz thought. "These are indeed very impressive, Mr. Mayor. My grandfather would be honored to assist you in adding to your collection," she said.

The mayor beamed and looked at her boss. "Mike, I like her already."

Mike nodded and glanced at Luz. By the look on his face, he was just as impressed as the mayor.

Luz took a deep breath. "Mr. Yates, do you have any more knives like the one that was auctioned off tonight?"

"I have similar makes but that was the only version of that particular knife I've owned. I really didn't want to part with it. I went through a lot to acquire it, but someone convinced me that parting with it would be a smart move on my part. As you saw by the bidding tonight, I have made quite an impression on the art community."

Seattle was known for its artistic history and way of life. Touching base with local artists and businesses would prove useful come election time.

"I noticed you've taken a lot of precautions to protect your collection. Have you had any break-ins?" she asked placing her hand on his arm.

The mayor scoffed. "I have a top-notch security system installed here, Ms. Santos, not only with the double doors, but on every glass case in the room. I've had each case de-oxidized," he said. "The oxygen has been suctioned out. Not only to preserve the items but also to ward against burglary attempts. Once oxygen enters the atmosphere inside the case, an alarm will sound. When unoccupied, this room has laser light beams that, when broken, will trip the alarm. Once the alarm is tripped, the room is sealed from the outside and the thief captured."

Mike let out a whistle. "Wow, Tony, you've thought of everything."

Yates nodded. "Yes, well, I value my possessions."

Luz stepped back from the large case at the center of the room and glanced at the ceiling. She counted fifteen cameras mounted around the room. "So you're saying it is next to impossible for these knives to be moved without your knowledge?"

The mayor chuckled. "My dear woman it *is* impossible."

"And no one knows the codes except for you?"

"That is correct," he said, looking a little put off. "Why are you so keen on knowing these things?"

"I'm a detective, Mr. Mayor. It's in my nature to question security." She saw that his suspicion hadn't eased. "If my grandfather were to sell you a knife, even at the right price, no amount of money would comfort him if he were to learn that the item could be stolen."

The mayor looked at her blankly, then slowly nodded. "I understand your concern. But I have had this system custom made for my use only."

She feigned relief, sighing slowly. "That's all the reassurance I need. Thank you. Shall we rejoin the party?" she asked, glancing toward the door.

"Of course. I hope you enjoyed my little tour and please feel free to visit anytime. There's much more of the property to admire."

They walked back to the ballroom and the mayor excused himself and went in search of the district attorney. Luz and Mike mingled a while longer and decided they'd stayed long enough. When they got into the car, Mike couldn't hide his amazement.

"You were incredible, Santos. Your grandfather would be proud."

"What grandfather?" she asked.

He looked at her, confused, then his face lit up. "There *is* no grandfather. My god, Luz, you had *me* convinced."

She wiped her hands and grinned. "All in a night's work. For the record, my grandfather passed away thirty years ago, may he rest in peace. Now I'm ready for a good night's sleep," she said, then yawned.

"I'm with you on that one," Mike said, then shook his head at what his words implied. "Not like that. You know what I meant," he clarified, flustered.

"Yeah," she said and rested her head back on the seat. They rode in silence and enjoyed the passing scenery. She was replaying the night's events in her mind when her eyelids grew heavy and she dropped off to sleep.

The blood-drenched boy pointed, indicating something behind her. His face was pale, though with fear or blood loss, Luz wasn't sure. "Run!" he screamed and ran from her.

"Stop! What's your name?" she called after him, but he was running so fast. Suddenly she heard footsteps behind her. She spun around, drawing her weapon in the process.

Blood.... So much blood

"Dammit, Santos, wake up now!" her boss ordered as he shook her shoulder.

She snapped awake, her heart beating out of her chest.

"What's wrong? One minute I'm making notes and the next you're flailing your arms and making enough noise to scare the driver."

The last thing she wanted was Mike questioning her ability to do her job, so she shrugged it off. "It must've been a nightmare. I get them once in a while if I'm not properly rested."

"Well you scared the living daylights outta me. I didn't know you were that tired. You must still be recovering."

"Something like that," she murmured.

"Yeah, well, I'll wait until I see you go inside before I take off."

"Thanks for a wonderful night, Mike. See you at work."

"G'night Santos, get some rest. It seems you need a lot more of it."

She crossed the parking lot quickly and as she neared her boat she heard Cheech's excited barks. "Mike, I'm really sorry I worried you. A little sleep and I'll be just—" she started but stopped short when she noticed the note pinned to her door. She took it down.

In small, typed print it read:

    You were blessed with a watchful eye.
    Keep it open or you will die.

CHAPTER ELEVEN

I found the nest of my enemy
And left a note for her to see
She can run and she can hide
But by my rules she will abide

MAY 22ND, 2002 9:18 A.M.

Luz woke up disoriented; it took her a moment to remember where she was. Room twenty-six at the Ramada Inn. The bed was uncomfortable, and the room smelled musty, but at least she was safe.

After finding the note, Mike insisted she stay somewhere else for the night. He argued with her when she told him she didn't want to stay with family. Upsetting them was the last thing she wanted to do after her recent incident. So they agreed she would stay in a hotel—more like a motel—but it was the cheapest motel near the police department and if they were going to pick up the bill, she wasn't complaining. Besides it would only be for a couple of days.

She threw the bedcovers off, climbed out of bed and pulled

back the thick curtains that covered the window. The sun shone but clouds gathered in the north. The weather mirrored her thoughts of the night before. The night had gone well, despite Annabel Yates's rude appearance. But after finding that note, unease had stayed with her.

She felt something press against her leg and looked down. Cheech stood upright with his front paws on her leg. She had picked him up after her primping session yesterday and dropped him at home before leaving for the mayor's auction. Just thinking about how close a stranger had been to him yesterday while she was out left her worried. She felt guilty about the lack of attention he'd gotten lately, but like any dog, he was quick to forgive his master's shortcomings. She bent down and picked him up, inviting all the licks of affection she received.

"I'm sorry, boy. I'd have more time to spend with you if some madman hadn't decided to carve up homeless people around town." He stopped licking her and stared at her with a tilted head as if thinking over what she'd told him. She kissed his face and put him down. He ran to the door and whined softly.

"Let me wash up real quick and we'll take a walk, okay?" she said, heading toward the bathroom.

After a quick shower, she dressed and took him out. They walked down Fifth Avenue and after a few blocks they arrived at Denny Park and she let Cheech sniff around. After he had done his business and continued to explore his new surroundings. Luz sat on a bench and watched him; soaking up as much sun she could before it decided to rain. It would rain, not because it was Seattle and it was the norm, but because the air around her felt thick with it.

As if reading her mind, a voice behind her spoke. "Looks like rain."

She jumped, swore then quickly turned around and found Nicholas Mason staring down at her, looking amused.

"Your choice of words never ceases to amaze me," he joked, and she watched his grin broaden.

"Your sudden appearances and knack for sneaking up on me never ceases to scare the shit out of me. Why do you keep doing that?" she asked.

"It wasn't my intention to startle you. I was just trying to make small talk," he said glancing up at the dark clouds in the distance. The silence stretched for a few seconds, then he stared at the empty seat beside her on the bench.

Her eyes followed his and she sat up, suddenly remembering her manners. "Would you like to sit down?" she asked. He was dressed in black slacks and a turtleneck sweater that gave him a GQ sort of look. Or it would have, had he been able to fill out the clothes properly. Luz guessed it would take him a while to put some weight back on after being homeless for so long.

"Are you okay?" he asked.

Realizing she'd been staring, she quickly looked away and found Cheech digging a hole under a flowering bush a few feet away. "Perro! Knock that off," she yelled, and Cheech sprang up and ran to her, his tail wagging wildly.

"Is that his name?" Nick chuckled, his eyes full of amusement.

"No, his name is Cheech. 'Perro' means 'dog' in Spanish. When I call him 'perro', he knows he's in trouble. You know, like when you were a kid and your parents called you by your first and middle name?"

He laughed again and reached down to pet the chihuahua, but Cheech wouldn't be caught off guard. He growled and snapped at Nick's fingers. Nick pulled his hand back, his eyes wide.

Luz picked up the dog and rubbed his head. "It's okay, Cheech, Nick's a good guy. He won't hurt you." She looked up at Nick and smiled. "He gets a little protective," she explained and scratched behind Cheech's ears.

"Do you live near here?" he asked.

She hooked a leash to the dog's collar. "No. I live north of here, but I'm temporarily staying in town," she said, choosing her words carefully. She didn't want to tell him what had happened the night before. She didn't want him to think of her as vulnerable. Her father was right, she *did* come off a bit too independent, but she didn't care. If she scared Nicholas Mason off it wouldn't matter.

"You know," he began. He opened his eyes and sighed. "I don't have much to do now that I've taken my life back. I just sit around all day wondering what to do next. When I was on the streets I would move around the city constantly, finding new places to sleep, new missions to visit, those types of things. Now there's so much I've missed, from pop culture to technology... I feel so out of touch. I've come to the realization that I can do more for the homeless by reconnecting with society and becoming a resource for those who are looking to better their circumstances. I will soon be starting a few proj-ects that will help me do just that but for now, would you like to grab some lunch?"

Luz stared at him for a beat before answering, trying to sort through all the words he'd just said. She understood that he hadn't been back in society for very long, so she decided to excuse his rambling. To ignore it. "Well, if you have absolutely nothing to do, I guess I can swing lunch. But I have to stop in the office to check on some things. Did you want to meet me back here in two hours?"

She thought she saw disappointment in his features but then he smiled. "Sure, I'll be here."

"Good. See you soon." She got up and walked Cheech down the path to the sidewalk. She felt Nick's eyes on her back, *or was it her ass,* she wondered, and smiled. She resisted the urge to turn around. She was in the middle of a murder case; involvement with one of the suspects wasn't a good idea. Though he wasn't a suspect anymore, she reminded herself.

• • •

She walked into her office fifteen minutes later and found a note from Mike asking her to call him. She unhooked Cheech and let him run free. Her office was small, limiting the space he had to scamper around, but he was content with all the nooks and crannies her furniture provided for him to investi-gate. She had just picked up the receiver when Mike popped his head in.

"I was just about to call you," she said, lowering the phone and placing it back in the cradle.

"Sure you were. And I was about to swear off women for good," he teased and bent down to pet Cheech who was practically crawling up his pant leg, wagging his tail.

"No, really. I was. What did you want to chat about?" Luz asked.

"Just making sure you got a good night's sleep, that's all. Notice anything different today?"

Luz surveyed her boss but could find nothing different about him. "You got me Mike, what's up?"

"There was no body found this morning. We went twenty-four hours without a new one. What do you think that means?"

"It means the killer was too busy trying to find me to bother with choosing another victim, that's what it means," she replied. That note had left her more rattled than she'd thought.

He frowned at her. "You're no fun, Santos."

"I didn't think *fun* was in my job description," she retorted.

"No, that's *my* job description." He emphatically pointed at himself.

Luz leaned back in her chair and looked up at him. "Why? What's happened now?"

"I have DHS on my A-S-S. They're asking what we're doing to help protect the homeless from this homicidal maniac."

The Department of Health and Human Services not only provided help to the homeless but had high expectations of the community and its leaders to assist them unfailingly. Their PATH programs (Project for Assistance in Transition for

Homelessness) had helped many families living on the street and had a positive effect on the communities. The programs tended to exclude those homeless people with substance abuse problems; they focused more on those who were mentally ill or unstable. DHS was more likely to secure funding to help the sick, even though drug addiction *was* a disease. Unfortunately, it all boiled down to politics. Luz had gotten a call from them herself but hadn't called them back.

"Did you tell them that when the federal government kicks in some money that we would be happy to help?"

"Yeah, yeah. They were going on about the money in our Victims Assistance fund. I told them that money is used for emergency housing, medical care, food, financial assistance, and language interpretation for actual victims of violent crimes. We can't afford to help everyone on the street," he said, exasperated.

"Besides, if anyone was a victim of murder, they wouldn't need assistance," she added.

"Another good point." He shook his head.

"We couldn't touch that money if we wanted to. The police department guidelines are very specific about the use of those funds," Luz noted, a bit frustrated.

"I tried to explain all of that to them, but DHS is like a tick, they crawl under your skin, bite down and hold on."

"Wish I could help, but I have my hands full with the press. They are not satisfied with the statement the mayor issued at the press conference. They want more and won't stop until they get it. I'm going to have to charm my way out of it or they'll say that the department was uncooperative, leading up to the fact that we're hiding something from the public that they have a right to know."

"No problem. I don't need help. I just stopped by to see how you were. I'm going to grab lunch, you want anything?"

Luz thought of Nick and smiled. "No thanks."

"What the hell was that?" Mike asked, eyeing her face.

Automatically, she reached towards her face. "What?"

"That goofy smile?"

"Mike, lack of food has you hallucinating. Go eat." She shooed him with her hands.

"Sure, whatever. I know what I saw."

"They say the sight is the first to go," she said and turned toward the other messages on her desk.

"You're starting with the old jokes? You must be hiding something big." He grinned.

She stopped shuffling the papers on her desk and looked up at him. "If you must know, I'm having lunch with a guy."

"Lopez finally got through your defenses?"

"Not Eddie," she said curtly, slightly taken back, wondering if everyone thought she was so hard to get close to.

"Who?" he asked.

"You wouldn't know him."

"That means he's not a cop, but I might. Try me." He leaned against the doorframe and crossed his arms.

Irritated at his lack of courtesy she blurted out Nick's name. She'd anticipated the silence that followed. "Before you start in, let me assure you that I'm not looking for a boyfriend. He just asked me to lunch."

But Mike didn't say a word. His lack of response made her a little nervous. "What?"

"Be careful, Santos," he said. "The guy's been living on the streets for a good chunk of time, seen some awful things. I'm not sure what that does to a person. Just keep your guard up." He tapped the door jamb and left.

His words rang true. What did she really know about Nick? Who he was, how he went from a prominent social figure to a homeless man on the street. How had his wife died? There could be something seriously wrong with him. She looked at the clock and decided she would learn nothing new about him if she missed lunch. She turned on her computer and logged in. After she returned about two dozen emails and composed a few of her own, she got to work.

Turning towards her computer, she logged into the criminal database with its endless amount of information.

The first thing she decided to research was the mayor and his collections. Anthony Yates was born and raised in Seattle, Washington. He attended Garfield High School and graduated valedictorian of his class in 1996, which made him about fifty-two years old. After graduation he moved to California to attend the UCLA School of Law. When he held his law degree he surprised his family by becoming a police officer in California instead of an attorney, claiming he wanted to make a real difference. Luz knew firsthand how his family must have reacted to his decision.

He was on the force only six years but had risen to captain

in that brief time. Finally deciding that politics held his interest, he left the force and moved back to Seattle. He worked closely with the city council until being elected as the chairperson of police, fire, courts and technology. *That would explain his custom-designed security system*, thought Luz.

Yates worked on that committee for ten years and was then named council president. Working closely with the mayor's staff, he eventually left his post at the council and settled for a job as the senior policy advisor for the previous mayor of Seattle. He handled public safety and human services issues and excelled in that position due to his law background. Three years before, he was elected mayor, encouraged to run by his own boss because he showed potential in politics, given all his years of public service.

She read rumors of Yates running for governor after completing his first term as mayor. Some political big wigs went as far to say that one day Yates might make a great leader as president of the United States. After meeting Yates, Luz prayed he would never get the chance. The man was not president material. He lacked the compassion and unbiased social stature. He would need to run a country diverse in financial status and cultural differences. All in all, he was a greedy man, and in the end, he would only put more pressure on the average blue-collar citizen.

She checked the clock and was surprised to see she'd been reading about Yates for a good hour and a half. She rubbed her eyes and pushed her chair from the computer. Her back cracked as she stood, and her knees were stiff from sitting so long. Cheech must have sensed it was time to go because he went to the door automatically. She scooped him up and headed out, closing the door to her office behind her.

She rode the elevator to the ground level and walked outside. She noticed the ground was damp and the cars parked along the street were sprinkled with water. It must have rained while she was working.

She walked along the street, careful not to let passersbys trod on her dog. It was more difficult because instead of avoiding their feet, Cheech walked right under them. Twice she had to pick him up, fearful he would get trampled. Cheech, of course, didn't understand her caution and soon became too squirmy to hold, so she put him down and shook her finger at him.

"Fine, but if you so much as get your tail stepped on, I don't want to hear a peep!" she scolded.

"Do you always yell at your dog in public?"

She knew who it was before she turned around. "There you go again, sneaking up on me."

Nick held his hands up. "Hey, you told me to meet you at the park. I was on my way there, but some lady was yelling at her poor dog and distracted me."

Luz wondered how long he'd been following her but decided that it didn't matter, since they were headed to the same place anyway. "What's that?" she asked pointing to the large paper sack he was holding.

"You'll find out when we get to the park," he said. He continued walking on without her. She followed him up the street and into the park to a bench and sat down with him.

After watching Cheech run around for a bit, her curiosity got the best of her.

"Okay, now I'm dying to know what's in the bag," she said, trying to sneak a peek but he grabbed the bag and placed it out of her reach.

"Stay right there, I'll be back." He got up from the bench and walked to the other end of the park behind a small grove of trees. She couldn't see what he was doing but that made the wait more fun. She didn't know why but she felt like a school girl, which didn't make sense considering she knew nothing more about this man than that he was a homeless lawyer with a stroke of bad luck. That thought discouraged her feelings of joyous wonder and she doubted Nick's intentions.

She called Cheech back to her and fastened his leash. She went to find Nick to feed him some lame excuse about having no time for lunch. But the words died in her throat. Behind the trees was a blanket laid out with an assortment of food from sandwiches and soup to butter rolls and fruit.

"Hey, I told you to wait over there," Nick admonished, looking up from a small plate upon which he arranged an array of doggy treats.

Cheech ran over and feasted on his treats, obviously pleased with the buffet provided. Luz, however, was reluctant.

"What's wrong?" Nick asked, seeing her less-than-enthusiastic reaction.

"Is this all for me?" she asked. She felt a bit of pressure seeing the lengths he'd gone to for a simple lunch.

"No. I was planning to eat as well." He sat on one side of the blanket and picked up a sourdough roll. "Unless, of course, you're really that hungry?"

His smile lured her to the blanket and she sat down, feeling less than thrilled. "I... I really don't know what to say," she stammered.

"Don't say anything, just eat. I know it's a little much."

Luz surveyed the food once more and decided to start with a chicken salad sandwich. It was, to her surprise, very good. They ate in silence for a while, enjoying the sounds of the park, before Nick spoke up.

"I'm sorry if this seems like a lot. I must be out of practice," he said looking abashed. "On the street, this would feed me for a week if I stretched it, not that I ever got my hands on a spread like this. I guess my eyes were bigger than my stomach at the store. I hope this doesn't mean I've scared you off."

It was like he'd read her mind. She met his eyes. "It takes a lot to scare me off. This just surprised me is all. I'm not used to picnics in the park. I appreciate the gesture though. This is rather pleasant." She leaned back on the tree and closed her eyes, enjoying the moment.

• • •

They talked for a while, learning about each other's interests and views. Luz steered the conversation from her dating life as Nick avoided talking much about his late wife, yet the conversation ebbed and flowed naturally as if they were old friends.

"I love this park. They keep everything maintained. And in the spring the flowers bloom so beautifully," Luz said. "My grandmother had the most amazing garden in Mexico. I spent a lot of time there with her brilliant, multi-colored flowers and all their scents. Roses, lilies, carnations… there really was no flower she couldn't grow, though the lilies were always my favorite. I'd go with her on the weekends into town to sell them at the market. Whenever I see beautiful flowers, it makes me think of her and that makes me smile."

Nick nodded. "I know what you mean. My grandfather was the green thumb in my family. He always had to have the biggest and brightest garden in the neighborhood. He'd spend hours cultivating that garden, but as a kid I didn't appreciate the patience and skill it took to keep a garden like his in top condition season in and season out. It was a lot of work and it gave him a sense of pride when people would stop and admire his flowers. After he passed, Grandma wasn't in good physical or mental condition, and she wasn't able to keep up his garden. Sadly, it became overgrown with weeds. It broke her heart but there was nothing she could do, so I hired a gardener for her. The change was almost immediate; the family started seeing the light in her eyes again. It really was worth every penny."

"That was a really sweet thing to do. I'm sure she appreciated it," Luz said.

As she spoke, Nick watched the shadows of the leaves dance on her face; she was like no one he had ever met. In addition to being sexy, exotic and strong-willed, yet amiable, she was also easy going but cautious and still managed to look independent and seem vulnerable at the same time. The concoction of those elements was interesting to say the least. Her thirst for justice and life in general reminded him of his wife, but Luz's approach to life's challenges and her cultural pride gave her an identity all her own. He found himself wanting to know more about her. She captivated him, and that terrified him. His heart pumped harder, and his head felt light and warm. His breaths became shallow.

He stood quickly and brushed the remaining crumbs off his trousers. "I've got to go. I… just remembered an important appointment I have this afternoon."

Luz stared at him for a bit, clearly confused. He knew she'd seen right through the lie when a look of disappointment coated her features. *She's a damn detective, idiot. Of course she sees through you.* But instead of challenging his words she simply started packing the food away.

"No problem. I'll help you with this," she said wrapping the sandwiches in plastic.

"Don't worry about it. Everything here is disposable except the blanket. Just throw it away and keep the blanket as a gift. I really have to go." He looked towards the grass as he rambled, growing even more annoyed that he couldn't meet her eyes. "Maybe… maybe we can do this again sometime?" He forced himself to look at her again when he heard the softness in her tone.

"Whatever you're comfortable with Nick," Luz replied, her eyes searching his face. "Take your time adjusting. I know this must be overwhelming but you're doing just fine. Baby steps, right?" She finished folding the blanket and tucked it under her arm.

Nick looked down at his feet. "I really am sorry."

She whistled for the dog and hooked on his leash "Don't be sorry. Just pace yourself. You've had an exciting few days. Get some rest and take care, okay?" she gave him a small wave and left.

He watched her walk away and was overcome with a heavy sense of guilt. All she wanted was someone to talk to, someone with whom she could share a quiet afternoon and she would have had it if he hadn't panicked.

He hung his head in his hands and leaned against the nearest tree. He felt the tears threatening to break loose. "I'm so sorry, Leah," he whispered softly and walked in the opposite direction Luz had taken.

CHAPTER TWELVE

I have stopped hunting those on the street
My bitter vengeance tastes all too sweet
Now's my turn to have some fun
With the setting of the sun

MAY 22ND, 2002 1:39 P.M.

Eddie Lopez watched the scene from his truck. He watched Luz walk from the office to the park, meeting Mason along the way.

Eddie was off duty and a lot less conspicuous in his Ford Ranger, parked in a space across the street.

Captain Andrews had called him an hour before and asked him to follow Luz at lunch. Eddie was not only surprised but worried. Everyone knew that when the captain of the force called you for a favor you don't take it lightly. The guy they had pulled in for the murders downtown a week ago had asked Luz to lunch, and Andrews was uncomfortable with it. Even though they cleared the guy, Andrews maintained a rotten feeling about Nicholas Mason.

So Eddie had agreed, but he didn't think it would be such a difficult task. Watching from his truck, he painfully endured every smile, every laugh and every look Luz bestowed upon Mason. Mason had planned a picnic for them—a romantic setting indeed—the gesture likely not only lit a flame between the pair, it also fueled the jealous fire within Eddie.

Four times, Eddie found himself clenching the steering wheel until his knuckles were white, and he had trouble observing them laugh and lean toward each other. He had the key in the ignition and was ready to drive off when their little excursion came to an abrupt end.

Mason jumped up and prepared to leave, wiping something from his pants. Luz looked disappointed. Her brow furrowed as she spoke with Nick, then she got her dog and walked quickly and purposefully back towards the precinct.

Mason watched her helplessly. He looked lost; out of place. Then he propped himself against the nearest tree and cried. Eddie observed for a minute, a smile playing across his face— Mason wasn't a threat to him. Or to Luz.

Eddie started the truck as Mason packed up the remains of the lunch and dumped them in the trash. Eddie turned his head to reverse out of his space and saw a glint of silver through the corner of his eye; felt the cold metal of a nine-millimeter against his temple and he froze.

"Get out of the truck."

He was surprised to hear Luz's voice and he tried to turn his head and look at her.

"Don't try to look, asshole, just step out of the truck."

He complied and slowly opened the door. Once he was outside, he put his hands on the canopy and assumed the position.

"Turn around, Lopez," she ordered. He turned to face her. "What the fuck do you think you're doing?"

He tried to look innocent but thought better of it. She wasn't stupid.

"I was keeping an eye on you," he mumbled, his heartbeat returning to normal. Even as a cop he wasn't used to having have a gun pulled on him.

"You were *spying* on me. Goddammit, Eddie. I don't need a babysitter. There are laws against stalking people in this state."

"I wasn't stalking you Luz—" he began, wishing she would put away her gun.

"Bullshit! You think I got my job sleeping my way to the top? I'm a detective, Eddie. I know when I'm being followed. I'm going to give you two minutes to explain yourself, then I don't ever want to see you again. Go."

Stunned, Eddie didn't know where to begin. Luz holstered her weapon and pointed to her watch.

"Time's ticking, Lopez, spit it out."

"It was my day off. Andrews called. Told me he had a bad feeling about Mason and asked if I would follow you two at lunch. I agreed and here I am."

Luz appeared dumbfounded. "Andrews called you?"

He nodded.

"What the hell is wrong with men?" she threw her arms in the air.

"Luz I'm sorry, I didn't—"

"Save it, Lopez, I'm through with you. It wasn't your idea, but you didn't have any qualms about stalking me around town, did you? Had to check out the competition, didn't you? Well fuck you, Lopez." She turned and walked away.

He immediately gave chase. "Luz! Please listen to me. I was only looking out for you. I care about you," he pleaded, hoping she would reconsider writing him off.

She stopped and turned. "You know what's sad? I was starting to care about you, too, but you blew it Eddie. I can't trust you anymore. This is great. I have a killer stalking me, two guys shut me out and now I get to chew out my boss. Anything else you want to throw my way?"

Eddie was shocked. "A killer is stalking you?"

She brought her gaze back to him and smiled mockingly. "Oh? thought *you* were the only one stalking me? I don't need your protection, Eddie, and I don't want it. Find someone else to follow," she said, her voice taking on a tired note.

Eddie watched her until she disappeared around the corner. Then he slumped against his truck and slapped himself on the forehead. How could he have been so stupid? Not only had he blown any chance of ever dating her; she couldn't stand the sight of him.

He climbed back into his truck and considered calling Andrews to warn him that Luz was on the war path but decided against it. Mike would have to hold his own. Eddie looked up and found no trace of Mason. He hoped the man hadn't witnessed the episode Luz had created.

Dejected and feeling like a top-notch ass, he drove home.

• • •

It was better than any movie I've seen—complete with romance, conflict and a promising ending. The only thing missing was a tub of popcorn and a comfortable seat. The bench I perched upon suited me just fine. I had a clear view of the detective's surprise lunch and the woman's blow out with her cop friend. The episode was rather amusing. I enjoyed every minute of the drama.

Luz Santos was a very attractive woman and likely had numerous suitors waiting in the wings. Too bad she didn't know that the closer she got to these men, the more devastated she would be when she lost them.

And she *would* lose them. I was torn between going after Nicholas Mason or Eduardo Lopez. There was also Ben Torres, who came to her rescue after my attempt to finish her off. All those men seemed equally interested in the detective, but which one would Luz miss the most? Decisions, decisions.

It doesn't matter. I will kill them all.

MAY 22ND, 2002 7:14 P.M.

Luz had been trying to work for the past five hours but keeping her mind from the events of the day was impossible. After her fight with Eddie she'd tracked Mike down and given him a piece of her mind, and almost her resignation.

175

Nothing bothered her more than being lied to. That people she had chosen to trust had tried to deceive her hurt more than anything else.

She wanted to be alone. Watching the gloomy masses of soot-grey clouds roll across the sky from her office window, she grew overwhelmed. The stress and tension that had built over the past week found its release and she wept uncontrollably.

She cried for the victims of the murders; she cried for her family; she cried over her near-death experience. She cried for Ben and the loss of what they once shared; for the betrayal of her coworkers; for the walls Nick had put up when she was feeling comfortable with him. Most of all—she cried for herself.

Why couldn't she have a meaningful relationship? Why couldn't she share herself with a man without feeling threatened?

She thought about the death of her mother, wishing she had someone close she could confide in. But she'd never been good at forming relationships with other women. Growing up without a female influence had scarred her in some way. Sometimes she was too proud to change, even if it meant she could then reach out and develop healthy relationships.

She reached for a tissue and remembered that Antoinette Peterson had emptied the box last week. She wiped her face dry with her sleeve. The skin around her eyes was tender. She fished for her mirror and fixed herself up the best she could. *Suck it up, Santos, and do your job.*

She'd spent the afternoon seeking the list of collectors who bought the twenty limited edition knives. After talking to the bladesmith in Georgia, she had found the list, which she could only obtain through showing the bladesmith her credentials. Once she had the list she went to work hunting down the knives. She came up with a half-dozen addresses for each person on the list. There were two museums listed—one in Florida and one in Japan—both of which she called, and both assured her that the knives were locked up tight.

Anthony Yates was the fifth name on the list. She learned that he'd acquired the knife some years ago, having bought it directly from the maker and it was placed straight into his collection. She thought about that for a moment and decided to take a different approach to the mayor's collection.

She pulled her chair back up to the computer and logged onto the database. She typed in *Anthony Yates* and *knife* and pressed "enter". She waited five minutes for the results. She scanned past the articles about past auctions, tributes to his police and political career and was ready to give up when something caught her eye.

Toward the bottom of the page was an article titled "Anthony Yates found innocent of the Mason murder." She brought up the entire article; it was three pages long and gave a detailed account of the case. Luz was shocked when she learned that the victim, Leah Mason, was Nicholas Mason's wife. *Shit, shit, shit.* Feeling guilty, she continued to read.

Leah Mason died at the age of twenty-seven. A neighbor found her in the dead of night, on her houseboat, with her throat slashed. A witness claimed he saw Anthony Yates at the scene earlier in the night, but the witness changed his story during the trial. Yates's lawyer had proven beyond a reasonable doubt that Yates was innocent. Even though he owned a knife that could have been the one used to kill Mrs. Mason, he got off clean. According to his lawyer, that knife was locked up and sealed tight, and he had the documentation from the security office showing no disturbances to the display case on or around the time of the murder. Yates also had the ticket and flight times proving he was out of town during the time of the murder and that he hadn't returned home until the week after the body was found.

Nicholas Mason had made it his sole mission to ensure Anthony Yates went down for the murder of Leah. Mason was a prominent attorney; a partner at his firm with more wins under his belt than average for someone his age. Nick seemed to have been the golden boy at his firm and on the fast track to success. The case had then been taken on by another law firm due to conflict of interest and the whole thing appeared to swirl down the toilet. The other witness had been proven unreliable, evidence disappeared and justice was ripped from Nick's grasp.

The media was not sensitive to his grief. They portrayed him as a crazed widower out for revenge.

After Luz finished the article, she searched Nick's name, but only found articles praising his ability as a prosecutor, the murder trial and a mention in his wife's obituary printed in the Seattle Times. His record at the DA's office was impressive, and Nick seemed to have had a promising future ahead of him.

She searched for any mention of Nick after Yates was found innocent—but came up empty. It was as if he had dropped off the face of the earth. What better way to disappear from society than to live under it. And that was the life Nick had chosen for himself.

She was understanding, piece by piece, what drove Nick Mason to give up on the system and leave everything he had known behind. In a way it was almost romantic, giving up his life when his wife's murderer was still free. She blinked and looked up from the computer screen.

She checked the time, deciding she was delirious from working so hard. She found Cheech asleep, sprawled out on the chair opposite her desk. She pulled on her windbreaker and packed her research into her briefcase. She decided against popping a couple of painkillers; she needed a clear head to drive and would take them once she got "home". The gash in her side was healing but some redness and puffiness remained. She hoped infection wasn't setting in and wondered for the umpteenth time if checking out of the hospital so soon was a mistake on her part. It didn't matter—she would keep an eye on it and if she ended up with gangrene she'd check herself back in. A few days' rest sounded appealing to her since she'd put in so many twelve-hour days.

She finished off her warm apple juice and picked up Cheech, who woke up for a moment then dropped back off to doggy dreamland. The office was deserted and most of the lights were off. She hurried through the eerie silence and pushed the "down" button when she reached the elevators.

Nerves she couldn't shake had her turning to scope out the building. No one was there.

She rode down to the parking lot level and walked toward her car. Without warning, Cheech jumped from her arms and crouched low to the ground, growling loudly. Luz stopped walking and drew her weapon.

"Who's there?" she asked, her echo the only answer. She crept forward a few steps and Cheech barked wildly. There were six other cars in the lot but hers was the farthest back and it sat in the shadows. Cautiously, she walked towards her car, keeping an eye out for any movement.

Luz was five feet from her car when the scent of death reached her. She walked with her gun pointed in front of her—the safety off. She could see no disturbance to her vehicle, but the smell of blood grew stronger the closer she got to her car, almost choking her with its coppery odor. She walked around to the driver's side and found the source of the sour scent. Written in blood on the door of her Eclipse were the words **FEELING HOMELESS YET?** Lying near her rear tire was the body of a massive rat. Its head hung limply from the rest of its body and a small puddle of blood had pooled from its neck. Luz gagged and held her breath, simultaneously pulling out her phone and dialing her boss's number. It took a long time for him to pick up.

"Mike, it's Santos. I had another visit from the killer, and this time he took out his anger on my car. Get down here pronto."

"Son of a bitch! The precinct garage? I'm sending down some uniforms. Wait for me on the street. See you in ten."

She confirmed and hung up. Cheech shook and growled at the dead rat. Luz carried her dog to the street and waited for Mike. She was growing concerned for her safety and the safety of those around her. Could she inadvertently get someone killed? She shuddered and held Cheech close to her heart for comfort, but it would be a long time before she felt safe again.

• • •

I watched with pleasure as Luz emerged from the parking lot holding her canine friend. The look on her face was priceless. I snapped a picture of her so as to freeze her fear in a tangible way. A strong sense of power surged through my body. How satisfying it was to be so close to her, to watch her horror up close while she had no idea how much danger she was truly in. *Time to step it up a notch.*

CHAPTER THIRTEEN

Shaken up and confused
My victim isn't so astute
Her resolve is wearing thin
Let the ruthless games begin

MAY 22ND, 2002 11:42 P.M.

Nicholas Mason woke to loud, angry voices in the hall. He stretched the stiffness from his body. He'd been sleeping on the floor, as the bed proved uncomfortably soft for someone accustomed to sleeping on concrete. Old habits, he guessed.

He wasn't sure how long it would take to adjust to even the smallest luxuries—like warm water and clean socks. Time would tell.

He stood slowly and approached the door. A man and a woman argued loudly about hotel security. He heard the voices more clearly when he entered the bathroom and realized that he recognized them both; Luz and Captain Andrews.

After stepping out of the bathroom he listened at the door to hear what the ruckus was about.

"I'll be fine, Mike. I'm an adult. I can take care of myself," Luz said.

"Like you took care of your car? What if that crazy person had still been there?" Captain Andrews replied.

"Then I would have blown his head off with my .22, that's what. Listen Mike, it's been a long day. All I want to do is sleep," Luz said sounding tired.

"Fine, go to sleep, but if this shit happens again you'll be sleeping in a cell surrounded by guards so no one can get at you, understand?" Andrews said.

"Okay Mike. Thanks for everything. See you tomorrow," Luz replied.

Nick heard footsteps retreat down the hall where a door opened and closed. Luz was staying at the same Inn, but Nick wasn't clear on why. From the conversation it sounded like she'd been attacked or harassed in some way.

He felt the need to check up on her. The scene from earlier that day in the park played through his mind. Luz wouldn't want to see him after his panic attack ruined their meal.

He walked to the desk in the corner of his room and wrote his thoughts on a pad of paper. He then lowered himself back down to his blanket pile on the floor and forced himself to go back to sleep.

MAY 23ʀᴅ, 2002 8:02 A.M.

Luz woke up with the sort of headache that comes with a hangover. After what had happened, she could have downed a bottle of José Cuervo. She needed something to calm her nerves.

The night before, Mike arrived with a crew of detectives, and Luz was forced to stay at the scene. They combed over her car, searching for signs of tampering or bombs. After photographing everything, they packed the rat up and sent it to the lab and the blood was wiped clean and sent for testing.

She expected something like this to happen after her attack; it was the delay that bothered her the most. Was she close to finding his identity? Was that why the killer was focusing on her? Instead of scaring her off, the killer had signed his own death warrant.

With new resolve, she hopped out of bed, momentarily forgetting her headache. She wouldn't allow it to slow her down. There was no time to lose.

After showering and dressing, she gave Cheech a bath in the bathroom sink. She was drying him off when there was a knock on her door. She wrapped Cheech in a towel and looked through the peephole.

"Go away, Eddie. I'm not ready to speak to you yet."

From the other side of the door she heard a muffled string of curses. She watched Eddie retreat then walk back and knock again.

"Come on, Luz, open up. I've got something you'll want to see."

She hesitated with her hand on the lock, but curiosity won out and she opened the door. Eddie handed her a piece of paper with tape on it.

"This was on your door," he said.

She stared at him and snatched the paper from his hands.

"I didn't read it. I promise," he said with his hands up. She cautiously unfolded the paper, worried it was another nasty threat from her would-be killer. Instead, it was a note from Nicholas Mason. He wanted to see her again. She scowled at Eddie.

"Are you sure you didn't read it?" she asked, not buying his boy scout routine.

"Yeah, I'm sure. I didn't come here to argue. I heard what happened last night and I just wanted to see how you were. I also came to apologize for spying on you. I should have known better."

"And?" she asked.

"And… I'm glad we've gotten to know each other, and I would hate to lose the friendship we share. Please don't write me off, Luz. I don't think I could take it. You're the closest thing I have to a real friend in this city."

He looked so pathetic. She punched him in the arm playfully. "Eddie let's get something straight to avoid further confusion," she said and stepped back, letting him into the room. Cheech was instantly alert and barked at Eddie.

"So this is Cheech, huh?" he asked. He kneeled on the carpet with his hand held out in front of him. Cheech kept his distance and barked furiously, but when Eddie didn't move, his barks subsided into growls and he inched closer. Finally, the growling ceased, and Cheech sniffed Eddie's hand. Luz kept one hand on Eddie's shoulder so that Cheech would know he was a friend. Then Cheech wagged his tail and licked Eddie.

"Good boy," Eddie gently told him and pet Cheech on the head.

"For being a victim of a dog attack, you're good with dogs," Luz said. She sat on the end of the bed. "Eddie, I know you don't want to hear this but it's about time you knew."

Eddie shook his head. "Don't tell me; you're a man. I knew it!"

Luz rolled her eyes. "Watch it, wiseass. One snap of my fingers and that little dog will bite your balls off."

Eddie looked down at the Chihuahua laying on his back begging to be rubbed on his stomach. "Whatever you say," he replied. "So, what's up?"

"Eddie, I'm glad I got to know you better, but you feel like a brother to me—a big brother. I don't have romantic feelings for you."

She watched him hide his disappointment and she felt guilty. But if he was going to hang around, it was something he had to know. With how mad she was at him the day before, she was surprised to find that most of that anger had burnt out and she was almost appreciative he had tracked her down to apologize and check on her well-being. That was something friends did for one another.

He was quiet for a moment and then spoke. "I understand. I kinda had a feeling that was the case." She heard the resignation in his voice "But it's no problem. I can respect that. When I saw you with Mason I thought 'hey, so she likes white meat' but it turns out that I was never in the race anyway."

"Race?"

"Come on Santos; don't tell me you don't know that half the force wants to go to bed with you."

Luz was surprised. "I… I knew that a few of the guys were interested, but *half* the force? Come on Lopez, give me a break."

"Stay in denial all you want but those are the facts. Anyway, I'm a little hungry, did you have plans for breakfast?"

She thought of the note taped to her door and took her time deciding what she would do. She'd already let Eddie down once. Nick would have to wait.

"Nope, let's go." She slid on her shoes and whistled for Cheech to follow. They left the room and walked down the hall toward the exit. The last door on the right opened and out stepped Nick.

"Hello," Nick said looking from her to Eddie and back. Luz could only imagine what was going through his mind; after all, they *were* in a motel. Her face burned slightly, and she turned to Eddie.

"Wait for me in the car?" she suggested.

Eddie looked at Nick with contempt, then walked around Luz and out the door.

"I get the feeling that guy doesn't like me," Nick said.

Luz smiled. "No, he doesn't, but that's not your problem, it's mine." When he looked confused she laughed and held out the note. "I got your message."

He looked a little embarrassed. "Yes, I heard you and Captain Andrews come in last night and I thought I'd slip you that since I wasn't sure you wanted to talk to me."

Luz shook her head. "Oh, you mean yesterday? Don't worry about that, I—" the horn of Eddie's truck honked loudly and cut her off.

187

Irritated, she looked out at the parking lot and sighed. "I have to go. My friend is taking me to breakfast, so maybe we can talk later? I forgot you were staying here. I'll come see you after I eat."

"Sure, see you then."

They stood awkwardly for a moment and Eddie honked the horn again. Without another word, Luz turned and left.

MAY 23ᴿᴰ, 2002 10:14 A.M.

After breakfast and a long lecture on why she shouldn't date murder suspects, Luz decided to return to the office to catch up on her other cases. When she got in, she noticed a message on her door from Sonny. It read: *Luz, call me I got a match.* She opened her office and the smell of flowers greeted her. On her desk sat a beautiful arrangement filled with tiger lilies.

After a minute she found a small envelope with her name on it, she pulled out the card and read it:

Detective Santos, had a wonderful picnic with you. Maybe we could try that again? Start fresh. I'd like a second chance.
Waiting patiently,
Nick

Luz set the card on the desk and smiled. She thought it had been wonderful too, and she was touched he remembered her story about her grandmother's garden and her favorite flower. Their conversation had only lasted an hour or so, but she found him to be intelligent and mature; compassionate with a sense of humor. He was still rough around the edges but with a history like his, why wouldn't he be? Maybe Nick really just needed someone to understand that he was struggling. So she decided to be a little more patient when it came to his reintegration process. She knew a few things about struggling and having someone to talk to could maybe help them both.

It surprised her that she looked forward to seeing him again. She had a lot going on in her life and they both had a lot of baggage. That little voice in her head warned her that dating got complicated, which was why she'd been avoiding it for so long. Maybe a fresh start was what they both needed.

"What did you do to deserve those?" Mike asked from the doorway, breaking her from her reverie.

She turned to him and scowled. "None of your business. What do you want?"

"That's no way to treat your boss, Luz," he said, stepping into her office.

"Just because you came to help me out yesterday doesn't mean you're off the hook for spying on me. I don't forgive that easily—or forget."

He winced and shook his head. "You know, I did what I did out of concern for you. You can take it or leave it."

"I can take care of myself, Mike. Just because I have tits doesn't mean I need protecting. I don't need big macho men to make me feel safe."

"It didn't seem that way last night. *You* called *me* for help, remember?"

"Yeah. You're my boss, captain of the force, and a crime was committed. So… I called you," she said indifferently, but she remained grateful that he'd been available to help her.

"You know what, Santos, you pretend you don't like the fact that people care about you, but I know different, so cut the act. I didn't stop by to discuss this. Have you spoken to Sonny?"

The change of subject happened so quickly Luz didn't get a chance to retort. "No. I was going to, but the flowers distracted me," she said.

"They are nice, but you really need to see Sonny. He found a match on those prints. I think we're finally getting somewhere."

"I'll be there in a minute, just let me straighten up here," she said rounding her desk and shuffling papers.

"Fine. We're meeting in the Storm Room. Don't take too long gawking at your flowers," he said and shut the door behind him.

Luz glared at the closed door and put down the papers she'd been holding. She got up and smelled her flowers again. She had received flowers before, roses mostly, but they were either from Ben, or as a token of congratulations. She'd never received flowers as gratitude for time spent with a person. Somehow, lilies were sweeter than roses.

Reluctantly, she put the vase back on her desk and left the room. She met Eddie at the elevator and they rode up together.

"What were you doing on my floor?" she asked him.

A blush crept up his neck and he scratched his head. "Just visiting," he replied sheepishly.

"Visiting who? The captain? Who else do you know up here?" He was silent.

"Fine, you don't have to tell me if it's that top secret," she said. The doors opened, and they walked down the hall toward the Storm Room. Everyone involved with the case would be there, brainstorming with and updating each other.

They found seats on the far side of the large conference table. The room buzzed with discussion and Luz wondered what the development was. Before she could ask, Mike walked in and the room fell silent. He cleared his throat and took his place at the head of the table.

"First of all, I want to thank everyone for putting in all this overtime. I appreciate all the help we can get with this case. Except," he said looking pointedly at Luz, "those who get too involved."

Most of the heads in the room turned in her direction but Luz watched Mike expectantly, concealing her annoyance. Mike went on.

"We've had a break in the case, but it needs a little follow-up. In fact, it could turn into quite a problem if we can't locate the suspect." He turned and motioned Sonny forward. "The floor's yours, Malone," he said and stepped back.

Sonny stood up straight and his voice boomed like that of a drill sergeant. "Let me recap what we have, people. Murder one was Mildred Jamison. The incision on her neck was made by a Reaper, that's the name of the knife. It was produced in 1926 by Uprising Smiths in Atlanta Georgia. They specialize in reproductions of knives used in eighteenth-century France during the French Revolution. They only made replicas of those swords and knives that are kept in museums, but they sold millions of knives before deciding to stop manufacturing and focused more on the marketing aspect of the goods. They made only twenty versions of this particular knife, so we're in the process of hunting down the location of all the existing knives.

"We've done a search of anyone released from prison recently who has an interest in cutting people up. Surprisingly, the list was short. Most of the men are back in prison and the others have found God and moved on to live productive lives." This evoked laughs around the room. Any cop knew that finding God was just an excuse to keep the police off their asses and out of their business. Those prisoners who found God were the ones watched the closest; after all, people did many bad things in the name of God. Sonny cleared his throat and continued:

"So that was a dead end. On the evidence end of this we have nothing. The lab's still processing the trash we brought in but it's a tedious process. We've been looking for any Hondas missing a hubcap and a blown out rear windshield—nothing there. Detective Santos has checked all the major windshield companies and alerted them to the Honda. She's had nothing pop thus far. As for the prints," he paused and smiled proudly. "I have found a match; the only problem is the person they belong to has disappeared. Last known address was New York City."

One of the officers raised his hand. "Where in New York?" he asked.

"Son, if I knew that would I be here asking you for help?" Sonny asked, eyebrows raised.

Mike rose from his chair and placed both hands on the table. "Now listen up, someone in the department has been leaking information to the press about our recent findings. If I find out who it is, that individual will sit in jail for a while for interfering with the investigation and when they see the light of day they will be jobless. After I get through with them, IA will rip them apart. The information we're going to share needs to be airtight. No leaks if we expect to find the killer. Is that understood?"

The room was silent as everyone nodded. Satisfied, Mike sat down and gave Sonny the floor again.

"Okay. I've traced the prints throughout the national database and come up with nothing. Then I had to take the grueling approach and search each state separately. I still came up empty. After that, I narrowed it down to the major cities: Seattle, Portland, Los Angeles, Las Vegas, Chicago, New York, Boston, Dallas, you get the point; but nothing came up. Exhausted and at my wits' end, I was about to give up but a buddy of mine in New York had a case like this thirty years ago, where homeless people were murdered. Though the people were found in New York City, three of the six victims originated from a small town upstate. So, on a hunch, he sent the prints there and—voilà! We found a match. The prints belong to a Francis Aberleen. Not only is this our suspect, but now suspected to be the person they've been looking for."

Luz spoke up. "So our killer murdered someone thirty years

ago. How old would that make him now?"

"She. How old would *she* be now?"

That remark was met with shocked silence. Luz eyed him with surprise. "A woman? I don't know about that. The person who attacked me that night was very, very strong."

Mike stood again. "You said Antoinette Peterson looked strong enough to overpower these homeless people. I'm sure there are other women just as strong."

Luz thought about that. "These killings seem so cold, so personal, it's hard to believe a woman could have... I guess you could be right," she conceded.

The room was silent again.

"Back to your question, Miss Aberleen would have only been fourteen years old."

Everyone seemed taken aback by this information. Sonny chuckled.

"That's not the best part; the three victims from her home town were none other than her mother, her brother and her sister. So we're basically dealing with a cold-hearted bitch with a chip on her shoulder. The problem is this woman hasn't popped up anywhere. There's no record of her even having a life, no addresses, no bank accounts and no arrests. That's where I'll need your help."

Luz listened but her mind was sorting the information. She tried to remember the attack. *Could* it have been a woman? Why was that idea so hard to grasp? She herself had had days when she wanted to kill everyone in sight, but that was due to a monthly hormonal change—not psychotic impulses or a mental break of some kind.

"Earth to Santos, come in Santos."

Luz looked up and everyone was staring at her.

"I'm sorry. I was thinking about something."

Mike sighed. "I asked you if you wanted to add anything."

"Umm… everyone already knows about the harassment I've been getting. What about the fact that the mayor used to own a duplicate of the murder weapon?"

Shocked whispers spread around the room.

"The mayor is a suspect?" asked Eddie.

Mike sighed and glared at Luz. "Detective Santos and I attended a charity auction at the mayor's the other night and one of the items sold was a knife matching the one we found at the second murder scene. There are eighteen other knives floating around and we are not pursuing the mayor as a suspect. After reviewing his impenetrable security system, we have concluded that it would be impossible for anyone but the mayor to have access to any of the knives in his collection. The mayor was out of town at the times most of these murders took place. He is under constant surveillance by his own security team and we've ruled him out as a suspect."

The whispers continued and Mike, looking irritated, raised his voice. "Let me remind everyone that this information stays in this room." He looked at Sonny. "Anything else, Malone?" Sonny shook his head. "Good. We'll meet on Monday to discuss further details of the case. Meeting adjourned."

Everyone filed out of the room, but Luz stayed where she was, thinking about the fact that the killer was a woman. She decided to pay Antoinette Peterson another visit.

CHAPTER FOURTEEN

My rage for now is kept at bay
Though my thirst for revenge must be obeyed
They believe they've found their horror-host
But they merely chase a vengeful ghost.

MAY 23ᴿᴰ, 2002 12:49 P.M.

Luz went back to her office to get Ms. Peterson's address. She knew if she called for an appointment the woman would only hang up. She would use the element of surprise and hopefully get some useful information this time around. She washed down a few aspirin, happy her wounds were healing. She could almost tie her shoes without wincing in pain.

On her way out, she went by Mike's office to tell him she'd be away for a couple of hours. Passing his secretary's desk, she was surprised to find Eddie in deep conversation with Rosa. He sat with his back to Luz, so she couldn't see him but by the look on Rosa's face, there was some flirting going on. She stopped to watch, amused.

Rosa caught her eye and stopped twisting her hair around

her finger.

"Did you *need* something, Santa?" Rosa asked. Eddie stiffened and turned around.

Luz looked at him and shook her head. "No. I just wanted to stop by and say hi," she said, suppressing a laugh. Eddie looked uncomfortable. "Bye." Luz waved, and Rosa glared at her.

Luz high-tailed it to the elevators but Eddie managed to catch up to her. He stopped to catch his breath.

"Luz…" he began.

She held up her hand. "No need to explain, Eddie. I told you how I felt."

"Just let me explain. Rosa… she's just a friend."

Luz looked at him squarely. "Eddie, frankly I could care less. I told you that I think of you as a friend. If you want to chase tail, that's none of my business. I could comment on your taste in women but again, it's none of my business. So go ahead and flirt. I. Don't. Care."

Eddie still looked guilty. Luz gave him a hug. "It's okay, Eddie, really… now go and charm Rosa the way you charmed me, and you'll have her in bed by midnight," she joked.

A smile tugged at his mouth and Eddie gently slugged her shoulder. "I guess if I can't have you, I'll have the next best thing."

She held up her hands "Whoa, I wouldn't go that far but yeah, Rosa's nice enough. Just be careful; she's got a mean streak."

I like 'em sassy, gives me a challenge." They laughed, and Luz got on the elevator and waved goodbye. When she stepped off, she came face to face with Nick. His sudden appearance startled her.

"What are you doing here?" she asked.

"I was beginning to think you would stand me up for lunch, so I thought I'd stop by and make sure we're still on."

Luz looked at her watch, then back up at him. "Sure. I need to run home and drop off my things. My captain says I'm clear of any danger, so I can move back home. That of course means he's got plainclothes posted in my neighborhood, doing drive-bys"

"Mind if I tag along?"

"No, not at all. I need to take Cheech for a walk anyway; he's been cooped up in the room all morning."

They walked back to the motel and Luz packed her things and put them in the car. They took a leisurely stroll down to the park where they had eaten before. With the reminder of the previous day's visit, Nick spoke up.

"I'm really sorry about yesterday. It's been so long since I've felt that comfortable with a woman— or anyone—and it kind of scared me a little bit," he admitted.

Luz watched Cheech chase a squirrel around a bush and up a tree. He barked at it from the ground for a while before losing interest. Luz chose her words carefully.

"Nick, I'm not expecting anything from you at this point but friendship, and I certainly don't want to put pressure on you for anything else. Especially if you're not ready. You have a lot going on and I don't want to add to that."

He looked pensive for a moment before replying. "I'm not going to lie, I *am* attracted to you, but I think we both know it would be inappropriate to explore those feelings until this case is solved."

Even though his words shocked her by creating a tingling sensation throughout her body she held her poker face. "I'm happy you feel that way and I fully agree with you," she replied with a nod.

"Now that that's out of the way, can we eat? I'm famished," he asked rubbing his stomach.

Luz whistled for Cheech, and after re-leashing him they walked to the station's parking lot. Luz headed toward her car, keys in hand.

"This is *your* car?" Nick asked enthusiastically. Luz thought he looked like a kid on Christmas morning.

"Yeah. What did you think I drove?"

"I don't know. I thought you were a Jeep or Volkswagen kind of woman or at least a department-issued Crown Vic."

"Nah, too rugged, too boring and too cliché. I prefer speed over popularity. Everywhere you look there's a new Jeep, Beetle or Jetta and don't get me started on the crap the city wants us to drive. But how many cars do you see that look like this?" She swept her hand over her car, happy she'd gotten it back after the fiasco yesterday, they'd even managed to get the blood off the paint.

"You have a point there. This car is unique, especially with all the modifications you made to the body and no doubt to the engine." He winked at her.

"You have no idea, get in. I'll show you."

She took the long way home, winding up and around the highway to show off the speed and agility of her car as well as her ability to handle it. By the time they got off the freeway she could tell Nick was impressed, though like Eddie, he gripped the door handle. Feeling satisfied, she smiled to herself.

"Sorry about that. I can get carried away. It's been a while since I got to take her on a drive."

"I'm fine," he said, breaking his hold on the door. "It's been a while since I've been in a car. I'll just have to get used to it."

As they pulled into the Lake Union Marina parking lot, Luz noticed the silence that stretched between them. She parked the car, grabbed her dog and bags and headed towards the docks. She noticed Nick wasn't following her and she stopped and looked back.

"Are you coming?"

He looked lost in thought for a moment and reluctantly stepped forward. They walked down the dock to her houseboat and she let herself in. She checked her messages and refilled Cheech's food and water bowls. When she looked up, Nick was nowhere to be found. She checked the bathroom and kitchen, but he wasn't there. Finally, she opened the door and checked outside. He was still standing on the dock, looking out across the water.

"You *are* welcome to come inside," she said, wondering why he hadn't. He looked at the boat like it was a forbidden place then shook his head.

"I-I can't, not right now," he said softly. "I'll go wait by the car."

Luz watched him walk away; completely baffled until the words from the article came to mind: Leah Mason was found on the deck of her houseboat lying in a puddle of blood. Luz shivered and watched Nick cross the parking lot and take a seat on a bench. It occurred to her that maybe he hadn't completely gotten over his wife's death. He might even blame himself. She tore her gaze from him and went inside.

When she returned to the parking lot, he was waiting at the car. But instead of walking to the car she passed him up and kept walking.

"Where are you going?"

"I thought you were hungry?"

"I am, but…"

"Then follow me."

They followed the walkway and came to a large two-story building that faced the water.

"This is Maggie Bluffs. I eat here all the time. Best fish and chips around and if you don't like fish, try their burgers, you won't be let down," she said, smiling.

• • •

He smiled back but even he knew that it didn't reach his eyes. He didn't want to spoil their lunch like he had yesterday. He hadn't known that Luz lived on a houseboat and arriving at the Marina stirred up all kinds of memories of Leah, the sharpest of which was the night she was found with her throat cut. He tried to clear his mind while Luz took care of things inside, but the memories lingered. His inability to protect his wife left him with doubts about getting involved with anyone again. In any capacity. He knew the two should be separate—that Luz and Leah were different—but his mind wove them together and bound them tight.

They put in their order then went outside to choose a table. They settled on a comfortable spot where the breeze from the water was gentle and its salty fragrance filled the air. They sat and admired the view of the bay as they waited for their food to arrive. It was a warm day and many boats were on the water. Nick decided to tell Luz about Leah. If he had any intention of anything meaningful happening between them—even if it turned out to be a friendship—she deserved to know.

He looked over and found her gazing out across the marina; her green eyes aglow with the reflection of the sun on the water. She looked so lost in thought, he didn't want to break her away, instead he took this time to study her. Her hair was freshly brushed and hung around her shoulders in long dark waves and her tanned skin looked soft. Her nails were cut and manicured. Clearly, she prided herself on her looks.

"Your meal," the waiter said snapping each back to the present. They ate mostly in silence—the only sounds came from the chewing of their food and a passing comment about the weather. A very different situation from when they had lunch at the park and couldn't stop chatting. It took some effort on Nick's part not to grab the extra rolls and wrap them in a napkin to take with him. He had to keep reminding himself that he had the means to feed himself whenever he was hungry. There would be no more hoarding food. Mentally, it was a struggle for him to retrain himself, but he was making progress. Nick insisted on paying for the meal.

"Luz," Nick said, stopping her on their way back to the car and spinning her so that they faced each other. "I need to tell you something."

She stared at him warily for a moment and nodded. Nick realized he didn't know where to start. He was quiet for a moment before he began.

"Leah, my wife; she was murdered seven years ago." He nearly choked on the words but forced himself to continue. "I was a hotshot lawyer back then, caught up in my success. I was on the fast track to make DA and that meant a very busy schedule. One night there was a celebration dinner. I had just won a huge case and brought in a substantial amount of money and good press. Um, I was the guest of honor. So when Leah told me she wasn't feeling well, I dismissed her concerns and asked her to get ready. She complained and asked me to go alone. I got angry and we argued. I eventually decided to go without her; but not without making her feel guilty for not supporting me in my career. She was crying when I left that night." He paused and stared through Luz, imagining his argument with his wife so vividly, he could practically see Leah's image beyond what was before him. "If... if I would have known that the last words she would hear from me would be harsh I would have..." he stopped, and his eyes were glossed over. "I would have told her how much she meant to me... how happy she made me... she always supported me, and I couldn't protect her..." he trailed off, breaking eye contact with Luz.

Luz touched his shoulder. "Nick, you don't have to tell me this."

He looked up at her. "Yes, I do. If not for you, then for me. I haven't talked about this for so long. I need to let it out."

Luz stood motionless then told him to continue. He took a deep breath and wiped his eyes. "I... I came home that night still angry at her, but the alcohol had softened me up a little. I could never stay angry with her for very long. She had a way about her..." he drifted off, again lost in his memories. "I remember walking down the dock and wondering why the lights in the houseboat were still on. The closer I got, the more alarmed I became and when I stepped onto the deck..." Nick began shaking and Luz led him to the nearest bench. His face was streaked with tears and his eyes were shut tight, but he didn't care how he looked.

"...she was laying there. Dead. Blood all around her. Her beautiful hair was matted with blood and her eyes were fixed in horror and I... I screamed. My neighbors came out to see what had happened. One of them called the cops but I didn't move. I couldn't stop staring, not wanting to believe my eyes, not wanting to accept that she was gone. My heart... hurt so much... I remember not being able to breathe and not wanting to. At that moment my life lost all meaning. Without Leah I had nothing, I *was* nothing. All my success meant nothing if I had no one to share it with." He smiled, imagining what could have been, what *should* have been his last words to Leah. "I should have told her that before I left that night, and she could have died knowing I loved her, appreciated her... cherished her. Instead, she died with my hurtful words echoing in her mind, my blatant ungratefulness and arrogance was the last image of me she saw." He broke down and sobbed. Luz put her arms around him.

Her touch was warm. Comforting. Her voice held the same features. "Nick, it was just one night of anger. Think of all the happy, special nights you spent together. Even though you fought, she knew you loved her deeply. Every couple fights once in a while. You weren't responsible. Whoever killed your wife is responsible. Do you hear me?"

He stopped crying and shook his head. "For days I blamed myself, I walked around like a zombie, consumed with grief. Then the day after her funeral I got a call, it was from a man who swore he saw Anthony Yates that night walking down the dock that led to my boathouse and drive away. Suddenly, I became angry and obsessed with putting that man behind bars. We put together a case with two witnesses. One was the man at the marina and the other swore he saw Yates board a plane at a private airport that night, heading to Phoenix. This case was all-consuming. I didn't sleep well; I had lost weight, but I couldn't stop until I found the man responsible and made him suffer the way I was suffering. Every day I woke up with this gaping hole in my chest, missing her with every fiber of my being. Someone had to pay." He took a deep breath and shook his head. "I went through great pains to make the case airtight, but it came apart at the seams in the courtroom. It was like Murphy's law. It crumbled, and we lost. Yates was free." Luz covered his hands with hers and he appreciated the comfort she gave him.

He continued, almost in a whisper, "It was then that I gave

up on the system, because that system—the system I had sworn to protect—had failed me. Without Leah and without justice, I couldn't bear to go on, but I was too much of a coward to kill myself. It would have been the easy way out, an insult to Leah's death. So I punished myself. Dropped out of society and, except for my accountant friend, I told no one of my plan. I just vanished. Seven years I've been on the street, hiding from my past."

He cleared his throat and squeezed her hand.

• • •

Luz was at a loss for words. A deep sorrow radiated from him and wrapped her up. Her heart ached for him. "Nick, I'm so sorry," she whispered, wishing there was something more she could do. He was so hard on himself, punishing himself for something he had no control over. Nick was stronger than he was giving himself credit for.

He sat quietly, the shaking had subsided, but the tears still fell. The two sat together, hand in hand, for an hour, Nick reflecting on his past and Luz pondering her future. Nick was a lost soul, searching for someone to help him lessen the burden of his wife's death. If it were anyone else, Luz would consider a relationship with him to be a rebound, but this man was so emotionally frail, she doubted he could stand losing someone again. That thought brought perspective to their situation in a way that saddened her.

"Luz, I'm sorry. I shouldn't have put this on you. I'm sorry if I've made you uncomfortable," he apologized, releasing her hand and wiping his face with his sleeve.

"Nick, you're hurting. If talking about it helps, I'll be here to listen. She was special to you and she should be remembered, but don't blame yourself anymore, you'll never heal, you'll never move on."

He shook his head "A couple of nights ago, I went to her grave for the first time in seven years. It was so hard, considering I had avoided facing her for so long. Oddly enough, I felt better after spending a couple of hours there, but my guilt didn't lessen, not one bit."

"It will take time." She rubbed his back.

"I know." He met her eyes. "Thank you, Luz, for being here with me. It's been ages since I've had someone to call a friend."

Luz smiled, but inside she wondered how smart it would be to get involved with a man haunted by his wife's death. On the other hand, he had chosen her to confide in, her shoulder was the one he chose to cry on. She pushed her doubts away and kissed him on the cheek. The sadness in his eyes faded and was replaced with a look of surprise.

"What was that for?" he asked.

She smiled. "For finally facing your ghosts. You're stronger than you think."

Tires screeching.

Headlights sliced through the dark.

"Run."

She took a deep breath and exhaled. Her own ghosts were

another story entirely. She tried to blame the attack and lack of sleep for the nightmares, but she knew deep down she'd soon have face up to what they meant. She looked over at Nick. He did appear to be a bit better. Talking about someone else's problems seemed easier than sharing her own, but maybe it wouldn't hurt to find someone she could confide in. She couldn't carry this around too long or it would start to affect her job and she would *not* allow that to happen.

He let out a shaky laugh. "I just wanted you to understand why I tried pushing you away yesterday."

Luz smiled at his confession. "When you're ready, you will know. In the meantime, don't worry about me. I can protect myself and I'm not going anywhere."

He squeezed her hand again. "You're amazing. Thank you."

She got to her feet and curtsied. "No problem, but I have to get back to work. There *is* a killer running around."

He rose and smoothed out his slacks. "Of course. I apologize if I took up too much of your time."

"Nonsense. I liked spending time with you today," she replied waving off his apology. "Let's go."

They walked back to the car and she dropped him off at the hotel before returning to work.

On the way back to the precinct, she played their conversation over in her mind. Nick was struggling to adjust after his period of homelessness; she could tell it would be a while before he was comfortable with his place in the world again. But did she want to be around to witness his transformation? Sure, she loved spending time with him, but would anything come of it? A better question would be would she *let* anything come of it? She had her routine, her family and her job, and for the most part, that was enough for her.

But on her loneliest nights didn't she wish she had someone to open up to, someone who understood her on many levels, someone she could be herself with? She wasn't placing any bets that Nick would be that person. She barely knew the man, but she'd never find a friend or a partner if she didn't loosen up and allow herself to be vulnerable.

She sighed loudly; frustrated that her mind was wandering to places she rarely allowed it to travel. Well, if Nick could find the courage to change, she could, too, right?

CHAPTER FIFTEEN

The rage came, and my patience was tried
Such loose ends were left untied
Now I must go; must kill again
Another life that I must end.

MAY 23RD, 2002 8:30 P.M.

Elaine Murphy was preparing for bed. She had turned off all the lights in the house and was climbing the stairs to her room. She took longer these days going up the stairs and knew that soon she wouldn't be able to climb them at all. Halfway up the staircase she was halted by a knock on the door. The time on the hall clock read 8:30 and she wondered who would visit her at this hour.

Slowly, she backed down the stairs, careful to hold the railing tight. The visitor knocked again as she peeked through the curtains next to the door. Cliff stood on the porch looking distressed. She unlocked the door and pulled it open.

"Hello, Cliff, what brings you here so late?"

He stood at the door, arms crossed tightly with a grim look on his face. "I think we did a very bad thing selling that knife, Elaine."

"Whatever do you mean?" Elaine asked. She peered outside and opened the door wider. "Come in and I'll make tea." Cliff grabbed her hand and held it tightly—a little too tight for her liking. She glanced back at him and was startled at how pinched his pale face looked and how his eyes darted around the room.

"I can't stay but I brought you this," he said shakily and held out a newspaper. "There's an article in there about a knife. There's no picture but from the sound of it, I think it's the same one you sold last week."

Elaine shook her head, trying to comprehend what he was telling her. "Cliff, you know my eyes are bad. Won't you come in and read it to me?" She turned and took a small step towards the parlor, but Cliff wouldn't leave the doorway.

"I can't stay, but I will summarize it for you. There have been numerous murders in Seattle involving a knife that matches the description of the one you sold. I think whoever bought that knife is killing those people. Since I didn't see the man who bought the knife, you have to call the Seattle Police and give a description right away," he pleaded.

Something cold slithered inside Elaine's stomach and she felt sick. She gripped the doorknob for support.

"Are you okay, Mrs. Murphy?" Cliff asked, concerned enough to step into the foyer.

Elaine was lightheaded and weak. Cliff took her arm and helped her to the couch. He sat with her until her breathing evened out, then got up to leave.

"Please, Elaine, call the police. You could save lives," he urged her. "The phone number to the detective running the case is at the bottom of the article. Call me if you need anything."

He opened the front door and shut it behind him. Once he was gone, the house settled into an eerie silence. Elaine fetched her reading glasses and picked up the article. She read it with shaking hands and circled the phone number at the bottom, then grabbed her phone and dialed. She listened to the other line ring and ring until she got the voicemail. She left a message stating her name and number and the purpose of her call and asked for a call back. When she hung up, she felt anxious and mentally exhausted. The fact that Eugene's knife might've played a part in a murder was too much to take in.

Please, God, don't let this be happening, she thought. The guilt from selling the knife returned and she knew she would visit Eugene's grave again the next day. But at that moment, she was tired and wanted more than anything to sleep. She pulled herself off the couch and slowly climbed the stairs to bed. She settled in and clapped the lights off. Elaine was grateful for the gift her grandson had given her. Without it, she was likely to fall out of bed reaching over the nightstand to turn off her lamp.

She pulled the quilt to her chin and closed her eyes. She would deal with the police first thing in the morning.

MAY 23ᴿᴰ, 2002 11:30 P.M.

Luz retrieved her Snickers bar from the vending machine,

then walked down the darkened halls, returning to her office. When she sat down she noticed that her voicemail light was on. While she dialed in her password she assumed the message was left recently because she'd been doing paperwork most of the night, tracking leads and pulling files. She only left her office one time and that was to empty her bladder, stopping for the candy bar on the way back. She quickly dialed in the code to retrieve her latest voicemail.

An old woman's voice spoke in her ear and at first, Luz thought it was Nelly, calling to invite her down for a visit, but the caller identified herself as Elaine Murphy. Luz bolted up in her chair as the message wore on. Apparently, this woman sold a knife exactly like the one described in the Seattle Times and only four days ago. Luz listened a little longer as the woman explained that she would call back in the morning and Luz made sure to save the message.

She decided it was too late to call the woman back. She thought of the killer; if the old woman had seen the killer, then she was in danger. After the one-legged bum's murder, Luz didn't want to take any chances. If she could prevent the old woman's death, she damn well would. She picked up the phone and dialed.

• • •

Elaine Murphy opened her eyes and listened to the sounds of her old house as it settled for the night. Normally, the sounds were familiar and comforting, but something about them that night made her uneasy. Her mind wandered to thoughts of the killer and for the first time in her life she wondered how safe she was living alone. For a moment she considered moving to a nursing home. At least she would have friends around her; at least it wouldn't be so disconcerting jumping at every little sound.

Maybe it was her old eyes, but she thought she saw a shadow move near the door of her bedroom. She tried to focus but couldn't make out the shape of anything significant. She was about to clap on the lights when her phone rang. The sound nearly gave her another stroke. She reached over and picked up the receiver of her antique Danish phone.

"Hello?" Elaine answered in a voice that shook from her little scare.

"Mrs. Murphy?"

"Yes, this is she."

"This is Detective Santos with the Seattle Police Department. You called earlier about a knife you sold a few days ago. You say it was a gentleman who came to your house for the knife?"

"Um… yes, that's correct. Miss Santos, it's almost midnight, why on earth are you phoning me so late? I would have called in the morning."

There was a long pause on the other end of the line before the detective spoke. "I know you would have. I just wanted to make sure you were okay."

Elaine looked around the room, searching for moving shadows but found none and felt foolish for being spooked so easily.

"Thank you for your concern, but I'm fine," she said, much more confidently than she felt.

"Are your doors locked?"

Elaine mentally traced her steps through the house after Cliff's visit and it occurred to her that she hadn't locked the front door after he'd departed. But she didn't want the detective to worry on her account. "Yes. Everything is secure."

"Are you sure? You live in Carnation, is that right? If you want, I can send a police officer over to keep an eye on your house."

"No, no, dear, that won't be necessary. I'll be fine," she said more firmly. She would not be scared in her own home.

"Okay. I'll see you tomorrow morning, then. Thank you for tolerating my interruption so late."

"Good night, detective," Elaine said softly, the lack of sleep and events of the day catching up with her.

"Good night, Ms. Murphy."

Elaine descended the stairs at a snail's pace. Her body wasn't used to the extra exercise she'd gotten lately, and she felt the ache in her bones. She reached the front door and threw the bolt down, securing the front entrance of her home. Again, she began climbing the stairs—it was an arduous task with her weak bones, but she made it to the top without incident.

Suddenly, her feet were no longer touching the hardwood floors of her hallway. She was flying. He arms flailed and she felt as if she were flapping like a bird.

She saw the stairs pass beneath her in slow motion, and she

swept her eyes up over them, all the way up to a dark figure at the top, and the light from her room caught on the metal object in his hand.

She then became aware that she was not flying but falling. She closed her eyes tightly, preparing herself for impact. She bounced off the last step and landed in a crumpled heap. She knew at once that her hip was dislocated but she couldn't place the pain that stabbed at her neck and shoulder. Dazed and in tremendous pain, she opened her eyes, but the figure was no longer at the top of the staircase.

She tried to turn her head, but the pain was so great she nearly fainted, so she closed her eyes and remained still. Heavy footsteps came from behind her.

Her final thoughts as the knife cut through the wrinkled flesh of her neck were of her late husband, Eugene. Soon she would apologize to him herself. Face to face.

MAY 24TH, 2002 2:01 A.M.

Luz checked the map again. She had driven across the 520 bridge to highway 202, and now she was on a road named Tolt Hill. She had been on the road for some time and wondered when she would see civilization. Driving through the country brought up memories of her childhood and she was occupied with them for most of the trip, but she was getting impatient. She crossed over a bridge and saw the distant lights of the small town. Soon she found herself at a crossing and took a left on Tolt Avenue. She drove through the town and, after a few more turns, pulled up in front of the Murphy house.

The house was old and falling apart in a few places, but it held up well for its age. Mrs. Murphy had kept the house looking nice, as well as the surrounding land. There were rose bushes around the porch and the grass looked freshly mowed. Luz could tell a landscaping crew had been there recently. Dark shutters flanked the windows and the porch wrapped around the front to the back of the house. It was beautiful but much too large for an old woman living alone. Luz caught sight of a swing hanging on the porch; she had had her first kiss on a porch swing like that.

Smiling, her eyes moved from the porch to the doorway and her heart skipped a beat. The huge oak door was ajar, and the breeze stirred the curtains just inside.

A heavy lump formed in her stomach and she immediately called 911. The operator came on the line.

"My name is Luz Santos. I'm a detective with the Seattle Police. I'm in Carnation at Elaine Murphy's place of on Bagwell Street. I need back up for a possible assault or homicide situation."

The dispatcher patched her to the police department and she repeated her request. She also told them that she was going in the house in five minutes whether they were there or not because Mrs. Murphy might be in danger. The sheriff told her to stay put and she hung up on him.

She kept her eyes on the front door and when she felt she couldn't wait any longer she un-holstered her gun and got out of the car. Creeping up the walk, she stayed as silent as possible but when she ascended the steps to the porch, an old floorboard groaned loudly with her weight. At that point she gave up on being quiet and opted to use speed. She kicked open the door and shouted "police", but the silence dragged on.

With her gun drawn, Luz stepped across the threshold, keeping her back to the door. A few steps into the foyer and the smell of human waste hit her hard. She reached for the nearest switch and turned on the lights. After seeing what the light revealed, she wished she hadn't.

Elaine Murphy was on her back at the foot of the stairs; her blank stare fixed at the ceiling. Her legs were bent at unnatural angles, and her white hair was soaked with blood from the puddle that had formed under her neck. The expression on her face struck Luz as very odd. The old woman had died with a smile on her face.

Sickened, Luz ran outside and leaned on the porch railing while nausea washed over her. She let the results spill all over the rosebushes. She heard sirens coming closer and decided she would wait for the locals to arrive.

How many more bodies would she have to see before they stopped this madness?

MAY 24TH, 2002 7:45 A.M.

"A smile?" Mike Andrews asked.

"Yeah, like she saw what awaited her in the great beyond and was happy about it. It was strange," Luz replied, trying to shake the image from her memory where she was sure it would remain for a long time.

"Or maybe the killer told her a joke before she cut her throat," Eddie added.

Luz shot him a look. "First of all, that was not funny or appropriate; second of all, Elaine told me it was a man who came to see her, mustache and all."

Eddie's face flushed but he continued. "It's not hard to find a disguise, you know. If it is this Aberleen woman, I'm sure she could find a fake mustache."

"I spoke with a man from Elaine's church, Cliff Saunders, and he said that whoever bought that knife must have been a man, and the voice over the phone was male. The email address they had for the bidder was lost when they shut down the website. Cliff said if he happens to remember it, he'll give me a call."

"He didn't write it down? If someone harassed me for weeks, I would remember the address," Eddie said.

"Apparently the man works for a small software company and deals with hundreds of emails a day. Plus, the fact that it's been a few weeks since the killer emailed him. We'll have to wait to see what we can recover," Luz said, placing her hands on the table.

After the Carnation police had processed the murder scene and asked her questions, Luz had driven back to Seattle, first to let Cheech out and second to call everyone back for an emergency meeting. Sonny was sitting across from her staring at his coffee cup, Eddie was on her right, Mike at the head of the table and two other officers flanked Sonny. For three hours they had worked with the Carnation police department on evidence and theories; they had nothing to show for it. All they knew was that this event was connected to their case and that they were running out of time.

Luz was tired and running on a short wick. "I'm going over to see Antoinette Peterson. She deserves a closer look." Luz stood up and prepared to leave.

"That is not a good idea, Luz. She filed a complaint against you, and she could sue for harassment if she's innocent," Mike warned.

"No she couldn't. I'm conducting an investigation. The only prints we have are from a woman and so far, she's the only female suspect we have," Luz snapped.

"I don't care, you're not going over there. I'll send Harris, or Lopez but not you." Mike's voice left no room for argument.

Luz glowered at him then sat back down. "Fine but send Eddie not Harris. He'll be anything but nice and you will have more than one complaint on your hands," she said. She noticed Eddie leaned toward Mike and whispered something in his ear.

"Hey!" she yelled. "What the fuck? This is a meeting. Anything you need to say should be said for all to hear."

Eddie stopped what he was doing and avoided her eyes. She looked at Mike and he did the same thing.

"What's going on?" she demanded and the silence that followed was uncomfortable. Luz considered what they could be keeping from her and figured it out. Instead of getting upset she remained calm and collected. "You still consider Nick a suspect, don't you?" she asked without blinking.

Mike met her gaze. "We don't think there's one killer. It might be two people and yes, we were considering Mr. Mason again."

Even though the thought that Nick could be involved was like a punch in the stomach, Luz nodded. "He's staying at the Ramada Inn. You should send someone down to question him right away."

Eddie's eyes narrowed into slits as he studied her. She was so mad she could burst. Instead, she reined her anger and sugarcoated it.

Ssomewhere in the farthest part of her mind Luz wondered if Nick was involved.

With all her heart, she hoped he wasn't.

• • •

Nick sat on his bed, propped up by pillows. He was reading the Seattle Times. There was an article about the murders and he wanted to keep himself up to date on any recent events. There was a knock on the door and he slid off the bed and peered through the peephole.

Luz stood outside, looking sullen. He opened the door quickly. "What's wrong? You look like someone ran over your puppy," he said.

Just then, Officer Lopez stepped out from behind the corner. "Heya, Nick, how are you doing?"

Nick looked from one face to the other, confused, before he remembered his manners and invited them in. Luz sat at the desk, but Eddie remained standing, towering over Nick by about five inches. Eddie rested one hand on the butt of his gun and the other hung loose at his side. He seemed relaxed, and kind of happy, as if he were enjoying a private joke. Luz, on the other hand, was the complete opposite. She stared at the wallpaper like it was the Mona Lisa, studying it intently.

"What can I do for you, detectives?" Nick asked, taking a seat on the edge of the bed.

"Nick—" Luz began.

"Mr. Mason where were you last night?" Eddie asked, cutting her off.

Nick looked around the room. "Here," he said. "Why?"

"Never mind that. Can you provide proof that you were here the entire night?"

"I ate down in the restaurant last night. You can ask the waiter who served me."

"What time was that?"

"Around nine or so."

"Where did you go then?"

"Back here."

"Can you prove that?"

"What's going on Luz?" he asked, raising his eyebrows.

Eddie tried to cut in again, but Luz was faster. "Lopez, take a seat. I got this one." Eddie stayed where he was, keeping an eye on Nick.

"Nick, last night there was a murder in Carnation. An old woman is dead because she saw the killer's face. I spoke with her only hours before this happened, and she swears it was a man she saw. So naturally the police department has to check out everyone and unfortunately, that includes you." She swallowed hard.

He sat on the bed and nodded. "I understand," he said and then brightened up. "Last night around midnight there were a bunch of teenagers in the next room throwing a party. I'm assuming they came here after prom. Anyway, I called the front desk to complain about the noise. The man at the front desk will tell you it's true."

Luz looked relieved and looked at Officer Lopez. "Anything else, Officer?" she asked, placing her hands on her hips.

Eddie's face was set in a grim expression. He put his notebook away and headed for the door. "No, but if your story doesn't check out, we will be back," he said.

Luz followed him into the hall and turned to thank Nick for his cooperation.

"Thank you, Mr. Mason. We apologize for disrupting you," she said.

"It's no problem. I enjoyed your company." Nick winked at her, then stepped back so that Eddie wouldn't see him as he mouthed the word "dinner". Luz nodded, quickly tamping down the thrill she felt.

"We need to get back to work, detective," Eddie said.

Luz waved goodbye to Nick and walked out the door.

Nick felt the tension drain from his muscles. While jail was somewhat comfortable for him, he didn't want to go back.

CHAPTER SIXTEEN

Another life greedily taken
Another human noticeably shaken
The game is growing harder to play
And I want them to know that I like it that way

MAY 24ᵀᴴ, 2002 6:30 A.M.

Cliff Saunders had never been so scared in his life. He shook from head to toe and for good reason. In his hand he held a piece of paper with a death threat written on it—and it wasn't just *his* death promised in the letter; his family was also in danger.

After speaking with the police at Elaine Murphy's house he had driven home, shaken and sick to his stomach. He filled his wife in on the events of the morning and she listened attentively, assured him that things would be all right, then returned to bed. It was early in the morning and his two children, Lisa and Jeremy were still asleep, but he was too anxious to get any rest.

He went downstairs and made himself some coffee and toast and thought about poor Mrs. Murphy. When he finished eating he went back upstairs, but not straight back to his bedroom. He felt the need to check on his son and daughter. He loved his children more than life and his job was to keep them safe. First, he went to Jeremy's room. The ten-year-old was laying on his stomach, snoring softly, with a peaceful expression on his face. The room was dark, but Cliff could see the posters of racecars on the walls and the model cars on the dresser. Jeremy loved everything about cars and his father dreaded the day he got his driver's license. Cliff walked over to the bed pulled the blanket up and kissed his son on the head before leaving the room.

Tiptoeing down the hall, he stopped at Lisa's room. Her door was cracked, and he could see the glow of her princess nightlight from the hall. He stepped into the room and smiled. It was like stepping into a fantasy land. Lisa was six years old but demanded her walls be pink to match her princess blankets and sheets. Dolls of all sorts and pictures she had drawn in class decorated the room. Lisa took pride in her accomplishments, no matter how small. Cliff knew she would grow into a beautiful successful woman someday.

He moved closer to the bed and stopped dead in his tracks. Icy dread filled his chest and a bead of sweat formed on his upper lip. There was a folded piece of paper with his name on it resting on his daughter's chest. He watched it for a while as it rose and fell with her breathing, willing it to be his imagination. When he couldn't take it any longer he carefully picked up the paper, then he kissed his daughter's head and left the room.

He stood in the hallway, shaking and holding the note in

his hand. He unfolded it and read it: *If you help the police find me I'll find you and you'll find yourself dead along with your beautiful wife and precious children. You've been warned.*

Cliff leaned on the wall, weak and scared. The killer had been in his house; had seen his family, had touched his daughter. It was too much to bear. He felt so helpless.

He walked down to the dining room and picked up the phone but put it down quickly when he considered that someone might be watching him.

He went to the kitchen and took a knife from the cutlery set on the counter, then he searched his house, room by room, his heart pounding fiercely against his ribs. At one point he stopped and looked at the knife in his hand, *what are you doing, man?* he asked himself. He wasn't Indiana Jones or John McCain. If he did encounter the killer, he doubted he'd be able to overpower him.

But he thought of Elizabeth, Lisa and Jeremy and his resolve returned twice as strong. He had cleared the upstairs and most of the downstairs, the living room and the den remained. He stepped into the living room and crept into every corner, knife held in front of him protectively—no one was there. Slowly, he entered the den and found the same was true, the house was empty of intruders.

Deflated, he sat on the nearest couch to catch his breath. He didn't realize he'd not been breathing. Instinct told him to call the police, but his love for his family overshadowed that instinct, and he was left powerless and totally at the killers will.

Eyes closed, he thought of Elaine's murder and cold shivers

ran over his skin like icy rain. He stood and went to the closet of the den and pulled out a sleeping bag, he would booby trap the back door and stand guard at the foot of the stairs all night if he had to.

All morning, he stayed awake; a dutiful sentry, and by the time everyone else woke and began their day, he'd come up with a plan. If he couldn't go to the police for help, he would track down the killer himself.

MAY 24TH, 2002 9:53 A.M.

Antoinette Peterson had woken up early that morning; today was her first wedding anniversary with her dear husband. He had left for work but promised her he would be home early to celebrate. She smiled in anticipation, surprised he could still give her butterflies.

Normally it was her day to host the neighborhood card game, but the other women had pushed her up to next Friday so she could pack and prepare for the special weekend trip Alan had planned for them—he'd kept the location a secret.

She was up half the night trying to guess where he would take her. She knew he'd pick the perfect place. She really was a lucky woman. She'd hinted to him on a few occasions that she would love to go up to Vancouver, Canada or down to Seaside, Oregon, but she had a feeling he'd chosen another destination and the anticipation was killing her.

She remembered Mildred and all the other victims of the murders and decided that using the word "killing" probably wasn't the best way to describe her excitement. She put down the laundry she'd been folding and fought hard to hold back tears. Every time she thought she was over Milly's death she found herself crying even more. She would never be able to undo her actions from that fateful day when Milly had approached her and asked for help; and she would have to live with that guilt for the rest of her life.

That obstinate detective at the police station would never understand the immense weight of the guilt she carried.

What was her name? Santa? Santo? That was it. Detective Santos was not only rude but unforgiving. Antoinette knew she had to live with the consequences of her actions, but that detective had rubbed Antoinette's nose in it and smeared it around to the point where she felt she *was* the one holding the knife that killed her friend.

She took a deep breath and began folding the laundry again. There was no point in rehashing the whole thing. She had already played it over in her mind a million times; Milly approaching her that day, and instead of what Antoinette did, in her head, she imagined herself walking away from her friends, taking Milly into her arms and telling her she could live with her, and she could stay as long as she liked; and they would have lived happily ever after. But if she was ever going to move on she needed to concentrate on *her* life. Was that just as selfish as turning down a friend in her time of need?

A knock at the door interrupted her thoughts and she grabbed the basket of folded clothes. She opened the door prepared to smile and invite in whomever was on her porch but when she saw who her guest was, her smile disappeared, and she started to close the door.

"Mrs. Peterson, don't you dare close that door. I have a few questions for you."

"I have nothing more to say to you, detective. Now, good day," she said. She tried to shut the door, but it wouldn't close. She glanced down to see a large tennis shoe wedged into the doorframe. Her eyes traveled from the shoe up to the face and she opened the door. "So, you brought back up this time."

Eddie smiled and nodded. "Ma'am, we just have a few quick questions. We realize it's an inconvenience, but this won't take long."

Antoinette considered that for a moment and put down the laundry basket. She stepped out onto the porch and closed the door behind her, walking past them to the porch swing and taking a seat. "You have ten minutes, then I want you off my property," she said.

The two looked at each other and Santos stepped forward. "There was another murder last night," she said, letting the words sink into Antoinette's mind.

"What does that have to do with me?"

Luz ignored her. "Is Antoinette your birth name, Mrs. Peterson?"

"Yes, but I don't understand how this is relevant—"

"Have you ever been to New York?"

Still confused, Antoinette decided to cooperate to get everything over with. "No, never. I told you I grew up in Spokane. Can't you check these things on your computers?" she asked.

Detective Santos narrowed her eyes. "Yes, but the

information on the computers isn't always correct and there are certain things you can't get from a computer."

"Like…"

"Like nervous ticks or evasive eye contact—physical impressions, if you will. I like to give my prime suspects a chance to come clean themselves. It makes it easier for them." She stepped back.

Without another word Antoinette got up from her seat and walked back inside. Before closing the door in their faces, she looked straight at Luz and said, "See you in court, Ms. Santos."

• • •

Eddie followed Luz down the steps shaking his head. "You've done it now, Santos, Mike's gonna shit a brick if she sues."

Luz didn't bat a lash. "She won't sue," she said flatly and opened the car door. Eddie got into the passenger side.

"What do you mean she won't sue?"

"If she sues, her past will be made public."

"And…?"

"And that means her perfect little façade will crumble right before her eyes. Her friends don't know she was homeless, they don't know where she came from or who she used to be, and most of all, they don't know that she abandoned a friend in her time of need because she was too afraid of how people would react knowing her past. Believe me, she will *not* sue. She has too much to lose."

"You amaze me, Luz," Eddie said, chuckling.

"I try. So, any more leads?" she asked.

"Nothing so far and you'll be happy to know that your little boyfriend is cleared of all suspicion. His story checked out."

Luz smiled at Eddie. "I knew it would. I told you, he's innocent. Woman's intuition."

He rolled his eyes. "Whatever. I just thought you'd want to know."

She grabbed his hand. "Now can we go back to being friends?"

She watched his eyes soften. "That never changed. Friends watch out for each other and that's all I was doing the other day, watching out for my friend."

She squeezed his hand and shifted into third as she got back on the highway. "I know, but I was so pissed I couldn't think. We'll just call a truce now and go on with our lives."

"Sounds good to me," he replied looking out the window.

They drove back over the bridge into Seattle and back to the station. Eddie went to work, and Luz went upstairs to do the same.

She stopped by Mike's office and warned him that Mrs. Peterson might be calling, but the woman had beaten her to it. After a very long, very boring lecture on harassing law-abiding citizens she went to her office.

A fresh vase full of yellow carnations was on her desk and she was pleasantly surprised. After their visit this morning sending flowers was the last thing she expected Nick to do. She found the card and it read: **Rendezvous carnations, rendezvous at seven tonight, see you soon.**

She turned the card over in her hand for a while, debating

whether she should accept that dinner. She had a lot of work to do and Mike would need her to work overtime if they were going to catch the sick individual who was knocking people off left and right.

She picked up the phone and dialed the Ramada. The receptionist transferred her to Nick's room but there was no answer. The receptionist came back on and asked if Luz would like to leave a message. She declined and hung up. She would try again later. If he didn't pick up, she didn't know what she would do. She couldn't very well stand him up because that would be horribly rude, and she was worried about disappointing him, or giving him the wrong impression. She didn't even know what impression she *wanted* to give. She leaned over and smelled the flowers and the spell their scent cast over her made her decide to go to dinner after all. She mentally chose the dress and accessories she would wear for the evening, saving herself an hour once she got home.

She turned her focus to her work; typing up reports and reading through evidence files. She took another look at Antoinette's profile, did some checking on her background and, to her dismay, it all looked legit. It looked like she owed the woman an apology. She would get around to that. She tried to concentrate on her work but once in a while the scent of the flowers wafted over to distract her. Finally, she got up, took the vase and placed it on the file cabinet across the room. But her eyes wandered back to the sun-colored petals so often, she ended up taking them out of her office and putting them on her secretary's desk.

Satisfied that she'd removed all distractions, she returned to her office and to her work once again. But it didn't take long before thoughts of Nick crept back into her mind. Frustrated, she put her head down on her arms and groaned.

"Luz, you are twenty-eight years old, get a grip," she scolded herself.

She picked up the phone and set an appointment to get her hair and nails done. She was such a sucker for flowers.

MAY 24ᵀᴴ, 2002 2:30 P.M.

The sign said NO SWIMMING, but Kenny didn't care. He'd been swimming in these waters for most of his twelve years. Some stupid sign wasn't going to stop him. He stood on the wall that separated the land from the water. He was barefoot and wore only his swimming trunks. It was unseasonably warm for May and he was going to cool off at his favorite swimming spot.

He looked around, searching for prying eyes. Finding no one, he dove head first into the icy waters of Lake Washington.

His brain registered two things. The first sensation came from the temperature of the water. It was a shock to his body. The second sensation was pain. It came when he was submerged but he had yet to complete the dive. He slammed, mid-plunge, into a hard, large object with enough force that pain exploded throughout his body with surprising intensity.

Paralyzed with agony, he let himself float to the surface. Once he sucked in some air, he kicked weakly to the wall. The action was incredibly painful, but his vision was blurred, and his head felt broken. He managed to pull himself out of the water and looked back, hoping to see the object that caused him such disorientation but only saw the dark water lapping lazily against the partition.

He used his hand to feel the top of his head and it was painful to touch. When he brought his hand back down it was sticky and covered in blood. Worried, he tried to get to his feet, but a light flashed before his eyes and he fell to the ground unconscious.

The sun kissed the horizon before anyone came looking for him.

MAY 24TH, 2002 9:40 P.M.

I cannot sleep! I keep waking up covered in sweat. Is it from a dream? I can't remember. My stomach is upset, and I feel like I will vomit. The champagne I drank earlier burns my stomach and I wish I would have waited to celebrate. But I deserved it, dammit; I've outsmarted the police, cut off all leads to my identity and disposed of evidence. That was cause for champagne.

From the bathroom I walk around my expansive room, from the large floor-to-ceiling windows back to my king-sized bed then back to the windows. I don't want to look out into the night. If I do, I will lose myself once again.

In the beginning I killed who and when I wanted. *I* was in control of my hunger. But lately I haven't been able to resist the need. Even when I don't want to kill, I still take a life. The word "escalation" floats through my mind but I shake it off. I *am* still in control.

Instead of accounting for this strange obsession—I've tried to think of it as a game.

A game with high stakes and real blood.

Blood. What is it about watching the life flow from my victims that captivates me so? Why do I suddenly feel like a player in a game instead of the one in control?

The thought takes root in my mind and this time I can't shake it loose. I walk back to my bed and climb under the covers. My breath comes too fast and hard and I hear my heartbeat pound my eardrums. I'm frantic.

It's happening again.

I try to fight it. I squeeze my eyes closed, but then the itching begins. My skin is on fire, and I start scratching before I realize what I'm doing.

Eyes shut, I resist it as long as I can but when it feels like every cell in my body will tear apart, I give up. I give over to the pull and I dress quietly. Tonight, I am alone in the house. My absence won't be detected. Taking the stairs two at a time I descend at a rapid pace, almost catching my foot on the bottom step. The itch is excruciating, and I wish I had taken the time to rub on the calamine lotion.

Then, I'm there. And the knife is so beautiful.

I pick it up and the wretched itching subsides. The temporary release of the torturous burning is such relief. It's as if the knife promises me sanctuary if I choose to use it.

My mind wanders to the streets of Seattle, where the filthy people live like rats and soon my hatred merges with the promise of the knife.

I am unstoppable.

The hunt is on.

MAY 24TH, 2002 10:13 P.M.

Nick and Luz walked along the street, hand in hand, oblivious to the world around them. They didn't talk much, but the silence they shared was warm and comfortable.

He took her to an older part of Seattle, where most of the buildings showed their age with chipped paint and broken windows. Nick stopped in front of an old brick building.

"We're here," he announced with a flourish. The small sign on the door read: Mary's Place, but nothing else about the building hinted as to what kind of business went on inside.

"Where are we?" Luz asked.

"This is Mary's Place. It's an emergency shelter for women and children who have no place to go. I like it because they empower these women to reclaim their lives. There's no shame, only acceptance and dignity as they work to better their circumstances. It can be a long process for a lot of them, but they provide warm meals and a place to sleep for women and their children if they need it. I thought we could help them out with dinner tonight."

The passion in his voice stirred something within her. This beautiful man cared so much for his community. And it made him that much more attractive to her. She walked up the stairs and pushed open the door, throwing him a look over her shoulder,

"Are you coming or what?" she asked playfully. He laughed, and he joined her inside.

• • •

They spent the next two hours lending a hand wherever they were needed. Nick watched Luz ladle soup into bowls and hand them out with smiles to the long line of hungry women and children. Her hair was piled on top of her head in a messy bun, but a few tendrils had escaped and framed her luminous face—the honey streaks contrasted well with her smooth dark skin.

He realized she likely spent some time getting ready for their date but any guilt he might've had vanished when she rolled up her sleeves, pulled her hair up and got to work.

When it was time for a break, they grabbed bowls of soup and some rolls and found seats at a crowded table. Luz spoke with those at their table with ease. It was when she made a silly face at a particularly sad-looking toddler—making the girl laugh—that he knew he'd made the right decision about their date.

• • •

They stood shoulder to shoulder at the large industrial sink in the kitchen, washing the last of the dishes.

"So, did you have fun tonight?" he asked.

"Of course I did," Luz responded, wiping the sweat from her brow with a wide grin. "Were you worried I wouldn't?" She shoved his shoulder with her own and laughed.

"Well, not many women would think this was romantic at all," he said, glancing around the kitchen. When he brought his eyes back to her she pulled her hands from the sink and held them out.

"I see why you brought me here. This place makes a difference. It truly is amazing, and I can guarantee you this won't be my last visit. I got just as much out of this date as those people did, so stop worrying, my nails will survive," she said, plopping a few suds on his nose. She giggled and started washing the last pan.

"Oh is this how we're going to play, detective?" he said, grabbing a handful of soapy suds. He watched her eyes widen as she realized what he was going to do. He dropped the suds on the top of her head and she squealed as they dripped down her face.

"I can't believe you just did that!" She grabbed the now-clean pan, filled with soapy water and tossed the contents at him, instantly soaking his shirt through. He reached out and snatched her hand, pulling her toward him, quickly eliminating any chance of escape. He put his arms around her and trapped her in a very wet hug.

"There," he said as she tried to wiggle free, "now we're even."

She quit struggling and went still looking up at him, even

in her current state of disarray he found her the most beautiful woman he'd ever seen. Those eyes full of mischief and something else… longing, maybe? He leaned down and captured her mouth with his. He felt her hesitate for a fraction of a second and then her arms slid around his waist and she gave into the kiss. When they broke away, they were breathless and began laughing at the same time.

"Look at us! We're a mess," Luz said.

"Come on, let's finish up here and go get ice cream, I know a place," he replied

"You had me at ice cream."

• • •

They took their ice cream to go and walked down to the water. Luz told him about her job and her family and Nick shared more about his life before the tragedy of his wife's murder. He was native to Washington, and only left to attend law school. He confessed that once his career advanced, he found a lot of his identity wrapped up in his role as a prosecutor. After Leah died, the distance from who he had become helped to put everything in perspective.

Luz couldn't begin to imagine what he'd gone through losing his wife then living on the streets all those years, but she was glad that he seemed to have taken away good lessons from his nomadic lifestyle.

They found themselves walking through a touristy area of the boardwalk and Nick suggested they take a ride on a horse drawn carriage. Sitting in that buggy with their bodies so close caused certain senses to awaken that had been dormant inside Luz since the end of her relationship with Ben. Sensations she learned to keep in check were slowly fighting their way loose and leaving her shaken, but giddy.

Thinking about the horse ride made her feel warm all over and she squeezed Nick's hand and when he squeezed back she wondered if he was thinking the same thing she was. They returned to the hotel and she walked him to his door.

"Thank you. I had a wonderful time," she said looking into his eyes. Her senses were on fire. She wondered how much longer she could deny the physical effect he had on her.

"That's all I wanted. For you to enjoy yourself. You've been under so much stress. I knew you could use a night off." He stared down at her and she was suddenly aware of how little space separated them.

"Goodnight," she said, backing up a step.

"Goodnight," he said, stepping closer. He pulled her toward him and pressed his lips to hers. Every alarm in her body went off at once as she lost herself in the moment.

He pulled away with a smile. "Do you want to come in?" he asked cautiously.

"Are you feeling lucky, Nick? Because I'm not that kind of girl." Luz gave him a wry smile and watched a blush creep slowly up his neck.

"Um, that's not what I meant at all. I don't know if this is the sugar talking but I'm really not that tired and was thinking about renting a movie on the TV. You game?"

Again, she hesitated. But she'd had a lot of fun and didn't want the date to end. "Can we at least rent one with a car chase in it?"

She saw relief pass over his features when he answered. "Of course, I know my way to a woman's heart."

• • •

Nick lay next to Luz, watching her. The weight of her in his arms was comforting. She had fallen asleep midway through the movie and was now slumped into his side. A sense of peace stole over him and he could do nothing but enjoy the feeling of her body next to his.

He had never expected to fall for her so quickly, but from the first time he saw her in that jail cell he'd been unable to think about much else. But now, because of her, he wanted to stop thinking about his past and start thinking about a future. A future that hopefully included Luz.

His own eyes were heavy, but he wanted to remain awake as long as possible to savor the moment. He had hidden away for seven years but she made him want to start living again.

He slid off the couch and shifted her into a horizontal position before placing a comforter over her. He thought maybe he should wake her but with the case taking up almost all her time, he imagined she needed the sleep.

• • •

A scream broke the silence and he was instantly awake and searching the room for the source. Finding no immediate threat, he crossed the room to check on Luz. She was thrashing on the couch. Her blanket lay in a heap on the floor. He approached her slowly, remembering that doctors advise to never wake someone from a nightmare. That course of action dissolved when he heard her crying. He gently nudged her shoulder, hoping it would wake her.

"So much blood," she whispered and started shaking. He couldn't allow the nightmare to continue so he called out to her. "Luz, you need to wake up right *now*."

He watched her eyes open and focus on him. "What happened? Was I snoring too loud?" she sat up and rubbed her eyes. She acted so put together, but Nick didn't miss that she wiped her tears with the heel of her hand.

"No, but you were having a nightmare and it sounded pretty bad. Something about blood?" he asked and instantly wished he hadn't. She went white as a sheet and looked away.

He grabbed her hand. "Luz, you're safe here. You don't have to leave but you do have to move to the bed."

The corner of her mouth lifted. "Hey, you wouldn't be taking advantage of the situation, would you?"

He wasn't in the mood to joke with her. "Tempting, but no. You need to rest, and the bed will be easier than the couch. Go ahead and get comfortable. I'm going to grab you a glass of water." He headed for the kitchenette.

When he returned with her water, he stopped upon noticing that Luz had gotten up and was observing the fully-made bed which was missing a single pillow. She had one hand on her hip, and the other ran along the comforter. His stomach dropped. She walked to the side of the bed, and there, wedged between the bed and the wall, she found the spare blanket he'd grabbed from the closet and the pillow missing from the bed. She placed a hand over her mouth.

He felt his neck heat, but he didn't want to be embarrassed. It was who he was. He shouldn't be ashamed. He cleared his throat, and Luz jumped a little. She turned to face him, but it was so dark he could only see the slightest glint in her eye. He hoped she didn't pity him. He'd have to put a stop to that if it were the case.

"Yes, you guessed it. I sleep on the floor. I really don't want to. I want to turn the page, get on with the next chapter of my life, move *forward* but... I don't know if I can explain it. Yes, it's more comfortable than the bed but I feel safer down there too. I know it makes no sense but—"

"Shh," she said, wrapping her arms around him. "You don't have to explain a thing to me. As you can see, I'm not without my own demons. I don't want to talk too much about mine, but just know that I had to make a hard decision on the job one night and the consequences kind of sneak up on me when I'm asleep. I'm sorry for waking you."

"What do you say we get some sleep?" he asked. He watched her climb into bed and dropped a kiss on her forehead before lowering himself back down to the nest of blankets on the floor.

"Hey Nick?" he heard her whisper.

"Yes?"

"Thanks."

"Back atcha, detective," he replied. "Now go to sleep."

CHAPTER SEVENTEEN

The night was long, the itch remained
I have to kill to stop the pain
People walk all around
Another victim in the ground

MAY 25TH, 2002 8:15 A.M.

Nick and Luz woke to a sharp knock on the door.

"Who could that be?" Nick asked standing to stretch.

From the bed Luz groaned. She knew who it was, and she didn't want to be caught in Nick's hotel room even if she'd slept fully clothed. Eddie would assume that they'd slept together, and she didn't have the energy to deal with his reaction. After her middle-of-the-night crisis, she had slept surprisingly well. Maybe sharing part of her past with Nick had helped. She certainly felt lighter, and as though they were exchanging things. She was communicating, and while she hadn't told Nick everything, she was proud of herself for admitting any sort of weakness and for talking about her trauma, even if it was only in vague terms. She jumped off the couch and collected her purse and shoes from the floor.

"I'll be in the bathroom. Whatever happens, I'm not here," she said walking past him. He grabbed her arm and pulled her in and kissed her. She walked away from him with a smile. The knock came again and she hurried into the bathroom where she saw her phone charging. *Shit 2 missed calls.* She thought when she checked the screen.

"Mr. Mason, it's Officer Lopez. I need to speak with you," Eddie called from the hallway. Luz scurried into the bathroom and peeked out as Nick pulled on a sweater and opened the door a crack.

"Yes, officer? What can I do for you?" he said. Eddie craned his neck trying to look past Nick into the room, but Nick stepped into his line of sight.

"Is… is Detective Santos in there?" Eddie asked with a hint of uncertainty and reluctance. Like he knew the answer but didn't want to hear it.

Nick cleared his throat and shook his head. "No," he answered.

Eddie eyed him, then smiled. "If you see Detective Santos," he said a little too loudly, "please tell her I have urgent news for her."

"I certainly will. Thanks," Nick said, quickly closing the door. Luz watched as Nick looked through the peephole.

Luz stepped out of the bathroom with her hair slightly mussed after not being able to find anything larger than a comb. She was worried for a moment about how she looked and what Nick would think of it. Nick stared at her with a sort of longing in his eyes that gave her chills, and she started toward him when her cell phone chirped and broke the moment.

They stood in a shocked silence before Luz winced and answered the ringing phone in her hand.

"Santos."

"That is so weird. I'm standing outside of Mason's room and he just told me you weren't there, and I call your phone and hear it ringing from the hallway. Coincidence? I think not. Open the door, Santos. I know you're in there."

Luz hung up and stomped toward the door. Nick stopped her again on the way and kissed her again, *I could get used to this*, she thought happily. She opened the door and the look on Eddie's face was enough to make her want to smack him. His expression was somewhere between amusement and disappointment.

"Well, well, well, Santos, I gotta hand it to you, you—"

"Save it Eddie. What's the *urgent* news?" she asked.

"We found the car," he stated, looking her up and down, his eyes hovering a little too long on her breasts. Luz was in business mode, so she ignored his behavior.

"Where did they find it?" she asked.

"You'll never guess. It was underwater somewhere across the lake."

"What? In Lake Washington?" she asked, her eyebrows shooting up.

"You got it."

"Did they trace it?"

"Listen, I don't know all the details. The meeting starts in twenty. It was my job to track you down. After going to your boat, this was my next guess. It turns out I was right," he said, smiling.

"I'll need to run home and change. I'll see you at the office," she said, shutting the door, then thinking better of it. She stuck her head out.

"Eddie!" she called.

"Yeah?"

"I would appreciate it if you would keep this little episode between us," she said softly, but in what she hoped was a firm voice.

"My lips are sealed." He mimed zipping his lips and throwing away the key.

"Thanks," she said, sighing with relief as she closed the door and faced Nick. "I have to go now, but I'll call you later… if I'm not too busy." She picked up her purse and grabbed her keys from the desk.

Nick strolled over and wrapped his arms around her, bending down so that their foreheads were touching.

"You are the most amazing woman I have ever met. Thank you for the most fun I've had in a very long time. I know you have to leave but I want to know when I will see you again."

She flushed, and he dropped a chaste kiss on her mouth. He pulled away, giving her a knowing look and walked to the bathroom. "I have a few things I have to take care of today so if you come by and I'm not here just leave a message for me at the front desk," he called from inside.

She opened the door to the hall. "Will do. And, Nick… thanks." He peeked out from the doorway, giving her a little wink. She left the room and walked to her car with a spring in her step She thought about him all the way home and to the office.

• • •

She arrived in the Storm Room thirty minutes later. When she walked into the room she heard a few snickers from the back, so she threw Eddie a look. But it didn't faze him. He stared at her defiantly, grinning.

Keeping her temper in check, she took a seat at the table and Mike began the meeting. "Thank you all for showing up," he said, looking at Luz. "Even if some of you arrived late. We have found the car the killer was driving the night Santos was attacked. Unfortunately, we've had a citizen suffer an injury, which is how the vehicle was discovered. Kenneth Bradley, a twelve-year-old boy from Juanita, was severely hurt. He decided to go swimming in a restricted area of one of the parks over there, and when he dove, it was headfirst into the trunk of the Honda.

"I don't know how long the car was sitting there. We have the lab guys working on that. But it is a 1995 Honda Accord, missing a hubcap and a bullet hole in the back windshield. So we know it's our car, now what it was doing there is what we'd like to find out. The boy's brothers found him late last night passed out on the grass near the water, a huge gash in the top of his head. He was still wet, so they knew he must have been in the water. His parents took him to the hospital and the boy sustained a serious concussion and had to have eight stitches in his head. After hearing what happened they called the police, who pulled the car out and gave us a call. So, we have the car. It might not be much but it's something. And we haven't had anything on this case since recovering the knife."

"What about the tags?" asked Luz.

Sonny stood up. "We ran them, and they belong to a Buick Regal that was reported stolen a few years back, so we ran the VIN number to the car and it's registered under the name…" he paused looking at the captain for approval and went on; "Leah Mason."

Luz's heart stopped for a second and she looked at Mike. "That was Nick's wife," she said. "Are you sure?"

"Leah Marie Mason, born January seventh nineteen-sixty-seven in Issaquah, Washington. Married to Nicholas Mason in the summer of eighty-nine, died in July ninety-four. Yes, I'm sure," Sonny said looking down at her sadly. "Sorry kid."

Her head spun, and the bitter taste of betrayal filled her mouth. She was going to be sick. "I… I need to talk to Mr. Mason," she said, holding her head in her hands.

"He's in custody downstairs," Mike said softly. "I had Lopez pick him up this morning after…" he trailed off, but Luz got the point. Fuming, she glared at Eddie and stormed out of the room. Without stopping to breathe, she rode the elevator to the ground floor and took off towards the holding cells. She snapped at the guards to follow her and unlock the cell.

Nick stood up and walked toward her. "Luz, what's happening?" he asked but once inside the cell she brought her hand up and slapped him hard across the face.

"You fucking bastard! You've been a part of this all along and you let me think you were this nice guy!" she screamed, beating his chest furiously. He grabbed both her hands and shook her.

"Listen to me! They told me what happened, and I can explain. Listen, dammit!"

She stopped struggling and dropped her arms, the fight leaving her. "Please explain fast because I think I'm going to be sick," she whimpered. He led her to the bench and they sat down.

"When I disappeared seven years ago, I left everything I owned in storage. The house was sold as well as the cars. I paid someone to take care of the entire deal. I was too involved in my own grief to worry about it. My friend told me everything went smoothly and that's when I took off. Whoever bought my car must have never transferred the title."

She wiped her eyes and thought this through. "Was the title signed?"

"Yes, everything was in order."

"Who is this friend of yours you trusted with all of this?"

"His name is Fredrick James. He is, well, *was*, my attorney on all matters of my estate. His wife worked at the credit union where my money is. They were good friends of ours— of mine, and I felt I could trust them. I went to high school with Candace, Fredrick's wife. She's a good person." He paused when Luz stood up and took a pad of paper out of her back pocket. "What are you doing?"

Luz jotted down the information. "Taking notes. I'll need to know his address, age, phone number…"

"Luz, that's the thing I was going to do today. This man controls all of my money and I can't find him." He looked up at her, his expression jumbled and a bit hurt.

She sat in stunned silence for a minute. "What?"

"It's true. I've been trying to locate him all week, but I've had limited resources."

Luz asked him to give her any information he could remember about Fredrick James and she wrote it all down. Then she called to the guard to open the door, stepped out and let the door close and lock before turning to speak to Nick. She had to choose her words carefully, so he understood why her reaction to the new intel seemed so extreme.

"Listen, I'm sorry I flew off the handle there for a moment. I don't trust easily and after last night I feel like I can be honest with you. This just came as a shock, after I thought I knew enough about you to believe you wouldn't lie to me. Come here," she ordered softly. He walked over so that their faces were inches apart. She reached in and caressed the cheek she had slapped. "Sorry," she said. She could still see where she'd made contact; the skin was pink, and a slight outline of her hand remained. "It was too much to handle when I heard what I heard upstairs. If I get you out of here soon, will you forgive me?"

He covered her hand with his own and smiled. "I'll forgive you either way, however it's a relief to know you believe me. No apologies necessary. Now go work. I'll stay here and nap. I was up late last night." He wiggled his eyebrows at her.

She giggled and turned to leave. She hurried to the elevators and rode back up practically running back to the Storm Room. She entered and interrupted Eddie who was explaining that he had searched Nick's hotel room and come up empty. Everyone stopped and watched her when she went over and whispered her findings to Mike, then she handed him her notepad and took a seat.

"All right, people, listen up! I need a full check on a Fredrick and Candace James. He was an attorney seven years ago in Seattle and she worked at Northwest Credit Union. They are both thirty-nine and they have one daughter named Chloe. She's currently attending the University of Washington. I have an old address that needs to be checked out and all this other information needs to be logged. We'll meet back here at four, understood?"

Everyone continued writing then looked up one by one and nodded. Luz watched them leave and approached Mike.

"Thanks Mike," she said.

"It might turn out to be nothing, but it's the only lead we have. Your boy Mason will have to stay locked up until we come up with something solid."

"No problem. Thank you so much."

"Don't thank me yet, Santos. I just hope Mason's not lying, for his sake *and* yours."

MAY 25TH, 2002 10:01 P.M.

Nick sat in the cell and moped. He had sat in this very cell only a week ago and he wasn't too happy about being back. What the hell was happening to him? Accused twice in one week of murder when all he wanted to do was get on with his life.

It would be okay. He had faith in Luz's abilities, and she was on his side and pushing hard for him. Memories of the previous night seeped into his thoughts and he smiled remembering the water fight in the kitchen. How he longed to hold her that close again.

But he would have to wait until his innocence was proven and he was let free. Even then, he would have to wait because he wanted to get his life in order again. He couldn't possibly offer Luz anything if he didn't take charge of his situation, and he wanted to be able to give their budding relationship a chance.

His thoughts drifted to his late wife. What he and Leah shared was special. She truly was his everything up until the day she was so brutally taken from him. There was a time he thought he'd never find happiness again, but Luz was slowly showing him there was still plenty of life worth living.

He would not mess up this time.

CHAPTER EIGHTEEN

I've grown reckless, careless and unafraid
Of the bloody mess of death I've made
No fear of discovery haunts my mind
I'm running the board and they're running blind.

MAY 25ᵀᴴ, 2002 12:14 P.M.

The young woman sat in the shade of the trees, reading over a stack of papers, her pencil poised over the paper.

She stared as Luz covered the last of the distance between them. The young woman set aside her paper and waited for Luz to stop.

"Chloe James?" Luz asked, holding out her badge.

"Yes?" Chloe answered cautiously.

"I'm Detective Santos with the Seattle Police Department. I have a couple of questions I need to ask you."

The young woman quickly put her books to the side and perked up. "Is this about those murders downtown? Because I have a few theories on why the killer is targeting homeless people. It all begins when they are young, about three or four years of age the human mind is most susceptible to—"

Luz cut her off. "I'm not interested in your psycho-babble. I'm not here about the murders. I came here to ask you about your parents."

Chloe pouted and refused to talk to Luz until she got an apology, and Luz threatened to arrest Chloe for interfering in a police investigation, then got down to business. "One of your father's old clients can't seem to locate your father. This man hasn't spoken with your father in seven years, but he left him in charge of a very substantial amount of money. Money he would like back. Now if you could just tell me where I can find him, we could talk this out."

The young woman's face grew blank and Luz allowed the girl time to think. She scanned all the books that surrounded Chloe, all related in one way or another to psychology. The girl was serious about her studies.

"Does my father owe this man money?" she asked slowly.

"No, nothing like that. My client left your parents with money for safekeeping. Now that he's back he would just like to check on his funds."

Chloe was silent for a moment then scribbled something on a sheet of notebook paper. She hesitated for a minute before she handed Luz the paper. Luz took it and read; it was her father's name followed by a phone number. Luz looked up at the girl and smiled.

"Thank you so much, Miss James. This will really help." She shoved the paper into her pocket.

"I hope you aren't lying to me about why you need to speak

with my father. I'm trusting you, Detective Santos," she said.

"Don't worry about it. We just need to speak with him," Luz said turning to leave. "Oh yeah, we just may need your help on the case. A fresh point of view is welcome in our line of work. Can I contact you?"

Chloe's face lit up and she quickly scribbled on another sheet of paper. "Sure. Here's my number and dorm number. Call or visit. Or I could come down to the station. I'm a psych major and think I could help you profile suspects and such. Just let me know." Chloe eagerly handed over her information.

Luz took the second slip of paper and smiled. "Your assistance is appreciated, Chloe. Thank you." She walked back down the grass hill and along the path to her car. She got on the radio and called Eddie.

"Is she getting up?" she asked softly, not wanting her voice to carry too far.

The radio burped back. "Yeah, she's packing up her books now. I'll tail her until she gets to a phone then I'm gone."

"Good." Luz hung up the radio and picked up her cell phone. She dialed the number for Fredrick James and waited for someone to pick up.

"Mayor Yates's office, how may I direct your call?" answered a voice on the other line.

Luz was confused. "Mayor's office?"

"Yes, how may I direct your call?" the woman asked again, clearly annoyed.

"Um... Fredrick James, please," Luz requested. She wasn't sure how the two men were connected but was happy Chloe had given her solid information.

"One moment."

Luz exhaled loudly when she was put on hold. She didn't have to wait long for the receptionist to pick back up.

"I'm sorry, Mr. James is on a call. Would you like to leave a message?"

Luz left her name and number but left out her title for the sake of gossip, then she hung up and waited. After a few more minutes the radio chirped, and she picked it up.

"Go ahead."

"You were right. She called her dad right away, told him about your visit and now she's heading back to the dorms."

"Thanks, Eddie. Mr. James works for the city council now. Let's go pay him a visit."

"Meet me at the north parking lot, see you in five." He cut off and Luz turned on her car and drove away, confused, but intrigued.

MAY 25TH, 2002 1:50 PM

Eddie and Luz arrived at city hall and rode the elevator to the mayor's office on the twelfth floor. The receptionist told them that the mayor wouldn't be available for another hour, so Luz asked instead to speak with Fredrick James. She dialed his office to announce their arrival and after a few minutes he met them in the foyer.

Fredrick was five feet, seven inches tall, small for the average man, and looked about twenty pounds overweight. He had red hair, pale skin and freckles dotted his face giving him a Tom Sawyer look. If it hadn't been for his age and his receding hairline, the man could have pulled it off. He wore a wrinkled suit and scuffed shoes.

"Detective," he said looking at Luz carefully. His eyes slid down to her legs and back up to her face, then to her breasts. Then he smiled and held out his arm. "What can I do for you today?"

Repulsed, Luz briefly shook his sweaty hand, resisting the urge to wipe her palm on her pants afterwards. "Mr. James, I'm sure your daughter called to tell you we were trying to locate you. If we could just go to your office I'd be happy to discuss the matter," she said, gesturing toward the direction he'd come from.

He stared at her for a moment and then at Eddie. Something close to fear crossed the man's face but he replaced it with a smile and beckoned them to follow him. Luz saw that the receptionist was shooting disgusted looks at Fredrick's back. It seemed Luz wasn't the only one who got the sleazy treatment from that man.

They followed him to a corner office on the west side of the building facing the water. From what Luz could see from the doorway, the view was spectacular.

"Mr. James, what is your title here?" Luz asked.

He followed her eyes out the window and cleared his throat. "I work as the assistant to the city solicitor, Bob Ackers, who serves as legal counsel to the mayor, city council and city administrative team. I used to work for a firm downtown. I was an attorney, a damn good one, I might add." He puffed out his chest a little with the admission. "Graduated from Harvard back in sixty-seven, tenth in my class, pretty good, considering the woman who graduated first currently works for NASA," he said, taking a seat behind his desk.

It was the longest answer to a question she'd heard in a while. Not only had he stated his title but he managed to ramble on about his past, sound bitter, and proud all in the same sentence. In short, he was babbling.

She took a seat in the vacant chair across from the desk and Eddie sat by the door. The office was sparsely decorated. There were a few plaques and certificates on the wall accompanied by a diploma from Harvard. There were also photos of James with important city officials all wearing the same worn-out grin. On his desk were pictures of him and his daughter with an attractive older woman Luz assumed was his wife. Chloe had been lucky and inherited most of her mother's features. Clearly, she had her father's eating habits. The girl she had spoken with on campus was a little on the pudgy side but with the academic knowledge and determination Chloe had shown, Luz knew that physical traits weren't important to a girl like that. It was the psychological patterns of the mind that intrigued her.

Luz found Fredrick James to be a bit out of place in the large office. Someone of his stature on the mayor's staff shouldn't have been on the same floor as the mayor, let alone in a giant corner office with its own view of Puget Sound.

"Now, what is it you came to talk to me about Miss…"

"Santos, *Detective* Santos. I work homicide for the Seattle

Police department, and this is Officer Lopez. He's with me today for observation purposes only. Shall we begin?" she asked.

"Yes, of course," he said reaching up to smooth his right eyebrow.

"Do you know a man named Nicholas Mason?"

"No, I don't believe so," he stated quickly.

"You don't?" Luz asked.

"Hmm," he said and smoothed his eyebrow again. "Nicholas Mason. The name sounds familiar, but I'm not sure I can place it."

Luz looked at Eddie, but Eddie's eyes never left Fredrick's face. Luz pulled a file out of her bag, opened it and read silently. After a few moments she looked up at the man seated across from her.

"So you're telling me that you're holding over nine-hundred thousand dollars and over 1.4 million dollars' worth of assets for a Nicholas Mason and his name doesn't ring a bell?" she asked, closing the file and setting it on her lap.

Fredrick looked shocked for a moment. Then he clasped his hands together and held them tightly, his knuckles white from the pressure. After taking a few gulps of air he brought his hand up to his right eyebrow once more. The action was starting to irritate Luz.

"Well?" she asked, looking at her watch.

He smiled then gasped loudly. "Oh, yes! I remember Nicky. We never called him by his full name. Of course, of course," he nodded vigorously. "I haven't seen him in years. How is he? Is he in trouble?"

Luz sidestepped the question. Nick hadn't wanted Fredrick to know too much until they found out what happened to his funds and property. "How much exactly were you asked to hold, including stocks and bonds, as well as property, Mr. James?"

"I have the information at home. I'll have to review it and get back to you on that, Ms. Santa."

"Santos, Detective Santos, if you please," she corrected. She'd had enough with the mispronunciations that week. "And a rough estimate will do. I trust you're using an accountant to help track the interest?"

"I'd say about 2.9 million, which included Leah's life insurance. The house in Kirkland was about one million, the houseboat was about three hundred-thou, and Nick's cars together sold for about a hundred twenty thousand. The rest went into storage. My wife works for a credit union and has been monitoring his stocks."

"How much would he be worth now? Everything included. Give us a full, round figure, Mr. James," Eddie ordered. It was the first time he had spoken. Fredrick frowned and reached up to smooth his eyebrow again.

"Well, I'd say…" he opened his desk drawer and removed a calculator, but Luz had a hard time believing that he needed it. "Roughly five-million dollars… give or take."

But was he giving or taking? thought Luz.

Eddie whistled low and shook his head. "And he trusted you to watch all of that? You two must've been tight, like brothers. I know I wouldn't trust anyone outside of my family

262

with that kind of money. Hell, I might not trust my *own* brother with that much money." He chuckled, then dropped back into serious mode.

Fredrick nodded slowly, and Luz took advantage of his silence. "What was your relationship with Mr. Mason?" she asked.

"Was? Is he dead? What happened, detective?" he asked but Luz detected a stale note to his voice that sounded vaguely like relief.

"Sir, would you answer my question, please?"

Fredrick blinked and rubbed his head. "Nick and I—" he began.

"Don't you mean 'Nicky?'" Eddie asked.

"Well... yes... Nicky." He gave them a weak smile. He stood and went to the window looking out over the waterfront before taking a deep breath. "Nicky knew my wife, Candace, in high school. They even dated a little junior and senior year. But they had known each other since the fourth grade. They grew up on the same block and were neighbors for years. both their parents knew each other and their parents, you get the point." Luz and Eddie nodded, and Fredrick went on.

"I met Candace in college and we hit it off, and after a few years we decided to get married. She always spoke well of Nicky all through college and I had met him a few times. After graduation, Candace had talked him into getting me a job downtown. As young as he was Nick... er... Nicky had proven himself valuable to the powers that be and had great influence over the decisions to hire. It wasn't much at first, low profile cases, some pro bono work, but it was *something* and I appreciated it."

"Your wife spoke of him often, and there was no jealously on your part? You two just became buddies?" Eddie asked.

"Well... yeah... something like that. I mean, at first, I thought I couldn't compete with this man my wife put on a pedestal but after meeting him and seeing them together I could tell there were no romantic feelings between them— only friendship bred from years of familiarity and history. Mason was a top-notch attorney. He made a lot of money and was a very busy man. We had lunch and had him over to dinner once in a while. We went to his wedding. I'll tell you I've never seen two people more in love." He stopped and seemed to reminisce.

Impatient and annoyed, Luz turned her attention to Fredrick. "Mr. James, can we jump to the part where Mr. Mason asked you to control all of his money and estate?"

Fredrick stared at her blankly for a moment and leaned back in his chair as if he were relaxed, but his tense body belied the image he projected.

"In the summer of ninety-four Leah, Nicky's wife was murdered on their houseboat while we partied it up downtown. Nick had won a really big case. Somehow, Anthony Yates was tied into the whole thing, but obviously he wasn't convicted, as he is now mayor and my boss." He laughed, and his hand shot toward his eyebrow, but he stopped mid-gesture and placed his hand back in his lap.

Luz stood and paced the room. "So Mason becomes obsessed

with putting Yates away and when he failed he just... disappeared?"

Fredrick nodded emphatically, reminding her of a bobble-head doll. "Yes, that's pretty much how it happened. The day of the trial he came to us, he was cool and calm, and we knew the shock had numbed him completely. We tried to talk him out of it, but he had all the paperwork filled out and ready to be signed and filed away. Power of Attorney and things like that. He wouldn't tell us where he was going or when he would be back. All he wanted was for us to take temporary control of his things. His last wish was that Leah's money and possessions not be touched."

"Even her car?" asked Eddie.

Fredrick looked from Eddie to Luz and back again. "What?" he asked.

"Her car. Her Honda. What happened to it?" Eddie asked again.

Silence filled the office and Fredrick jumped up like he'd been shocked. "Oh. Yes, the Honda! She could be so stubborn about that car. Nick drove a Mercedes, wanted her to have one as well but she'd had that Honda since college and wouldn't let it go." He chuckled to himself and looked up at them. "It was stolen."

"The Honda was stolen?" Luz asked. "When did this happen? Did you file a police report?"

"The car was kept in a storage garage. It was the cheapest place we could find to store it. The owner assured us it was safe. Then, three years ago, someone broke in and stole it. The guy, Emmanuel, I think his name was, told us he called the police and filed a report, and then refunded us the rest of our deposit and sent us on our way. We were never told if the car was found. I know it would devastate Nicky if he found out Leah's car was gone."

"That's it? You never looked into it?" Luz asked.

"Candace and I were unsure what to do. Emmanuel never called us. So Candace began a fund in Leah's name. The proceeds go to the families and friends of murder victims, to help them, you know, cope with the pain. The Leah Mason Fund, it was called. I have all the paperwork at home." He shrugged. "I would be happy to have a copy couriered to you after the long weekend first thing Tuesday morning," he added hastily.

"Please do," Luz said, gathering her briefcase and coat. Eddie rose and headed towards the door. Luz reached over the desk to shake Fredrick's hand, which was cold and clammy. She pulled herself from that grotesque grip as soon as she could and wiped her palm on her coat, trying to piece together why this man was so nervous. They opened the door to leave and, unable to contain himself any longer, Fredrick blurted out; "Is he alive?"

Luz turned to look at the man and said nothing. She let the silence drag out until she saw beads of sweat pop and glisten on the man's forehead again, then she left, closing the door behind her. The last thing she saw was his hand fly up to his right eyebrow. *Good*, she thought, *he'll have something to wipe away this time.*

MAY 25TH, 2002 3:00 P.M.

"Shifty little shit, isn't he?" Eddie asked as they got into the car.

Luz groaned. "Yes. He's hiding something but I'm not sure if it has anything to do with this case. Don't you find it peculiar that a man of his... stature holds such a prominent job at the mayor's office? I'm going to run his credentials to see how the hell he ended up there. I want you to check out the car story, see if you can locate that police report. In the meantime, we'll have to wait until he sends me more information."

Eddie was silent for a moment and then spoke up. "His daughter, Cooley—"

"Chloe," Luz corrected.

"Whatever, anyway, when we checked on her we found that she didn't go to college on a scholarship. Actually, she used to be a pretty troubled kid, she's got an MIP on her record."

"What's your point? Hasn't every other kid gotten booked with a possession charge in their teens?" Luz demanded.

Eddie sighed. "My point is, how does someone like her afford four years plus at the U when her parents barely had enough money to pay the mortgage on their house?"

Luz thought about that. "You may be on to something, Sherlock," she teased.

"Elementary, my dear Santos, elementary," he replied and laughed

"Fuck elementary, we have a lot to do. Shit, we've got all these trails leading nowhere. Every time we get something new, it turns us in another direction. It's driving me crazy," she said, rubbing the back of her neck.

Eddie put his hand on her shoulder. "Don't worry, Santos.

Mason will be fine. He can use his time to think about how lucky he is that he snagged you."

Whether he was reading her mind or making a guess, Luz was grateful Eddie was on her side regarding Nick. If only she could convince her boss to do the same.

CHAPTER NINETEEN

I realize now I've lost control
My taking of lives has taken a toll
My mind and body are beginning to fail
But I refuse to become soft, lost or frail

MAY 25TH, 2002 6:20 P.M.

"So much for Memorial Day weekend." Mike shook his head and looked across the desk at his top detective.

"Come on, Mike, I know you can authorize his release," Luz huffed.

"Dammit, Santos, can't you see this is for your own good? If he turns out to be involved with the killer, you could be in danger. I don't want to risk that."

Luz stood and leaned over the desk. "We've been through this, Mike. I don't need a babysitter. Nick's innocent, and I'll prove it."

"And when you do, I will release him," Mike said.

"Dammit! Why do you have to be so goddamn stubborn?" she said and resigned herself to the visitor's chair.

"Does this have anything to do with your feelings for him because if it does—"

"It doesn't," she said flatly.

"Then you can't let that affect your job performance. If this were any other Tom, Dick or Harry, you wouldn't be pushing this hard and we both know it."

Luz stood up and went to the door. "Listen, Mike, you've always told me to listen to my gut and for years, it's never failed me. I've interviewed many suspects and I've conquered the art of interrogation, so I *know* the good guys from the bad guys and Nicholas Mason is *not* a bad guy. His story rings true," Luz said. Mike started to speak, but she held up her hand to silence him.

"I'm not finished. I know you may think that because I'm a woman I'm more emotional about this than let's say that asshole Harris, or even Lopez, but that's where you're wrong. I've viewed this case from an emotionally detached point of view, by the facts only and even though Nick's name has come up many times, there's been no strong proof that he's linked to the murders. Just go with me on this, will you?" she asked.

Mike put his head in his hands and exhaled loudly then he pulled out his wrinkled pack of Marlboros and lit one. He took a couple drags before he spoke, letting the smoke wisp out slowly while he weighed his options.

"Santos, if you make me regret this, you're out of a job. Are you willing to stake your career on this man?" he asked, his eyes boring into her.

Luz's eyes didn't waver. "Yes, Mike, I am."

"Shit, then you got it worse than I thought," he said, putting his cigarette out in an old cup of coffee on his desk.

"Got what?" Luz asked sharply.

"Nevermind, I'll call down and get your boy out. He's to stay with you at all times. I don't think it will be a problem for you. Watch yourself, Luz. I don't want you hurt again, and I meant what I said about your job being on the line," he threatened but the fight seemed to have gone out of him.

"Thanks, Mike. I owe you big time," she said leaving the office. She rode the elevators downstairs and cleared the release with the guard on duty. As she walked to Nick's cell, she wondered if she'd been right to push his release. All she had been doing to Mike lately was pushing him. In one week their professional relationship had changed. She hoped it was for the better. Mike wasn't only a good guy but a great boss and a greater mentor.

When she reached Nick's holding cell and saw his hopeful face, she forgot all about Mike's opinion of her.

"Come on, Nick, let's celebrate." She unlocked the door.

7:00 P.M.

Nick and Luz ended up at the Seattle Center for the annual Folklife Festival. There was food from around the world as well as dancing, music, theater, vendors and booths. They started off at a Filipino food stand and ordered barbeque pork on skewers and washed it down with fresh squeezed lemonade. They saw street performers, families having picnics on the grass and groups of teenagers hanging out listening to the live bands.

Luz insisted they go to the main stage where one of her favorite Salsa bands was playing their set. They listened for a while and Luz decided to get up and join the crowd to dance. Nick watched her sway to and fro, her hips moving with the beat flawlessly. It was mesmerizing and somewhat arousing. The woman was quickly becoming important to him. He was surprised that the thought came with none of the usual guilt he was so used to feeling. He was finally healing, and it felt good. Even more so, it felt right.

Luz danced her way back to him and took ahold of his hand. "Come on!" she shouted above the noise with a huge smile on her face.

Nick wasn't sure how much he remembered from the salsa class he'd taken in his youth, but Luz was aglow, and her energy was infectious. She led him back to where she danced before, and he grabbed her hips began to dance.

"Wow! You dance well for a gringo!" she shouted over the music

"I'm not sure if that is a compliment," he shouted back and took her hand and spun her around. They came chest to chest and began moving together step to step. Their proximity only proved to heighten his already strong attraction to her.

"It is," Luz replied and clung to his shoulders. They continued to spin and turn until the song finally ended. They panted heavily as they clapped with the crowd, then decided to take a walk.

They strolled toward the north entrance. The farther they

went from the festival, the less populated the walkways became.

"It's getting late," Luz said, staring up at the sky. The clouds were wispy, and the air was humid, but she could almost smell the oncoming of rain.

"Did you want to leave?" Nick asked.

"Oh no, my week has been *way* too hard, I deserve this," she replied. He stopped and wrapped his arms around her pulling her close.

"Luz—" he began.

"Elephant ears!" Luz screamed.

Nick looked around, expecting to see an elephant stomping through the crowd. "Wh-what?" he asked, and she grabbed his hand and pulled him to a booth. The smell of cinnamon drifted from the small tent. She ordered and the man behind the counter handed her something warm wrapped in wax paper. Luz paid him then found a seat on the grass. Nick sat beside her and waited for her to tell him what she'd bought. She opened up the wax paper to reveal a large piece of fried dough coated in butter with cinnamon and sugar.

"This is an elephant ear. In Mexico, we call them churritos but here they serve them long and flat like this so that they resemble the ears of an elephant," she said tearing off a piece and handing it to Nick before popping a piece into her mouth and moaning with pleasure.

Upon seeing her reaction Nick popped the piece of dough in his mouth and began chewing. It was warm and melted in his mouth. It was a bit too sweet, but it tasted wonderful.

"So what do you think?" she raised her eyebrows. "I know

it's a lot of sugar. Every mother's worst nightmare, but it's worth it, que no?"

Nick swallowed, tore off a big piece and shoved it at Luz. He noticed too late that the piece was massive and watched with intrigue as she opened her mouth and bit off about as much as she could fit.

"Now that your mouth is full I want you to listen," Nick began. He took her hands in his and looked into her eyes. "Luz, I don't know how to thank you for all you've done for me. I don't know what I would do if I had to sleep one more night in that cell. But I also want to thank you for believing in me. It's forced me to take a good look at myself and change who I was before it was too late. Thank you for giving me my life back."

Luz finished chewing then she slugged him hard on the shoulder. "That wasn't very nice!" she scolded. "I could have choked and all because you wanted center stage."

Nick laughed. "I knew you'd forgive me." He reached up and wiped some sugar off her cheek.

She laughed but stopped when she spotted something over his shoulder. Nick turned following her line of sight and saw Officer Lopez headed their way. He was never comfortable around the man. It had a lot to do with the way they kept running into each other under unfortunate circumstances. But he could see that Luz held some affection for the guy, so Nick decided he could tolerate the officer a little longer.

Eddie reached them and smiled at Luz. "Hola senorita." He turned to Nick and held out his hand. "Hey, Nick. Sorry about before, police procedure and all…" Eddie trailed off.

Nick shook his hand and nodded. "I know all about police procedure. I know you weren't to blame. Don't worry—I don't hold grudges."

He was grateful that Luz didn't mention his seven-year grudge against Anthony Yates. She seemed pleased that he and Eddie were getting along.

"What are you doing here?" she asked Eddie, who was in uniform.

"Mike wanted to bump up security for the festival. Homeless people from all over town flock here whether it's to dance, sing, eat food that's left sitting out or beg for money. Either way, we need to patrol the whole area all weekend. It's easy pickings for this killer and we'd rather be safe than sorry."

Most of the passersby were families and couples but they spotted a few bums wandering around alone. One homeless man sat with a cardboard sign asking for money or food.

"This is going to be a long night," Eddie said, turning back to them. "But I'm sure you two wouldn't mind a long night."

Luz gave him a withering look. "Eddie…" she began.

"Okay, okay I'm going. You two be careful. By the way, Luz, I ran a check on local garages in the area. Emmanuel Altek works at Benny's down south. He wasn't working today but was lucky enough to have to work on Memorial Day."

Luz placed her hands over her ears and hummed loudly. Both Eddie and Nick laughed, and Eddie backed off. "All right no talk about work. Enjoy yourselves and I'll call you, Luz."

Luz stopped humming and waved goodbye, then leaned

back on the grass and watched the sky get darker in the north. "Looks like rain."

"Nah, it should pass by and miss us. Too far to the north," Nick said.

"Oh yeah, don't tell me you used to be a weatherman too," she joked.

"No, but my uncle used to take me sailing. He taught me to watch the weather closely for signs of storms."

"Wow, a man of many traits. How ever did I get so lucky?" she said in a southern belle accent, causing him to chuckle.

"How did *I* ever get so lucky?" he looked at her with genuine adoration, then added; "So, what's the story with you and Eddie?"

Luz stopped smiling and slapped him roughly on the arm. "Hey, I only got to know him this last week. He's helped me on the case from the beginning. He was open with me about his crush and I made it clear that I didn't return his feelings. Now we're good friends and plan to keep it that way. But it was sweet and *nosey* of you to ask."

"I'm sorry if I'm being intrusive."

"Nick, I haven't dated anyone for two years." She lay back down on the grass.

Nick was about to plant a kiss on her cheek when he paused and looked into the distance. He leaned over and whispered in Luz's ear.

"Don't look but there's a man sitting across the way there and I think he's been following us for a while."

"Why do you say that? Roll over. I need to see him," she said kissing him and laughing. Nick was surprised how at ease she seemed even though she knew they could be in danger. With Nick on his back she pretended to kiss his neck, trying to spot the man he spoke of.

"The one with the blue sweatshirt and funny hat?" she whispered, staring through the strands of her long hair.

"He sees me staring, he's up and moving toward the crowd, he's not looking back. Let's go." Nick had to run to catch up with Luz, and together they tracked the dark hat among the crowd of people.

"Still see him?"

"Barely. He's moving fast. I think he knows we're following him," she said, picking up speed. They walked faster, passing the dome-shaped fountain in the middle of the center. Children screamed and ran in the water while parents watched from afar, preferring to stay dry.

Mimes, petitioners and vendors walked in their path. The crowd grew thicker and Nick could tell Luz's patience was wearing thin. A few steps past the kiddie rides, and he was gone.

"Shit! Shit. Shit. Shit. We lost him," Luz cursed.

• • •

Luz pulled out her phone to call Eddie and quickly filled him in on the man and the chase. He asked her to meet him back on the north end of the center, but he didn't sound happy.

It took them ten minutes to trek back to where Eddie was. He stood next to a body covered with a white sheet. Leroy was taping off the area and people were herded from the scene.

"What happened?" Luz asked, deflated.

"Our guy strikes again. I was patrolling this area and I heard a scream. That woman," he paused and pointed to a small booth where a woman packed up her hippie-style shirts and skirts and glanced uneasily about. "She found the body. She said he'd been wandering by her booth all day and about an hour ago he decided to camp out on the stump over there. The guy is, well, *was* homeless, and he sat down with a sign reading WILL DANCE FOR FOOD. After he sat down, this woman gets nervous, says she doesn't trust bums, says they steal things from her cart every year, so she asked him to leave but all he did was shake his head and grunt. She didn't see him dance all day. After that, she left him alone. Apparently, her booth got busy. So it comes time for these vendors to start packing up and she sees him still sitting here. She also sees one of the bracelets from her stand around his wrist. So she marches over here to ask him where he got it. Well, the guy doesn't answer so she kicks his sign and he falls over. That's when she noticed he was dead."

Eddie pulled up the sheet. The old man had white hair with a matching beard, looking almost like Santa Claus. But Santa never wore sunglasses with a worn-out army coat over torn-up jeans and old galoshes.

"This is getting ridiculous. If we don't find who's doing this, we'll all be out of a job with a pile of bodies to show for it," Luz said, her face on fire.

"There's a job opening at the morgue, Litebrite," Ben said walking up to the body. "But that's not your thing, is it?" He smiled and put his arm around her shoulders. Luz looked at Eddie who was watching Nick, but Nick didn't so much as flinch when Ben bent down and gave Luz a peck on the cheek.

"You're in a good mood for just having been called to a murder scene," she said, pulling away. She could only imagine what Nick thought of the familiarity between her and her ex.

"It's been a good day. Until now, of course," Ben said, pulling on his latex gloves and kneeling beside the body. He placed and ran a finger along the gash in the neck.

"Same kind of knife, but this gash is messier than the previous few I've seen." He made some notes on his pad before continuing his preliminary exam of the body.

"Which means the killer is either losing his touch or blowing off some serious steam," Luz speculated and added, "We were just trying to question a guy who was watching us. It was probably him."

"Well something's going on. Could be a new knife, but he went from killing once a month to once a week to once a day, then twice a day and now this. The morgue's never been this busy. I had to call in Severson from Stevens to help."

"What do you mean?" Eddie asked. "This is the first body we've seen today." Even as Eddie finished his sentence his radio chirped, and he picked up the call. When he hung up his face was pale. "Luz, they found three more bodies around the park. Mike's notifying the Director of Northwest Folklife and the Center's facilities director. We're shutting down the festival until the bodies are examined and the scenes processed."

Luz kissed her weekend goodbye and pulled out her cell

phone. She called Mike, who was busy, and said he'd call back in a minute. So she called Sonny at the office.

"We got bodies everywhere. Did you follow Antoinette?"

"Yup, she's in Hawaii. She and hubby drove to Sea-Tac this morning and hopped on a plane."

"Damn!"

"I know you were hoping she would be the woman you were looking for but it's not her. Sorry, Luz. Can't win 'em all."

"Thanks, Einstein."

"Whoa, hold on there. I've got other news. After carefully draining the car found in the lake, we found some brown hair on the seats and floors. Now we're just getting started on it. I'll call you with the results as soon as I have them."

"Thanks Sonny." Luz hung up and thought about the man they were chasing. He had brown hair. Her phone rang again, and she picked it up. It was Mike.

"Yeah, Santos, it's a fucking circus out here. Wrap up there and come down to the south entrance. The press is here, and I need some help until the mayor's press conference. Shit, this is going to look bad on my resume if we don't find this psycho."

"Ben says there's an opening at the morgue."

"That's sick, Santos."

"Hey, keep your options open. If we don't close this case, beggars can't be choosers."

"Yeah but apparently, they can be murder vics. See you in ten."

She hung up and closed her eyes. When she reopened them, Nick was staring at her with obvious concern.

"Are you okay?" he asked.

"I'll be fine when this is all over. Let's go." She began walking away but quickly walked back to the body and tapped Ben on the shoulder.

"Hey, who quit at the morgue?" she asked him.

"Me." He smiled. "It seems I had a long-lost uncle. I didn't know him, but he knew me and left a pretty big inheritance."

"How big?"

"Let's just say, by this time next month, I'll never have to work again. Isn't life great?"

Luz snorted and shook her head. "Tell that to the guy under the sheet," she said and walked away.

CHAPTER TWENTY

The walls of my mind are closing in
A pressure born from all my sins
Now I loathe the smell of blood
I would stop this madness if I could

MAY 25ᵀᴴ, 2002 10:59 P.M.

The dreams are killing me inside. The dreams make me kill. I've just woken, and my stomach is tied in knots. I must not get sick this time. If I get sick, I itch. I must clear my mind. The sign said *no swimming*. How did they find the car? I've made too many mistakes. The police are getting closer.

The feeling of superiority comes and goes but I no longer think myself invincible. I've gone from being the hunter to the hunted and back again. The power is like a high but the vulnerability that follows is unbearable.

Goddamn my mother! All I wanted was a normal life and the bitch couldn't give it to me. Now look at me. Look at what I've become—and all because of her.

I shake my head. She doesn't deserve all the blame. I've lost control of myself, and I've lost control of the need.

I walk into the bathroom. The smell of disinfectant makes me nauseous, but I refuse to vomit. I must find a way to get well quickly. Once I regain control, I can resume killing at will. Instead of a curse, the murders will become a pleasure once again; a hobby, even.

Catching my reflection in the mirror, I jump. I barely recognize myself. My hair is matted and there are bags under my eyes. I wonder how much longer I can keep this up. It's a huge strain, physically and mentally, to focus on my daily life when the burning inside me never subsides; a constant longing for death that grows with every passing day.

A vision from my dream floats through my mind. My body surrenders, and I retch into the sink, unable to stop. I hear my cell phone ring in the other room, but I cannot move. I'm paralyzed with sickness. For a moment I wonder why I'm not afraid, with all the lives I've taken, with all the witnesses around, and with all the loose ends. I should be falling apart.

Then I remember seven years ago when Leah Mason died by my hand and the retching stops. Looking at my face in the mirror, I catch a smile forming on my lips. It had to be done. She would have ruined my life. She would have thrown me back from whence I came. But I wouldn't go back. I *won't* go back, ever, no matter the cost.

With that last thought my body shudders and I know what is next. I quickly turn on the shower and set the temperature to blistering hot. Shedding my robe, I step in and scream as the water scalds my skin. The painful sensation is both inviting and agonizing. Surely, I will have second-degree burns. But it relieves the itching. Sobbing, I give myself over to the pain and the itch is soon forgotten.

MAY 26ᵀᴴ, 2002 7:45 A.M.

Cliff Saunders rubbed his eyes and turned off his laptop. He feared the killer could somehow link into his home PC and track his movements, so he brought a laptop home to work on his investigation.

He'd been up all night and his mind was fried, even if he could track that email address back to the owner, how would he get a message to the police? Assuming, of course, that he could track it, why would the killer continue using it? Any and all links to the emails could have been destroyed. The two years he had attended at ITT Technical Institute had taught him that much. Unless the killer wasn't knowledgeable in computer systems. Was that why he had been threatened, so the killer could buy time to figure it all out, or hire someone to do it for him?

That thought stuck in his mind as Cliff turned the laptop back on, beginning to work once more. Elizabeth had come into his office around six to check on him, wondering why he hadn't come to bed. Instead of telling her about the note left by the killer, he told her he had a big project at work. With that explanation he was left alone for the weekend, but he knew she was getting restless with the lack of time he was spending with her and the kids.

What she didn't know was that the sacrifice would pay off if it meant that the man who violated their home and threatened them with death could be found and put away for life, leaving them safe from harm.

He rubbed his eyes again and refilled his coffee mug. He went back to work and would continue working until he found answers. Even if he hit a dead end, at least he'd know he'd done all he could to save his family. Looking at the laptop screen he wiped the tears forming at the corners of his eyes and resumed his search.

MAY 26TH, 2002 8:10 A.M.

Luz woke slowly, her eyes taking in the details, the light filtering through the curtains of her bedroom window, the sound of the water lapping against the hull of the boat, and the unmistakable scent of bacon wafted to her nose. She inhaled deeply and smiled.

She had so many conflicting feelings when it came to Nick. Sure, they got along, had a lot in common—but there was a small voice in the back of her mind that warned his feelings for her might stem from the unconventional way they met. It was the way he was always thanking her for saving him. She could tell he was grateful for the second chance at life but how could she be sure he liked her for the right reasons? These doubts had nagged at her for days but as a cop she felt she could rely on her intuition and her gut told her he was a good guy.

She would still take things slow. The man came with a lot of emotional baggage and she wanted to be sure she gave him enough time and space to work through his ghosts. She could use that time to sort out her own feelings about him. After processing the scene at the festival, they had come back to her place for the night. She had been worried about how he would deal with her boat, but there had been no hesitation when she invited him in. She took that to mean he was making progress with his trauma. The thought made her smile.

Neither had been talkative after the grisly things they had witnessed and agreed that sleep was the best option—him sleeping on the couch and Luz in her own room. She didn't remember anything after her head hit the pillow. All the events of the previous week caught up with her and she quickly fell asleep.

Her stomach growled, interrupting her thoughts. She got up, grinning, and went straight for the bathroom to make herself presentable. Her reflection was less than impressive so she pulled out a brush and dragged it through her hair. After pulling it back with a claw clip she brushed her teeth and washed her face. Surveying herself again she noticed the dark circles under her eyes. There was no helping those. This case was taking its toll and it was bound to show on her one way or the other, but it was unflattering nonetheless. At least her wound was only a minor annoyance at that point.

She grabbed her robe and strolled to the other side of the boat where the scent of bacon, eggs and onions was the strongest. She walked into the kitchen and Nick looked up from the stove and frowned.

"You ruined the surprise. Go back to bed," he ordered pointing her in the direction of the bedroom.

"I'm still surprised. Besides, I have to work today. Better sooner than later."

"Oh. Well, I was just finishing up my famous omelets de Nick."

Luz walked over and saw the eggs cooking along with peppers, mushrooms and bits of bacon. "A man of many talents. I'm impressed. But where did all this food come from? The last time I went grocery shopping was before the case."

"I took the liberty of running out and stocking your fridge for you."

A frown creased her face. "Nick, what happened yesterday has clearly taken you off the list of suspects, but you need to be careful. There's a killer out there and I'm in his crosshairs. I'd hate for anything bad to happen to you.

Nick raised his hands in surrender. "I'm really sorry Luz, this is all new to me. For seven years I went where I wanted, when I wanted without needing to check in with anyone." He flipped the omelet once more, placed it on a plate and sprinkled it with cheese. "Go sit down. I'm just about done." He put the plates on the table where he had already cut some fresh cantaloupe and apples. He poured each of them some coffee and sat down. They ate in silence except for the groans of satisfaction that came from Luz every time she took a bite of the omelet.

"If you don't keep it down, I'm going to need a cold shower," Nick teased while he sipped his coffee.

"Sorry, it's just… this is so delicious. I'm not spoiled like this too often. Who am I kidding? I'm not spoiled like this at all," she said taking another bite.

Nick smiled at her, "So, what's on the agenda today?"

"What else? Murder"

After breakfast, Nick helped her clean up and they got ready to go. It was nearing nine-thirty and she knew Mike and the team would be waiting for her at work.

"I'll be back around three," she said.

"Why don't I come with you?" he asked, tying his shoes.

"Not today. I don't need any distractions," she said pointing her finger at his chest. "And you, sir, are a distraction."

He smiled down at her. "Fine, but if you're not back by three, I'm coming to get you." He leaned down to kiss her nose. They embraced for a while longer, not wanting to separate, but it was Nick who finally pulled away.

"Go to work. I'll stay here and keep Cheech company."

She looked around for her dog and found him sleeping under the window next to the bed. She patted him goodbye. Cheech lifted his head and licked her hand. "Poor baby, I'm never home to walk you anymore, am I? Nick's gonna walk you today, okay boy?" she asked. and Cheech wagged his tail. She stood up. "I think you made a friend. There's a trail that runs behind the marina. Feel free to walk him whenever you want. He hates being cooped up on the boat, so he'd be grateful." She kissed Nick once more and grabbed her coat. "See ya," she said.

MAY 26ᵀᴴ, 2002 10:00 A.M.

"Santa, Mike wants you upstairs pronto," Rosa snapped as Luz got off the elevator. *Bitch*, thought Luz, but she smiled at Rosa and thanked her, leaving the woman confused once more. Luz wasn't going to let Rampage Rosa ruin her day. She never understood why Mike kept Rosa around. Hell of an admin, sure, but she made everyone's life miserable. Lately she was downright hostile, glaring at Luz whenever they crossed paths. If Rosa didn't improve her attitude Luz was going to talk to Mike about it... again. Rolling her shoulders back, Luz shook off the bad mojo. Maybe things hadn't worked out with Eddie and Rosa was a woman scorned. Not that it mattered—Luz wasn't going to make that *her* problem.

She rode the elevators and got out, heading directly to the Storm Room. When she opened the door, all eyes turned to her. Mike, Sonny, Eddie, and two of their tech guys were sitting on the far end of the table, but there were three men in gray suits seated closest to the door—one of whom rose when she entered the room.

"Detective Santos, agent Blue Adams," he said, holding out his hand. They shook, and Luz took her seat, raising her eyebrows.

"Blue? Is that some new FBI agent coding or something?" she asked.

The man's serious countenance slipped for a moment and she saw the hint of a smile at the corners of his mouth. "No. My parents were hippies. My brother got it worse. His name is Rainbow. My full name is Blue Sky Adams, call me Sky if you want, people seem to settle better with that one."

Luz skipped the formalities. "And you are here…" she led.

"Because there's a serial killer running around that you people can't seem to catch," he finished and looked at her as if daring her to challenge the observation. Luz shrugged and leaned back in her chair.

"So you were called in to solve the case. My hero," she drawled. A few people in the room laughed quietly but Adams's face was like stone.

"Detective, with that attitude it's no wonder you haven't caught the killer yet. And yes, I'm here to clean up after you. You've got evidence in the news and plastered on the cover of all the papers, the killer is running free, and from what I hear you're sleeping with the main suspect," he shot back.

Luz jumped out of her seat and marched up to him. "First of all, every single person in this room has been working day and night on this case. I've got the bags to prove it," she said, pointing to her eyes. "Not to mention a concussion and this pretty little scar," she said, lifting up her shirt.

"Which you got because you didn't call for backup and—"

"Second of all," she interrupted, "there's someone in the department leaking to the media, and we're working on squeezing that shut, but it can't be helped. It happens with these big cases. And lastly, how dare you come in here from god-knows-where and judge my personal life? Nicholas Mason has been cleared of all charges. His innocence had been proven, so if you have anything relevant on this case, say it and then get off of mine."

The room was silent as Blue and Luz stood face to face. Agent Adams mumbled an apology and, satisfied, Luz took her seat.

Adams cleared his throat and began. "So far we've got zilch on the killer's identity. We traced a woman called Francis Aberleen back to New York but that's as far as we got. You all know the file, but there's nothing else to go off of. That's where we come in. I'll need to set up a task force. Agent Walker and Agent Knutson are here to help with that. I'll expect full cooperation," he ended, looking around the room.

Mike stood and addressed the group. "Did you hear that? Full cooperation? Understood?" Everyone nodded. "Good. Dismissed." As the others left, Mike waved Luz over to him.

"Mike, was this all necessary?" Luz asked.

"Listen," he whispered, "I didn't call them in. The mayor did."

Luz was stunned into silence for a moment before she could speak. "Yates called the FBI. Shit. We must be making him look bad."

"Yeah. Anyway, I want you to find this man or woman who's slashing up my town. I don't want this thing solved by a bunch of out-of-state suits with egos, got that?"

"Sure."

"That means no more dates with your dream guy. I want you on this twenty-four seven. If you have to sleep, I want it to be at your desk. I'm serious," he added when he saw her smile.

"I got you, boss. I'm all over it. I'll report to you every few hours. I won't rest until we find out who's behind this."

"Good, we need this to end," he said and threw two Rolaids in his mouth "I've never had heartburn this bad my entire life."

Luz returned to her office and called Nick to tell him not to expect her but to make himself at home. She could hear the regret in his voice, but work was work.

"I've been out of the work force so long that I forgot how long the hours on tough a case can drag on. So when will I see you?" he asked.

"You could come here," she suggested.

"No. I've been kind of working on something."

"Really? What?" she asked.

"Well, I really enjoyed being an attorney; even when I was homeless I helped a few people on the street. People who were wrongly evicted, young mothers who needed state help, wives who didn't know they had a right to sue their husbands who beat them, things like that. I've missed doing it a lot." Luz was silent, and he went on. "Anyway, I was thinking of opening a small firm, maybe doing independent work. But I need my money, I was going to talk to Fred and ask him—"

"Don't."

"What?"

"Don't go to him yet. I have a funny feeling about him. First, he disappeared. Seven years ago, he was making ends meet and now he's got a daughter in a four-year university and a beautiful new house, not to mention he works for the mayor."

"What?" Nick gasped. "He works for Yates? But how... how..."

"I know. So please, don't go see him. We're still investigating him, trying to figure out how he climbed the political ladder by skipping a few rungs. Please promise me you won't go see him."

The line was silent for a while and finally he agreed. "It's Sunday. The mayor's office is closed anyway."

"Nick, I know how stubborn you can be. Please let me take care of this for you. Just lie low for a while. Fredrick doesn't even know you're alive. Just let it go for now."

"Fine," he replied tightly. "I'll go check on a few friends downtown. I'm trying to convince my friend Andy to give up life on the streets and get his butt into rehab. That alone will take up the rest of my day."

She sighed, relieved to have won that small battle. "Thank you. I know it's hard but he's one of the first leads we're going to follow. It's just so coincidental that he works for Yates and that Yates had a duplicate of the murder weapon. I'll keep you updated, okay?"

"Okay. Thank you, Luz, I'll call you later."

"All right. I'll be here. If not, call my cell."

"Luz?"

"Yeah?"

"Be careful"

Luz was glad he couldn't see her face as it went through ten shades of red. "Will do. Bye." She hung up the phone and smiled at it for a minute before getting to work.

She reviewed Yates's file and could find nothing of use, so she moved on to the file she had Sonny compile on Fredrick James. It was a relatively short file. The man hadn't accomplished much in his forty years. She dialed her house again. Nick answered the second ring.

"I have one more question for you, and then I won't bother you."

"As if you could bother me. What do you need to know?"

"What was Fredrick's job at the DA's office?"

"He worked as a lawyer. Well, actually, he was very green when I worked there with him."

"Oh?"

"Anyway, Candace, his wife, and I had been friends since I put glue in her hair in fourth grade. We dated for a while in high school and kept in touch throughout college. Our families remained close. When she was married I came to the wedding, and I became Chloe's godfather."

"Wow, that's a lot of information. Go on," she urged him to continue.

"Well, her husband, Fredrick, was a nice guy all the way around, so when she asked about openings downtown I told her I'd do what I could. At that time, we didn't have any openings, but I convinced the big guys to give him a job. I put myself on the line for the guy. But after he started working there, I realized he must have cheated his way through college because the man wasn't very bright. My boss came to me and we agreed to give him the low profile, easy win cases, which he barely handled alone. After that he was put on cases as second chair only. We couldn't afford to lose any more cases due to his lack of knowledge. From there it seemed to work out fine. I didn't think much of it when I left. He didn't last, did he?"

"No, but then why would you choose to leave everything in his charge?"

"I was grief-stricken, and all out of friends. Candace was the one I'd known the longest. She's a beautiful person, Luz. I don't think she would have let anything happen to my money."

Luz didn't share his trustworthiness, but she kept silent. "Okay, that helps a lot. I'll call you if I need anything else. Thanks." When she hung up she checked the dates of employment for Fredrick downtown and she found he had worked there up until three weeks after Nick disappeared. Had they gotten rid of him that fast? She called there again and left her name, number and badge number asking for someone to call her back as early as possible the following day.

She worked through the afternoon, stopping briefly to buy a candy bar from the vending machine. Around three-thirty Sonny called and told her that the hair turned out to be artificial, meaning the killer wore a wig or toupee. No DNA to trace; it was a dead-end.

She let out a frustrated sigh and left her office, walking toward the other end of the building. The last thing she wanted was to talk to the cop shrink they'd nicknamed Quinn the Quack. Quinn Presley was the department psychologist. She counseled cops who had discharged their weapons, saw something awful or were involved in traumatic incidents on duty. Luz had only been forced to see her once and that was after she was involved in a case where she had to shoot to kill. Squeezing her eyes shut, she relived the incident over again.

It was one of those nights in the summer where it was too hot to breathe. She hadn't yet made detective and was out patrolling when a little boy ran into the street in front of her car. She slammed on the breaks and got out to check on him.

That's when she noticed the blood all over his little hands and tears streaming down his face.

"What happened to you? What's your name?" she asked, trying to keep the panic from her voice.

He stared up at her with wide eyes. "Run!" he yelled. He ran away from her.

She started after him but heard footsteps behind her. She spun around, drawing her weapon in the process, but something struck the side of her head and she went down. She heard yelling, and then that little boy screamed.

Gun in hand, she struggled to her feet. She turned to find the boy in a heap on the ground, blood pooling around his tiny frame. A man stood over him holding a baseball bad coated in blood—a crazed look in his eyes. She yelled to him, identifying herself and hoping to distract him from the brutal beating he was delivering to the helpless boy. When he turned his soulless eyes to her, she understood there would be no reasoning with that man. He'd crossed the line from sanity into insanity long ago.

"You don't know ME!" he screamed, marching her way, bat held high. She backed up and came into contact with the hood of her car. There was nowhere to run.

"Police! Put down your weapon!" she screamed, bracing the gun in her hands "Put it down now or I'll shoot." An icy panic slid through her whole body, but she'd been trained for situations like that. She took a deep breath and steadied her stance. Her confidence rose just enough to keep her in control.

He sneered at her. "You shoot me? I don't think so." He

lunged at her, bat swinging high. She pulled the trigger. That moment still played through her mind every now and again. She shuddered thinking of the wet sound the bullet made when it tore through the man's chest, and the way his face expressed shock and then nothing at all when he collapsed on the street, never to move again.

The man she killed that night, Clancy Keane, was chasing his son from their home with a baseball bat. They later learned that he had snapped and already bludgeoned both his wife and their daughter to death in their home. The poor kid had seen his own father kill his mother and sister. He ran out of the house in panic to get away from his deranged father and right into Luz's path. She could still recall the abject terror on his face when her headlights illuminated him.

She wouldn't, she *couldn't* imagine what he had been through that night, but she knew in her gut that she wouldn't have changed the way she handled things because the boy had lived. One year of excruciatingly painful physical therapy and more years of psychiatric therapy and the boy recovered from most of his injuries, both the physical and the mental ones. His grandparents raised him after that and every Christmas she had a Christmas card with his picture on it as proof that she'd done the right thing.

Quinn Presley though, had her own opinions on what happened that night and took Luz through it over and over, dissecting every detail. Going over other ways that night could have played out, questioning Luz's logic and methods. Trying to dig into her personal life, saying her own experiences may have played a role in the decisions she made. It got under her skin and left a bad taste in her mouth. She knew the shrink was just doing her job, but she was no one's lab rat. She attended every session, stuck by her story and eventually was cleared for duty and had given Quinn a wide berth from that point on.

But now she needed her—not only was she the on-call head doctor, she also dabbled in profiling and with her assistance, many cases had been solved or prioritized. Luz needed someone to get inside her suspect's mind, peel away the layers to see why this person was killing so many so fast. It was obvious the killer was escalating, and she needed all the help she could get to find some clues into his or her psyche.

She knocked on the door and heard Quinn call for her to enter. She was a petite thing, not more than five-two, blazing red hair, pale skin, large brown eyes that flashed surprise when she looked up from her files and saw Luz in the doorway. "Santos, what can I do for you?"

"Hey, doc, I'm sure you've heard about my homeless killer case. I brought in my notes and was hoping you could add some weight to the profile I've started on her."

For the second time the shrink's eyebrows shot up. "A woman…" she mused "I could see that…"

"So you are familiar with the case?"

"I've scanned over the data, yes. It looks like your killer is on a spree to rid Seattle of its homeless population. This person has justified these killings in his or her mind. They may feel like they are doing the citizens of Seattle a favor." She paused, shuffling through the files on her desk and pulled out the case file. After perusing the case notes she looked up again.

"He—or she—has no remorse, which could mean this person has crossed the line and isn't coming back any time soon. The attempt on your life may have led them to escalate their plan. They see it as a challenge now that the police are involved. Patrols were doubled and you, yourself were at the Folklife festival, pulling off those kills would've acted as a rush, a release if you will, for the killer. Using the knife makes this personal. This person feels they are righting a wrong, perhaps someone close to them betrayed them. Seeing as you do have a woman suspect in mind, I'd guess she's young, maybe twenty-five to thirty. She would have a decent job, a way to blend in. However, I wouldn't rule out a man just yet. It would take a lot of strength to pull off these murders. Whoever this is, they probably feel like the end game is coming. At first, they were in charge, merely blowing off steam, but with the escalation comes a kind of panic, almost a frantic need to keep up the pace. Their social life will suffer. The façade they kept up for so long will begin to slip. This person is now a slave to their addiction, but like every addict, they will hit rock bottom, and in this case, that could be a very dangerous thing." She shook her head and looked at Luz.

Luz decided to add the information to her notes for the captain. "I appreciate your input, Presley." Luz turned away.

"Do you?" the doctor asked.

Luz knew immediately that the doctor was referring to the personal sessions they shared. "Look, I know we didn't see eye to eye on my own situation. Sometimes it is just what it is: self-defense."

"You're saying there are times when the memory of that night doesn't surface and punch you in the gut?"

Luz threw up her hands angrily. "Of course it does. I wouldn't be human if it didn't, but the job is the job and sometimes I *have* to make hard decisions. That night a demented man was coming at me with a baseball bat covered in the blood of his wife... his fucking daughter... I'd be a robot if that didn't bother me now and then."

Quinn studied her quietly for a moment. "And what of the life you took that night? Yes, he was deranged, but did he deserve to die?"

Anger simmered to the surface and Luz stuffed her hands in her pockets, hoping to avoid taking a swing at the shrink.

Quinn must've sensed her anger because she held up her hands in surrender. "I'm not defending that sicko. What he did was unforgiveable on every level. I was only ever worried about you. Killing someone can take a toll on a person, cop or not. How often are you thinking about it, detective? PTSD is a pretty serious thing. Ignoring it instead of working through it can be more damaging in the end. When I poked and prodded you I was only making sure you were okay. Like you, I was only doing my job." She folded her arms and leaned forward on her desk, waiting for a response.

Luz let out a long breath. The anger she'd felt dissipated. "I know, I really do. Other than family, I'm not used to people worrying about me. I usually take care of myself."

Quinn smiled warmly and asked; "Doesn't that make you tired sometimes? Always watching your back, looking out for yourself? Isn't it time to let someone else take care of you?"

Thinking of Nick taking care of her made Luz smile. "Maybe. Thanks, doc, I appreciate the time."

"Anytime you want to stop by to chat—on or off the record—I'm here for you. Don't be a stranger"

Luz nodded, closing the door behind her. She found herself warming up to the Quack... who knew? Maybe one day they'd be friends... maybe.

Luz pursed her lips and thought through the details of the murders again. Yes, this person was losing their edge, but an animal backed into a corner was dangerous. She had to stop the killer before someone else got hurt.

Eddie called and asked if Luz would need him to accompany her to the car garage where the Honda was stolen from. Emmanuel didn't work until ten o'clock that night, so they set up a time to meet beforehand. They discussed bringing Leroy along. Even though he was a sweet guy, Leroy was the biggest, tallest black man Luz had ever seen except other than NFL players. They decided that Leroy would do well for the purpose of intimidation and she asked Eddie to bring him along.

Eddie and Leroy picked her up around ten and they drove down south along Highway 99 toward the airport. Passing the airport, they kept an eye out for Benny's Park-n-Store.

"So, where's Nick?" Eddie asked.

"Back at my place. Why?"

"Mike wanted him to stay with you, so I thought he'd tag along."

"No, he's been cleared. He needs some time to work things out. Besides, I sent a patrol car over to check on him occasionally."

"Ahh the joys of dating." Eddie chuckled.

"Shut up, Lopez. I had to do this. He knows he's being watched. I explained it to him."

Changing the subject Eddie said, "So what's with the FBI moving in?"

"The mayor's worried about his image, so he called them up and they send down Mr. Blue's Clues to close the case," Luz said.

Leroy laughed but Eddie seemed confused. "Blue's Clues?"

"Yeah that little blue dog on TV that finds clues, it's a children's show. Don't you have nieces or nephews?" Luz asked Eddie.

"Back in LA so I don't get a chance to watch shows with them, but I get the point. Good one, Santos."

"The joke was lost on you but whatever," she said, pointing to a green sign that read "Benny's" across the street. "Take a left here."

Eddie signaled and pulled into the parking lot. It was dark along the side of the building and Luz could just make out a neon service sign toward the back. They parked along the fence and got out of the truck. Luz led the way and they entered the business. The front desk was unattended, and the lobby was a mess. Car magazines were strewn all over the chairs and the small table with the coffeemaker was covered in sugar and cream.

"Nice place." Eddie snorted and rang the bell on the counter.

A large, round man poked his head out of a doorway across the room. His hair was dark and looked as if it had never seen a comb or brush. He sported an overgrown, unruly goatee.

"Yeah?" he called but made no move to come out.

"We're looking for Emmanuel Altek," Luz said, flashing her badge.

The man stared at them a moment longer and spat. "What for?"

"There was a break-in here a while ago and we need some answers."

"A break-in? You sure you got the right place?" he called, still making no move to come out of the office.

Eddie stepped around the desk toward the man. "Why don't you come out where we can see you, sir?"

The man's eyes grew wide. "No, no. Don't come back here. Get back!" he whined, nearly falling out of his chair. Eddie approached the office, but by that time, the man had gotten to his feet and attempted to shut the door. But Eddie was too fast. He used his shoulder to block the door and pulled the man by his collar out of the room. The name on his shirt read "Manny".

Luz clicked her tongue. "Refusing to cooperate with the police is a bad thing, Mr. Altek."

He looked at her then back toward his office. "Leroy, would you go see what Mr. Altek was so busy doing in his office?" she asked, never taking her eyes off Altek. Leroy walked past them into the office and Altek's face fell.

"Well, well, well, looks like our man has a problem," Leroy called from inside. They waited for an explanation and got it when Leroy stepped out, holding a small plastic bag full of white powder.

Luz shook her head and turned back to Altek. "Tsk, tsk, tsk, Emmanuel. You're bad news, aren't you?"

Altek looked from Eddie to Leroy and shrugged. "That ain't mine."

Luz raised her eyebrows. "Then whose is it?" she asked.

"I'm holding it for a customer. This is a storage place."

"Auto storage last I heard," Eddie said giving him a little shove.

"Whatever," was the man's response but he was starting to sweat.

Luz walked up to Altek's face. She could smell alcohol on his breath. "Whoa. Manny, is that vodka I smell?"

He looked at her and swore under his breath. "Yeah. I grabbed a drink before work. So?"

His indifference irritated Luz. She raised her hand to Altek's face and squeezed his nose hard and held on. His scream resembled the sound of a teapot at boiling point. When she finally let go, his hands covered his nose and he fell to his knees, whimpering.

"You fucking bitch… you… fucking… bitch, that hurt!" he repeated as he rubbed his nose. Then he jumped to his feet and lunged at her. Both Leroy and Eddie caught him by the shoulders and held him back. Looking pathetic, Altek glared with undisguised hatred.

"Lying to the police is worse. Now, we came here for answers. All you've proven just now is that you're a liar. Judging from the pain you're obviously in, that coke is yours. I came for the truth, Manny. Why don't we start over?" She walked back to the door and rang the bell on the counter then waited expectantly.

Altek looked at her for a second then got up and walked to the desk. "M-may I help you?" he stammered.

Luz flashed her badge again and smiled. "I need to speak with Emmanuel Altek, is he around?"

"That's me. I'm him," he replied pointing to himself. Luz felt sorry for the man. His nose was bright red and there was blood around the rims of his nostrils, but she had no time to play good cop.

"I'm Detective Santos with the Seattle Police Department. We're working a murder case downtown and need do ask you a few questions."

"S-Sure." He clasped his hands together.

"Fredrick and Candace James stored a ninety-five Honda Accord here up until it was stolen two years ago. What happened to it?"

He stared at her, his face blank.

"Maybe you want to pull up the file," she said flatly, pointing to the ancient computer at the end of the counter. He went to the computer and typed slowly. The machine was dated, and Luz knew it would take a while. After a few beeps, Altek nodded and waved her over.

"Yeah, it was never found."

"Was it ever lost?" she asked.

"What? I don't understand," he said. More beads of sweat formed on his upper lip.

She placed both hands on the counter and Altek moved

back a step, watching her closely like he was ready to jump back if her fingers came anywhere near his nose.

"Why wasn't it reported?" she asked, and he opened his mouth to speak but she cut him off. "And don't bother lying. You reported a Honda stolen that night, but you reported a Honda *Civic* and you gave the wrong tags. I looked it up. What happened to the Accord?"

Altek was silent for too long. Eddie came up behind him and barked in his ear. "Answer the lady," he ordered. Altek shrugged.

"Well?"

"I don't know," he said softly.

"I think you do, and if you don't want me to adjust your nose again, you'll tell us now. But if you lie, you're not only going down for possession of cocaine. We'll stack on attempted assault on an officer—that would be me—interfering with an investigation and falsifying a stolen vehicle report."

The sweat flowed freely at this point, but he shook his head. "Lady, I got a family. I know I dabble with drugs, but I've worked here for ten years, I could lose my job."

"You'll lose it either way. I've got sources that tell me you sell stolen parts out of vehicles you're supposed to be keeping safe. Others tell me you deal drugs out of here as well, so if you don't feel like helping us, we're not going to feel like helping you. But if you give us the information we need, we might just act like we never stopped by. Get it?"

He took a seat on the old rusted office chair behind the desk. Luz gave him time to think but motioned for Eddie and Leroy to stand by. They walked up behind Altek and took their seats on the desk.

"Well?" she asked.

He sighed heavily and began. "A few years back I did a little dealing. Drugs and parts, out of the garage but shit kept going wrong and the cops wouldn't leave me alone. It was those fucking chinks. Never kept their mouths shut about anything."

Eddie spoke up. "The proper word would be 'Asians'."

Altek looked up at him, surprised. "Excuse me, Mr. Politically Correct, can I continue?" he asked. Eddie rolled his eyes and looked at Luz.

"Go on," she prodded

"As I was saying, this was all a few years back. I don't mess around like that no more, bad for real business. So one day this chick walks in and asks about some Honda we were holding."

Luz stopped him. "It was a woman?"

"Yeah, but she didn't fit in, ya know, her clothes were too nice, ironed and all that shit, and she smelled clean. Anyway, I tell her all records are sealed from the public, only the owners can see the cars. Well, she shoves this fifty in my hand, telling me she just wants to see it. So I show it to her and she freaks out, says that she has to buy it. I tell her that this is a storage place, not a car dealership and she gives me this crazy look like she's gone over the edge.

"Then she reaches into her pocket and pulls out a lot of money. She counts out two thousand dollars and hands it to me. I'm thinking 'shit', so I go back inside and make a copy of the key for her. Then I just gave it to her. She gave me six hundred dollars to never mention it and then that crazy look. At that point, I was scared, but I asked anyway. 'What if the cops come around?' and she did the weirdest thing. She scratched her arms—like a lot and, well, that was enough for me. I told her to beat it, that I would take care of it and you know what she says to me? She says, 'Better to take care of it then to be taken care of.' Strange bitch. I just nodded and said 'sure' and she drove off. So then I call in the stolen Accord with a different VIN and tags. The police really didn't bother. They never do in this part of town. Well that was before you guys showed up."

"Yeah, then we show up," Leroy echoed getting to his feet.

"Jesus, Manny, you've broken so many laws, and I'm sure the owner of the car won't be too happy to hear this." Luz said.

Altek shot out of his chair. "What? I thought you weren't going to say anything?" he shouted.

Luz backed up and smiled. "I don't remember making any agreement like that."

Altek's face scrunched up and he pointed his finger at her.

"Don't get all worked up, Manny. If we could just get a description of the woman, I'd be in a negotiating mood. How about it?" she asked, pulling out her notepad.

He stared at her for a moment. "Lady, I really need this job," he said slowly.

"And I really need this information," Luz replied.

"What if she comes after me? What if she sends someone? If she's the killer you've been looking for?"

"If you don't tell me, she will be the least of your problems,"

Luz said grabbing hold of his nose again, but she didn't squeeze. Instantly Altek's forehead was coated with sweat.

"P-Please don't... she was tall, and skinny," he blurted, and Luz let go.

"And?"

"It was hard to tell. She wore a long coat. Actually, she was dressed more like a man," he said and scratched his head.

"Excuse me?" Luz said.

"Yeah, I remember now, she had a brown wig and a funny hat and one of those stick-on mustaches."

"How did you know she was a she?" Eddie asked.

"When she handed over the money I noticed her nails. They were long and cut real nice, and she had no apple."

"Adam's apple?" Luz suggested. He nodded pointing at his own.

"And her voice, I could tell she was trying to disguise it but after she freaked out about the car, she must have forgotten cuz her voice went back to normal."

"Shit!"

"You know her?" Altek asked, eyebrows raised.

Luz put her notepad away, headed out the door and told Eddie and Leroy to come with her. Altek hurried after her and called to her from the doorway.

"Hey! So does this mean I'm off the hook?"

"For now," Luz replied.

"Well what the fuck is that supposed to mean?"

"It means for now. Get back to work, Manny," she said and climbed into the truck.

• • •

After they got on the freeway Eddie broke the silence. "A woman. Well at least that's consistent with the actual evidence we've got."

"But where does Fredrick James come in? I mean why does he work for Yates all of a sudden when Yates was suspected of killing his good friend's wife? It doesn't jive," Leroy added.

"There's no doubt the guy is hiding something. He was shaking like leaf in a windstorm. What if he killed Leah for Yates and as a reward Yates set him up with a job and paid for Chloe's college?" Eddie surmised.

Luz looked at Eddie, reached over and patted him on the back. "Shit, Lopez, I didn't know you had it in you. You're gonna make detective someday."

Eddie looked embarrassed but managed a small smile.

"First thing tomorrow we visit Mr. James again. But right now, we need to find out what's going on with this he/she Altek told us about. If I can put together a photo-line-up maybe he'll pick her—or him—out. We're getting somewhere," she said. "Finally."

CHAPTER TWENTY-ONE

I've gained control of this horrible curse
I feel much better, no longer act worse
Pleasure is now the name of the game
But still I feel I'm going insane

MAY 26TH, 2002 11:50 P.M.

Candace James could not sleep. Her husband was going to go to hell and there was no way she could prevent it. For three years now, she had lied to herself about the money, but now Nicholas was back, and everything was starting to come together.

After Nick disappeared, she and her husband had taken care of his estate, from the house to the money to the stocks and bonds. Everything was safe and secure—at least that's what the paperwork said.

But that evening, she thought differently. Since yesterday Fredrick had been tense and short tempered. She tried to talk to him about it when he got home the night before, but he refused to speak. He went straight into his office, made some calls and looked through files then he closed the door and stayed there all night. Candace had no idea what had gotten him so upset so she waited and asked him after church that morning. He didn't answer, only claimed that he had errands to run. The desperate note in his voice scared her. He left in a hurry, and Candace had no idea what was happening.

Chloe came for dinner, like she did every Sunday night, and she asked if her father's absence had anything to do with the police and his old client. Nearly choking on a piece of roasted chicken, Candace waited until the coughing subsided to ask her daughter what she was talking about.

Chloe filled her in on the visit a detective had paid her at the university and the conversation she had with her father on the phone. Candace had tried to enjoy the rest of the meal for her daughter's sake, but her mind was working on what this all might mean. They finished their meal and Chloe had to get back to cram for a test but asked Candace why her father had yet to tell her about the detective. Candace shooed her daughter from the house, giving her a hug and a kiss. She promised they would meet for lunch the following week.

After Chloe left Candace began to tremble. The small seed of doubt that sat in her subconscious for years had finally found the room to grow and it left her sick to her stomach. She went straight for her husband's office, but the door was locked. She searched their bedroom and found a spare key taped under the second drawer in his nightstand.

Once she'd unlocked the door, Candace made haste, fearful her husband would return and find her rummaging through his things. Then she chided herself. This was her house, too.

She could go into any room she wanted to.

She saw her husband's desk, covered in records of Nick's account as well as statements of transfers from other accounts she couldn't remember ever seeing.

She found deposits that been transferred into an account with her husband's name on it. The amounts varied from a thousand dollars to ten-thousand dollars and her blood ran cold. Where was this money coming from? *Who* was it coming from?

She found a recent statement from American Bank, showing three transfers from the unknown source but five more from Leah's Fund. She gasped and covered her mouth.

"Candace! What the hell are you doing?" her husband shouted from the hallway. He stood outside, peering in at her. The look on his face was that of a guilty man.

She spun and looked at him, studying him as hard as she could. She had trouble reconciling the man she married with the possibly illegal dealings she'd seen in his records. "What have you done, Fred?" she asked softly, but the anger was building, and she felt it surface.

"Get out of my office. I have work to do," he demanded as he walked around his desk.

"Fuck you," she said.

Utter shock crossed his face. Candace never spoke to him like that. "Excuse me?" he asked.

"I said 'fuck you'. Did I stutter, dear? Now tell me, what is going on? Where is all this money coming from? Who is it coming from and why?" she shouted, beginning to shake again.

313

A few moments passed as the shock of her demands sunk in. "Let me explain…" he started, wiping his eyebrow.

"No!" she shouted back. She didn't want to be lied to anymore. "Is this how Chloe got into the U? Is this why we own three cars and a boat? Did you buy this house with that money? Fred, that is Leah's money! Blood money!" she spat. "You said you got a promotion at work with yearly bonuses. You lied!" she took a few steps towards him.

Fredrick tried to tell Candace that he had done it all for her and their daughter. She wouldn't hear it. Instead, she walked up and slapped him across the face. He grabbed her arms and shook her, which frightened her, but not enough for her to flee.

"Dammit, Candace just listen. Listen to me!" he yelled. "There was no other way. I wanted the best for my family, and we would have never gotten the opportunity to rise above without the help. The cars, the vacations, the university, I did it for us!"

She stared up at him, tears streaming down her face and shook her head. "You did it for *you*. You were never happy with what we had, with what *you* had. Always wanting more since the day I met you. So goddamn selfish, so don't you *dare* justify this with your family, with us." She said "family" with loathing. She watched her husband wince at her words, then she shoved him away from her. He let her go.

Now she lay on the bed in their guest room, looking up at the ceiling and feeling torn. After the guilt and betrayal receded she was left wondering what she was going to do. What her husband did was not only wrong but very illegal.

Should she turn him in? Would she? Could she?

The fury returned for a moment and she picked up the phone, intent on calling the police, she dialed the area code, then hung up. She knew they would lose everything. Her daughter might even have to leave the university. She didn't want to be responsible for ruining Chloe's promising future; that was Fred's responsibility.

She climbed out of bed and unlocked the guestroom door. Locking it was a last-minute decision. She needed time to cool off and didn't want Fred popping in with more lies. She couldn't handle any more lies. She padded down the hall and up the stairs. Seeing the light still on in her husband's office she walked toward the door, mentally preparing the ultimatums she had carefully thought up earlier.

But she never got the chance to speak. She had just taken a step into the office, just made eye contact with her husband when she saw the flash of dark metal catch in the light. She was frozen as he raised the gun to his temple and pulled the trigger. Her screams echoed through the house.

MAY 27TH, 2002 1:30 A.M.

The phone rang, startling Luz awake. She groggily rolled over and picked up the phone.

"Can't a person get some sleep?" she said into the phone.

"Not tonight. Sorry, Luz, but we're going to need you on this one," Mike said sounding like he, too, had just been awakened.

"What happened? Another body?" She wasn't sure she could take another victim.

"Yeah, but this wasn't murder. It was suicide."

Luz jolted upright, accidentally kicking Nick in the leg. "What? Who?" she asked.

"Fredrick James. He shot himself an hour ago. Used a .22 and blew half his head off."

"Aw shit, I'll be right there," she said and hung up the phone. Nick turned to her, rubbing his injured shin, but she didn't want to be the bearer of bad news.

"What happened, Luz?" he asked but she got up and pulled on the shoes that Nick must've taken off her when she passed out. *How sweet was that?* she thought.

"Sorry about the kick. That was Mike. We got a sui-situation and they need me. Sorry."

"A suicide? Who was it? Do I know…" he trailed off when he looked her in the eye. She saw when the pieces slid into place and he realized it was probably someone he knew. "Fredrick?" he whispered, and she nodded. "Are you sure?"

"I'm sorry, Nick. I know you two were close."

Nick looked at his hands started dressing himself.

"Where do you think you're going?" she asked, pulling on her holster.

"With you. Candace will be there. Besides Chloe, her family has moved out of state. She'll need someone to comfort her. We've been friends for a long time, Luz. She's like family to me."

Luz looked at the alarm clock across the room and debated whether to leave without him. "Fine, let's go. But I can't have you interfering. It's bad enough you already know these people."

"Whatever you say. Let's just go."

She watched the pain contort his features and wondered how well he would hold up once he saw the body. She would have to risk it. She had to go and fighting with him would only waste more time. They left the boat and drove through the city toward the James residence.

While she drove, Luz brooded. Her only lead had just slipped away.

• • •

Luz pulled up to the scene and found Chloe James rushing out of her Volkswagen Passat toward the house. The officers posted at the door stopped her from entering and she became distraught. After asking Nick to wait in the car, Luz walked up the steps and took hold of her shoulder, telling the cops that the girl could enter.

Chloe allowed herself to be guided inside to the living room where her mother sat on the couch. Luz watched as the girl ran to her mother's side, but Candace wouldn't acknowledge her daughter's presence. She gazed at the coffee table, but her eyes were set somewhere no one else could see. Chloe shook her mother's shoulder, then collapsed on the floor in front of the couch, begging her mom to see her.

The whole scene was especially painful for Luz. She had never grown up with a mother and couldn't imagine having one who wouldn't acknowledge her when she most needed her to. She bent down and put her hand on Chloe's head.

"Chloe, your mother's in shock," she explained softly. "It will be some time before she's ready to talk about what happened. Why don't you just sit here with her, maybe hold her? On some level, she'll feel the comfort. Just be her rock, okay?"

Chloe looked at Luz then back at her mother. "Okay," she whispered getting up and sitting beside Candace. She slid her arms around her mom's shoulders and wept; Luz left them alone.

She followed an officer upstairs and down the hall to where Ben stood. He gave orders to bag up what remained of Mr. James. Luz still wasn't sure how she felt about Ben quitting. He turned when she approached him and smiled grimly.

"This is getting to be too much. I wanted to go out with a bang but come on…" he shook his head.

"I know. This man was the key to our investigation. Without him, we're back to square one." She looked through the door to the office. "What do we got here?"

"The man was definitely hiding something. He left a note for his wife, but she hasn't read it. Too shook up. There's a bottle of Jack Daniels, two-thirds empty on his desk and another empty bottle in the trash. He must have needed a lot of liquid courage to shoot himself."

Luz nodded and walked into the room where the crime scene crew was working. The photographer had just finished taking pictures of the scene. And what a scene it was; blood and chunks of skull were spattered on the far wall behind the desk. The chair was being cleaned. She saw Mac Dudley working on the gun and approached him.

"Hey, Mac. Flat out suicide, right?"

"Pretty much. The only thing the autopsy will show is that the guy was highly intoxicated at the time."

"No signs of foul play?" Luz asked, hoping the killer would be connected in some way.

"No. The wife saw it all happen; poor woman may be scarred for life."

"Thanks," Luz said and wandered back out into the hall. She could hear Nick's voice from downstairs and she cursed under her breath.

"Boyfriend blues?" Ben asked, and she turned around.

"No, it's just... I didn't want Nick involved. I have a feeling he'll come into play somehow."

"I wouldn't worry about it. Let him help her any way he can. She needs *somebody* right now."

"I know. If he can get her to release those records, maybe we can piece together some things, maybe find out if he's connected to the case. Getting a warrant for it will take too long and time is not something I have in abundance on this case. Take the computer and the files in here and we'll see what else we can get from the wife. I just spoke with the man two days ago and he was nervous about something. I need to find out if it's relevant to the case."

Ben sighed. "Just give it time, Litebrite. These people are going to be hurting."

"I know, and I'll wait but not too long. We need to put a lid on this thing. The media is all over us for closure."

"The media can wait. Just do what you can for now. Chase

a couple other leads and come back to this one later, maybe a day or two."

"Eight hours, tops. There's no way I can wait days," she said reluctantly.

"You look happy, though," he said, catching her off guard.

"What?" she asked, looking around the death scene.

He followed her gaze and shook his head. "Not now, but the other day. You looked happy. I'm guessing Nick's treating you all right."

She was uncomfortable discussing her love life with an ex-boyfriend, but she answered. "Yeah, he makes me happy."

"Good, now hold tight to that feeling this time and don't let your ego get in the way."

The words hurt but rang true. She swallowed hard, ready to argue that things were different, that she was different, but Ben held up his hand.

"It's okay. I'm not trying to attack you. I'm just saying that if he makes you happy there shouldn't be anything more important than that, nothing, not even the job. Don't make the same mistake we made, letting the job get in the way all of the time. We had our ups and downs but we're better as friends. I want you to be happy," he said, reaching out to rub her arm.

Nick cleared his throat and walked up to them. Luz hadn't heard him coming. She wondered how much he had overheard.

"Luz, Candace's doctor is on the way. Her daughter gave me the number, and she's going to break down if we don't get a sedative into her. She's barely talking to me. Just words; no complete sentences but she keeps apologizing to me. She keeps saying sorry to me over and over again. Then she rubs her hand over her arms."

Luz thought about the itching woman at the car garage that Manny Altek had mentioned. "Is she rubbing or scratching?" she asked quickly.

Nick looked puzzled. "Uh… like this." He held both his arms with the opposite hands and rubbed. It didn't look like itching to Luz. "Why?" he asked.

"No reason, I just thought of something, that's all. Don't worry about it. Did she say anything else?"

"No, not really. She just seems really numb right now," he replied, glancing down the hallway towards the living room.

"Let me know when the doctor gets here. I need to ask her some questions."

Nick looked wary. "Luz, we don't want to upset her further. Can't we do it some other time?"

She looked at him then at Ben, who gave her a warning look. "Sure. I can wait," she said a little too quickly and Nick looked at Ben, eyebrows raised.

Just then Mac came out of the room. "Nothing much left to do here," he told Luz and spotted Ben. "Hey Torres! What's happening? I heard about the inheritance thing. Congratulations, man! Some guys get all the luck," he said smiling broadly then turning to Luz. "Too bad you two couldn't work things out. You would've been a rich woman, Santos, had you a real sugar daddy," Mac said, elbowing her slightly in the ribs.

Luz elbowed him back roughly. "Thanks, Mac, but I'm seeing someone right now," she said, tilting her head toward

Nick. Mac's eyes widened, and he backed up a step. "Oops my bad," he mumbled, then went back inside the room.

"Sorry," Luz said, turning to Nick. "Mac's a little outspoken."

Ben laughed "That's a severe understatement. The man talks too much. I'd bet you anything he's the leak. I hear he's screwing Emily Watkins from Channel Four."

"Shit. Mike's gonna love that," Luz said, letting the implications sink in.

Ben turned to Nick. "I'm sorry, Nick. I guess no one told you that Luz and I were involved. A little over two years ago, but we're friends now."

"Good to know." He gave Luz an amused look. "We haven't actually put a label on it yet. So I hear you helped Luz the night she was attacked."

"Yeah, she called me after she was stabbed. Scariest hours of my life though." He gave Luz a stern look. "Don't do that to me again."

"Would you stop talking about me as if I'm not standing right here?" Luz asked.

They laughed and shook hands. Luz hoped they would be friends. But she had more important things to worry about. "Nick, would you go down and see if Candace is talking? I'm going to run around town. I'll be back in an hour."

"I don't think she'll want to talk…"

"That's okay. I'll stop by, just in case."

Nick walked over to her and gave her a hug and a peck on the cheek. "Okay. See you soon."

She watched him walk down the stairs before turning to

Ben. "Call me if anything unusual comes up."

"Will do, but don't push this." He walked back and told Mac to finish up. "She's gonna need some time."

Luz started down the stairs and turned back. "We don't have time."

MAY 27TH, 2002 2:40 P.M.

Luz went back into her office to type up the Altek report. She reported that the woman wore a brown wig, which indicated she might have been the killer, since synthetic hairs were found in the car. Luz didn't know how that would be proven but it was the first connection they had. Second, she noted that after the auction of the knife that matched the one they had in evidence, the victims were still being cut with the same knife. There was another version of the knife floating around.

She picked up the phone and called everyone on the collector's list, asking them to fax her proof that their knives were still in their possessions. This resulted in a lot of very annoyed knife collectors, but soon her fax machine hummed with activity as they came pouring through.

Then she went online to double check the quality of the knife and printed herself a copy from her color printer. She went downstairs to get a closer look and met Eddie on the way down.

"What's up?" he asked her. He wore plain clothes.

"I'm just on my way to check something. Where are you headed?"

"I just got off. I have some things do to before my date

tonight," he said and wiggled his eyebrows.

"Well, well, well. Rosa finally lowered her standards, huh?"

"Hey," Eddie replied in mock offense.

"I'm kidding, Eddie."

"I know. I heard about Fredrick James. Too bad, huh?"

"Yeah, he was our only real link to anything. Nick's over there now comforting Candace and Chloe. I just hope he pushes Candace to release all her husband's records. They could be the key to a lot of things."

They rode the elevator to the ground floor and got out. Eddie followed her to the evidence locker, still chatting about the case. They stopped at the desk and gave the officer the evidence bag number. He looked it up on the computer and came up empty. Luz looked at Eddie in shock, then back at the officer.

"Excuse me?" she asked, her heart beating wildly.

"I'm sorry, detective. I don't have anything filed under that number."

"Please check again," she said and repeated the number.

The officer looked at her blankly and re-keyed the numbers. He looked up, shaking his head. "Nothing," he said. "How about date? We can look it up by date," he suggested, his hands poised over his keyboard ready to enter the digits.

Luz looked at Eddie who said. "May 16th, the Jamison Murder downtown." They waited as the officer typed in the new information. When he looked up at them, Luz noticed the sweat running down his hairline.

"I-I'm not showing a listing of that item under date or case name or number," he stammered. He flinched when Luz slammed her hand down on his desk. She pushed him out of the way and typed furiously, almost desperately. The system showed no proof that the knife had even been logged. How could that be? Ben told her the knife was found and brought in. Where was it?

"Luz, are you okay?" Eddie asked.

She looked at her clenched fists and then at the officer standing beside her, who himself looked befuddled and a bit wary. She backed away from the computer and took a deep breath.

"What is your name and department code?" she asked the officer and wrote down what he told her. "Now, you listen to me, I want the name and department code or badge number of whoever worked here two days before, on and the week after the sixteenth up to today. Once you get that, I want a list sent directly to me. The item that's missing is very pertinent to the case we're working on."

"The Seattle Slasher case?" he asked.

Luz looked at Eddie and then back at the young officer. "Excuse me?"

"That's what the news is calling the case," he said, a little slower as if he wasn't sure if he'd crossed a line.

Luz shook her head and rubbed her temples. "I can't believe this is happening." She looked at Eddie again. "Tell me this is a dream. Tell me I'm going to wake up in my nice warm bed and this is all a fucking dream."

Eddie smiled slowly. "Hey, I would if I could, but this isn't a dream. It's a fucking nightmare."

CHAPTER TWENTY-TWO

Control is what I seek
My façade makes me weary makes me weak
Soon my resolve will tear, will break
Leaving more bodies in my wake

MAY 27TH, 2002 3:30 P.M.

"What the hell is going on?" Mike roared. "Evidence doesn't just disappear!"

Luz tried to stay calm after her episode downstairs. Eddie had convinced her to relax before she approached Mike with the news. It was a good thing, too, because Mike looked like he was going to have a stroke. "I know, but it was never brought in as evidence in the first place. I'm trying to track down every officer and person at the scene, but I got there so late, the knife was already taken in, at least that's what Ben told me," Luz explained in a tight voice. It was taking a lot of effort to control her anger over this mishap.

"Then talk to Ben. Ask him who had the damn thing and where they were taking it! We cannot afford to lose this!"

Mike roared.

Eddie spoke up. "We know it left the scene and was brought in and photographed. The next step should have been to tag it, bag it and lock it down in evidence. We figured whoever was handling it here in the building would know what happened to it."

"So who would that be?"

Eddie shrugged. "We don't know yet, the report wasn't signed."

"Well, who had access? Who took the photos of it?"

"Mike, we're looking, we should know by the end of the day." Luz explained.

Mike leaned back and sighed. "I can't believe this. We're going to look like idiots! Our only evidence and we lose it? Wait a minute…"

Luz saw a flicker in his eyes. "What is it, Mike?" she asked.

"Davis."

"Who?"

"Last week you told me Davis down in evidence said that knife was worth a lot of money. He said something about his grandfather collecting knives or something like that."

"I remember, but I don't know the guy. His name tag said Officer Davis. Let me call over to human resources." She picked up the phone on Mike's desk. After speaking with HR, she hung up slowly and looked up at them.

"What?" Mike asked when she didn't immediately volunteer information.

"The only Davis who works here is John Davis over in Sex Crimes and he's black. The guy I spoke with downstairs was possibly Caucasian, maybe Hispanic. Shit, Mike, I think we've been scammed."

Mike grunted, picked up the phone and dialed. Luz had only what Mike said to go on, but it was clear how the conversation went on the other end. "Yeah, Sonny?" Mike waited barely a second before speaking again. "Who brought you that knife for examination?" Mike tensed up, closed his eyes and sighed. "Uh-huh. Some guy named Davis from evidence. He took it back when you were done?" Another pause. Mike balled his hand into a fist. "Great." Mike opened his hand and clutched it again. "No, nothing. Don't worry about it, but thanks again. Bye." He hung up and stared at the Luz and Eddie. Without a word he pulled out his pack of Marlboros and lit one. After a few drags he peered through the smoke at Luz.

"Santos, if we don't get this guy, we're all out of a job. We really messed this one up. Go. And don't come back until you've got some good news."

Luz closed the door behind her and slapped her forehead. "I can't believe I forgot about that Davis guy."

"Hey, you've been under a lot of stress. Just try to stay calm and look at this from all angles." Eddie said.

"I'm glad I have you to help me. I have to call Nick and tell him I won't be home again tonight."

"Sorry, Santos, I can't stay. It's my night off and boy, do I need it."

"What? Eddie come on..." Luz groaned.

"No can-do, Luz, I'm taking Rosa up to my cabin tonight and I'll be back tomorrow afternoon. I'm turning my cell phone off at midnight and that's that."

Luz eyed him. "Are you seriously telling me that you are putting off this case, so you can get laid?"

"Let me remind you that I work beat. I volunteered to help out, but I'm not obligated. I'll leave the detecting to you, *detective*." He winked at her.

She sighed and walked away feeling hopeless and Eddie followed her to her office. "Leave me alone. I have *detecting* to do, remember?" she snapped.

"Yeah okay, but don't be mad. When this thing is over, you and Nick can come up and stay at my cabin."

"Great, I'll keep that in mind. Now get out," she said.

Eddie waited around, probably for her to say something else, but left when she read through the reports on her desk without giving him another glance. After he left she picked up the phone and called the James' household to speak with Nick. Chloe picked up.

"Hello," Chloe answered. Her voice was weak. Broken.

"Chloe? This is Detective Santos; can I speak with Mr. Mason, please?"

"One moment." The girl called for Nick. He replied and picked up on the other line.

"Luz this really isn't a good time. The doctor's here and we're trying to get Candace to lie down."

"Call me back soon, Nick. She may know something. We want her consent, but I'll get a warrant if I have to," she said. Nick sighed.

"Luz, now is really not the time," he said, sounding a bit irritated.

"Nick, it may never *be* the time. The woman saw her husband kill himself, but we need to know why. Eventually, she'll need to know why for closure. This case may weigh on that information, so please try and push it."

The other end was silent, then Nick mumbled in agreement.

"Good. Call me back."

"Fine," he said.

Luz hung up. She knew he was mad and protecting his friend. She probably sounded like a cold-hearted bitch, but it was her job and she couldn't afford to lose this case. Too many people counted on her and she didn't plan to let them down.

MAY 27TH, 2002 5:00 P.M.

Cliff Saunders had been up for forty-eight hours straight and thought he was hallucinating when he saw the name on the screen. Five o'clock that morning he had called a friend at work who was known for being a hacker—Marty Benedict—and asked him to come over to help track down the killer's identity.

Marty showed up in khaki shorts and a Hawaiian shirt completing the look with white socks and sandals. Cliff thought he looked way too relaxed for the task at hand, he half expected him to pull a margarita out of his messenger bag. As the day wore on, things got more intense and Marty sat beside him, sweating with his shirt wrinkled and a look of disbelief on his face.

Cliff filled him in on the emails but didn't tell him of the threat to his family. He explained that he wanted to help the

330

police find Elaine's murderer. Marty had asked why the police weren't searching themselves, when they had a lot more computer experts at their disposal, but he didn't question Cliff's explanation, or why he seemed hell-bent on finding it himself.

So they worked through the day, resting only for coffee or snacks but Cliff wouldn't allow himself any sleep before he found what he was looking for. But nearly three days of searching had come to an end. The result was on the screen in black and white, but Cliff couldn't believe it.

"Maybe I did something wrong?" Marty said, looking at him.

"I'm kind of hoping you did. This can't be right, what would a man like that need with a collector's knife?"

"Or why did he buy it from Mrs. Murphy? He has enough money to have a new one made."

Cliff scratched at his two-day beard; this was too much to work out. He needed privacy to plan his next course of action. He got up and paced the room, stopping behind Marty's chair.

"Thanks, Marty, I owe you one."

Marty turned to look at him, mouth agape. "That's it? You're going to sit on this? This is *big*, Cliff. I mean, really big."

"I know. It's just… I may be wrong. Imagine what these kinds of implications could do to that man's career."

Marty shook his head. "It doesn't matter. We have to tell someone."

"Not *we*, Marty, just me. *I* will tell someone. But not yet."

"Man, I wish I had never picked up that phone this morning. I don't feel safe knowing this." He shoved his hands in his pockets and shifted his weight from one leg to the other.

Cliff thought about the note the killer had left him and shuddered. "Marty, you should be safe, as long as you let me handle this from this point on, understand?"

Marty got up and shrugged. "Sure, no problem. Just promise me you'll call the cops soon, okay?"

Cliff clapped a hand on his shoulder. "Okay. Now, I've got a lot to finish up. I'll let you know when this whole thing blows over." He walked his friend out to his Toyota and waved goodbye. Marty backed out of the driveway and rolled down the window.

"Cliff, man, I'm serious; don't wait on this one," he pleaded.

"Don't worry about me. Thanks again, Marty," Cliff replied.

Marty gave him a disapproving look but put the car in drive and took off down the street. Cliff watched him disappear around the corner and quickly scanned the block for anything unusual; unmarked cars, strange people who could be watching him. But all he saw was the neighbor mowing his lawn and children running in the sprinkler across the street. He breathed a sigh of relief, but his heart pounded furiously.

Turning around, he heard the phone ring inside the house. He walked through the foyer to the kitchen to answer it.

"Hello?"

Silence. He said hello again, but no one replied. He was about to hang up when he heard breathing on the other end.

"I can hear you breathing, who *is* this?" he asked.

The breathing stopped, and a voice came on the line. "You were warned, and you broke the rules," the raspy voice said. "Marty will die because of you." The line went dead.

Cliff clutched the phone and began to shake. He had been so careful and now his friend's life was at stake. Without thinking he grabbed his car keys and hopped in his Volvo, taking off in the same direction he'd seen Marty go. But his friend's Rav4 was nowhere to be found, so he drove to Marty's house and waited for him to come home.

After an hour of waiting he feared that Elizabeth would be home with the kids soon and they would be unprotected at his house. There was no doubt in his mind that the killer knew where he was and what he was doing. His fear for his family overrode the fear for his friend. He turned around and went home.

• • •

Marty was involved; he was always involved; he hated that. He wished he'd slept over at Nina's house the night before. Then he wouldn't have been home when Cliff called so early in the morning.

But it was too late. He knew what he knew, and he couldn't do a thing about it. Could he? Cliff told him not to tell a soul what they learned that day. Cliff trusted Marty to keep his mouth shut, and he would. Not many people trusted him, but Cliff was different; even though he knew what Marty did outside of work, he never let it affect their friendship.

Cliff had been a good guy from the start; he always respected the opinions of those around him and appreciated the help he got from his coworkers. Though Marty was twelve years his junior, Cliff always treated him as a peer, and Marty appreciated that.

It had taken him three years to get out of the hacking business. It all started as a hobby late one night and he was surprised how good he became at it. One day, he got too good, and somebody noticed. Instead of getting him in trouble, that person asked Marty for his services. After that, Marty had many people calling him to hack into files and networks he'd never heard of. Soon he was working with two other guys and they started a small business that made a large amount of money. The only problem was that it was made illegally.

Clients ranged from suspicious husbands or wives wanting a peek at their spouse's private filings and financial records to money hungry business owners wanting one up on the competition. Whoever his clients were, they weren't good people, but their money was good and back then, that was all that mattered to Marty.

As time went by, the money became less important; during one of his earlier jobs he had hacked into the police department's mainframe for a rogue cop and found out that someone was tracking his every move. He immediately ended the job, returned the cop his money and got rid of his equipment. He laid low for a while, expecting the FBI to pound down his door any minute, but they never came. Eventually, he picked up where he'd left off and was fine until he encountered the tracking system again, but this time it wouldn't let him out of the system. It froze his computer and tracked him down frame by frame. He panicked again and barely got out before their search was complete. Again, he threw away everything he had just replaced, down to the last disk, thousands of dollars' worth of equipment, destroyed to protect himself.

It all paid off when the police stopped by to search his house. Supposedly the FBI had narrowed the activity down to a small area in which the hacker could have lived, including Marty's house and a four-block radius. It was all too close for comfort and Marty was sweating profusely long after the cops had come and gone.

After that day, he never thought he'd turn on another computer, never mind becoming a network manager at a software company. But he'd used his skills to get a legitimate job, and though there were those at work who suspected he might have been a hacker, the subject was never brought up. He still did small jobs once in a while but if he got so much as a whiff of trouble he backed off.

That day had been different. Instead of backing off, he dove in head first and was right back where he started. He was in his car stopped at a red light when he noticed the police station across the street. He stared so long he didn't notice the light turn green until the person behind him laid on the horn.

He drove around the block a couple of times, mulling over whether to stop. After the fifth time around the block, he was a little dizzy. He decided to sleep on the decision and call Cliff in the morning. He checked his watch, six-fifteen. Nina would be off work soon. He decided to go home and wash up to surprise her with a night out. As he pulled into his driveway, he could have sworn he saw Cliff's car driving down the road.

He shrugged it off and went inside.

• • •

Cliff hung up the phone. He had called Marty's house repeatedly, but no one picked up the line. He wasn't sure if Marty had gotten home or not and he was sick with worry. Elizabeth arrived home soon after him and could tell something was wrong, but he put her off and continued dialing his friend's phone number. This time he left a message.

"Marty, if you get this message, don't waste time calling me back, just come right over, right away. You could be in danger; the killer knows you helped me; he threatened my family if I told anyone and now he knows you're involved. Please come over right away. Do not, I repeated, *do not* call the cops. he'll kill my family. I have to go. Bye."

He hung up and waited with baited breath, what would he do if something happened to Marty? How could he forgive himself? Silently, he cursed Elaine Murphy for dragging him into this nightmare, then scolded himself for dishonoring her memory. She was just a nice old woman who didn't know what she was getting herself into. And he was the one who convinced her to sell the knives.

"Oh god," he moaned dropping his head into his hands. It *was* his fault. It was all his fault and he hid out while the killer kept on killing. But his family; he couldn't risk losing his family. He tossed around that thought for a while until an idea came to him. He went to the kitchen where his wife was preparing dinner, walked up behind her and kissed her neck. She relaxed against him. "Well, that was unexpected."

He frowned. Had he been too busy to kiss his wife? He slid his arms around her waist and held her close. "I'm sorry, Lizzie. I know I've been busy, but I'm just about done now. I'll have a lot more time to spend with you and the kids. Forgive me?"

She turned from the stove and looked him in the eye. "Only if you promise to never take on that much work again. I never want to feel neglected like that, and I don't think the children liked it either."

"I promise," he said holding up his fingers in a boy scout salute. She laughed and hugged him close. He buried his face in her hair, breathing in the familiar smell of her lavender shampoo.

"Now get out of the kitchen until dinner is ready," she said with mock severity, pointing the wooden spoon in her hand at his chest.

"Okay," he said and kissed her again. On his way out of the kitchen he spotted her cell phone on the charger and unplugged it. Once he was out of the kitchen, he went into the garage and dialed 911. The operator came on and he covered his mouth with his hand, disguising his voice.

"I think someone is in danger at 13452 Park Lane. Please hurry. He might be dead."

The voice cracked on the other end. "Sir, where are you?"

"Please help him. He's my friend," Cliff said and hung up. Breathing easier, he hoped he had done the right thing. He went back inside and did something he hadn't done in days— he played with his kids.

• • •

Marty showered and put on the cologne Nina bought him. He wasn't particularly fond of the smell, but it drove Nina wild, so he didn't mind smelling a little off once in a while. Besides tonight was her night—he would make it her night. He needed to keep his mind off the name he saw on Cliff's computer screen.

He checked his wallet for cash and went to grab his car keys when the phone rang.

"Hello?" he answered.

"Mr. Benedict, this is the Carnation Police Department. Is everything all right?"

Marty was confused. He hadn't called the police. "Yeah, I'm fine. What's going on?"

"We got an anonymous call about a disturbance at your residence. Are you sure you're okay?"

"I'm fine. I don't know who made the call, but I'm okay." He verified his information until the officer was satisfied it was him.

"Okay. I'm sorry to disturb you. Have a nice night," the operator said, then ended the call.

Baffled, Marty hung up the phone and noticed the blinking red light on his machine. He had two messages. He reached over and pushed play and his blood ran cold as he heard Cliff's scared voice rambling about the killer. When the message finished, he picked the phone right back up and dialed; he got Cliff on the second ring.

"Jesus Christ, man, your message scared the shit out of me! What the hell is going on?" he demanded.

"Marty, thank God you got my message. I even called the cops to come check on you. Are you okay?"

"I'm talking to you, aren't I? So it was you who called the cops. Boy you panicked," he replied.

"This is serious. Marty," Cliff said. He relayed the events of the past few days including the note he found on his daughter the morning of Elaine's murder. When he finished, Marty stood weak-kneed and worried. He wished he'd never met Cliff Saunders.

"Marty, you there?" Cliff asked guardedly.

Marty wiped the sweat from his forehead and took a deep breath. "Yeah, I'm here; barely. Cliff, I'm coming over right now and—" a sound behind him startled Marty, and he jerked around sharply, his breath catching in his throat.

"Hello? Marty? Say something dammit!" Cliff yelled on the other line.

The silence was long as Marty collected his wits. "I'm here, man. Biff, my dog just made me shit my pants. Fucking dog." At the mention of his name the golden retriever's tail wagged and he licked his owners shaking hand.

"I thought… well, you know what I thought. Get over here and we'll discuss this."

"Fine, just let me call Nina and cancel our plans, she's going to be pissed. I promised her a night out tonight."

"Marty, that should be the least of your worries," Cliff scolded.

"I know. I'll see you in about fifteen, okay, man?"

"Yeah, and Marty… hurry."

Marty hung up but the urgency in Cliff's voice left a nasty residue in his mind. He called Ixtapa, the Mexican restaurant where Nina worked as a bartender, and told her he would be running a little late. After all, how long would it take to convince Cliff to call the police? Marty and Nina agreed to meet at her place around nine-thirty and said goodbye. He locked up the house and left; he never heard the second message on his machine.

CHAPTER TWENTY-THREE

Chaos all around and nothing I can do
I must see this all the way through
The demons inside are tearing me apart
I fear that blackness coats my heart

MAY 27TH, 2002 6:00 P.M.

Candace James opened her eyes and stared at the textured ceiling above her bed. What was she doing in bed, she wondered. Then everything came back to her in a painful, world-crushing rush. She gasped and began to tremble.

"It's okay," came a voice from beside her, and she felt a hand on her leg. She lifted her head and saw Nick sitting in a chair beside her bed, a worried expression on his face. His presence alone seemed to ease her mind.

"Nick, it's so good to see you after all these years. You look... good," she said softly, trying hard to keep the memory of the night before under the surface.

He stood and placed his hand on her shoulder. "Thank you, Candy, but let's catch up later. You need to rest."

It was true. She could still feel the effects of the sedative the doctor had given her earlier, but she needed to talk. She didn't know how long Nick would be around and she needed to apologize for her husband's actions while she could.

"Nick," she began, unsure where to start. "Fred took... and I'm sorry... never should have touched the money... and Leah."

"Shh. Later, Candace. It can wait," Nick said.

"No. It can't. My husband is dead, and it can't wait!" she shouted shaking her head and pulling herself up into a sitting position. "Please listen to me, Nick, I'm apologizing for my husband—for his greed, for what he's done to you, what he's done to us..." she trailed off, her eyes filling with tears. Nick walked to her nightstand where the doctor had left a bottle of sedatives. Candace held up her hand.

"Nick, wait, please don't. I don't want to black out again." She'd taken two the night before and barely recalled any of it except the parts no drug was strong enough to erase.

"Candy, you won't black out. The doctor says these will help you calm down and sleep," he said, unscrewing the bottle and shaking a pill out into his hand. He took the pill to her and handed her a glass of water, but she kept her hands up in protest.

"I don't need one of those horrible pills; they make me queasy. I'll be fine, Nick." But when Nick shook his head her voice took on a desperate tone. "No! You don't understand. When I sleep, when I close my eyes... the only thing I see is... is Fredrick in his office at his desk with his gun... blowing his brains..." she shuddered and wailed uncontrollably.

Nick barely caught her when she collapsed off the bed. He held her tight as she released the pain all over again. She knew this wouldn't be the last time she broke down. The doctor said it would be a while before she would begin to cope with the situation, assuming of course that she would cope with it at all.

Nick held her trembling body and she prayed she would find the strength to get through this, not only for her own sake but for her daughter's. Nick convinced her to take a pill and rest and she didn't argue. Instead, she thought of the escape the pill would provide and greedily washed it down with water. Soon the edges of her vision blurred, and she sank back into blissful nothingness.

• • •

Chloe was holding up surprisingly well compared to her mother, but she wasn't present when her father ended his life. Nick went downstairs and peeked into the living room to check on her. She was still on the couch, staring out the huge bay window that displayed a beautiful view of Lake Washington. From where he stood, he could see sailboats floating across the lake in the distance. The sun was setting, and the sky had turned from blue to a deep red, creating a breathtaking view.

But that beauty was lost on Chloe. She sat stiffly on the sofa, her eyes swollen and tears running down her face. Even though she had aged seven years since the last time he'd seen her she still looked like a little girl. A frightened child. He took a seat beside her, hoping to offer some comfort, but Chloe didn't so much as blink when he put his hand on her shoulder. She kept her gaze straight and continued crying silently.

"Chloe," he said her name softly and she came out of her daze at the sound of his voice. She turned toward him, but her eyes still held that faraway look. He wasn't sure if she was in shock or if she was too exhausted to answer. "Chloe, your mother is doing better," he lied but he was at a loss. "She's sleeping upstairs, and I was wondering if you wanted to lie down for a bit."

She was silent for a few moments before she shook her head. The motion was slow at first but soon she was thrashing her head back and forth so rapidly he feared her neck would snap.

"Chloe, stop it," he said gently and placed his hands on the sides of her head to stop the thrashing, but she fought him. "Stop it!" he demanded and held on to her tightly. Then, like her mother, she wailed loudly and began to sputter.

"M-My father is… d-d-dead, he sh-shot himself, m-my father is dead h-he shot h-himself, my father i-is d-dead he shot hims-self…"

She repeated the phrase as if she were trying to convince herself it was true. Nick stared at her until he could take no more. He took her into his arms and began rocking. "Shh… Chloe, it's okay, honey, shh…." He tried to quiet her down. Her body relaxed in his arms and she ceased chanting the disturbing mantra and clung to him, sobbing uncontrollably.

When she finally fell asleep he laid her down on the couch and covered her with the throw from the recliner across the room. He was surprised at the softness of the blanket and checked the tag to see if it was cashmere. He was taken aback when the tag read one-hundred percent Pashmina. Throws like the one he held ran for three-hundred dollars or more in boutiques across the country. For the first time since his arrival he noticed how richly furnished the space was.

He walked through the house, stopping to look in the bedrooms and admire the décor. He was impressed by the interior design of the home as well as the taste in art that hung on the walls. He stopped to examine the study where Fredrick had committed suicide and was equally impressed at the furnishings in the room.

The huge desk set in the center of the office was mahogany and matched the bookcases and credenza that lined the walls. There were Remington lamps and framed paintings around the room that gave it a cozy feel. He walked closer to the desk and saw a cedar cigar box sitting on the edge of the desk. He opened it and found a half dozen Cubans inside. To be sure of their authenticity he took one out, held it under his nose and inhaled deeply. He smiled; it had been a long time since he'd smelled a cigar like that one. But what was Fredrick doing with them?

When Nick had worked for Knotts, Cane & Associates before his move to the DA's office he had been successful and could afford luxuries like cigars and well-furnished homes, as well as boats, cars and trips to Cancun but Fredrick's salary was miniscule in comparison. After working there for a year, Fredrick couldn't afford a new car. Nick knew this because he'd offered to cosign when Candace mentioned it. So why did they now have this beautiful house with a view? Why was Chloe's tuition of the University paid in full? And why were there three new cars and a boat in the garage? Did working for Yates pay that well?

He spotted a photograph on the credenza behind the desk and almost answered his own question. He picked up the picture of Fredrick and the mayor shaking hands. The sight of Anthony Yates made him sick to his stomach, but he went on staring. He couldn't comprehend why Fred decided to work for Yates after the bastard was accused of killing Leah. Luz said he had looked out of place in the mayor's office. She said his office had been lavishly furnished as well and also included a waterfront view. How did a man go from barely making ends meet to living as large as this?

Nick almost sat down in the chair but thought better of it, remembering that a dead man occupied it less than twelve hours before; instead he sat on the couch by the window. He thought back to Candy's apology about Leah and let the thought drift around his mind for a while. Then something occurred to him and he jumped up from where he was lounging and went to the desk.

MAY 27TH, 2002 6:50 P.M.

Mike's office was filled with smoke, but Luz wasn't about to comment on it. It was an old building and the alarms on this floor never seemed to work. He was in one of his moods, and

346

lack of sleep and pressure from the city weren't helping.

"Mike, I don't want to push too far. She could snap completely, burn the files and we'd never know a thing."

"She better not, unless she wants to sit in jail for obstruction."

Luz gave him a wry look. "You're going to put a woman who just saw her husband kill himself in jail?"

Mike took a long drag on his cigarette and exhaled. "Well, shit, Santos what the hell should I do? Everyone is on my ass to solve this thing. We can't keep this from the FBI any longer; they'll have my ass if I don't cooperate."

Luz looked at her watch. "I'm going to head over there now to talk to Nick. Give me until tomorrow to get ahold of any other records and files. I called Candace's doctor and he thought it would be better to give this at least twenty-four hours."

Mike looked thoughtful for a moment then snubbed his cigarette out on the paperweight that sat on his desk. "Fine. I'll tell Agent Adams in the morning that, as far as they know, Fredrick James's suicide has nothing to do with this case but it's only a matter of time before they figure it out," he said and lit another cigarette.

"Mike, you should really cut down on the smoking." Luz suggested, waving her hand at all the smoke that accumulated around her.

"And you should cut down on the nagging. Enough with the bullshit. Just go."

Luz turned and left the smoke-filled office.

MAY 27TH, 2002 7:45 P.M.

Candace James woke up crying. She didn't wait for the memories to flood back. She sat up in bed and wiped her eyes. She listened to the silence of the house, wishing she wasn't alone. Slowly she went to the bathroom to wash her face, but when she saw her husband's robe on the door she decided she would avoid anything that reminded her of him. But that would be difficult, considering all the time they spent in the house. There was so much of him left that she didn't know how she would survive the challenge. Maybe it was time to move away, start a new life. With Chloe in school, those things would have to wait.

She opened the door to her bedroom and saw the light on in the office down the hall. As she neared the room she heard a man's voice. For a moment, she hoped with every fiber of her body that her husband's suicide had all been a bad dream. But when she rounded the doorframe, she stopped short when she saw Nick sitting at the desk instead of Fredrick.

Nick saw her and stood up. "Candy, I'm so sorry, after what's happened I'm sure it's hard for you to see this room," he said, walking to where she was leaning on the wall.

"For a moment I thought... I thought maybe Fred..."

She didn't have to continue; Nick put his arm around her. "It's okay Candy, I shouldn't even be in here. I'm sorry if I've disturbed anything."

Candace looked around the room and shook her head. "No, it's okay. You of all people should know what happened."

Nick cocked his head to the side. "I don't understand." But Candace wasn't able to finish the explanation she started. She simply stared at numerous things in the room as her eyes quickly filled with tears. Nick grabbed her shoulder and guided her out of the room. She didn't resist until they came to the door of her room.

"Where's Chloe?" she asked in a soft voice.

"She's downstairs. Do you want to see her?"

"Yes."

He helped her down the stairs and into the living room where Chloe slept peacefully on the couch. Candace walked over to the sofa and looked at Chloe. She reached down and touched her daughter's face.

"She shouldn't have to go through this; she was doing so well. This trauma might stunt her emotionally and academically."

"Candy, it will take her time to grieve and deal with all of this, but she'll be fine. You will both be fine."

"I know. But I don't know if I'm strong enough," she said, her voice trembling.

"You are, and so is your daughter," he assured her.

Candace didn't respond she just lay down next to her daughter on the couch and caressed her face.

"I'm going to be upstairs," Nick stated softly. It was the last thing she heard before she fell asleep.

MAY 27TH, 2002 8:06 P.M.

Luz knocked on the door, but nobody answered. She knocked a few more times then tried the handle; it was locked. She pulled out her cell phone and dialed the James's number; she could hear the ringing through the door. A groggy voice came on the line.

"Hello?"

"Chloe, it's Detective Santos. I'm at the front door. Can you let me in?" She heard shuffling around and the deadbolt pull back before the door opened. She hung up her phone and stepped inside.

"Where's Nick?" she asked looking around.

"I don't know. You can ask my mother though. She's in the living room," Chloe said shutting the door and beckoning Luz to the room on the left. Candace sat on the edge of the couch, looking as if she had just woken up.

"Hello, Candace, how are you holding up?" Luz asked.

The woman turned to her with a haunted expression and instead of speaking, she shook her head.

"Is Nick here?" Luz pushed.

"He was upstairs last I knew."

"Can I go see him?"

"Sure," she answered curtly.

Luz checked all the rooms on the second floor but didn't find Nick. She returned downstairs to the living room and found the mother and daughter embracing and sobbing on the couch together. She didn't want to interrupt them but before she could step aside, Candace caught her eye.

"He's not upstairs. I looked in every room," Luz said.

Without letting go of her daughter, Candace shrugged and looked out the window. "Then I'm not sure where he went.

He mentioned something about getting food earlier so maybe he went out," she said, rocking with her daughter in her arms. Luz felt that it wasn't the time to push for the information she needed. Seeing two people in so much pain—there was no way she would interfere. The FBI would have to seize the records in the morning. Mike would be pissed but Luz couldn't add to the stress and sadness the family was going through. She would, for the first time in her career, back down.

"If he returns, can you tell him to call me?" Luz asked tentatively, and Candace nodded in response.

Luz decided to drive around for a while and figure things out but after a half hour she realized she was more tired than she thought, so she drove home hoping that Nick would be waiting for her. When she opened her door, Cheech was the only one who greeted her. She called Nick's phone and left a message, letting him know where she was and to get in touch with her. After taking her dog out for his nightly ritual and a brief belly rubbing session, she settled down and went to sleep.

MAY 27TH, 2002 11:00 P.M.

I can't control this urge any longer; the marks on my skin are physical evidence of that fact. It has only been an hour since my last kill and yet I feel the need once again. Killing has become necessary for my survival, like an addiction that cannot be broken. I can no longer go out in public without feeling the need to take a life.

I should stay home, but that's next to impossible. I have

obligations to keep with the public; it's part of my job. I've worked my whole life to get where I am today. I've pulled myself up from who I once was, and remade myself into an intelligent, valuable person. Now I'm surrounded with everything I ever wanted yet faced with the possibility that I'll lose it all.

That will not happen, I will not let it happen. There are ways I can finish this thing. I need to find the person who started this madness in my mind; I need to find Nicholas Mason.

• • •

Marty and Cliff had been arguing for hours about the police. Marty wanted it all to be over but Cliff's fear for his family had him thinking irrationally.

"Cliff, for the last time, if you do not call the police then I will."

"You don't understand. The killer knows my every move. If I even attempt it, he will kill us all. Don't you get it?"

"Get Lizzy and the kids somewhere safe and Nina and I will hide out. Then you can call the police. How does that sound? Because I'm not going to sit here and argue with you anymore. This is it, Cliff, either you agree to do that, or I'll call the police." Marty stood his ground. The whole thing had gone on long enough and wasting time talking about it wasn't worthwhile.

Cliff was silent for a moment, then said, "If you call the police now, we could all be in danger but if you called it in later after we find a safe place the police could start investigating the lead. I don't want to be away from my family, but I don't want to be selfish; it could cost us our lives. So, fine. Go get Nina and we'll decide where we can lay low until this thing blows over. Meet me back here in forty-five minutes. I'll have everyone ready to go."

Marty was stunned that his ultimatum had worked. It had been over three hours since they started talking, and he didn't think Cliff would fold. But he was glad the man was finally thinking rationally.

"Okay. Nina won't believe all this, but she'll come along. I don't want her in danger. See you in forty-five," he said, grabbing his coat and racing out the door. He hopped in his Toyota and took off for the west side of town, wondering how in the world he was going to explain everything to Nina. He had a tough time canceling his plans with her earlier, but she understood and agreed to see him later at her house.

Marty drove up the hill she lived on and parked the car at the curb. He got out and ran to the front door, hoping to catch her still awake. But when he saw the bent doorframe, his blood ran cold, and he was unable to catch his breath. He burst into the house, screaming her name but there was no answer. He ran upstairs and found both her bedroom and the guest room untouched. Sweating and panting, he ran downstairs to the dark kitchen. Two steps into the room at full speed, he tripped over something big and landed on his face. He instantly felt his cheek swell and started to get up. There was little light to see with, but Marty had already guessed the cause of his fall. He squeezed his eyes shut to hold back the flood of tears that threatened to burst free. Then he felt around with his hands until they found a handful of the soft, silky substance that was Nina's hair.

It was then that he cried. The tears came fast, warm, and uninhibited. But the grief soon turned to anger, and Marty got up and felt his way across the room to the phone. He picked it up, dialed three digits, and waited for help.

CHAPTER TWENTY-FOUR

I've made a decision and it's not too late
To find and kill the one I hate
I can be free to live again
And this cursed nightmare will come to an end.

MAY 28TH, 2002 1:30 A.M.

Luz was already awake when the phone rang beside her bed.

"Santo. Speak," she said into the phone.

"This is Agent Adams. We have a situation here, and we can't get answers until this man talks directly to you."

The agent's derogatory tone irritated Luz and she snapped back. "Well then let me talk to him."

She heard Adams call the man over and tell him that she was on the line.

"Hello? Detective Santos?" asked a shaky voice that was vaguely familiar to her.

"Yes, this is she. Who is this?"

"This is Cliff Saunders. I don't know if you remember me, but I'm the man who helped Elaine Murphy sell her knife collection."

Luz placed the voice with the face and moved on. "Okay, I remember you. But what is it you need from me?"

"I'm so scared. My family is in danger. The killer told me that if I helped the police find out his identity, he would hurt my family. But I kept researching even though I wasn't sure how I would get the information to you once I had it. Well a friend helped me and now his girlfriend was murdered—"

"Murdered?" she jolted upright and swung her legs over the side of the bed.

"Yes, and he called the cops and sent them over here. If the killer finds out, we'll all be dead."

"Just tell me who the killer is, and we won't let that happen, sir."

"No."

"What do you mean 'no'? We could end this nightmare now if you would only tell us what you know."

"I'm not sure my information is correct. But before I say a word, I want my family relocated quickly to a safe place."

"I'll take care of it. Put Agent Adams back on the phone." Luz got up and put on a robe. It was hard to be authoritative wearing her worn-out academy t-shirt.

"Yes," Adams barked into her ear.

"What the hell are you doing there?" she demanded. "This is my investigation."

"Not anymore, detective. I have orders from the top that if one more body is tied to this investigation—we step in. And guess what? We found a body, so you can either back out gracefully or fully cooperate. And I do mean fully."

"Now you listen here—" she began but he interrupted.

"No, *you* listen, Santos. We've stood by and watched this maniac hack up people all over town and we're not about to let it continue. This is my investigation now, got it?"

"Then you can deal with Mr. Saunders, good luck," Luz said, then hung up. She was fuming. It was the first time she'd lost control of an investigation. The fact that she has lost it to the FBI was what bothered her most. How had she let this happen? Why on earth hadn't she found the killer yet? There were clues everywhere. What were they missing?

She opted to continue working the case from her office. After a quick shower and a cup of coffee, she grabbed Cheech and headed out. Instead of taking her car she decided she would jog to work. She could feel the tension in her shoulders and hoped the jog would loosen her up and give her some time to blow off steam. She threw her holster on under her windbreaker and clipped Cheech to a leash. After locking up the boat she took off running.

She had five messages from Agent Adams when she got in the office. She chose to ignore them out of spite. But after fifteen minutes of trying to work on the case she gave in and called him back.

"What do you want?" she asked, disposing of formalities.

"Mr. Saunders refuses to cooperate with me. Would you please speak with him?" he asked sounding a bit embarrassed and quite irritated.

"Why? Just give him what he wants."

"What he wants right now is to talk to you."

"Fine. Put him on." She waited a moment and then spoke to Cliff. "Mr. Saunders, why won't you cooperate with the FBI? You could get into a lot of trouble if you don't."

"I can't trust anyone, but I can trust you. Please help me." He sounded desperate.

"What do you want me to do?" she asked.

"Move my family to an undisclosed location and I'll give you the name of who I think might be the killer."

"*Might?* I need to know for sure." Luz didn't want to risk accusing the wrong person.

"It's the best I can do. But my friend, who helped track the email is a professional. He never makes mistakes."

That was enough for Luz. "Okay, I'll be there soon, just sit tight." She hung up walked across the larger office to talk to Mike. She was surprised to see the light on in his office and knocked softly on the door.

"Come in," he replied. She stepped into the office and closed the door behind her. But before she could speak he held up a hand to silence her.

"There's nothing I could do about the FBI guys taking over so don't bust my balls okay?"

"That's not why I'm here. It's about the Saunders thing."

"You mean that guy in Carnation? The one who's driving Agent Adams crazy with demands? He sounds a little off center if you ask me."

"If there's truth to what he's saying, he has reason to be. That psycho threatened his family and someone he knew was murdered last night. I believe he can help us on this. What

I need from you is authorization to use our safehouse in Redmond. He won't speak unless he and his family are safe."

Mike sighed, and Luz noticed the bags under his eyes and the drawn look of his face. She admired his dedication to the case, but it was killing him.

"You got it. I'll make some calls and get back to you. About the Fredrick James situation, did you get authorization?"

"Nick is working on it as we speak," she lied.

"Good. So far the FBI hasn't tied him in. Keep pushing, okay?"

"Will do, but I need to drive out to Carnation and I need a squad car."

"Why? Your Eclipse could get there a lot faster."

"I know, but I jogged in and my Eclipse is at home."

Mike appeared incredulous. "You what? There's a killer wandering the streets of Seattle, looking for either his next victim or for you, and you decide to take a nice jog to work?"

Luz realized his reaction stemmed from his concern for her, so she let it go instead of pressing the matter. "Let him or her come after me. I'm ready for this to end."

Mike sighed again. "It's not up to you to play bait, Dirty Harriet. Be more careful. That's an order. I'll call downstairs to get the list of open cars available." He picked up the phone and talked to someone in the garage. When he hung up he looked at her and shook his head. "They've got one gassed up for you. Be careful, Santos."

She smiled and opened the door to leave. "I'll call you soon, but until then, Mike, get some rest. You look like shit."

He grunted and gave her the finger.

• • •

She pulled into the Saunders's driveway a half-hour later and found two FBI agents waiting for her on the porch. She would've gotten there sooner but had to drop Cheech back off at her brother's place, much to the delight of the children. That dog was so spoiled.

"It's about time," one of them said. Luz ignored the comment and went inside. Cliff sat in the kitchen with the local sheriff and Agent Adams. He looked up when she entered the room. He stood and walked over to her. There was prominent relief in his eyes.

"Detective, thank you for coming. Is everything in order?" Cliff asked her.

"Yes, but I need a word with Agent Adams before we leave."

"I don't want anyone to know where we are going. Please… it's important."

"Don't worry. I won't say a word. I have other things to discuss with him."

Cliff nodded and joined his obviously shaken family in the living room. Luz turned back to Blue and smirked.

"Needed my help after all, didn't you? I told you, this is my case, and it will stay that way. I don't care what you or your superiors think of that. I'm moving this man and his family to a safehouse, and when I get a name, I'll contact you. Then you will work with me. Not the other way around. We want this bastard as much as you do, understand?"

He looked at her for a moment, then flashed a cold smile.

"Whatever is in the best interest of the case," he said.

His voice was strained but Luz was happy he complied. She nodded and went into the living room. Cliff's daughter cried uncontrollably, and he and his wife were trying to get her to calm down.

"Is everything all right?" Luz asked, feeling out of place.

Mrs. Saunders looked up at her. "No, everything is not all right. We're being forced out of our home because you guys can't catch this maniac."

"Lizzie, calm down, you'll just frighten Lisa even more," Cliff scolded, then led them to the front porch.

"Wait. I'll drive the cruiser into the garage—that way you aren't so exposed," Luz said hurrying down the steps. After packing them into the car they hit the road. The ride was silent except for the few whimpers from the small girl, but Luz was anxious to get them to a safe place, so Cliff would give her the information she needed. She kept checking her rear-view mirror to make sure they weren't being followed.

They pulled into a residential area about three o'clock and Luz had to check the address to make sure she had the right street. After several turns they came upon a salmon-colored house with white trim. Luz pulled up and opened the door, beckoning them to follow. They reached the door and she unlocked it.

"Mommy, this house is perfect for a princess," Lisa said. "It's even pink, like my room."

Elizabeth smiled weakly at her daughter and inspected the interior of the house. "How long do we have to stay here?" she asked, observing the décor and lack of furniture.

"Hopefully not too long," Luz said, smiling at Cliff, hoping he would take a hint that she needed his information on the killer.

"Where are the bedrooms?" he asked, and Luz told him. "Good. Now you guys unpack while I thank Detective Santos for keeping us safe," Cliff said. Luz followed him into the kitchen and he held a disk labeled *Elaine*.

"Everything you need is on this disk. The name, how we got the name, and all the information from the emails I received from Elaine's knife website."

"With all due respect, Mr. Saunders, can't you just tell me?"

He looked around the room as if he were searching for surveillance equipment of some kind. "Just look at the disk. I don't want to risk anything."

"This place is not bugged Cliff," she stated, running out of patience. But he wasn't going to be convinced.

"Just please, look at the disk," he urged again.

Luz sighed heavily and nodded. "Fine. This is the only copy, right?"

"Yes, and I've carried it with me since I made it. No one else has had access to it and I smashed up my hard drive, so I wouldn't be responsible for any info leaking out."

"Good man. Okay, I'll view the disk and be in touch. You and your family can get some rest. The fridge is stocked and the cupboards as well. I'll call you if I have questions."

"Thank you for all your help."

"One more thing—your friend, the one who found his girl-friend dead. Didn't he want protection? He's still in danger."

Cliff swallowed hard and tears filled his eyes. "The agent at the house didn't tell you?"

"Tell me what?" she asked.

"After Marty found the body, the killer found him."

• • •

After leaving the house Luz called Agent Adams for an update on the murders. So far, they had cleaned up the scene and found no new evidence. They would continue working the case. Frustrated, she hung up and headed back to the office.

As she drove, she thought about Nick and why he hadn't come back to her place the night before. The last time they talked she'd been a little cold but that had nothing to do with him and everything to do with her job and she hoped he understood that. It had been admirable of him to go comfort the family of the man who stole from him and his dead wife. But Luz couldn't help missing him when he wasn't with her. She was better off, she reasoned, she had a case to solve. Even so, she pulled her phone out and dialed her home number to see if he was there.

Instead of ringing, there was a strange buzz on the other end, and a recorded voice told her the line was temporarily out of order. She dialed again, waited, and got the same response. Puzzled, she decided to check home before returning to the office. It was only three thirty; it wasn't likely Mike was expecting her back so soon.

She drove through Redmond and hopped on State Route

520 back to Seattle. She took the familiar route home and was about a block from the marina when she smelled the smoke.

She rounded the corner and saw the devastation of her home. She screamed and pressed on the gas, driving up to the docks with the cruiser lights on. She hopped out and started rushing down the dock, but was held back by a steady arm.

"Luz! Thank god you're alive!"

She tore her eyes from the wreckage at the sound of Ben's voice. "Ben, what happened? My boat, it's gone." Shock rippled through her, quickly followed by fury.

Ben was astonished. "Who cares about the boat? For the last twenty minutes I thought you were *in* that boat. Litebrite, I thought you were dead."

Luz looked at him, noticing the tears on his face and her expression softened at the concern she heard in his voice. "Oh, Ben," she said and hugged him tightly. "That was my home," she said sadly. Then a thought occurred, and her stomach sank. "Shit, Ben. What about Nick?"

Ben released her and looked toward the end of the dock where her houseboat was burning itself out. He ran down to the team of firemen who fought to control the blaze and talked with them. Then he ran back looking optimistic.

"They have a team of divers on the way. They were supposed to be looking for your body, but I told them about Nick. Once they get the fire out, the divers will go in."

Luz exhaled. "Tell them to hurry. Call me as soon as you know."

Ben seemed shocked. "Where are you going?"

"I have to talk to Mike. Call me, okay?" she said and hopped back into the cruiser and took off. What she had to say to Mike could wait but there was no way she could handle it if they pulled Nick's body from the bay right in front of her. She tasted bile in the back of her throat when she thought of Nick, dead. She drove the rest of the way to work trying to think of anything else.

MAY 28TH, 2002 6:00 A.M.

Anthony Yates watched the morning news and nearly choked on his toast when Emily Watkins of Channel Four reported that two more people had been murdered in connection with the Seattle Slasher case. He listened intently for any leads the police had, then checked the other channels for any clues about the investigation.

Yates was tired of Seattle. It rained all the time and the problems of the city only grew worse every year. He hoped that one day he would be governor or better yet, perhaps work with the president. He prided himself on his expertise and political standings, but this case could make or break him. As mayor, he strove to make Seattle the ideal place to live by ridding it of traffic issues, social problems and financial debt. Along the way his accomplishments had been added to his already long list of achievements but catching a serial killer would push him up considerably.

He finished his breakfast and went upstairs. His wife was sleeping soundly in bed, her lovely blond hair fanned out across her pillow. She was still as beautiful as the day they'd met, and he wondered why that wasn't enough anymore.

She was so hard on him sometimes and he couldn't figure out why. She was usually such a warm, giving person. She alone had led the city in a petition to make the schools a safer place for kids and provided them with better means to become educated. The response had been overwhelming. The city council had agreed to the new security measures, computers and books the schools received. She had always had a drive for obtaining justice that he found a little annoying at times, but that was because in his line of work, morals were the last thing considered.

When he met her, they had fallen in love quickly and she supported his every decision. While his popularity grew, he lavished her with attention and expensive gifts. At first, she refused them, telling him she didn't deserve material things as a token of affection, but as time went on, she accepted them freely, and after more time, almost greedily. She had blossomed into a woman of stature, surrounding herself with precious things. At first, he was happy that she had become so comfortable with sharing his wealth, but as he watched her collection grow he noticed an almost obsessive quality to her collecting. She went from being grateful and modest to flaunting herself and her possessions. But she always seemed to stay somewhat grounded. If it wasn't for her involvement with projects in the community he would have thought her snobbish. He was sure she gave that impression to more than one person, but if they got to know her they would see what a giving, wonderful person she was.

He watched her sleep for a while; caught up in the beauty of her serene expression, then he approached her and kissed her face; something he hadn't done in a long time, at least without the public watching. She shifted her position at his touch and he pulled away quickly, smelling her strong scent. He gave her one last look to make sure she was still asleep then went to his study to make a phone call. He sat in his leather chair and picked up his private line to dial. The call was answered immediately.

"Tony is that you?" came a sultry voice on the other end.

"Yes, Madeline. I won't be able to see you tonight," he said. Madeline was the curator of the Seattle Art Museum and they had met one night eight years ago at a Japanese Exhibition she had put together. He was deeply impressed at the detail and beauty of the project but even more impressed by the intelligence and attractiveness of the woman. After many subtle hints on his part and obvious flirting on her part, they decided to indulge the physical desires they shared, and the affair was still in full throng. But they were careful; both had reputations they couldn't afford to tarnish. The sex was good but not good enough to lose face over.

"What's wrong?" she asked, and he could picture her pouting on the other end. He loved the way her lower lip stuck out when she pouted, full and round and ready to nibble on. He shook the thought away and answered her question.

"Nothing's wrong. I just need to spend a little more time with my wife right now."

"That old hag? Whatever for? I thought you said you

couldn't stand being near the woman," she said, and he cringed at the loathing in her voice.

"But I can't give the public that impression. You understand, don't you?"

"Of course I do, it's all part of being the mayor, is it not? But I still get you this weekend, right? I'm bringing the red teddy…" she said, her voice dipping seductively.

Yates felt a tightening in his pants and he chuckled lowly. "You know me so well; yes, I'll see you this weekend. I have some conferences during the days but I'm all yours come nighttime."

"Good. Remember to wash up thoroughly; you know how I hate dirty smelling things." Madeline was compulsive about her cleanliness, but her body made up for her annoying little indulgence, and it he could easily overlook it once her clothes came off.

"You know I will. I always do. You wouldn't let me in otherwise," he whispered into the phone and smiled. "See you then." He hung up grinning, then remembered his wife in the other room and his face heated with shame. He was playing with fire having an affair; it could ruin him worse than any political scandal, yet he couldn't stay away from Madeline. She had him in a trance. Just thinking about her full-rounded and ample breasts, he felt his pants stiffen once more and tried to clear his mind.

Spending more time with his wife didn't come from the public's pressure—it stemmed from guilt. Annabel didn't deserve what he was doing behind her back. She had come a long way with him and they supported each other in every way but one. But just because Annabel had lost her sexual passion didn't justify his affair.

His office phone rang, and he was torn from his thoughts. "Yates," he answered.

"Hey, Tony, it's Mike Andrews. I'm guessing you saw the news already."

"I have and I'm disappointed, Mike. I thought your people would have ended this much sooner."

"I thought so too. I just called to tell you that, because the FBI is working on this case, the media is hungry for an update. So I was thinking we could put together a press conference later today. I've called in my people for a meeting around seven, can you make it?"

"I'll be there. My staff is up and working by now. See you soon." He hung up and called his driver to circle around the front. Forgetting his personal shortcomings, he left the house.

MAY 28TH, 2002 6:52 A.M.

"You've got to be fucking kidding me," Sonny shouted.

Luz saw people looking in their direction. "Hey, Einstein, can you pipe down? I don't want everyone to know what we're looking at," she said, nudging him with her elbow. She felt much better after Ben had called and told her they'd come up empty on bodies in the lake. Hearing that, she was able to concentrate more on the case. But she wondered where Nick was, and why he hadn't called.

Before looking at the disk, she wanted witnesses to verify

that she hadn't tampered with it. After calling Sonny and agreeing to meet at his desk along with another detective from computer forensics, they began to piece together the information on the disk, but they weren't happy with the result.

"This is going to make things a lot harder, you know this right?" Sonny asked, his brow furrowing.

"No shit," the other detective added.

"We have to go to Mike with this. This is huge."

"He called a meeting upstairs that starts in about five minutes. Let's go," Sonny said, grabbing the disk from the computer. Luz agreed to meet them upstairs after she ran to her office. She checked her voicemail for any messages from Nick but found none. An uneasy feeling knotted her stomach, but she had to deal with one thing at a time. She left her office and headed upstairs. She saw Eddie and Rosa in the hall; Rosa looked angry, as usual, and her skin was an odd shade of pink.

"What happened to you?" Luz asked as she passed them.

Rosa shot her an icy stare. "Why are you always so nosy, Santos?" She sneered and scratched her arms, leaving angry red marks on her already pink skin.

Eddie looked at Luz apologetically. "We were at my cabin last night and decided to take a late walk. So we took a path headed toward the lake and on the way back up to the cabin Rosa starts itching, a lot. At first, we thought it was a bug bite but her skin turned red, which was not consistent with a bite. I walked the path again to find the source. Sure enough, there were about six poison ivy plants spread out along the side she'd walked. I ran up to tell her and to try to find some aloe or calamine lotion but —"

"But the idiot didn't have any and the next store was ten miles away. Idiot." Rosa spat, looking at Eddie.

Eddie blushed and looked sheepishly at Luz, but Luz didn't bother to control her laughter. "Tough break, Rosa," she said but kept smiling. She couldn't help but absolutely revel in Rosa's physical misery. At least she could associate the action of arm scratching with something that brought her joy instead of sorrow.

"Fuck off, Santa." Rosa pushed past Eddie and stormed back to her desk, scratching furiously the whole way. Once she was out of earshot Eddie joined Luz and laughed a little.

"I really do feel bad, but you should have seen her itching and bitching, it was hilarious. But I think I lost my date to the policeman's ball."

Luz chuckled and checked her watch. "I gotta go, man, meeting upstairs."

"Okay, I'll see you around. I've got vacation hours left and I need a nap."

"See you around then," she said stepping into the elevator.

Eddie waved and then stopped the doors from closing. "Luz, I heard about your boat. I'm sorry."

She'd been trying not to think of the incident and his words made her heart sink. "Yeah, tough break for me," she said.

"I'm not trying to get into your pants but, if you need a place to stay…"

"I'll be fine, but thanks."

He let go of the doors and before they shut he yelled to her;

"At least you don't have poison ivy!" She laughed the whole ride up.

• • •

Luz opened the door to the Storm Room and took her regular seat to the right of Mike. She leaned over to speak to him, but the mayor interrupted her.

"Detective Santos, I'm glad you're here. We could use your perspective on the status of this case."

Luz jumped in her seat and saw Sonny stare at her from across the table, a pained expression on his face. She gathered her wits; forced a smile.

"Yes, well so far we've followed every lead and we're making progress. We have evidence in our possession that will wrap this case up in twenty-four to forty-eight hours."

Stunned whispers erupted around the room and the mayor looked shocked.

"You mean, you've found the killer? You know who it is?" he asked.

His genuine interest and blunt statement threw Luz for a loop. She glanced back at Sonny and could tell he was thinking the same thing.

"We don't know yet but it's working itself out. It's only a matter of time before we see the big picture."

The mayor slapped Mike on the back. "That's what I wanted to hear! I will tell the public that the case is nearly closed."

"I wouldn't advise that, sir," Luz added quickly.

"Why not?" he asked.

"We don't want the killer to hear. He might make a run for it. Or worse yet, kill again. Just let them know that we're utilizing all resources in order to solve the case and that you're positive that you will see results soon."

He looked at her with what she could only guess was a twinge of pride. "Detective, you should have worked my campaign; you have a way with words." He chuckled and turned to his advisor. "Did you write that down, Gregory?" he asked grinning.

Luz smiled weakly and looked around the room. Everyone appeared confused at this turn of events; Agent Adams looked irritated. It wasn't a good look for him.

They wrapped things up and the group split and went separate ways. Agent Adams, Mike and Sonny surrounded Luz.

"You wanna explain that little episode, Santos?" Mike asked.

Luz opened her mouth but once again the mayor interrupted her.

"Mike, I have some last-minute things to ask you about," he said, demanding the captain's attention. "In private," he added.

"Sure, let's go down to my office," Mike said. Luz got up to leave also.

"Detective Santos, I want a word with you," Agent Adams called from across the room.

Luz winced at the tone of his voice. She didn't want to discuss her findings with anyone until she'd had a chance to speak with Mike. "I'm really busy right now, Blue. Maybe later," she said absently. He walked up to her and leaned in close.

"If you have information pertinent to this case and refuse disclosing that information to me, you could find yourself in a lot of trouble," he said.

Luz just looked up at him. "Now why in the world would I do that?" she asked, smiling at him.

He shook his head. "Suit yourself, detective." He walked out of the room.

Sonny gave her a sympathetic glance. "Oh, Santos, you're in for it now. The FBI will have your balls in a vice if they find out you're hiding something from them."

She smiled, grabbing her crotch. "Then I guess I have nothing to worry about."

CHAPTER TWENTY-FIVE

I strive for love from those around
But emptiness is all I've found
Within this void I grow alone
I'll show the world all I've known.

MAY 28TH, 2002 9:15 A.M.

"He's still in there?" Luz asked Rosa, who stood guard outside of Mike's office.

"Yes. He's with the *mayor*, Santos," she stated then began typing only to stop to scratch at her arms again.

Luz smiled. "I know, which means he's probably in there blowing hot air around the room. Can you call me when they're through?"

"Yeah, whatever," Rosa said. She grabbed a bottle of calamine lotion and squirted a quarter-sized glob onto her hand. Before rubbing it in she looked up at a smiling Luz. "You think this is funny, Santos?" she asked. "I hate the smell of this crap and now I have to work all day with it and I'm uncomfortable to top it off, so get off my case, will you?"

"Sure. Sorry, Rosa," Luz said, heading for her office but when she heard Mike's door open she turned around.

"Okay, Tony. Thanks for coming by," Mike said shaking the mayor's hand.

"No problem. I'll be out of town this weekend, so—" the man stopped as though he'd hit a brick wall. His nose scrunched up. "What is that? Is that calamine lotion?" Yates said sniffing the air. "What a god-awful smell. Who is that?" he demanded.

Rosa quickly closed the bottle and put it in her drawer, but her pink skin gave her away. Yates pointed at her.

"You there. Is that you?"

Rosa's cheeks reddened slightly. "Yes, I got poison ivy this—"

"Never mind that," Yates interrupted. "My wife has diabetes and sometimes it causes her skin to dry out and itch, but no matter how many times I ask her to use aloe she insists on calamine. I have a… friend who uses calamine for her skin as well; she has some sort of blood disorder that also dries her skin out. With all the lotions and creams they have out nowadays you'd think there would be a better treatment but everywhere I look—there's calamine," he ended gruffly. A tense silence followed.

"Well, Tony, thanks again for stopping by," Mike said breaking the strain.

The mayor's attention turned back to business. "Sure. If you need to reach me call my cell. I want to be the first to know when this case breaks."

"Will do," Mike replied. After mayor was out of hearing

range, everyone turned to Rosa.

"What was that about?" Mike asked.

"The man obviously hates the smell of calamine," Rosa replied, watching the mayor retreat toward the elevators.

"With a passion," Luz added.

Mike placed a hand on Luz's shoulder. "We need to talk. In my office."

Once inside Mike's office, Luz could barely contain herself. "I think we've got something," she said.

"After that little scene upstairs, I figured as much. Fill me in," Mike said, arms crossed.

Luz took a deep breath and spoke. "Anthony Yates."

"What?"

"That was the name on the disk Cliff Saunders gave me."

"What? The guy who tracked the email from the Murphy murder?"

"Yes. He tracked it on his own; actually, he had a friend help him. I had Sonny look into the friend and he used to be a professional hacker, kind of a legend in that realm, so he knew what he was doing. I did a background check on him and as far as I could tell, the man has no connections to Yates, therefore no reason to sabotage the search to point it toward the mayor."

"That can't be right, Luz. We've checked Yates. He's clean."

"I don't think you wanted to investigate hard enough and I understand why. The man's your boss, but I think he deserves a second look."

"Luz…" he said holding his head in his hands. "This is the

last thing I need right now."

"Dammit, Mike, if he is the killer—or if he's connected to the killer—we have to know about it."

"So wait… you're telling me that *this* is what you meant when you told the mayor you had a lead? Shit, Santos." He slammed his hands down on the desk.

"Why are you fighting me on this? This is the first piece of hard evidence we've had, and you're refusing to acknowledge it."

"No, I'm refusing to acknowledge what it could mean." He sighed heavily. "Fine. What do you want me to do about this?"

"Nothing obvious to start with; just keep an eye on him. Day and night."

"Do you know how hard that will be? He's got a small army watching him already."

"I know you can do it, Mike. We've got the resources," she said.

"Fine. Anything else?"

"Yes. I'll need a record of where he was every minute for the past ten days."

"You want miracles, Santos," Mike said, rolling his eyes.

"No, Mike. I just want answers," she responded, staring at him.

"Fine. I'll get people on it right away. Where are you going?"

"First of all, I need a place to stay,"

"Any idea on who might have done it?" Mike asked, referring to her now-burnt down boat house.

"No. But whoever it was thought I was home. My car was there. It has to be the same person who defaced my car. I must be getting close for the killer to try to burn me to death. I'm just glad I took Cheech with me before I left and I'm glad

Nick wasn't there. I still need to find him."

Mike gave her a questioning look.

"Don't even think about it, Mike. He's got nothing to do with this case anymore. I haven't heard from him since yesterday and I'm starting to worry."

"Worry about what?" he asked.

"Well, he was at the James's residence all day then he just up and left."

"Speaking of that, has Candace consented to release the files to us?"

"No. That's another thing I need to do today. I've already called in a warrant so if she refuses, I'll have to take them by force. Hopefully that's a last resort."

"Good. Tell me what you find. You might want to take Sonny along—those computer files will have locks on them, but he can bypass them. We searched Fredrick's office downtown earlier and came up empty. All we know is that he wasn't well liked, and nobody there seems to miss him. Not even the mayor seemed distressed, but he'll change his tune once the press asks him about it. Fredrick James didn't leave much behind."

"For our sake, I hope he did. I'll call you later with what we find. Until then, I want you to promise me you'll take this mayor thing seriously."

"I told you I would," Mike said with a scowl. "Just worry about your part."

Luz left the office, but she could smell the smoke from his cigarette before she closed the door.

MAY 28ᵀᴴ, 2002 11:15 A.M.

Nick woke up to pure darkness. His first reaction was to feel around for his surroundings but when he tried to move he found his arms and legs were tightly bound with a rope. He took a deep breath to fight down the panic that threatened to overwhelm him, but his heart was beating too fast.

Where am I? What am I doing here? How did I get here? Who brought me here? He tried to remember where he was before blacking out, but his memory was hazy. He concluded that haziness was due to a sore spot he felt on the top of his head, where someone must have struck him—hard. He rolled off his side onto his back and took another breath, trying to find a more comfortable position. It was then he felt the material covering his eyes; he was blindfolded.

The last thing he remembered was walking downtown, on his way back to the marina to find Luz when… when someone hit him? He couldn't remember what happened next. All he knew was that he was in a dark place. Alone.

He thought back to what happened before he left the James's house. After Candace curled up on the couch with her daughter, Nick went back up to Fredrick's office to finish the research he'd started. Up to that point he'd found nothing more than a few statements from the bank showing large deposits from an unknown account and illegal withdrawals from the trust fund set up in Leah's name. So he kept looking. But once he found what he was looking for, he was sorry he'd found it.

Someone was paying Fredrick James an immense amount of money in exchange for his cooperation. He didn't know why, but the funds were coming from an account in Oregon. The name on the account was A. Yates. After learning this, Nick had gone straight to Yates's house to confront him but thought better of it when he pulled up to the house and noticed the security measures Yates had in place. Instead, he turned around with the intention of getting help from the police.

The only thing that bothered him was the fact that the money started coming to Fredrick a week after Leah was killed. Different questions came to mind when he found this out; did someone pay Fredrick to kill Leah? Why? Is that how he accumulated his wealth? The timing was too coincidental, but the only one who knew for sure had shot himself two nights before. So that left the person who had paid him to do the deed.

Nick tried to convince himself that Fredrick wasn't capable of killing, but the more he thought about it, the less likely it seemed. Nick remembered seeing a note under the pillow on Candace's bed. Was that a letter from Fred? A suicide note? Of course Fred would have left some sort of confession in the letter. He'd have to check that. He pulled at the rope that bound his hands behind his back and huffed through the gag.

He might never get the chance.

MAY 28TH, 2002 12:52 A.M.

Candace James stared out the window towards the lake; her

eyes swollen from crying. Just when she thought she had dried up, the tears came harder and faster. In her hand she held the answer to her husband's suicide. The letter he left for her dangled from her shaking hand. She discovered it when she woke from her nap and found herself cradling Fredrick's pillow, the sharp point of the paper poking her hand. She'd immediately shoved it back under the pillow, not wanting to read it, not wanting to know the last words her husband wrote for her.

The decision to read the letter came from the overwhelming need to justify her husband's actions over the last seven years leading up to his death. Even though she had proof of his wrongdoing right in front of her, in his own handwriting, it was too difficult for her to believe he was capable of such malice and scandal.

But it wouldn't be difficult for the media to believe, and they would not only believe it—they would make sure everyone else did, too. She wouldn't let that happen, she couldn't; it was bad enough Fredrick had killed himself. She would not have his name, or hers, publicly slandered.

She sighed, all she wanted was to mourn in peace and move on with her life the best she could. Handing the letter over to the police could only mean trouble for her and her daughter. Poor Chloe. If the letter went public she'd deal with nothing but ridicule at the university and in her fragile emotional state, Candace doubted she could handle it. She looked down at the tear-streaked paper in her hand. She stared long and hard before she made her decision, but before she could find a match to burn the letter with, Chloe entered her room.

Chloe found her mother in the den staring out the window. "Mother there you are," she said, crossing the room to embrace her only parent. She saw her mother tense up and shove something behind the couch. "What was that?" she asked.

Her mother's brow furrowed then quickly smoothed out as a smile came to her face. "Just some tissues, honey, I've been leaving them everywhere."

"But why hide them?"

"I wasn't hiding them from you; it's just that I want to be strong for you. I can't be crying every time you see me. It will only upset you more."

With the reminder of her father's death, Chloe forgot her suspicion and hugged her mother close. "I miss Daddy," she said in a little girl's voice and Candace's chest tightened. She reached down and caressed her daughter's face. "I do, too," she said, promising herself she would destroy the letter on the floor behind the couch.

CHAPTER TWENTY-SIX

MAY 28TH, 2002 1:30 P.M.

A door opened, and Nick's body stiffened with fear. He held his breath and listened for movement. He heard footsteps as someone crossed the room and stopped in front of where he lay. Then, with a crushing blow, his captor kicked him in the ribs. His muffled scream caught in the gag and he twisted against his bonds.

"Good, just making sure you were awake," a cold, feminine voice announced.

Nick stayed still. The woman clicked her tongue. "Tsk, tsk, Nicholas Mason. You have caused me so much trouble. I thought I would kill you the moment I found you. But after thinking about it; maybe you can play a bigger part in my scheme."

Nick moved his head and struggled to see through the crack of his blindfold, but the woman kicked him again, this time in the head. Pain exploded, and lights flashed behind his eyelids. His body spasmed wildly. The woman's laughter echoed through the room.

"See what happens when you try to resist? Do it again and I won't stop kicking until I see a crack in your skull," she warned him.

Nick moaned, and she bent down so close he could smell the coffee on her breath. There was another scent as well—*is that calamine?*

"Are you trying to say something?" she asked, removing the gag. "Here's your chance.

Nick tried to gather the scattered thoughts in his mind but all that came out was one word. "Why…"

"Why, you ask? Well it's a long story. But I'll indulge your request with a shorter version. Your slut wife was at the wrong place at the wrong time and was disposed of. Since then, I've learned how to kill for the right reasons. Then you got in the way. I will deal with you when the time comes."

She replaced the gag and Nick heard her walk across the room and pick something up. The footsteps grew closer again and he winced, expecting more torture. But no blows came. Instead, his head was pulled up from behind and a cold steel blade rested against his throat. Death spoke in his ear.

"How does it feel, Nick?" she asked, breathing hard. "How does it feel knowing you'll soon join your beloved in the afterlife?"

Nick didn't flinch. The point of the knife was so close to his throat, one wrong move and she'd slice through. The woman laughed and removed the knife, landing one more kick before walking away. "I've got plans for you, Nick." The door opened and closed, and the lock slid into place.

His body went limp with relief and he lay on the floor gasping for breath. Anger replaced the fear that gripped him moments before. Who was this woman and what right did she have to say those things about Leah? Better yet, why did she hold *him* responsible for her rage?

MAY 28TH, 2002 2:30 P.M.

The woman left the room shaking. She wanted to take the knife and end Nicholas Mason's life. Holding herself back was a challenge she hadn't expected to face. She'd always been able to kill whom she wanted when she wanted; exercising self-control with a victim had never been an issue.

Soon, she told herself, *soon this will all be over.* Not only would she kill Mason, but she would kill Luz Santos. A slow smile spread over her face and quickly disappeared when the urge to scratch interrupted her thoughts.

She quickly walked to the bathroom and almost screamed from frustration when her calamine lotion wasn't where it was supposed to be. She composed herself, checked her purse and found it at the bottom.

Relieved, she lathered her body with the lotion and redressed carefully to avoid pink smudges on her clothes. She still felt the itching, but it wasn't so intense. She got into her car, and as she drove, she decided that the best way to stop the itching was to give into the need.

4:00 P.M.

Luz pulled into the James's empty driveway and got out. But before she got to the front door, another car pulled into the driveway. Candace and Chloe got out and walked to where she stood.

"Detective Santos, is there something I can help you with?" Mrs. James asked. Luz thought she looked nervous but shrugged it off; the woman's husband had just died.

"I tried calling earlier and couldn't reach you," she said.

"We've been making funeral arrangements for Fredrick," Candace replied, blinking back tears.

"Oh, I'm sorry," Luz said, looking at Chloe, who was also crying. "I need to ask you a couple of questions, if you don't mind."

Candace looked hesitant "Detective, we're in mourning. Can't you and everyone else leave us alone?" she snipped, turning on her heel toward the front door.

"Mrs. James, I understand you've been through quite an ordeal but—"

"You understand? How would you understand? Did your husband kill himself two nights ago?" she screamed, her face turning redder by the minute.

"Mother, stop," Chloe screamed and ran into the house.

Candance pointed at Luz. "Do you see what you've done?" she asked, still pointing. Her hands shook.

"I haven't done anything, Mrs. James. But I am going to have to do something soon if I can't get your cooperation."

"What is that supposed to mean?" Candace asked.

"It means that if we aren't allowed access to your husband's accounts, I can get a warrant down here in five minutes. But

I'm trying to be sensitive to your situation."

Candace looked at her and said, "Then I'll see you in five minutes." She marched into the house and slammed the door.

Luz looked at her watch. "Aw, shit."

• • •

Candace James walked quickly to the den knowing she had only five minutes to destroy the letter. She looked behind the couch but didn't find it there. Panicked, she moved the couch to look underneath and came up empty again. *What the hell?* she thought as she dropped to her hands and knees, frantically searching beneath the furniture.

"Looking for this?" Chloe asked from the doorway. Candace was so startled, she banged her head on an end table. She looked up at her daughter and gasped.

"Where did you find that?" she asked.

"You know where I found it, Mother, but I won't let you do it. I won't let you destroy this letter," Chloe said.

"You give me that letter right now, you hear me?" Candace started toward her daughter, but Chloe backed out of the room and ran upstairs.

"No!" Chloe screamed down the staircase. "I will *not* have both of my parents corrupt! It's bad enough my father was a felon. I won't have my mother break the law as well!"

There was a knock at the front door, but Candace ignored it. "Chloe, don't you understand? If the police get that letter, the media will too; and whether I committed a crime won't matter to them. They'll paint our whole family as crooks. *Everyone* will see us that way," she yelled up to the top of the staircase where he daughter stood, crying.

Chloe looked down at her mother and waved the letter around. "But at least I would know the truth; at least I would know that my mother did the right thing! And destroying this letter is not the right thing, Mom. It's too late for me to learn any more from Dad but it's not too late for you." Voice cracking, Chloe burst into tears again.

Candace looked up at her daughter and smiled sadly. The knock at the front door grew more insistent but she ignored it as the tears rolled down her cheeks. "I-I don't know what's right anymore, Chloe. I wish this would all go away," she said.

Chloe walked down the stairs past Candace to the front door. Before she opened it, she gave her mom one last look. Candace had never been prouder of her daughter and knew that whatever wrongs Fredrick had done, none of it affected his daughter's will. She smiled and nodded at Chloe.

Luz impatiently waited for the warrant to arrive and when Eddie pulled up and delivered it to her, she went right to the door and knocked hard. She waited a minute before knocking again and when she received no response the second time, she turned to Eddie.

"It's solid Oak but the lock doesn't seem too strong. You think you could take it?" she asked him. Before he had a chance to reply, the door slowly opened, and Chloe stood behind it, looking distraught and holding out a piece of paper.

"This is the letter my father left when he… died. My mother

and I... we're trusting you to be responsible with the information it contains," she said.

"Where is your mother?" Luz asked, a little annoyed

"She's inside but if this is all you came for, I'd rather you left us alone for a while."

Luz took the letter and skimmed it briefly. Fredrick James had not been a good person at all. So many lies, so much coverup and for what? Greed could really twist people up and Fredrick had been a casualty of his own greed and manipulation. How in the world was she going to break this to Nick? As far as she could tell, it was genuine. She looked up at the young woman who, at that moment, looked much older than her years, and said, "We may need to come by later for your dad's files, but this works for now. Thank you, Chloe."

Chloe nodded and closed the door softly. Luz looked at Eddie and he shrugged.

"Don't look at me like that. I'm just as confused as you are. But we got the letter. Let's go."

5:50 P.M.

The mayor checked the time and decided to call it a day. He had just returned to his office from a stressful meeting with the governor and was tired from the verbal combat that had taken place. It was time to go home.

But he didn't want to go home. The calamine incident at the police station had stayed in the back of his mind all day. He opened his top drawer and grabbed a ring holding two keys and unlocked the file cabinet across the room. He went through several keys and drawers before locating his hidden cell phone It was all so secretive, but he needed to keep some things to himself and the extra precautionary efforts had paid off. No one knew about Madeline. It was better that way.

He went back to his desk and notified his secretary to hold his calls for the next twenty minutes. Then he picked up the cell phone and checked it for tampering. When he'd ensured his own safety, he turned on the power and dialed a number.

"Hello?" said a woman on the other line; she sounded preoccupied.

"It's me, can you talk?"

"Let me go to my office." He heard her discuss work issues with others at the Museum and some shuffling sounds. Finally, he heard a door shut.

"I'm here, lover. What did you need?" she asked.

"I need you," he replied, already aroused by her husky voice.

"Well, you'll have me this weekend. Is that why you called?"

"Actually yes, it is…"

"Dammit, Tony, are you canceling on me again?" she asked, the sultry tone in her voice gone.

"Calm down. I'm not canceling. I'm actually calling to see if we could get together tonight."

There was a pause on the other end that stretched a little too long. "What is it? he asked impatiently.

"What happened to spending quality time with your wife?" she asked softly.

The question irritated him. He didn't feel he had to justify anything to this woman. "Listen, if you don't want to see me tonight you don't have to. I don't go where I'm not welcome."

"Oh, Tony, that's not what I meant. It's just, you sounded so insistent this morning and I wanted to be sure you wouldn't change your mind," she explained.

"So you will see me?" he asked.

"Of course. Oh… wait."

"What?"

"We're getting in some pieces from South America tonight. Midnight shipment," she said, a note of disappointment in her words.

"We'll be done by then. I can let you go back to work."

"Really?" she almost sounded disappointed and he hurriedly reassured her it wasn't his sexual performance that would cause the visit to be quick.

"Yes. This Seattle Slasher case is taking up all my time. In addition to that, I have nothing on my schedule that would take me out of town tonight, so I'll have to sleep at home anyway."

They talked a little more, dropping sexual innuendos throughout the conversation. Once everything was set for the evening they ended their call. The mayor went back through the routine of hiding his cell phone. He still had an erection when he left the office.

CHAPTER TWENTY-SEVEN

MAY 28TH, 2002 10:19 P.M.

For the first time in a long time, Mike Andrews was at a loss for words. For the last two hours his team of experts had worked on the James case from three different angles and every one of them led to the same conclusion—Anthony Yates was a killer.

"Do you believe me now?" Luz asked exasperated.

He turned to her and said, "Do you ever have those moments where you know that whatever you end up doing will be the wrong thing?" She nodded. "Well, this is one of those fucking moments. Christ, Santos." He buried his head in his hands.

"So Anthony Yates definitely had something to do with the murder of Leah Mason. If not, why did he pay off Fredrick James? All the money is from an out of state account under A. Yates. Plus, we can't account for his whereabouts for most of the TODs."

Before Mike could reply Sonny came running into the Storm Room, waving a newspaper. "You will not believe what

I just found out!" he yelled, jogging over and placing the paper in front of Luz. "Read the last article on the bottom," he said excitedly.

She picked it up and read aloud, "The Music Man will be performed at the 5th Avenue Theatre next month—"

Sonny interrupted her. "Not *that* article, the one next to it. Just gimme the paper," he said. He snatched it from her and read aloud:

"Mayor Sold a Fake. Ethan Petry of Petry's Rare Knives and Swords based in Philadelphia, Pennsylvania was the highest bidder on a collector's knife from an auction hosted by the mayor this month. The knife was thought to be the original copy but before adding it to his collection, Petry had the knife appraised. It was then he learned that the piece was a fake. Petry, who had paid four thousand dollars for the knife, says that he plans to speak to the mayor personally on this matter and blah blah blah, you get the gist of it," he concluded.

Luz looked at Mike who was searching his pockets for a lighter. "It's no use, Mike, you can't smoke on this floor. The sprinklers could go off."

Mike stopped his search and took the paper from Sonny. The room was quiet as they waited for him to finish reading. Finally, he looked at Luz. "I have one question. How does Francis Aberleen fit into all of this? Before today, we thought the killer was a woman."

"The only thing I could come up with that maybe Francis had contact with the knife after the first couple of murders. Since the knife was found on Nick, who was homeless, maybe

Francis is still homeless. Maybe she walked by and dropped it on him," Eddie suggested.

"Is that all we've got?" Mike asked. "We need to find a connection between that woman and the mayor before we move on this thing."

"She could be his mistress," Luz suggested.

Mike looked a little annoyed. "Now we are pulling at straws, dammit!" The phone on the table rang and Mike picked it up. After a few "yeahs" and "shits", he hung up looking forlorn.

"What happened?" Eddie asked.

"We got another body."

"Do we know where Yates is?" Luz asked. Mike gave her a stern look and picked up the phone. After speaking briefly with the mayor's office and his home security offices, he hung up.

"Shit. The mayor's missing."

Everyone in the room turned and looked at Mike.

"What do you mean the mayor's missing? Mayors just don't disappear," Sonny said.

"Well, this one did. He told his office he was going home, and he told his wife he was working late. According to his driver, his car's at the office but he isn't."

"You know what this means, Mike..." Luz began.

"It means we got ourselves a suspect," he said before turning to address the rest of the room. "Anyone got a fucking light?"

EARLIER 6:00 P.M.

Anthony Yates basked in the afterglow of his adulterous deed;

and it was because Madeline Baker was not only a generous lover—she was inventive as well. They were lying naked on her bed, still panting and enjoying the moment. Smiling, he reached over and stroked her hair.

"Woman, you've done it again," he said.

"Hmm?" she said lazily, reaching over to play with the hairs on his chest.

"That was amazing, I didn't think I'd be able to do it two times, but you proved me wrong. How do you do it?"

She smiled. "You bring out my wild side, Tony."

They lay there a little longer and when she tried to get up he protested and pulled her close to him. She resisted and left for the bathroom. He listened to the water running and became irritated. The woman knew how to please him but her constant cleansing routine ruined the mood. He sighed. He didn't know what else to expect from someone who suffered from obsessive compulsive disorder, and so he abhorred her rituals. The water turned off and she walked out of the bathroom in a silk robe.

"Tony, get up and wash. I have to take the sheets off the bed," she ordered quietly.

Yates reluctantly swung his legs over the side of the bed and got up. This wasn't his first rodeo. He walked to the bathroom and turned the shower on. He avoided looking in the mirror, which he always did at Madeline's house because he did not want to face himself; he did not want to see the guilty man staring back at him. He opened the shower door and stepped under the hot water, letting it wash away the smells of sex. As he reached for the shampoo, he heard the bathroom door open.

"Madeline is that you?" he purred. "Why don't you hop in here with me and we'll see if we can make the third time a charm?"

He stood under the water, his eyes closed while he rinsed the shampoo. He felt a sudden pressure as someone grabbed his face and yanked back his head.

"What the..." he began but never finished. He couldn't finish; he had a gaping gash in his throat. His last effort was to face his attacker, but he never made it that far. Instead his body slumped to the floor of the shower. He watched as his blood swirled down the drain until death claimed him.

MAY 28TH, 2002 6:52PM

Nick was nearly asleep when he heard the door open. He held his breath and waited for the brutal beating he was sure would come. But as time passed, the room remained silent. Then he heard her voice.

"I just killed again. It was almost too easy. I prefer more of a challenge but what's done is done." Her voice was sounded so detached, it scared Nick. This woman was escalating for sure. He didn't move. The silence stretched on again and then she spoke.

"People might call me a serial killer but I'm more of a..." she paused. "Cleaning service." She said it so matter-of-factly Nick was sure she believed it. It made his skin crawl; the woman was certifiably crazy.

"It's like the maids who come and clean for the rich people. They're doing a service for the people who would rather not deal with the mess but need it done. I do society a favor. The homeless are leeches on this city; filthy parasites who litter our streets and waste our resources. They are despicable, foul people who blame society for their misgivings. They don't take opportunities to better themselves when the resources are available all around them. They just sit in their dirty clothes, drinking and smoking and digging in the garbage. But you know what the worst thing is?" she asked slowly. "Those people, after living off the upper class, after deciding to live forever on the streets, they reproduce!"

She said the last sentence with such loathing that the hairs on the back of Nick's neck stood up straight. He didn't agree with her assessment of the poor and homeless people of Seattle. He believed most were victims of bad circumstances, but he kept his thoughts on the topic to himself.

As if reading his mind, she spoke up. "You think my opinions are misplaced, but that's because you were one of them. If I had seen you that night in the alley, I would have killed you. But I didn't see you. I tripped and dropped my knife. I thought I had tripped over trash, but I realized it must have been you." She was quiet for a moment before she continued. "But look at you, you are living proof that the homeless can rise up and be an active part of society. It's too bad I can't let you live to be an example to the others. You just know too much."

Nick wouldn't have been able to rejoin society if he hadn't stashed money away before becoming homeless. He also may have never made the move back into society without Luz's confidence in him. This woman, who claimed to know who he was, didn't seem to know him very well.

"My mother was homeless, the filthy bitch. She tried to raise me on the streets before giving me away to people even worse than her. I was made to live in a shithole. The people around me were horrible. My family consisted of prostitutes, alcoholics and drug dealers who only cared for themselves. It was the worst childhood and I didn't deserve to be put through that. No child does."

Nick expected her to go on but instead she retreated to the door, left and put the lock in place. He let out a sigh and freed his body of tension. He wondered if he would get out of this alive. Then he remembered his killer's promise of death and he knew he'd die at the hands of a madwoman.

7:20 P.M.

Luz was tired of looking at dead bodies and didn't know how much more she could take. The body she searched had no identification but there was no question the man had been homeless. She studied the wound in the corpse's neck. It wasn't the usual slash pattern.

"The killer's out of control," she said.

"All killers are out of control. It's in their nature," Ben replied.

"Well, this killer started off *in* control. He, or she, killed in a relatively controlled manner—a quick cut and that was it. But this looks like the killer hacked at this guy's throat. There are at least three separate cuts here. The killer's mind is slipping, and we've got to catch them before they go over the edge."

"You keep saying 'they' and 'them'. You've been on this case for two weeks now and you don't know if the killer is a man or a woman?" Ben asked, eyebrows raised.

"We've got it narrowed down and the signs point toward a male," she said, examining the body once more.

"Well I'll leave the detective work up to you, but it would have to be a pretty strong woman to take this guy down. He's got to be at least two hundred pounds."

"Yeah but the killer had the element of surprise —" Luz started to explain but was interrupted by her phone ringing. She answered it.

"Santos."

"Luz, you need to get over here right away," her boss demanded.

"What happened?"

"The mayor's dead."

• • •

She pulled up to the scene twenty minutes later. Mike met her halfway down the walk.

"The FBI has taken over the case, but I wanted you here anyway. I've already gotten clearance from Agent Adams for you to look over the scene after they've processed it."

"Bullshit. I'm going in now," she said and walked toward the house.

Mike sighed and let her go. Luz climbed the stairs and went into the front room where a man in a black suit stopped her.

"Excuse me, ma'am, but you can't be in here."

Luz flashed her badge. "Let me speak to Agent Blue Adams, pronto," she ordered, but the man didn't move. She tried to pass him, but he blocked her way.

"Listen, if you don't let me in now I will—"

"Let her in, Abe, she's here to talk to me," a voice came from behind her.

Luz turned and saw Blue coming her way. "My, my, my! You have a way with words. So you want in?" he asked.

She shrugged. "This is my case."

"Correction, this is *my* case now." He stared down at her. "But the damage has been done and we're pretty much done here so go ahead and take a look around. Let me fill you in, we have two bodies—"

"Two?" she interrupted.

"One is the mayor; the second belongs to a woman named Madeline Baker. She's the curator at the Seattle Art Museum. From what we've found, the two were having sexual relations, but we don't know for how long. She was killed downstairs in the laundry room and he was killed in the shower. Same knife that was used in the other killings."

"Who found them?" Luz asked, taking down notes.

"Andrew Netti. Ms. Baker's assistant at the museum. He was helping her with an exhibit from South America. Some pieces were flown in today and some were scheduled for a shipment later tonight. But the plane never took off and the shipment was rescheduled for tomorrow morning. When he called to let her know, she didn't pick up. So he tried her cell phone, which he claims she always answers, and didn't get a response. So he thought he'd drive over on his way home. He said the door was wide open when he got here and that's when he called the police."

"Where is this guy now?" Luz asked.

"He's outside sitting in the black BMW across the street. We checked his background and when nothing came up, we told him to go home but he's been there ever since."

"I'll be right back," she said, running outside. She spotted the car and crossed the street. The windows were darkly tinted, and she couldn't see inside. She knocked on the glass and the window came down about three inches, revealing wide, fearful eyes.

"Mr. Netti?" she asked.

"Yes?" he replied.

"My name is Detective Santos. I work with the Seattle Police department. Can I ask you a few questions?"

"The-the FBI already asked me questions." His red-rimmed eyes filled with fresh tears. She'd have to handle him with kid gloves.

"I understand that, but I would like to ask you a few more, is that okay?" She waited for his reply. Instead of agreeing verbally, he got out of the car. He wore a black turtleneck tucked into a pair of Dockers, and he was very, very thin. His eyes were swollen from crying and he looked frail.

"How long have you known Madeline Baker?" She pulled out her pad and pen.

"Well, about five years and four months now."

"How well would you say you knew her?"

"It was mostly a professional relationship."

"Mostly? Could you explain?" she prodded.

"Well, we worked together most of the time, but we would go out for dinner or drinks once in a while. I've been to her house maybe ten times for dinner parties and such."

"Was there any romantic involvement?"

He laughed quickly before answering. "No, there was no romantic involvement, Ms. Santos."

"Why is that funny?"

"It's actually not funny, seeing how they just trucked her body off to the morgue, but let me just say that Madeline and I had the same taste in men."

When she got the implication, she moved on. "So, was she ever involved with anyone else?"

"She dated a couple of men here and there but nothing serious. She gave off this vibe like she was already seriously involved with somebody."

"What made you think that?" Luz asked, thinking of the mayor.

"She was always taking secret calls in her office, always leaving work, you know, taking long lunches. She'd get flowers from an admirer, and extravagant presents. She also took more vacation days than anyone else in the museum. We all kind of guessed that she was seeing somebody, but we would have never guessed that it was the mayor."

"You keep saying 'we', who is 'we'?"

"Oh, that means me and a couple of other people on staff

who run in the same circles."

"Okay. On a different subject, has there been anything odd recently at the museum? Anyone suspicious lurking around?"

"Not that I've seen. Well… wait. A couple days ago a woman came in asking about Madeline. She said she worked for an art magazine and wanted to do an article on the upcoming exhibit. But when I went to fetch Madeline, the woman was already gone. We just dismissed it and went back to work. I didn't think of that until now. Should I tell the FBI?"

"I will let them know. One last thing—could you describe this woman in detail?" She wrote down the description as he told her and thanked him for his time. Then she crossed the street and entered the house, keeping her notes to herself.

The bodies had already been removed. Luz was grateful that she didn't have to see more bodies that day. She went to the laundry room where an FBI tech was still taking apart the place piece by piece.

"Anything?" she asked.

He looked up and shook his head. "No. This woman must have been compulsive about her cleaning, cuz I can't even find a dust bunny."

"From what I hear she *was* an obsessive compulsive," Agent Adams said from the doorway. "You probably won't find much, but if you do, I want to be the first to know," he said, glancing at Luz.

The tech continued working and Luz headed upstairs with Blue on her heels.

"Did Netti help at all?" he asked.

Luz stopped midway up the stairs and stared back at him. At that moment, her phone rang. She answered it but heard nothing.

"Hello?" she repeated.

"...Luz..."

It sounded like Nick. "Nick? Is that you?" She heard the something that could have been duct tape in the background, then someone came on the line.

"Missing your lover boy?"

The voice was electronically altered but she could tell it belonged to a woman. She took a moment to respond, pushing down the fear of what Nick must be going through. "Who is this?"

"This is the person you've been looking for. I've got something of yours," she teased.

"Where is Nick?" Luz asked as her heart skipped a beat. She tried not to let fear seep into her voice.

"He's here with me."

"What have you done with him?"

"Let's cut this short. If you don't want him to end up like the mayor, you'll back off this case."

"I can't do that," Luz said gaining back some confidence. But she didn't want to sound too arrogant; Nick's life was on the line.

"I knew you'd say that. That's why I have a plan. If you solve this case in twelve hours, Nick lives and you'll be the hero of the day. But if you don't, Nick dies, and you'll never find me. The clock's ticking."

The line went dead, and Luz sat down on the stairs. Agent Adams grabbed her arm. "What the hell was that about?"

She repeated what the woman had told her and by the time she finished he already had her phone tapped and ready for another call.

We'll have to wait for her to call again."

"She won't call again," Luz said and walked out the door. Blue followed her to her car.

"What are you going to do?" he asked.

"I have to solve this, or Nick is dead."

"I know that, but where are you going?"

"I'm going to the museum to get a security tape of last week. I'm hoping the woman who showed up there will be on the tape."

"What woman?" he asked, and she relayed her interview with Mr. Netti to him.

"We can help. We've got all the equipment you need."

"You want to help me?" she turned to him in shock.

"I want to help, period," he replied staring down at her.

She looked at him and smiled weakly. "Thank God, because right now, I need all the help I can get."

8:10 P.M.

Nick struggled with his bonds, but it was no use. He gave up and tried to relax, but after hearing what his captor told Luz, it was hard to calm down. He prayed that Luz would find him in time.

CHAPTER TWENTY-EIGHT

9:14 P.M.

Luz, Mike, Eddie, Sonny and Agent Adams gathered in the Storm Room, watching the surveillance tape.

"There!" Luz said. "Sonny, back that up." Sonny rewound the tape and let it play again. "Now freeze it there," Luz ordered.

The tape froze the scene, and everyone was silent.

"I don't see anyone who matches her description," Mike said.

Luz pointed to the upper right part of the screen and asked Sonny to zoom in.

"See? Right there. Hold on." She looked at Eddie. "Bring Netti in."

Eddie left the room and was gone ten minutes before he returned with Andrew Netti. Luz asked Netti to view that tape up to the point where she'd frozen it. She asked him if the woman on the upper right part of the screen was the woman they were looking for.

"That could be her, but I can only see her legs."

"But that's where she would be, right? That's where you spoke with her?

Netti looked at the screen for a few more seconds, then nodded. "Correct."

Luz looked at Sonny and gestured for him to play the tape. They watched for a few more moments until Netti came into the screen.

"There I am. Yes. That must be her. The timing is right."

Luz looked pleased, but Mike wasn't impressed. "But look, we don't have a front shot; we can only see the back of her head."

"Annabel Yates," Blue exclaimed.

"What?" Mike asked looking from him to Luz and back. "Somebody explain."

"A. Yates, we thought the A stood for Anthony, but we never considered Annabel."

"The wife?" Eddie asked, his face a mask of shock.

"Who else would kill her husband and his lover? The wife!" Luz said, not worried how visible her excitement was. *Nick, I'm coming*, she thought.

"One problem," Mike said.

"What?" Luz asked.

"The mayor's wife was in D.C. up until an hour ago."

Almost in unison the rest of the room said, "Shit!"

10:00 P.M.

Annabel Yates could not stop the itching. She had already used a bottle of calamine lotion since she got off the plane, but nothing helped. She hopped in the shower and rinsed it off, letting the hot water temporarily relieve the discomfort. After twenty minutes she turned the water off and got out. She was rubbing on more lotion when she heard the phone ring in the other room. She took her time putting on her robe. Then she walked to the bedside table and picked up the phone.

"Mrs. Yates?"

"Yes."

"This is Agent Blue Adams from the FBI. I'm working the Seattle Slasher case."

"Did you want to talk to my husband? He isn't here right now, but I believe you can reach him at his office."

"Actually, that is what I'm calling about."

"I don't understand."

"Mrs. Yates, your husband was found dead an hour ago."

Annabel squeezed the phone tightly before she fainted.

Fifteen minutes later, Luz arrived with her team in tow just in time to see the mayor's wife come to. "Where am I?" she asked softly.

Agent Adams responded. "You are in your living room, ma'am. You fainted and went into shock after my call, so we came over to make sure you were okay."

Annabel looked at Luz and Mike. "Michael, why are all these people here? Get them out of my house this instant."

"I'm afraid I can't do that, Mrs. Yates," Mike replied. "Or do you prefer I call you Francis?"

Luz watched Annabel's face for any flicker of recognition and when she saw one, she got out her handcuffs and started toward the woman. She grabbed both arms, cuffed them tightly and said, "Francis Annabel Aberleen, you are under arrest for the murder of Anthony Yates, Madeline Baker, and many others—possibly including Nicholas Mason."

Annabel looked confused then lowered her head. "I didn't kill anyone. I was in Washington D.C."

"That's what we thought, until we found out you took an earlier flight home. The time frame fits," Agent Adams stated.

Mike pulled out a picture of a young woman, but there was no mistaking that the woman in the picture and the woman sitting in handcuffs were the same person.

Annabel gasped. "Where on earth did you get that?"

"Well, it seems you left a trail. But when you disappear and start a new life you have to make sure all pictures from your past life are destroyed. Now, we searched old yearbooks, family photos, police records and we couldn't locate one picture of you. Until of course we offered a reward back in your home town. This picture was faxed to us a half hour ago from the town of Lyons, New York from a Miss Betty Ray. She used to watch you and your siblings before your mother dragged you to the city—"

Annabel shot up out of her chair. "NO! Leave me alone!" She tried to run but with her hands cuffed behind her she couldn't quite catch her balance and Luz tackled her to the ground. After securing her legs, the police searched the house while Luz met with Mike.

"Did you get the other pictures verified?" he asked her.

"Yeah. Altek, the man at the auto storage, says that the woman who took the car from him looked a lot like the picture of Mrs. Yates."

"Great. Good job, Santos."

"But he didn't sound too sure. Neither did Netti when I showed him the picture. They both agreed that the woman they spoke with closely resembled Annabel, but neither sounded like they were convinced."

Mike waved her off. "Luz, we've found the killer. This woman killed her own family—"

"Captain, we found something, over here!" one of the officers called. They all followed him through the house down to the building Luz recognized as the place Anthony Yates kept his knives.

The officer stopped short of the entrance and led them around the small structure to a metal box mounted to the wall. It looked like a fuse box of some sort but there was a pink smudge around the handle.

"Open it," Mike ordered.

The officer complied. And a knife fell to the ground. *The* knife.

Luz looked closely at it and verified it was the murder weapon. "Get this bagged up and sent to the lab ASAP. I want results in an hour on prints, DNA, or whatever else they can come up with," she told Eddie, then she turned to Mike. "But where the hell is Nick?"

11:25 P.M.

"New York wants her," Mike stated calmly.

"I don't care. This is our case and we're going to prosecute

411

her here first," Luz demanded. "She killed the fucking mayor, and I'll need to talk to her about Nick's location."

Agent Adams stepped forward. "Luz, she says she doesn't know a thing about Nick, only that she remembers him from the murder case her husband was a suspect in eight years ago."

"Let me talk to her," Luz said, coming out from behind the desk.

"All right. Follow me." Blue led the way to the interrogation room and opened the door. Annabel Yates sat at the table with her attorney and didn't look up when Luz entered the room. Luz closed the door behind her and asked the attorney to leave.

"I will not let my client's rights—"

"Robert, please go," Annabel said softly.

"But... you—"

"Go. Thank you," she said.

The attorney obliged, leaving Luz and Annabel alone. Luz took a seat across the table and stared hard at the woman in front of her.

"Where's Nick?" she asked.

"If I knew I would tell you, you nasty little woman."

"Do you remember Leah Mason?"

"The woman my husband was accused of killing? Yes."

"Do you remember much about her?"

"I don't see where you are going with this," Annabel said impatiently.

"Wasn't the story the prosecution used that Yates was having an affair with Leah and that he killed her after she threatened to go public?"

Her lip curled in disgust. "That was one of their stories, yes."

"Tell me about your childhood, Annabel. Or would you rather I call you Francis?"

Annabel scoffed. "Don't call me that dreadful name. I left that person behind years ago."

"You grew up on the streets. You were poor. Your mother was an alcoholic, your sister a prostitute and when your brother wasn't fucking her he was pimping her on the streets. Is that right?"

"You have no right!" Annabel screamed. "No right to my life. You have no idea what I went through as a child! Living in cars, in dirty boxes and wearing dirty clothes, digging through the garbage for food. I hated my mother for putting me through that. I begged my sister and brother for help, but they were lost in their lives on the streets. I didn't deserve it!" Breathing heavily, she sat back in her chair and looked down at her hands.

"But look at you now. You're a killer. No matter how hard you tried to leave your past behind, it still haunts you to this day."

Annabel looked at her squarely. "Look at me now, detective; I have more than you ever will. A beautiful house; beautiful things; a smart, successful family. I pulled myself up and remade myself into the beautiful, elegant person you met last week. I've got so much money now, so much prestige…" she trailed off her eyes defocusing momentarily.

Luz stayed quiet while she studied the woman in front of her. Finally, she broke the silence. "Leah Mason was a beautiful woman."

"I've never met her, so I wouldn't know," Annabel replied stiffly.

"She was successful. Came from money, and was very, very pretty. I could see why someone like, say, your husband would find her attractive."

Annabel bit down on her lip and stared hard at Luz. Luz continued. "If I were you and I found out my husband was sleeping with such a perfect woman, I would be pretty upset. I mean, it's hard for a person like you to compete with a person like her."

"You bitch!" Annabel screamed and dove across the table. She grabbed Luz's hair and punched her in the face. Luz struggled with her and shouted for help. Eddie and Blue burst into the room and tore the crazed woman off her. They led a shrieking, out of control Annabel out of the room.

"Damn, what did you say to her?" Eddie asked

"We got it all on tape," Blue said, holding up a mini recorder.

"Where was that?" Luz asked.

"Taped under the table."

"Let me guess, FBI procedure?" Luz asked wryly, then turned serious. "She didn't tell me where Nick is. I've got eight hours."

"Eight hours until what?" Eddie asked.

"When she called me, the killer said the clock is ticking. If Annabel Yates is the killer, she probably has Nick strapped to something that's on a timer."

Eddie's eyes opened wide. "You mean like a bomb or something?"

"Or something," Luz said with a grimace. "We've got to find him."

MAY 29TH, 2002 12:50 A.M.

Sonny was on his ninth cup of coffee and running high. He had already traced the bank account in California back to Annabel Yates and was still sorting through most of the records when Luz walked in.

"Have you found anything?" she asked hopefully.

"I'm still on the financial records. I've gone through the bank records and it looks like Annabel was paying Fredrick James for some reason. I'm guessing he somehow knew she killed that Mason woman and was milking her for all she had."

"That's great, Sonny, but I need some clue as to where Nick might be."

"If you want to stick around and wait, you're welcome to."

Luz pulled up a chair and sat.

"I'll wait. But dammit, Einstein, please hurry."

It was two in the morning when Sonny woke her up. She lifted her head and looked around. "I'm sorry. I didn't mean to fall asleep."

"I found it," Sonny said.

Luz sat up, instantly awake. "Found what?"

"Back in 1999, a small house on the lake, not too far from the mayor's house, was purchased under the name Annabel Aberleen. The mortgage loan was granted by a small private bank in Seattle."

"Call Mike and Eddie and have them meet me there."

"You're going alone?"

"Yes."

2:25 A.M.

Luz drove well. She pushed her car through traffic at eighty-six miles an hour. She looked at her watch, it was two-thirty, she'd be there in minutes.

She pulled off at the next exit and followed the directions through the residential streets to a small cul-de-sac. A house matching the description Sonny gave her sat at the rear of the street. She pulled up and got out of the car with her gun drawn. Crouching low, she ran to the front door and knocked hard.

"Police! Open up now!" she yelled. She remained crouched; out of view of both front windows. After getting no response she crept around the house and looked through the windows. From what she could see the house looked normal. The furniture was draped with sheets and the lights were off. She went back to the front of the house and knocked on the door again. She might have left then if she hadn't noticed a spot on the door frame.

She thought back to the search of the mayor's mansion and remembered how odd it was that Annabel Yates owned about a case of calamine lotion. She had just applied some before fainting and Agent Adams had wondered at her pink-tinted arms when they'd arrived at the house. Even though the mayor mentioned his wife's tendency to use the pink balm. Luz wondered why she needed so much.

Luz bent to sniff the rose smudge but couldn't quite make out the scent of calamine. She pulled out her phone and dialed. Mike answered almost immediately.

"Dammit, Luz, you can't just go running off—"

"Mike," she cut him off. "I need Sonny to bring me a bottle of calamine lotion and a lab kit."

"What the hell?" he said slowly.

She explained why her finding was relevant. It all added up to evidence, the more she collected the stronger their case would be when they caught this maniac and put them away. Mike said he'd be there in fifteen minutes. Luz waited until he pulled up behind her car and got out before asking him for the lotion. He walked quickly to where she stood. He instructed the crime scene guys to process the front end of the house and while they were busy, he scolded Luz for messing up a possible murder scene.

Luz took the scolding badly. "Murder scene?" she asked fearfully.

Mike ignored her and made a call on his cell phone. After hanging up, he spoke with the techs. Then he walked back to her, shaking his head. "Been inside?"

Luz looked at the house. "There's no way in without breaking down the door. Mike, I think Nick is inside."

Mike nodded. "I do, too, but we'll have to wait. I've got some guys coming who will make sure we aren't walking into a trap. When they give us the okay, we can search the house."

Luz exhaled. "How long?" she asked.

"As long as it takes. But there's no guarantee that Nick is in there. And if he is, there's no guarantee that he's alive."

"I know that," Luz snapped. With every cell in her body she wished for Nick to be alive.

• • •

Why is it so cold? Nick thought. He'd been shivering for what felt like forever and couldn't make himself stop. It was summertime. It should be warm inside the building. Unless he was in shock. Or underground,

He rolled over to get a feel for the floor. The second he touched it, he recognized the texture; it was concrete. He didn't know what he should do with his discovery. If anything, being underground lessened his chances of discovery.

He thought about his captor. She left him some time ago and hadn't returned. He tried to think which would be worse— starving to death or having his throat cut. Either way would be painful, but the latter would be quicker. He moaned loudly, it wouldn't matter what he thought about starving to death. The killer had been clear on her desire to kill him; she had meant it when she said she would end his life. *But then where is she?*

He forced himself to stop thinking about the woman who planned to kill him and thought of Luz instead.

He loved Luz; loved her more than he had wanted to admit so soon, and the fear of losing that love overcame the fear of losing his life. Tears of frustration welled in his eyes. The killer said she would take care of Luz; said she'd make her pay. It would be the second time he couldn't save the woman he loved.

He would rather die than live through that again.

CHAPTER TWENTY-NINE

MAY 29TH, 2002 4:58 A.M.

Luz never wanted to choke someone as badly as she wanted to choke Mike. She'd been waiting for close to two hours and still wasn't allowed to enter the house. It was like they were taking their time to piss her off. She shook her head and groaned; she understood procedure, and how long it took, but she couldn't shake the feeling that they were running out of time.

"Santos, over here!" Mike yelled from the porch. Luz rushed to meet him, but he looked unhappy.

Her first thought was that they'd found Nick and he was dead. Mike must have seen the color drain from her face.

"Calm down, Luz. We haven't found him yet, but we did find this," he said, holding up a plastic bag with a box inside. Luz took the bag from him and looked at the box closely.

"Did you look inside?" she asked.

Mike produced a second bag that held papers. Luz looked at them and gasped. "Mike, those are the papers to the knife that Elaine Murphy sold to the killer. Cliff told me she kept them in a box like this."

"Good. That's one connection. I'll send this to the lab and we'll know for sure in about an hour. It makes sense now; Annabel Yates would have been the only other person with access to the mayor's knife collection. This whole thing is a mess." He shook his head.

Luz was growing impatient. "Mike, can I go in now?" Just then, Sonny came out of the house shaking his head slowly. Luz's heart jumped to her throat at the expression on his face.

"He's not in there," he told her.

"Bullshit!" she yelled. "I know he's in there!"

Sonny stepped aside and pointed to the house. "Be my guest. We've cleared the house." Luz brushed past him and ran inside with her fists clenched. The techs gave her a look, but no one tried to stop her.

An hour later, exhausted and fear-stricken, Luz sank to the floor of the kitchen, her head in her hands. She heard someone walk through the doorway but didn't care. She felt so helpless and she knew others weren't used to seeing this side of her. They viewed her as being emotionally in check. She realized then that Nicholas Mason meant more to her than anyone had in a long time.

Luz looked up and saw her boss.

"Leave me alone, Mike."

"It's not your fault, you just need to—"

"I said leave me alone," she yelled at him. "Look at the time, Mike! I've failed! Nick is dead because of me!" She spun around and kicked the cabinets closest to her. The door buckled and flew open with the force of her kick. Luz and Mike stared at the opening in front of them. Instead of three large cabinets with separate doors—it was one large door made to look like a separate piece.

Luz started through the opening, but Mike held her back. "You don't know who or what is down there. If this is a trap, you'll be walking right into it!"

She shrugged him off and walked a couple of feet into the opening. Then she stopped when she noticed a blinking red light at the end of the short passageway. She turned and walked back out into the kitchen. Mike was shouting at Sonny to get a bomb tech down there fast and the tech guys prepared to follow her in.

"There's a blinking light on a console at the end of the passageway. There's a steel door at the end. I want that door opened *now*," she ordered Mike.

"I'm doing the best I can, Santos. Calm down and remember who's the boss here."

She took a deep breath and leaned against the wall. Eddie approached her and addressed her in a soothing tone. "If he's in there, Luz, we'll get him out."

Luz smiled weakly and nodded. "I know. It's just that… I wish I knew if he was still alive. If not here, then somewhere. I don't know if I could…" her voice cracked, and she left the sentence unfinished.

A tall blond man entered the room and Mike brought him over to Luz. "Santos, this is Cody Everett. He's the bomb tech. Walk him to the console you told me about and we'll see if we can get the door opened."

Luz shook Cody's hand and led him through the passageway to the steel door. She held a flashlight as he studied the console. Fifteen minutes went by and she couldn't hold her curiosity any longer. "What do you think it is?" she asked.

Everett had removed the console casing and worked his way through several wires underneath. He used his sleeve to wipe his forehead and turned to her. "Just your basic trip sequence. Had we tried to dial in the code it would have triggered an explosion of some sort. Except that these wires aren't used for an explosive device. From what I can see it looks like they connect to a pump of some sort." He got up and Luz followed him back out of the tunnel-like space to where Mike stood waiting.

"I'm going to need the blueprints of this property," Everett stated.

Sonny walked over. "I'm way ahead of you, I have them, but they aren't much help if there's a bomb." Everett went to the counter where the blueprints were laid out.

"What's this?" he asked pointing to the section of wall under the sink.

"Water pipes," Sonny replied, but Luz knew where Everett was going.

"No," she said pointing to another set of pipes on the drawing. "*These* are the water pipes, *these* are the gas pipes."

Everett stood and looked at a tech across the room. "Eric, come over here," he called, and the young man walked over.

"What do you suppose these pipes are for?" he asked the young man then explained that Eric had worked in home construction before joining the force. Eric leaned over the drawing, studied it intently, then stood up.

"Those aren't pipes; it's a ventilation system. Probably built to filter cold air into a refrigerated room of some sort."

Luz nodded. "Of course. It's a giant freezer. The mayor and his wife would have had small dinner parties here. This is where they must have stored the food for their guests."

Everett looked back to the blueprint and followed the pipes to the other side of the kitchen. He walked over to where a painting of fruit hung and moved the picture aside.

There, on the wall, were the controls to the freezing unit.

"Shit!" he uttered, and Luz walked over to where he stood. "The setting is jammed to high."

"But wouldn't we hear the generator powering this room?" Luz asked.

"We did," Eric said and they all turned to him. "We were down in the basement and assumed it was the furnace or something."

They followed him to the sound and Everett nodded. "That's it, but it doesn't sound like it's fully functional." Just then the mild hum they heard grew louder.

"What happened?" Luz asked and ran upstairs to the kitchen, she raced down the small passageway and saw that the red light was now green and felt that the steel door was growing cold. Fast.

"Everett!" she yelled. "Get in here now!" He came down the tunnel. "What happened?"

He studied the wires once more and shook his head. "I didn't see it before but there's a small timer on this and it stopped at twelve."

Luz looked at her watch; it had been exactly twelve hours since the killer had called her. Her blood ran cold. Nick was inside. She turned to Everett. "Get this door open now or Nick will freeze to death!" she cried frantically but Everett retreated out of the tunnel looking grim.

"The door is steel and sealed tight. The lock would take hours to break," he explained.

"Get started, then. We don't *have* hours," Luz ordered.

"I don't have the resources—" he started.

"The FBI will get you everything you need. Just, please hurry!" she said. They got to work.

• • •

Nick heard the hum get louder and didn't know what it was. Blindfolded, he couldn't see anything, so he was unable to guess at the source of the sound. But when the cold air filtered in and the temperature dropped, his guess was that he was in a giant freezer. *That would explain the cold*, he thought.

The temperature was decreasing at an alarming rate and his back was already pained from his constant shivering. *This is it; this is how I'm going to die*, he thought. At least with the knife he knew it would be quick, but freezing to death? He would suffer a long, long time.

Shaking uncontrollably, he closed his eyes and tried to prepare himself for the oncoming pain.

• • •

Luz tapped her foot on the tiles of the kitchen and looked at her watch for the hundredth time. She pictured finding Nick's cold, lifeless body frozen in an agonizing position on the floor of the freezer and her heart filled with pain.

Cody Everett had been cutting away at the lock for an hour and a half now and he was only halfway through. She couldn't wait another hour and a half; she had to get in. She pushed past the others in the tunnel and was about to call for Everett when they all heard a loud bang. She quickly made her way through the tunnel to where Everett stood with a big smile on his face.

"The lock gave way under pressure. It's all yours."

Luz wanted to kiss him. Instead, she turned to the ruined door and gave it a good kick. The lock fell through and Luz reached in and pulled the latch and opened the door. She burst into the room but didn't see Nick. She ran through shelves of frozen meat, but the room simply ended.

"What the fuck?" she yelled. She spotted a small door on the opposite wall with a simple deadbolt on it. She took out her gun, took aim and shot the lock off the door. At the sound of the shot the others ran into the room. She took no notice of them. She swung open the door and saw Nick lying bound and gagged on the floor across the room. The new room was colder than the last and Luz could see her breath clearly.

She rushed to Nick, overjoyed at having found him. Dread replaced her joy as she turned him over and felt his skin. He was ice cold and he didn't appear to be breathing. A thin layer of frost coated his face and his lips were blue.

Her eyes filled with tears and she let out a loud sob.

Mike, Eddie and Sonny ran over to her. "Luz, I called for an ambulance, they'll be here any minute," Eddie said.

But Luz ignored him. "Nick, I'm sorry. I'm so, so sorry. Oh god. Nick!"

The paramedics arrived. Eddie and Mike pulled her away so that they could take a look.

"He's still breathing," one of them said.

Luz clung to those three words all the way to the hospital.

10:30 A.M.

Nick woke up and saw Luz smiling down at him. "Hi," she said, and he smiled. "Don't try to talk; I'm just happy you woke up."

He stared at her a while longer and closed his eyes. Luz watched him drift off and bent to kiss his lips. She whispered, "I love you."

THE NEXT DAY

Annabel Yates would be tried for every murder in Seattle, but she refused to budge on her story. It was her resistance to cooperate that bothered Luz the most. She admitted to killing her family, claiming abuse from her mother, brother and sister. She also told them she'd known about her husband's affair years earlier but refused to admit to killing Leah Mason. Even after Nick had woken up, his statement about the woman who tried to kill him matched everything they had. But why then, wasn't Luz satisfied?

A knock at the door caught her attention. "Come in," she said, and opened the door to an enormous vase of tiger lilies. Nick lowered the vase.

"Hey beautiful," he said.

Luz stood up and came around the desk to take the flowers from him. "Hey. I thought they weren't going to let you out until this afternoon," she said, checking her watch.

"Well they checked me over and decided I'd be okay," he said, taking her into his arms. "Plus, I couldn't wait one more minute to see you." He kissed her lightly on the lips. They stayed locked together for a while longer, the kissing getting more and more hungry. All the tension and worry that had built up the last week leaked out with every touch, and the need to be together was stronger than ever. When Luz remembered where she was, she had to break the connection.

"I think I'll be getting off early today," she said a bit breathless. It felt so good to feel his warm skin on her own. She was still processing the horror of the last few days but the feeling of his ice-cold skin when she'd found him was one memory she was hoping to forget.

He smiled and took a seat. "So what are you working on?"

"The case, what else? But there are a lot of things we overlooked." She related all the details along with her doubts about the killer. Nick listened intently. "I think we were all so eager to find one killer that we didn't find *the* killer; you know what I'm saying?"

Nick nodded. "Can I be of some help? Maybe I can be a witness or something. I don't know, but I want that woman behind bars," he said with a shudder.

"No. We have enough witnesses so far. The problem is that their recollection seems to be hazy. But if we need you, we'll call you. Your testimony of her state of mind might be useful. Your captor's speech about being homeless and hating her family matches what Annabel—I mean Francis—told us about her past. Hopefully that will be enough for the judge. We also found out that Annabel knew the codes to her husband's vault of knives. She won't admit to using them but knowing them should be enough."

Nick leaned back in the chair. "So you've got your hands full." He sighed. "I was hoping maybe you would have some time for lunch."

"Sure. Just let me wrap this up here and we can leave. I'm so glad you're feeling better," she said placing some files back in her drawer.

About forty-five minutes later she'd sent the last of the reports to her boss and was ready to go.

She grabbed her jacket and opened the door but stopped when the phone rang. "Dammit. I was so close!" She walked back to her desk and plopped down in her chair. She pressed the speakerphone button. "Yes?"

"Santa."

"What, Rosa? What could you possibly want now?" The

woman exasperated her.

"I've been dealing with the press all day and I dealt with them all day yesterday. You need to come do your job." The admin sounded especially aggressive.

"Rosa, that's your job."

Rosa ignored her. "Mike is meeting with the city council about the mayor and I can't handle…" while she went on and on, Luz rolled her eyes and looked over at Nick. She ceased her mockery when she saw that his face was white, and his eyes were frozen, locked on the phone in her hand. Luz tried to get his attention by snapping her fingers, but he only stared, as though he were in a trance, or catatonic.

"Rosa, I'll have to call you back," she said into the phone.

"Oh no you don't. You will not ignore me!" Rosa yelled back.

"Dammit Rosa, Nick is in my office…" she began and saw Nick shake his head vigorously, but she didn't understand what he wasn't agreeing to. "…and we have to go."

The other line was quiet, then Rosa disconnected the call. Luz went to Nick and put her arms around him. "Nick, are you okay?" Nick's eyes held such a haunted look that Luz had to turn away. She sat next to him and waited for his panic to subside. When his breathing evened out he turned to Luz.

"That was her," he said, his voice barely audible.

"What? That was Rosa, my boss's assistant."

Nick turned to her, looking her straight in the eyes. "No. That was *her*."

Then, all hell broke loose.

CHAPTER THIRTY

MAY 30ᵀᴴ, 2002 11:45 A.M.

Eddie and Leroy had just finished closing off the front entrance of the precinct building when Luz ran toward them.

"They're almost done searching the building, but I think she's already gone," she said.

"There's no way she could have gotten out so fast," Leroy said.

"There are ways out of this building that you don't even know about," Luz said holding up a file. "I've got her information. I'm going to her house. Anyway, who's up to joining me?" she asked looking at Eddie.

"What about Nick?" Leroy asked.

"He's going to wait for me in my office. I said I'd be right back."

"But—"

"There are no buts. If I told him I was leaving, he would insist on coming and I don't want to worry about him again. I'll call him when I'm on the road and tell him. Better yet, Leroy would you go and tell him I was called out?"

Leroy backed up. "Oh no, I'm not getting involved—"

"Please. I need this favor. I'll owe you."

Leroy reluctantly agreed. "Fine, but you *do* owe me," he said.

"As long as you keep your mind out of the gutter, I'm all yours," she said and turned to leave with Eddie in tow.

They pulled up to a small apartment building ten minutes later and Eddie looked up at the place. "What are we doing here?" he asked.

"This is the address in Rosa's file."

"Well, this isn't where I dropped her off yesterday," he complained, and Luz double checked the file.

"But this is it; this is what the file says," Luz said, a sick feeling coming over her. She put the key back in the ignition. "Then show me where you dropped her off," she ordered him, and they tore away from the sidewalk.

He took her two miles north toward Greenlake and they stopped in front of an old house with a modest lawn and a tiny front porch.

"This is it," Eddie said getting out of the car.

Luz met him on the sidewalk with her gun out. "Call for backup. If she's in here, we'll need the street blocked off. We'll need four or five units immediately."

Eddie radioed it all in and they decided to enter the house through the front door. They got on the porch and Eddie knocked, staying clear of any windows or possible lines of sight.

When no one came to the door, Luz took a peek through one of the front windows. "Shit, have you ever been inside?"

"No, I just dropped her off. Why?"

Luz moved out of the way. "Take a look." They switched

places and Eddie looked inside.

"It looks vacant. I'm going to run the address," he said, reaching for his radio. A few minutes later he got an answer. "The house is under the name Francis Aberleen."

Luz looked at him. "What? What the hell is the connection?" Eddie shook his head and looked at her blankly.

Police cars pulled up to the house and Luz organized a barrier so that whoever they found in the house would not be able to go very far. Mike had arrived at the scene and beelined it straight for Luz.

"What the hell is going on Santos?"

"It's Rosa. She's the killer."

"That's what I hear but shouldn't we be looking for her at her apartment?"

Eddie spoke up. "This is where I picked her up and dropped her off."

"But she lives in an apartment. I already sent two units over there to secure the place."

Eddie was insistent. "This is where I picked her up and dropped her off. This house. I saw her walk out of this front door."

Luz looked at Mike. "We need to look inside. Set up an entry team and we'll go in and see. I need to know why Rosa was coming out of a house owned by the mayor's wife."

Mike raised his eyebrows but didn't say a word. He organized a team for entry. When everything was ready, Luz stood aside while the door was forced open. One by one they cleared the rooms of the house but found nothing. The only room that looked used was the upstairs bedroom and what they found in that bedroom chilled Luz to the bone.

"Christ, it looks like Hate fest 2002 in here," Mike said.

The walls were lined with paper clippings on all the murders from Leah Mason to the mayor's recent articles. Pictures of each victim were pasted in a row with a timeline drawn on the bottom with dates and words underneath. Under Leah Mason's picture was the word SLUT. Under Mildred Jamison's picture was the word WHY. Under the mayor's picture was the word SLEAZY and under Madeline Baker's picture was the word WHORE. What scared Luz the most was seeing her own picture; it was all over the walls. Pictures from articles in which she'd been recognized for her abilities in the field, and from various award ceremonies held at city hall. When she looked more closely she found a few snapshots of herself and recognized one of them from the picnic she had with Nick, while another was from her night out with Mike to the mayor's mansion. Some of her pictures were slashed up and others had tacks pushed so far in they looked permanently embedded into the wall. Chills ran through her. She swallowed hard, fighting down the terror that threatened to overwhelm her.

"Whoa," Eddie said in a scared voice and Luz understood his fear. Not three days before he had gone away alone with that woman. Luz wondered why she hadn't killed him then.

"It looks like she's fixated on me the most. I mean, looking at this timeline, she's tracking her killings one by one. Even here where she wrote the word 'why' under some of her victim's names, that shows her confusion and doubt. She seems to think she had motive killing most of these people, but the random killings show that her thinking became irrational and unjustifiable. She was having problems facing her crimes and—" Luz was interrupted

"Captain!" called one of the officers; "You better come see this!" Everyone stopped what they were doing and followed Mike into the adjoining bathroom.

"Oh shit," Mike said. The bathroom floor was littered with empty bottles of calamine lotion. The bathtub was filled to the brim with them, as were the sink and toilet. Everywhere they looked were piles of the pink bottles. Mike turned to the officer. "I want this place dusted for prints and sent off. I need to know if these prints match the ones in Rosa Acker's file." The officer nodded and set to work.

• • •

Francis Aberleen (a.k.a. Annabel Yates) hovered over the toilet with her nose crinkled in disgust. She rarely used public toilets due to the bacteria that surely thrived there, but she was forced to use the toilet in her cell. She had avoided using it for as long as her bladder would allow and now she tried her hardest not to touch the repulsive bowl, knowing that whoever used it last wouldn't have been hygiene conscious at all.

She finished and looked over at the roll of single-ply toilet paper bolted in the wall. The last thing she wanted to do was drip dry, so she took her chances with the tissue. Pulling off about five squares she folded them carefully, while keeping her balance, and wiped clean. She stood up and pulled her underwear back into place, letting her long skirt fall back to her ankles and sat down.

Thoughts of the murders rolled through her mind and she wondered anew how anyone would think her responsible. But she didn't wonder long because the same answer came to her over and over again.

She thought back to her life in New York, when she lived in her mother Meredith's beat up Cadillac with her brother and sister. Life had been tough back then, but that was no reason for her mother to make it harder. Her mother had married her father at eighteen and had all three children soon thereafter. But her mother had been an abusive and unfaithful woman and one day her father got fed up and left. After that, they lost the house and almost everything inside. Her mother had a hair-brained idea and that idea entailed going to New York City.

When they arrived, Meredith set to work trying to find modelling gigs for her oldest daughter Suzanne. Meanwhile, Francis and her brother, Ritchie, were left in the car almost nine hours at a time to fend for themselves. Most of the time they would venture out into the city in search of food or money, but they were so young, and the big city was a bit scary.

It didn't take long for the fear to wear off. When her brother turned fifteen, another birthday gone uncelebrated, he got tired of sitting in the car and foraging for food. He decided he would make his own money and disappeared for three weeks. When her mother found out she didn't seem to care; one less mouth to feed.

After that Meredith took her along on their daily outings to what Francis thought was a modeling company. Francis was thirteen years old at that time, but having lived on the streets for nine months, was no longer naive. The first time she had walked into the small building and seen the people and equipment inside she knew at once that it wasn't a modeling agency. It was a pornography studio.

Her mother made her sit and watch her sister being used day in and day out for months. The images of that time still made her sick. One day, her mother told her that the sleazy director had his eye on her and that he wanted *her* to star in a movie. To any other thirteen-year-old, acting in a movie would seem like a dream come true but Francis had seen enough to know that it would be a nightmare.

She pleaded with her mom for protection, but her mother just looked at her with disdain and asked why she didn't want to contribute to the family's wellbeing. Her mother explained that these movies were what had fed and clothed them for the past year. What Meredith didn't mention was that the movies had also supported her own addiction to alcohol and other drugs.

One morning her mother woke her up in the back seat of the car and told her that today was the day she would be a star. Francis resisted. She screamed, kicked and bit her mother so badly that Meredith left her and took Suzanne to work. That day Francis planned her escape. She packed up what little she had and decided to run away. She hadn't gone far when she ran into her brother.

He was on a street corner dealing drugs to a younger crowd when she happened upon them. Already upset that her own mother would subject her to perverts she took her anger out on Ritchie. She walked up to him and began scolding him loudly, making a scene on the street. Her brother's customers ran away, and Ritchie turned to her. Seeing his face, she knew he was not the little boy she had grown to count on as a brother. His face looked years older and his eyes were crazed and wild. He wasn't only selling drugs—he was taking them as well. He took one look at her and backhanded her across the face, sending her flying to the ground.

Crying, she picked herself up and started back toward the Cadillac. If she couldn't trust her family not to hurt her then she couldn't trust anyone else. He followed her to the car, ranting and raving the whole way. Francis was scared and locked him out of the car. He stood outside, sputtered obscenities and waved his arms. Seeing him like that, Francis doubted even he knew who she was.

Her doubts were confirmed when he broke the rear window and let himself in the car. He grabbed for her and she shied away screaming at him to leave her alone. He called her a bitch and accused her of stealing his money and then began beating her over and over. He only stopped when her cries ceased. He left her alone, bloodied and bruised, to suffer in peace.

Her mother and sister returned but neither of them seemed alarmed or offered help. Instead, they ignored her until most of her injuries healed. She hated them for that and she hated her brother for hurting her so bad. But she didn't say a word.

It would have fallen on deaf ears. She let the rage build inside, unaware of the damage she was doing to herself.

A year passed, and her brother had become a notorious drug dealer on the streets. Her sister was a prostitute and her mother was a drunken whore of a woman who cared for no one but herself. Francis managed to get paid washing cars. It had taken a while, but she had saved up two hundred dollars and hid it in the ashtray in her section of the Caddy. One day she came back to the car to find her brother and mother sitting on the trunk of the car smoking crack while her sister earned a living in the back seat.

Horrified, she yelled at her mother to make her sister stop and get out of the car. Her mother cussed at her and slapped her hard, warning her to keep her mouth shut. Francis lashed out at her mother, but Meredith only smiled and held up a small wad of money; her money. Full of rage, Francis ran at her mother, knocking her off the car and hitting her in the face. Her brother laughed and pulled her off and pushed her into the street. Her mother recovered and got to her feet, yelling at her to never come back, telling her she was good for nothing, calling her a little whore.

Francis ran and ran. Tears blinded her, but she didn't stop until her legs could no longer carry her. She rested for a while, still seething with rage at the betrayal of her own family; at the revolting things they did to survive, at the sickening things they expected her to do to stay alive. She was so lost in her thoughts that she didn't hear the man come up behind her. By the time she did notice him he was almost on top of her. She jumped to her feet, but he already had a hold of her. She struggled and screamed but he placed his hand over her mouth and began ripping off her pants.

At that point she knew what it was he wanted from her. There was no point resisting any further. He was too strong. Terror gripped her, and she fought him, but it was useless, so she lay limply, and he raped her until he lost interest, which didn't take long.

Hurt, abused, neglected and in pain, she plotted her revenge as she lay on the cold cement of the alleyway. Eventually she got up and went to the little smoke shop down the street. She had been in the store a couple of times and noticed that they sold more than cigarettes. She walked through the entrance and made her way to the back of the shop where they kept the shelves of knives. Then she counted her day's earnings—twenty-eight dollars and sixty-seven cents—and picked out the knife she could afford. She bought it without incident and left the store with blood on her mind.

It was dark when she returned to the Cadillac. Her brother was sleeping in the open trunk and her sister and mother were inside. She crept over to make sure they were all asleep and then took out the knife. She didn't allow herself the chance to second guess her next move. The horrific life she had been living had to come to an end if she were going to ever become a normal person.

She killed her brother first. He had barely woken up when she stabbed him in the throat and once in the chest. She listened to him choke on his own blood for a moment, then opened the back door. Her sister was asleep but smelled like sex and that smell nauseated Francis, fueling her fury. She quickly cut her throat, but not before Suzanne woke up and screamed.

Her mother woke in a drunken stupor and when she saw Francis she began screaming at her again. Francis merely pointed at her dead sister and held up the knife covered with the blood of her siblings. Her mother stopped mid-sentence and stared at her daughter as if realizing a mistake had been made. Francis told her mother of her hate, told her how much better she would feel after she killed her. Meredith pleaded with her daughter, telling her lies, telling her that she loved her and that she had always been her favorite.

Francis let her mother whine until she couldn't bear to hear the sound of her pathetic apologies any longer. She simply jammed the knife into Meredith's throat and twisted the handle until her mother's eyes were vacant and her breath no more.

• • •

Someone coughed, and Annabel looked across the hall to the occupied cell where an old man was staring at her. She lay down in bed and pulled the blanket over her. She didn't want to return to the past, but it was the only thing she could think about. Nothing came to mind in that hellish place other than what had put her there.

After killing her family, Francis roamed the city, increasingly aware of her growing belly. She had tried repeatedly to lose the baby—falling for no reason, picking fights with others on the street—but all her efforts failed, so she chose to ignore the fact that she was five months pregnant.

Surprisingly, the police never found her, if they were even looking. The bigger she got, the less work she could find for herself. No one wanted to hire a fourteen-year-old, pregnant and homeless girl. Instead, she spent her days in a library and her nights in shelters throughout the city. She taught herself everything from mathematics and science to history and art. Soon she began daydreaming about the life she would one day live, a life where she would have everything she wanted; where she would be respected and never have to live on the streets again.

She hung on tight to that dream and began educating herself so that one day it would come true. But she got so caught up that she had forgotten the baby she carried inside; one day on her way to the shelter she felt a strong pain in her abdomen and then felt warm liquid running down her leg and saw it puddling on the dirty sidewalk. The pain increased, and she barely made it to the steps of a nearby church when the pains developed into full-blown labor. She crouched on the steps of the church, crying out, wishing there was someone to help her, but no one came. The last thing she remembered was passing out cold.

She awoke in a warm bed unaware that a nun had heard her cries and taken her in. The baby, she was told, was alive and well and being cleaned and looked after in the other room. Not surprising at all that she didn't care much about the baby she had given birth to. It merely represented the traumatic events that were her pathetic existence up to this point. The only thing that mattered was the fact that she was closer to finding a better life for herself.

The nuns came to her with the baby, expecting her to be happy and ready to hold it. At first, she wanted nothing to do with the child, but curiosity won out and eventually she consented to seeing the child. Holding her daughter for the first time brought back memories of the man who raped her, and she called for the nuns to take the baby away. They didn't understand her repulsion with the baby but took her to the nursery anyway. Days later, one of the nuns approached her and asked her to name the baby. She asked them what they had been calling her and the nun told her they had given her the name Rosary—Rosa for short. Francis nodded and told her that that name would do and asked when she would be able to leave. The nun explained about the birth and how much damage Francis had sustained to her lower area and Francis cringed with the memory of Rosa's conception, remembering the pain of that night, not just the rape, but the murder of her family.

The next day she was preparing to leave when the same nun walked in carrying her baby and asking when she would leave with her child. Francis stated that she didn't want anything to do with the baby and the nun called her a bad mother. The accusation reminded her of her own mother and the life she had given her children; it was then that she decided to take her baby with her.

She found a place to live with a friend from her old job and set out to look for work. She was totally unprepared for the responsibilities of motherhood. The baby was too needy and suffered from colic and after three months she buckled and left her child with her friend, Lynne. She felt no remorse for her actions; instead, she felt an odd sense of freedom.

After that she made her way to Seattle. She had read that scholarships were vastly available to underprivileged kids of her age and felt she had a shot if she could just pass the test for her GED. Surprisingly enough, she did pass the test and began her new life, never looking back at who and what she left behind.

CHAPTER THIRTY-ONE

MAY 30ᵀᴴ, 2002 3:10 P.M.

Rosa Aberleen had a horrible childhood, and that was an understatement. She had blocked most of it out to get on with her life but every so often she would have a dream, or a flash-back and it would make her sick. Being beaten for no reason, being physically, sexually and emotionally abused. Having cigarettes put out on her hands and feet, being locked outside without food, sleeping on the street. Being forced to do the sickest things in order to meet her most basic needs. All these things and more were locked up in her mind, finally finding release. It was a release that made everything feel better, but unfortunately the only release she had was killing. Well, it was unfortunate for her victims. For her it was the only way to obtain the peace she so desperately wanted.

She had found her mother ten years ago, but the reunion was anything but loving. Her mother had shunned her, telling Rosa to stay out of her life, that she had no room for her now. But Rosa wouldn't listen. She insisted that she wasn't there to ruin her mother's new life; she just wanted to know the woman who had given birth to her. But Annabel wouldn't listen; she refused to acknowledge her own daughter.

That was over the phone. Rosa began showing up at her mother's place of work and her mother became afraid that those around her would learn of her background and the things she had done when she was younger. Rosa was the only link to her past and her mother wanted to keep her quiet.

Finally, she started to show love and understanding, promising that someday Rosa would be a part of her life again. She set up an account where money could be deposited, and she paid her daughter to stay away. At first, Rosa took the money, thinking it a token of motherly love, that her mother wanted a better life for her. But after her mother's husband became mayor she knew her chance at a real family was slipping away.

So she drove to her mother's new luxurious mansion, intent on asking why she wanted her daughter out of her life. But her mother wasn't there; instead she got a peek at the man she had chosen to marry. Curious and very interested, she followed Anthony Yates across town to a small marina. She watched him get out of his car and walk down a long dock out of sight. She waited two hours for him to come back to his car, but he took his time. So she got out of the car to find out where he had gone. It was dark on the dock and she couldn't see very far but when she heard voices, she hid behind the marina's supply shed and listened.

What she heard was not what she expected. Two people agreeing to meet again soon. One of them was Yates and the other was a woman. They were exchanging sexual suggestions and praising each other on their abilities in bed. The woman was insulting her mother, claiming she, the whore, was the one who could make him happy.

Rosa fumed, knowing at once what needed to be done. She waited until they had kissed goodbye and she watched Anthony Yates walk back to his car. She looked down the dock and saw a woman standing outside on the deck of a houseboat. She returned to her car, found some gloves under the seat and walked toward the boat. She assumed the woman was the mayor's mistress, she assumed this woman was the slut he was sleeping with, that this woman could cause her mother to lose everything; in turn causing *her* to lose everything. She was shaking with anger by the time she reached the boat, but the woman was nowhere to be found.

Climbing onto the boat, careful not to cause too much swaying, she spotted the open door and stepped quietly inside. One light was on down the hall but first she stopped in the kitchen for a knife. The kitchen was modern and bigger than she thought it should be for a boat. Frantically, she opened three drawers before she found a large carving knife. She then crept down the hall toward the back of the boat, as silent as possible. She reached the door of the lighted room and peeked inside. The woman was reading in bed, the lamp beside her was on. Rosa opened the door, but the woman didn't look up.

"Nick?" the woman asked. She looked up when she didn't get a response. Her eyes grew wide and filled with fear. "Who are you?" she asked but Rosa was already closing the space between them. Immediately the woman jumped out of bed and grabbed the lamp. Rosa held up her weapon and watched the woman shake as the implication sank in.

Before she knew it, the woman threw the lamp at her and ran for the door, but Rosa was quick and caught up to her as she was about to run onto the deck, probably to scream for help. Rosa tackled the woman and grabbed a handful of her hair and yanked her head up, almost snapping her neck. The woman cried and begged but her pleas went unanswered. Feeling with every bone in her body that it was right to do so, Rosa slit Leah Mason's throat.

She got up quickly to avoid getting blood on herself and left the boat in a hurry. When she got to her car she was breathing hard, but not from exertion. There was an excitement to what she had just done that, strangely enough, delighted her. In the back of her mind she told herself that it was wrong and that she was a monster, but she couldn't keep from smiling, from feeling the power she had never experienced before.

She brushed away all her thoughts but one; to find her mother and get her back.

• • •

Annabel stared at the ceiling of her cell thinking about her only daughter. Things should have been different, but it was too late to change anything. She should have put her daughter away a long time ago. Then she could have avoided this mess. *Why. Oh why didn't I do it?* She asked herself. But deep down, she knew the answer: *because she's your daughter and you are her mother*. It was a way to prove to herself that she hadn't completely failed Rosa. What gift is better than the gift of freedom? She sighed and looked around; freedom was a gift she herself would never receive.

She thought back to the night Rosa had come to her after killing Leah Mason. Rosa had called her and asked to come over. Annabel had refused on the spot, telling her daughter that it wasn't safe for her to do so. Rosa had threatened to tell the press everything about her mother and Annabel relented and agreed to meet her at a house they owned across town.

On the drive over, she wondered what could be so important that Rosa had to drag her out of bed in the middle of the night. When she got to the house she found her daughter smiling, almost giddy. Before she had a chance to ask what was going on, Rosa blurted out what had happened.

Horrified, Annabel had yelled at Rosa, explaining the enormity of the deed that had been done. Outwardly she was enraged at her daughter's lack of sense; inwardly she was fearful that her own legacy had been passed down somehow. She could almost picture the dark twisted strands of their shared DNA, knotted, bulbous and dripping with blood. Either way it was her own fault. She had left her daughter with people of questionable character. She'd left her child to suffer the same life she had tried so hard to leave behind herself.

Annabel looked at her daughter in a new light and listened to what she had to say. Rosa, with no remorse in her voice, told her that she had done it all for Annabel. She wanted her mother to know that her husband was cheating on her but that she had taken care of it all. The shock of Anthony's infidelity didn't outweigh the fact that her daughter was seriously disturbed. But instead of showing revulsion, Annabel simply smiled down at Rosa and thanked her politely.

Rosa beamed at the praise and after that everything between them went smoothly until the night Annabel got a call. It was from a man named Fredrick James, the man who knew too much. He told her that he saw Rosa leave that night and followed her to their meeting place, and after looking up the address he figured out that Annabel was the mayor's wife. He also assumed she'd ordered the killing of her husband's mistress and he knew that her husband would be the key suspect in Leah Mason's murder.

Annabel panicked and asked him what he wanted. It was simple enough: he wanted money. They worked out a deal: he would stay silent about what he knew—or thought he knew—and she would make his life very comfortable. She set him up with a job on her husband's staff, set his family up with a house and even paid for his daughter's tuition to college. She assumed that would be enough, but the man got greedy and made threats and she was tempted to kill him herself but the risk to her was too great. Instead, they set up a fund in Leah Mason's name, with which she could deposit a set amount of money and he would have access to that wherever and whenever he chose. This arrangement suited him just fine and it went on like that for nearly eight years until a few days before when the man took his own life.

She was grateful that she no longer had to pay for his luxuries; she didn't fear detection because the fund was legal in every aspect. But she was still stretched financially because she had bought a house in her old name so that her daughter would have a place to live. Rosa had rented an apartment so no one would become suspicious about her salary and the big roomy house she lived in. They kept in touch for the most part, secretly of course, but lately she hadn't heard from her daughter at all.

And then the killing began. Annabel tried to convince herself they had nothing to do with her daughter, but her heart knew the truth. She knew what her daughter went through after the first killing, the feelings of power and supremacy, and getting away with Leah Mason's murder had just added to her twisted ego. Annabel had gone through the same emotions after killing her own family but overcame the need to kill again by justifying her motive.

Her daughter hadn't done that. Rosa had given in to the need. Unlike Annabel, who after killing, vowed never to be a victim again, her daughter had worn her victim cape proudly, always feeling entitled, always justifying every wrong decision she made because she'd had a crappy childhood.

Annabel sighed. There was nothing she could do for her daughter. She had become someone and something else altogether and she had no desire to hold onto her any longer. But then why hadn't she told the police about Rosa? She could be exonerated for all the local murders and only stand trial for the ones in New York. Why was she protecting her daughter?

After all, Rosa had killed Anthony in cold blood. Lying, cheating Anthony and his whore of a mistress. She should feel grateful, but instead she worried that she would be next. Her daughter was sinking deeper into a black hole every day. What would stop her from turning on her own mother? Hadn't Annabel done that very thing?

Was it because she was already going down for three murders? Why not make it twenty? It wouldn't matter; she would sit in jail for the rest of her life anyway. It may even be the safer option. After trying so hard to live the life she'd always dreamed of, surrounding herself with rich and beautiful things, with powerful and wealthy people, she still ended up at the bottom of the barrel. What was that saying? *What goes around comes around.*

But her daughter deserved the punishment much more than she. Then she realized that any punishment Rosa was given would be better than the life she endured every day. That's why she was protecting her daughter; because it was the only way she knew how to love her.

Annabel had married, given birth to a son, and loved him with all her heart. Given him the childhood she'd always wanted, and he would be completing college in the fall and would grow up to be a very successful man. But what had she given Rosa? The answer was nothing.

That wasn't true; she had given Rosa something, the worst gift any parent could ever give: the need to kill.

• • •

Rosa stopped thinking about her past long enough to peek out of the vent. The hall was swarming with officers and she could feel the walls closing in. After hearing that Nick was not only in the office when she'd called Luz but had heard her voice on speakerphone, she hung up and ran. She knew the building very well. She had made a point of memorizing escape routes should she ever be caught. But how had they figured it out? How did they get Nick free in time? She left no clues. She clenched her hands hard, her nails breaking skin.

She had been so busy doing her job as executive assistant to the captain, dealing with the press, and the fact that her boss had become quite close-lipped about the investigation. She realized it was because he feared a leak in the department. For the last forty-eight hours he'd instituted a "need to know" policy around the office. If you needed to know, he'd let you know; other than that he held his cards close to his chest. At one point she tried warming up to Eddie, but he told her the investigation was on lockdown and that he couldn't share any details outside of the task force. But now, Nick was free of the trap she had set and now she was in big trouble. *How did this happen?*

The hunter had become the hunted. It was not a good feeling.

She thought of Luz Santos and anger boiled below the surface. She knew the itching would begin if she allowed herself to get worked up and it wasn't something she could afford to deal with at that point. Instead, she snuck another peek through the vent and waited for her chance to run. The sooner she got out of that stuffy place the better. It reminded her too much of the closet she was forced to sleep in as a child, but she wouldn't think about that.

The vent in the ceiling of the hallway that led to the reception area of her floor was the closest escape route she could use after learning that Nick was free and on the premises. She had run to the bathroom, praying no one else was inside. When she found it empty she jumped on the sink, pushed the drop ceiling tile over and pulled herself up. She had made her way above the hallway where the elevators were, so she would be able to leave the floor at the first possibility of escape. Those yoga classes she'd taken had really paid off as she easily and quietly worked her way through the building.

Since working at the police department she had begun physical training exercises to stay in shape, knowing that one day she might be faced with a situation like the one she was in. She was fit and intelligent and knew how to take care of herself. She had various disguises to avoid detection when she was out on the street and she'd learned to use different weapons with which to defend herself, but more importantly, with which to kill.

The knife had been her favorite early on but there needed to be a special connection with the knife and she had only felt that way about one knife. It was when she'd started learning about her mother; she used to dress up and attend functions at the mayor's mansion, touring with her boss and other people to different parts of the house. When she had been shown the extensive collection, she was captivated by a particular knife. After telling her mom of Leah Mason's death, she asked for access to that knife. Her mother outright refused but after some cajoling on her part, Annabel gave in. Rosa was given passwords and codes to the small building in exchange for distance from her mother and her mother's affairs. She had readily agreed and took the knife when she chose, at first just to get a feel for it, but the knife coupled with her lust to kill again gave her the extra push she needed into madness.

She put the imitation knife back into the mayor's collection and kept the real one for herself. When she lost the real knife, she panicked. She went back to the mayor's collection but found that the imitation knife had been auctioned off. So very carefully she had risked discovery when she recovered the knife from the evidence locker at work.

At first, she didn't know what to do; she couldn't just go around killing people without a purpose. She became obsessed with finding a reason to kill, never asking herself why she wanted to kill in the first place. She was on autopilot, the murder switch thrown. Then she thought of her childhood and where she came from and she made up her mind that the homeless were to blame. To anyone else it would sound irrational but to her it was a perfect fit, and how convenient it was that Mildred Jamison crossed her path on her way home one day.

After the first kill, the others came easily. Seattle had a vast population of homeless people and her selection was immense. Slowly she began to kill but then something unexpected happened. She lost all reason. She tried to control whom she killed and when she killed but she couldn't help herself. Then the itching came, relentless and unforgiving.

When she was a child and she was upset or mad with some-one, her skin would itch a lot, but she would calm herself by imagining hurting that person the way they had hurt her, and the itching would cease. Hives, the doctors told her. She'd been prescribed antihistamines and sent her on her way. She never took them; they made her groggy and with a hobby like hers, slow reflexes could mean the end to a murder career that had barely even started. It was the same when the desire to kill came along, except this time the itching was worse. It became unbearable. Her passion became a curse and she lost control.

Then Luz Santos got involved and she found her purpose once more. Kill all those who tried to learn her identity and all those who helped them. First, she tried to kill Luz but when that failed she began eliminating everyone who was a danger to her. She had started with Elaine Murphy, Marty Benedict, Nina Everly and almost Eddie Lopez, but that would have been too obvious, so she let him live. She paid dearly for that allowance; her itching was worse than ever. She had tried to kill Luz again, believing her to be at home sleep-ing when she broke in. But the place was empty, and, in her frustration, she torched the boat.

She clenched her fists in fury; Luz Santos had spoiled her plans and outsmarted her. She had arrested her mother on charges of murder and forced her to give up the deception she had worked so hard to keep intact. Luz Santos had ruined her life and now she would pay.

• • •

The guard let Luz into the holding room where Annabel was sitting. Luz rounded the table and sat in the seat on the opposite end of the table.

"How are you, Mrs. Yates?" she asked.

Annabel stared at her with obvious hatred. "Please spare me the nice cop routine, what do you want?" she said bluntly.

Luz cleared her throat. "Rosa Ackers is your daughter."

The silence seemed to last forever. Luz looked at Annabel and saw no sign of recognition in her eyes, but she could tell her words had affected the woman.

"I don't know what—"

"Don't bother lying. It won't help you."

"Nothing will help me, will it?" she snapped.

Luz went on, ignoring Annabel's attitude. "Rosa is your daughter, Annabel, or Christine, or whatever your name is," she led.

The other woman's head lifted, and she wore a look of surprise. "How did you know that?"

"The nuns who were there for Rosa's birth had pictures of you and your baby; it wasn't hard to see that it was you at fourteen. You told them your name was Christine."

"But how did you trace it? I was very careful, very, *very* careful," she insisted and for the first time Luz saw a chink in her armor.

"We found where Rosa lived. The apartment was under your old name. From there, we tracked down both your blood types to see if there was even a possibility you were related. Two murderers in one family, far-fetched, or it would seem so. The DNA matched so we started digging, calling up people and tracking the information. You might have been careful, but Rosa wasn't. After checking her employee file, we learned that most of her information was false, except for one of her references. A Ms. Rebecca Albert from Rosa's old neighborhood. They had an agreement that if anyone were to call, that Ms. Albert was to pretend she was an old co-worker and give the best reference possible. But when I spoke to Ms. Albert and told her what Rosa had done and is still capable of doing, she cooperated fully. I got Rosa's old address, if you can call it an address, and had the local cops visit your old friend Lynne Ackers. Does any of this ring a bell?"

Annabel didn't answer; she simply looked shocked. Luz continued. "So, Lynne tells them that you used to work together until you disappeared. When she saw you again, you had your new baby girl with you, and that baby's name was Rosa. You told her that you lived at a church; St. Joseph's. She said that you tried your best to be a good mother but ended up giving up and left your baby for her to raise. I asked her why she didn't try to find you or why she kept the child. She says she could never have any kids of her own, that her husband would beat her so badly every time she was pregnant, she'd lose the baby. In addition to that fact, they were poor and homeless a lot of the time. This way the baby was already born, and she decided to take her chances. She was hoping the baby could help her receive handouts that were previously denied to her." Luz looked straight at Annabel. "She didn't do a very good job. She told us that her husband didn't take to the new baby and was very abusive. Lynne, herself admits to abusing Rosa occasionally. I found hospital records showing broken bones at two and six years old, a concussion at seven and burns and bruises at ten, and that is just what was reported. I wonder what else she went through that no one ever saw. Sounds like a pretty shitty childhood if you ask me."

Luz watched Annabel closely; she knew that what she was saying was harsh, but she wasn't finished. "How could a mother do that?" she asked. "How could you walk away from your own flesh and blood?"

The woman glared at her. "Don't presume to know me, detective. You know nothing about who I am."

"What's to know? You murdered your family, gave birth to a daughter you left behind, started a new life here and lived under a false identity. What more is there?"

"Shut up!" yelled Annabel, visibly shaken. "I had my reasons and I don't need to explain myself to you!"

Luz leaned toward the woman. "That's where you're wrong. You *do* have to explain yourself to me. You are a killer and your daughter is killing people all over my city, so yes, you *do* have to cooperate!" She watched Annabel's hands ball up and remembered the attack the last time she visited. As much as she wanted to add assaulting an officer to the list of the woman's charges, she didn't want a black eye, so she stepped back.

"What my daughter does is none of my concern. I gave up being her mother a long time ago."

Luz was prepared for this answer and gave one of her own. "What about Theodore? Did you give up on him as well?" She could see the confusion on Annabel's face. "Rosa killed your husband. She wants her mother all to herself. What will stop her from going after your son?"

"She wouldn't…" Annabel started but didn't finish.

Her face went white "You have to help my son. Teddy doesn't know about Rosa, he doesn't even know about me. Nothing can happen to him," she implored, tears running down her cheeks.

Luz heard the desperation in her voice. "I'll help him, if you help me. I need to know everything about Rosa."

Annabel hesitated for a single second and began talking.

CHAPTER THIRTY-TWO

MAY 30TH, 2002 4:43 P.M.

Nick was upset. Luz had left him in her office to chase after the killer without knowing how dangerous she actually was. He would have followed her if he had known where she went, but all he could do was stay put. If any word came in about her, the police station was the best place to be. Officer Leroy Sacks had promised to keep him posted.

He was scared for Luz. She was unpredictable and impulsive; two traits that could cause both positive and negative results. He hoped this time they were positive. He hoped Luz found the woman who captured and tortured him with promises of death. Shivers raced down his spine and he folded his arms and leaned back in his chair.

Fatigue swept over him and he closed his eyes to rest. He was still recovering and not yet back to one hundred percent. He must have dozed for a couple of minutes before he was awoken by a small scratching sound. He opened his eyes a crack, but he was the only one in the office. He shut his eyes again to listen for the sound, but he didn't hear it and he dozed off once more.

Then all at once the noise returned, louder and the sound of something heavy dropping woke him. His eyes flew open and he found a woman standing in front of him. She was medium height and build with short blond hair that curled around her ears. The odd thing was that she was covered in what looked like dust and she was smiling but it didn't quite reach her eyes. He looked up and saw the vent in the ceiling had been kicked out.

"We meet again," she said, and Nick's mind spun with sudden recognition at the sound of her voice. She had come back, and this time she would finish him off.

• • •

Luz went back to the house owned by Francis Aberleen in Greenlake. Police officers and FBI agents were scattered all over the property, combing for clues to the killer's whereabouts. Agent Adams met her at the front door with a grim expression. Instead of stopping to chat, she brushed past him and motioned for him to follow. He followed her to the shed in the back yard.

"In the mood for gardening?" he asked when she started pulling out old flower pots. She gave him a wry expression and continued pulling out the pots until the floor of the shed was clear. Then she reached down with the butt of her gun and pounded on the surface. Agent Adams walked over scratching his head. "Hollow?" he asked, and Luz nodded.

Together they removed the metal sheet and found three small books containing about sixty pages each. Luz opened the first and read aloud. "The rage inside me has found its way free

The need for evil burns inside of me, the way to quench this thirst to kill, is to give in to this wicked thrill." She looked up at Blue with raised eyebrows.

"It looks like we have a psychotic poet on our hands," he said, scratching his head.

Luz read down the page and shook her head. "These are her diaries; this is a journal of her thoughts. I bet there are confessions of every killing in these journals." She skipped through the writings skimming each page until she came to a page where the writing was more erratic and less legible and showed it to Blue.

"The more I read the more obvious it becomes that her mental state is deteriorating. Read this section about her mother, this woman is in a lot of pain."

Blue grunted. "She'll be in a lot more pain before this thing is through."

"Her mother told me these were here. She said when Rosa resurfaced in her life that she held a lot of anguish and resentment. Annabel suggested she write down her feelings, hoping it would help. Rosa had told her mother of the diaries but not of the murders and atrocities that she wrote about." She looked at Blue and found him reading one of the books and shaking his head. He gave a low whistle and took out his cell phone.

"I'm going to need a shrink to decipher all this shit and

maybe it will lead us to where she's at now," he said before walking away, talking into his phone.

Luz continued to look through the writings, hoping she'd pick up a clue before the FBI had a chance to go after Rosa. She noticed a pattern. Rosa would regress into her past before her killings. On one occasion she had written for fifteen pages about her childhood before stopping. Always, the next entry mentioned a killing. Was it that she was trying to justify the killings? Was she telling herself that the homeless were responsible for her pain, and therefore didn't deserve to live? She worked herself into a tizzy, so amped up that the only way down was to take a life.

Luz was ready to give up when she picked up the third journal and began reading. This journal was newer. The binding was barely cracked, and the entries started with the date of only two weeks prior. The writings in this book were different. The other two were written in chronological order according to the killings. This book focused on Cliff Saunders, Eddie Lopez and Nicholas Mason. She read a little more and found her name among them and tried to find what one thing she and the others had in common. Then it hit her; she was one of the targets that got away. The killer had threatened Cliff but never got to him, Rosa wanted to kill Eddie but couldn't without attracting attention to herself, Nicholas had disappeared in the middle of her plan and Luz had escaped the killer more than once. The last entry was made a few days before, then nothing else. That worried her more than anything considering all of the daily entries she could see throughout the journals.

Chills ran down her back when she realized how enraged Rosa must have been when her continued efforts to eliminate these people failed time and again. Luckily, Cliff was in the safe house, which no one knew about except her and Mike. She and Eddie were armed and safe for the time being and Nick was back at the station. She pulled out her cell phone and called Sonny.

"Sonny, will you do me a favor?" she asked when he picked up.

"Sure, what is it you need, my dear?"

"Go to my office and check on Nick."

"Okay, did you want to stay on the line or should I call you back?"

"I can wait. Go ahead." She heard him open the door to his office and step into the noisy bullpen beyond. He knocked once on her office door. When there was no answer, Luz heard him open the door.

"You!" she heard him yell. There was a crash and the sound of someone falling to the floor.

"Sonny! What happened? Sonny!" she called but there was no answer. Then someone picked up the phone and spoke one word.

"Bitch."

The line went dead.

There was no mistaking the voice or its intent. Luz ran through the house calling for Blue to follow her to the police station where the killer was. Everyone stopped what they were doing and watched her run out the front door to her car. Agent Adams barely caught up to her before she sped away.

"You're serious?" he asked.

"We need to go!" she shouted. She left him on the sidewalk staring after her. She watched him in her rearview mirror as she drove away. He ran back toward the house shouting orders. She boosted her car to fifty and prayed to God they weren't too late.

• • •

Rosa stood over the limp body of Sonny Malone and smiled. "You were always too smart for your own good, Einstein," she said. She pulled the gun from his holster and pointed it at Nick.

She walked over to him and shoved the barrel of the gun in his face. "I hate guns; they give people a false sense of power. Anyone can shoot a gun, but not everyone can wield a knife like I can. Not everyone can stand to feel the life drain out of another human being."

Her words were ice cold and Nick felt a coldness run through his veins that made him shudder. At that moment, he would take a bullet over a blade; at least it would be quick and painless.

She shoved him toward the door and whispered in his ear. "But don't think for a minute that I would hesitate to shoot you if you don't do as I say."

She gripped him by the neck and opened the door. Everyone on the floor seemed to be busy doing their jobs and no one looked in their direction.

"Don't say a word and walk with me toward the elevators,"

she whispered sharply in Nick's ear.

They walked down the hall, past the officers at their desks. Nick desperately tried not to panic but he knew that once they were out of the building any hope of escape would wash away. They were almost to the elevators when Nick spotted Eddie across the lobby. In his mind Nick willed Eddie to look at him. *Shouldn't someone be watching the elevators?* he asked himself. But to his surprise, Rosa propelled him past the elevators and around the corner to a door leading to the stairs. Frantically, Nick tried to look back to where Eddie was standing but Rosa caught the effort and cuffed him hard with the butt of the gun. His vision blurred for a moment and he struggled to remain standing.

"Try that shit again, Nick, and you can kiss your life good-bye, now go!" she ordered and pushed him through the door. They were just through when they heard voices from the other side. Someone had seen them, and they were alerting the other officers. Rosa rushed him down the stairs, keeping the barrel of the pistol pressed firmly against his temple. Nick was terrified. One wrong step and Rosa would inadvertently blow his brains out. Not that it mattered. She would *intentionally* kill him soon enough.

But he had no time to think about that. He had to concentrate on putting one foot in front of the other and taking one flight of stairs at a time. The door opened above them and they heard voices from above.

"Rosa! Stop where you are!" Eddie shouted.

"Kiss my ass, Lopez! You come after me and Nick here gets

a bullet in his head!" she kept descending the stairs while she shouted, not slowing her pace. They could hear sounds of pursuit, but Rosa had no fear, she just stayed out of shooting range against the wall and kept going.

Suddenly the door opened one floor below them and Rosa pulled to a stop. She peered over the side of the railing. Then Nick saw the gun come up as she took aim and fired. The sound of the shot was deafening in the stairwell, but Rosa took advantage of the confusion it caused, grabbed Nick and started down once more. When they passed the fallen officer, Nick saw the blood pooled behind his head and his vacant eyes staring off into the afterlife.

Finally, they made it to the bottom and there were two doors, one leading to the lobby, which was sure to be swarming with cops and the other straight outside. Rosa chose the latter and opened the door with the intention of running. Slowly, she opened the door and shoved Nick out in front of her, using him as a shield.

That's when they saw Luz standing twenty feet from the exit. She had her gun drawn and pointed at Rosa's head. Rosa quickly pulled her pistol up to Nick's temple and backed up against the wall of the building.

"Rosa, put the gun down or I'll shoot," Luz said calmly but Nick could see the fear in her eyes.

"You shoot me, I shoot him it's as simple as that," Rosa spat in frustration. "Dammit Santos, can't you ever just let things go?"

"I know about you Rosa," Luz started.

"You know nothing about me!" she yelled back, slowly

backing away, dragging Nick with her.

• • •

Luz looked at the woman, her clothes covered in dirt and her eyes wild with a look of desperation. "What do you want, Rosa?"

Rosa stopped walking. "What?" she asked, looking around like an animal trapped.

"What do you want?" Luz repeated.

"What do you mean what do I want?" Exasperated and confused Rosa was sure the question led into a trap.

"I mean, what will it take to get you to stop this? Why are you doing this?" Luz asked again.

Rosa laughed. "I want to kill Nick, and when I'm done with him I want to kill you!"

"Then what?" Luz asked taking the tiniest step forward.

"Stop it!" Rosa screamed. "Stop trying to analyze me!"

"I'm just asking you a question. When will this all stop? After Nick? After me? We know you. You won't get very far."

"Don't be too sure. I got this far, didn't I?" Rosa replied a little less steady.

"It's over Rosa, put the gun down," Luz said.

Rosa pulled Nick along the wall, keeping her eyes on Luz. She stopped when she came to a dumpster along the wall, blocking her way. Frantically, she put as much room between her and the dumpster as possible. Luz saw this and wondered if it had to do with Rosa's obsession with homeless people.

"Afraid of getting a little dirty?" she asked nodding her head towards the trash bin.

"Dumpsters are filthy! There's no reason I should be near one."

"You used to climb in dumpsters all the time as a kid," Luz pushed while taking advantage of Rosa's agitated state to take another small step forward.

"Shut up! You don't know what you're talking about!" she screamed.

"Rosa, I know all about your childhood. I know about the Ackers and I know about the abuse. I know you used to sleep outside on the streets as well. I know all about the pains of being poor. I was poor myself once," Luz confessed.

"I know that! I know about you, too," she sneered. "About coming from a poor family but look at you now! Your clothes, your car, your house. You're fucking perfect and I hate you for it!"

Luz now understood why Rosa had chosen to fixate on her. She was living the life Rosa always wanted but never got. "But I was never abused, I was never homeless. Rosa, you need help. Let me get you that."

"I don't need your help and I certainly don't need your pity. I don't regret killing any of those people and I doubt anyone else cares that I took out those homeless morons. I did society a favor. If I enjoyed any of it, then we'll call that icing on the cake!" She laughed manically. "How fitting that I get to send Nick off like I sent his wife off."

She watched the blood drain from Nick's face but she pushed through her own shock to ask the question. "What are you talking about?"

A slow smile spread across Rosa's face. "Do I have to spell it out for you *detective*? I killed Leah Mason. At the time, I thought she was sleeping with Anthony Yates, my mother's husband. He could've ruined everything for me, so I had no choice. It came to light recently that it wasn't Leah he was screwing that night but some bitch in the boat next door. Madeline, I think her name was. She got what was coming to her eventually, but you know all about that right?"

Luz wanted to throw up. This fucked up woman was responsible for ruining so many lives, and Nick. Poor Nick. Leah's death destroyed him causing him to give up life as he knew it. "You're sick, Rosa, and you need help. What is happening to you mentally will kill you if you don't stop it all here and now," Luz promised but she knew deep down that there wasn't a shred of humanity left inside the monster that stood before her.

Rosa pressed the gun on Nick's temple and looked straight at Luz. Luz saw the madness take hold.

Headlights.

A baseball bat covered in blood.

Crazed eyes promising pain staring her down.

Luz blinked away the images. She couldn't afford to freeze up. She took a deep breath, steadying the gun in her hand. "If I die, Nick dies with me," Rosa said, and Luz could see her finger tense on the trigger.

Wasting no time, Luz held her breath and pulled the trigger.

• • •

After hearing Rosa confess to killing Leah, Nick barely heard the rest of the exchange. His mind grew fuzzy as he tried to piece together what it meant. He knew who had taken his wife from him. And it wasn't Anthony Yates. So much time wasted! Rage burned hot and strong in his belly and he felt it build until it was a barely contained explosion. Slowly everything came back in startling detail. In front of him, Luz tried to talk Rosa down but behind him Rosa was more tense and desperate, he could feel it in her grip. He felt the cold steel against his face and imagined how it would feel to die. Would he see Leah again? He could finally apologize… but for what? That some psycho woman killed the wrong person? There was no way he could've foreseen such a random act of violence. He felt the fight drain from him as the burden of her death finally lifted. In its place was the desire to live, to push on and honor her memory by living a full life helping others and forgiving himself for all those years of torment. Taking in the situation he was in, he wasn't sure he'd get that chance.

Suddenly, Luz took a shot and he felt the bullet tear into his shoulder and rip out of his back. He staggered back. Then, the edges of his sight blurred until they were black.

• • •

Rosa felt her control slip with every word Luz spoke, but she didn't want this to end quite yet. Her mind raced with options, but she kept coming up empty and her desperation grew. She couldn't figure out why Luz was trying to help her, after everything that has happened so far. Then she remembered Nick and Luz's blossoming relationship and realized that she was being talked down out of fear for his safety.

Angrier than ever, she held the gun tight against Nick's head and prepared to pull the trigger, but Luz was quicker and shot first. The bullet hit Nick in the shoulder and he lurched back with the impact.

Rosa was so surprised that Luz had chosen to shoot Nick that she didn't notice the bullet had gone through him and into her chest. It was when she tried to speak that she saw the damage done to her body.

Pain spread through her chest and everything went numb. She stumbled and fell, landing on the ground with Nick on top of her. She tried to push him off, but her strength failed her, and she lay gasping on the hard cement. *The dirty cement.* She knew her lung had collapsed, and she was losing a lot of blood. Too much blood. Thoughts of dying played in her mind. How sad that one who came from the streets would die on the streets. After everything she'd done to leave her past behind, it caught up with her. Her premonition about Luz had proven true and she would die. She wouldn't survive prison, anyway. At least the itching would stop. She closed her eyes against the pain and welcomed death with a smile on her face.

CHAPTER THIRTY-THREE

Agent Adams had witnessed the whole scene and was surprised that Luz shot Nick. He had only been five minutes behind her driving from the house and had just pulled up to the building. Running inside he found everything in chaos. One of his agents told him the killer had been spotted running down the stairs but that she had a hostage. They were standing guard at both staircase doors that led to the lobby waiting for her to emerge.

Frustrated, Blue opened the door and realized there was another door that led outside. He was about to go through the door when he heard voices on the other side. Detective Santos was involved in some sort of confrontation with the killer. He quickly ran back out of the building and circled around just in time to see Luz shoot Nick and he watched as both the hostage and the killer went down in one tangled heap.

He rushed to them, arriving at the same time as Luz, and he watched her face go pale. "Call for an ambulance!" she shouted to him. She moved Nick gently so that he was no longer lying on Rosa but flat on the ground.

Blue pulled out his phone and called for help but wondered

what good it would do; the man looked as if he had lost more blood than the woman the bullet was intended to kill.

Luz laid Nick out as gently as she could, but she worried about the damage she had caused. It had been a split-second decision; the only way for her to get Rosa was to go through Nick. Nick's wound was bleeding, spreading out on the cement. *Please don't die*, she thought, applying pressure to both sides of the wound.

She heard a cough behind her and turned to see Rosa's mouth spurt blood. She hated the woman but felt sorry it all had to end this way. "Rosa?" she said softly but could tell by Rosa's empty stare that she was dead.

Tears came to her eyes and she turned back to Nick. His face was pale and his breathing shallow. *Just one more miracle*, she prayed. Her prayers were answered when she heard sirens a block away.

• • •

Nick felt the sun on his face as he woke up. Someone had left the blinds open in his room. He heard soft breathing from the side of him. He turned his head and saw Luz asleep in a chair next to his bed. Her face devoid of the stress that usually coated her features when she was working on something. He took a few quiet moments to gaze at her before lightly tapping her shoulder.

She opened her eyes and focused on him, then she jumped up. "Hey, you. How are you feeling?"

"Groggy. How long was I out?" he asked. His voice was scratchy and his mouth felt like he'd been stuck in the desert for days.

Anticipating his needs, Luz picked up a nearby cup of water and brought it to him, sticking the straw in his dry lips and watched him drink. Her face was a mask of regret when she explained what happened.

"When you came in, they got to work on you right away. You lost a lot of blood, so they pushed you right through to surgery, worked on you for a few hours and put you in here to recover." She moved up to the head of the bed, looking nervous. "Nick I'm so sorry. I didn't want to shoot you. But I could tell Rosa was about to shoot you, so I did the only thing I could think of and took her out first. I was hoping for a clean shot, but she kept using you as a shield. The bullet did pass through your shoulder before killing her, but it tore through your muscle. The doctor feels that with some physical therapy you'll be back to a hundred percent in no time."

She reached up and brushed his hair from his forehead. He could see the emotions warring across her face. He imagined she was torturing herself with consequences of shooting him. He grabbed her hand and stared into her beautiful emerald eyes, watching her take a deep breath and exhaling.

"Nick, I'm so—"

He shushed her and pulled her closer. "Please don't apologize, Luz, you are a seasoned police detective. If you believed the only way to stop that madwoman was shooting her through me, then you made the right choice. I hold no ill

475

will towards you and respect the decision you had to make in such a tough situation. Please believe that, so we can move on from this."

Luz looked away for a moment then turned back to him, her eyes full of tears. "I thought I'd lost you," she whispered, and he felt something slide into place inside of him. This beautiful, intelligent, frustrating woman loved him and it made him feel like the luckiest guy in the world.

"But you didn't. I'm right here, so it looks like you're stuck with me." He tightened his hold on her with his good arm.

She laughed and placed a kiss on his mouth gently. "I wouldn't have it any other way."

THE END.

EPILOGUE

"I still have nightmares." Luz shifted on the couch, trying to find a comfortable position as she spoke to the department psychiatrist, Quinn Presley. It was funny she was on the couch but not as a patient.

"Do you feel they're getting worse?" asked the doctor and Luz thought back to the last few bad dreams she'd endured.

Blood

Darkness

The blast of a gunshot

Screams.

She shuddered.

"Not exactly. It's the same boy and it always ends with me shooting his father. So much blood…" she trailed off.

Quinn eyed her colleague and now friend. "What about what happened after that? I mean, does the dream stop after you shoot him?"

Luz nodded. "Most of the time it does. Sometimes he morphs into Rosa, holding a gun to Nick's head. It's terrifying. Brings back the pain and panic from that day. How am I supposed to move on when I have ghosts haunting me?"

"Ah, okay. So there's more recent trauma mixing with the old trauma," Quinn explained crossing the room and sitting down next to Luz. She placed a hand on the detective's arm. "Take a deep breath," she ordered. Luz complied, inhaling deeply and exhaling slowly.

"Now listen up because I'm only going to say this once," Quinn said, her tone serious. Luz feared what she was about to hear. "You, my friend are blessed. You have a wonderfully supportive family, a great career and I've heard through the grapevine that the FBI wants to make you yet *another* offer. You also have a very handsome, very talented boyfriend, who I hear is already making a difference in this community with his homeless shelter as well as offering his legal skills pro bono to those who find themselves in difficult circumstances." She smiled warmly but wasn't through yet. "And finally, not to toot my own horn, but you are recently befriended a pretty awesome chick here at work who won't stop helping you until she knows that you believe that you are one, badass woman."

Warmth spread through Luz's body and she couldn't stop the grin from spreading across her face. She and Quinn had visited a few times since the case closed and so far, it had proven beneficial in a multitude of ways. Besides a crass sense of humor, they found they had a lot in common and Luz believed the common ground they shared made a strong foundation for a friendship.

"Well I know I'm pretty badass, so you *might* know what you're talking about," Luz quipped, laughing lightly.

"All of those diplomas hanging on my wall say I *do* know what I'm talking about." Quinn sighed and got to her feet, pulling

Luz up with her. "It's time to let go, Luz. At this point I think you might be getting in your own way. Retrain your brain and start living your life again. You have so much going for you right now, try to enjoy—"

Luz's phone began ringing, cutting Quinn off. "Sorry," Luz said and answered her phone. It was short conversation and she hung up quickly, turning back to her friend. "Gotta go," she said grabbing her coat from the hook behind the door.

"I understand, call me later!" Quinn waved her off and Luz stepped into the hallway, closing the door behind her. She called Nick on her way out of the building.

"Hello beautiful," he answered.

"Hello yourself. Hey, I'm going to be late tonight. I just caught a case and it's bad. Real bad. Two parents dead and their eleven-year-old son is the primary suspect."

There was a pause on the other line before he asked. "Will you be okay?"

"We'll have to see. I have to go now. Just wanted to check in with you. I guess I needed to let a little light in before I wade through what should be a very dark crime scene"

Luz heard the concern in Nick's voice. "Okay but remember; I'm the light at the end of the tunnel, too. Take care of my cop."

Warmth

Safety

Love.

She was going to be okay.

"Always," she replied then hung up.

It was time to do the job.

479

Dear book lover,

Thank you immensely for reading my book. This story has been very close to my heart for many years, and I'm so grateful you've chosen to share this journey with me. I am truly humbled. I would be incredibly thankful if you took the time to leave a review on Amazon. A short, moderate or long review would be *just* fine. By reviewing my book, you will make such a difference not only for me, but for the readers out there who would love to discover this story.

I would be over the moon if you joined my book club at ByMelodieHernandez.com! I *never* share information so there's no need to worry about details being dispersed. I'm a private person, and I greatly respect the privacy of others. When you sign up for the book club, you'll receive updates on my newest releases. You can also follow me on Facebook, Amazon and Instagram. All three, if you're feeling saucy!

The next story in my *Forgotten* Series is currently in progress. **Please turn the page for a sneak peek of the next installment of the *Forgotten* Series: *Forgotten Pain*.** I am very excited to finish this story and share the next chapter in the *Forgotten* journey with you. Stay tuned...

Keep smiling!

Melodie Hernandez

FINAL THANKS

Way back in 2002 I had an idea for a story. I started writing down notes about characters and scenes, and soon those notes became paragraphs, which then became chapters.... Well, you get the idea. I pretty much grew up with this story and these characters. Throughout many of the major milestones in my life, I'd pull the manuscript out every now and then and work on making the story and characters feel just that much more genuine. As I matured, so did the story. And I'm so proud of, and at peace with, the finished product. It's been a long ride, but a great one.

And now, onto the thanks!

To my husband Del and my wonderful children, thank you for showing me what family truly means. I'm not sure I could've written about love and family so well if I wasn't experiencing it every day in my own home. I love you to the moon and back. Viva Hernandez!

To my mother, thank you for encouraging this story from the start. You were my cheerleader. Every chapter I gave you, you immediately read and gave me feedback that really pushed me to see the story through to the end. I love you. To my father, I am grateful for your support of this story from the start. As a longtime fan of crime fiction, your appreciation of this story holds a lot of weight with me. Thank you for making this the only book in your book club! I'll always love you for that!

Thank you to my family and friends who have read the book and encouraged me. Your support means the world to me.

I want to say ***muchas gracias*** to all of the strong Latina women in my life. Without, you Luz Santos wouldn't be the independent and fierce woman I wrote her to be. Her sense of self, of culture and of family comes from watching every one of you live and grow and own it in your own lives! Thank you so much for your love, support and friendship.

Finally thank you to my amazing editor, Melissa Carmean. This process was new and intimidating to me but you guided me through it like the pro you are. You took this story, this diamond in the rough and made it shine. I'm eternally grateful for your insight and encouragement because it made me a better writer. There are really no words to properly thank you for that, just know that you'll always have a special place in my heart.

SNEAK PEEK OF THE NEXT BOOK:

FORGOTTEN PAIN

BY MELODIE HERNANDEZ

Prologue

Silence coated the house and those sleeping within rested peacefully with a false sense of security. The boy crept through the house, carefully avoiding the floorboards he knew would creak. He knew the house well. It was his home, after all. More importantly, he knew the people who slept beyond the door he stood in front of.

He shifted the weight he carried from one hand to the other and tightened his grip in anticipation. Slowly, he pushed the door. It swung open soundlessly and he smiled. Oiling the hinges earlier had been calculated and guaranteed him easy access to the room without waking the occupants.

With his heart pounding in his chest and his breathing shallow, he stepped into the room and quietly closed the door behind him. He could hear the steady breathing of the man and woman, both of whom seemed to be in a deep sleep. An arrogant smile played across his face.

The moon shone brightly through the windows, lighting the way for death. He stole his way across the room, keeping to the shadows until he reached the side of the bed. *They are sound asleep*, he thought as he stared down at the serene expressions of the unsuspecting couple. *They'll never know what hit them.*

He lifted the baseball bat with both hands and whipped it up over his head with ease. The Louisville Slugger has a familiar feel to it; he'd used it time and again on the field at the school. But this wasn't a game. This was real — suddenly all too real — when he glanced again at their faces. The weight of what he was about to do became so heavy that doubt clouded his vision and he lowered the bat a few inches. *What am I doing?*

Then the rage returned, white hot and blinding. It brought with it his purpose. He swung the bat up again and brought it down hard and fast. He didn't hear the sickening thud the bat made as it connected with skull. He kept swinging, letting the fury burn through his body and his arms. He grunted with each swing.

In his bloodlust, he barely registered when the screaming began, the woman had woken during his assault and screamed. He stopped his assault looking from the bloody mass that had once been a human head to the woman who sat shaking on the bed, her face a mask of shock and horror.

"Ethan?" she began in a small terrified whisper. "Your father...what have you done to your father? How...c-c-could you do that to your father?" She sobbed and placed a hand over her mouth.

The boy ignored the terror and denial he heard in his mother's voice and slowly walked to her side of the bed, the bat lifted high, ready to strike. His mother's eyes grew wide. She quickly pulled herself away from the edge of the bed, away from her son.

"Ethan, honey it's me. It's your mother, please put the bat down," she begged as she tried to pull herself over her husband's body. She made the mistake of looking at the gory pummeled remains of his once handsome face and she froze again.

The boy stared at his mother for a moment. Her pleas fueled his rage. He brought the bat down in one swift swing, silencing the hysterical sobs that tried to break him down. Except for his panting, the room was silent, and he stepped back from the bed to observe his work.

His mother lay on his father's chest. She might have looked like she was sleeping except for the blood that dripped from her lips. And her misshapen, crushed skull. His father was no longer recognizable. Only a mound of mutilated flesh, brain and bone was left of him on the bloodstained pillow, duvet and walls.

Sighing deeply, he took off the plastic mask and rain slicker he'd worn and dropped them at the foot of the bed. A sound from the hallway caught his attention and he suddenly remembered his little sister. He readjusted his grip on the bat and started out into the hallway just as he heard the sirens down the street.

Panic had his heart pumping wildly as he called out in frustration. "Sissy I know you're here somewhere, why don't you come out so we can talk?" He listened for her but could only hear the sirens drawing closer. He quickly weighed his options and decided he would have to leave to avoid capture; he would take care of the little girl later.

He ran down the stairs, out of the house and into the night with the blood of his parents still on his hands *Happy 11th Birthday to me.*